CHRISTMAS ANGELS

By Dennis Smith

To Karla

Without Her Help And Inspiration

This Book Would Not Have Been Possible

MMXI

CHRISTMAS ANGELS

A True Story Presented As
Fiction With All Names Changed
To Protect The Guilty

MMXI

There is no living thing that is not afraid when it faces danger. The true courage is in facing danger when you are afraid.

L. FRANK BAUM, *The Wonderful Wizard of Oz*

Prologue

Sick, so sick. My face and body are on fire. My daddy is washing my face with alcohol. I have thrown up everything inside of me. The odors of alcohol and Pepto Bismol and Ginger Ale are all mixed together making me sicker. Can't throw up anymore. I can hear the voices of my grandmothers whispering. "It's the big red measles I reckon."
"Yes, it tis, but I've never seen a young'un that sick with it.
"Well, Henry's gone to get Doc Snow. They'll be here dreckly"
A man in a blue suit is pushing on my stomach. "Ya'll have got one sick boy here." I can see a big black bag. I feel the sting of a needle. "I'm going to have to paint his throat."
A wooden paddle with something purple on it is going down my throat. I can taste the awful purple. I gag and then it is gone. I turn my head a little and I can see my mother sitting in the kitchen staring out a window at the night. I turn my head a little and I can see the Christmas tree in the living room. I look at the Christmas Angel at the very top of the tree. Through my feverish eyes, the Angel seems to be looking at me.

1

Chapter 1

Bayview, Alabama - also known as "the camps" - was a peaceful little mining community in January of 1949. This, of course, was with the exception of my mother, Malva, who was prone to burst from the house at any given moment and take off running down the street screaming, "I'm dyyyying ! Jesus, help me, Jesus"! My daddy, Ben, would tail along after her and eventually get her in tow and bring her sobbing back to the house. At 7-years-old, this was a great source of embarrassment to me and, I was sure, a great source of glee to the neighbors. Many mornings I walked to school with my head down, positive that the people I passed in their clapboard houses were staring at me from behind their curtains. "There goes that Knight boy. He's the one with the crazy mama." I envied my sister, Marty, because she was only three, didn't go to school yet, and was spared the indignities I suffered. Everyone agreed that my mother's problems were her "nerves." All but Ma, my grandmother and my daddy's mother. Ma was old and the wisest person in the world. Even God revealed things to Ma that he wouldn't to anybody else. Several times a week I would head over to Ma's house. Ma and me would sit on her front porch drinking iced tea while Ma told me about the world and its evils. She was the littlest woman you ever saw and wore a sun bonnet that was so big you almost couldn't see her. Ma especially disliked women. She would tell me, "son, I won't live to see it but you will. You just remember what I say and watch for it. Women will be the downfall of this ol' world. Women are sorry and getting sorrier. It's not like it was when I was a girl. Now they want to boss the men folk and run everything and it ain't gonna bring about nothing but the end of time." I knew what would be coming next. "It's all in the bible, Daniel, if folks would just take the time to read it." This was always a little confusing to me because of Ma being a woman herself. But I never made any comment on it because I sure didn't want Ma to think I was foolish. As to my mother's condition, Ma had the diagnosis. "What your mother has, Daniel, is 'running fits'. It runs in her side of the family. Her daddy had 'em whilst he was living, and her mother has 'em (my other grandmother, Mama Davis). Ain't nothin' but the pure ol' devil."

Most times this topic would end with, "I'll never understand why your daddy married into that family with all their foolishness. Benjamin could have married Lorena Massey. She really loved him and would have made him a good wife with good sense." I would sit and nod in agreement with Ma and wonder why my daddy had not married Lorena Massey. I guess neither one of us stopped to think that if he had, I wouldn't be sitting in the porch swing agreeing with Ma.

Chapter 2

The majority of the male population in Bayview worked at one of the local coal mines. The few who didn't, worked at the steel mill. The steel plant was called TCI which stood for Tennessee Coal and Iron. These few lucky ones were always identified as "big shots." For example, if I mentioned the fact that, "Jimmy Spears got a lot of stuff for Christmas", it would be immediately pointed out that, "his daddy works for TCI, they're big shots."

There was a grocery store that everyone called the commissary. In years past it had been a "company store" where the miners had bought goods and payed with scrip earned working in the mines. Bayview had a sheriff of sorts. Sheriff Clayburn. He had a small brick building, with bars on the windows, just down the hill from the commissary. I never knew where sheriff Clayburn received his authority from and no one ever saw a prisoner in the little brick building.

We even had a village idiot that everyone called "Utah." I never met anybody who knew where Utah actually lived. Every morning he would station himself outside the commissary and remain there most of the day yelling remarks, nobody understood, at passing cars. All of us kids were warned to stay away from Utah because he was "not right in the head." Once, at 6-years-old, I had the misfortune of running headlong into Utah after dashing around the corner of the commissary. Of course he immediately jumped in front of me to block my path. It didn't matter because I was too scared to move anyway. Utah looked down at me and asked, "whar you think you going, boy"? I said, "I'm going home I guess." But Utah explained to me, "You ain't goin' anywhar till I talk to you 'bout babies. Do you know whar babies come from, boy"?

This was my first close up look at Utah and I couldn't help but stare at him. His hair was parted down the middle and looked like somebody had poured grease on it. His face was beet red and full of holes.
I said, "I guess so but I guess I don't, really."

Utah laughed. "You shore are stupid, boy. Doncha know a man sticks his peter in his wife's butt and pumps her fulla white milk, an' thas how white babies ar' made? A nigger pumps his wife fulla choc'lat milk and thas why they ar' niggers." My face flushed as tears welled up and I broke and ran as fast as I could. After a fair distance, I looked over my shoulder to see if Utah was gaining on me. To my relief, he was standing in the same spot hollering at a passing car. As I passed each house on the way home my shame was almost unbearable. I believed that every person sitting in their porch swing knew I had just found out the "facts of life" from Utah. "There goes that Knight boy. He knows where babies come from now. Utah just told him"

Chapter 3

The tranquility of the camps was sometimes shattered by the death of a miner. Once in a while this was caused by an explosion inside the mine. More often the reason was "a rock fell on him and cut his head slap off." In the early part of 1948, one of these tragedies hit close to home. My daddy had a sister named Doney Shook, who lived in Bayview. Her husband, Marvin, worked at Edgewater Mine. They had a daughter named Molly Faye who was my age and a son two years older, named Jerry Ray. Molly Faye and I were in the same class at Bayview School. One morning in February of that year, Mr. Wilson, the principal, cracked the classroom door and beckoned our teacher, Mrs. Hamrick, into the hall. A few seconds later, Mrs. Hamrick cracked the door and asked Molly Faye to "please come out into the hall". A couple of minutes later, to my surprise, the door opened again, and the teacher asked me to come out. When I reached the hall, there was no sign of Molly Faye. Mrs. Hamrick then broke the bad news to me.

"Daniel, your uncle, Marvin Shook, was killed in the coal mine early this morning, and I'm sure you would like to go on home for the rest of the day." I said, "Yes ma'am, I think so". I dashed back into the classroom, grabbed my book satchel, and bolted down the hall and out the front door. As I passed Mr. Earl, the janitor and bell-ringer, he inquired as to where I was going in such a hurry. I blurted out, "My uncle's been killed in the coal mine, Mr. Earl! A rock cut his head slap off!"

I hadn't seen Uncle Marvin more than six times in my life, but I was not going to pass up a day off from school. Nobody I knew of had a telephone in those days, and news traveled slowly. I ran the entire mile and a half hoping to be the first to tell my family the bad news. And I was.

My mother was sitting on the front porch reading a storybook to Marty. As I bounded up the steps, she swept Marty from her lap, jumped up from the porch swing, and demanded, "What are you doing home, Daniel Wayne? What in the world is wrong? Help me, Jesus!" I sure hoped she wasn't going to have a running fit. I could hear the radio playing back in the kitchen, ***"If I knew you were coming I'da baaked a cake, baaaked a cake."***
Almost out of breath, I finally got it out. "Uncle Marvin has been killed in the coal mines! Somebody came and got Molly Faye, and the teacher said I could go home too!"
Indoor plumbing had not been introduced in Bayview at that time. Our backyard was actually a small hill with concrete steps leading up to our "outhouse" as it was called. When I broke the news to my mother about Uncle Marvin, my daddy happened to be occupying the outhouse. My mother tore around the side of the house toward the backyard with me on her heels. We bounded the concrete steps two at a time. My mother beat on the tin door shouting, "Ben, Marvin has been killed in the mines!"
My daddy's voice came back, "Get the hell away from this damn door and let me do my business!"
My mother, sure he had not understood her, pleaded again. "Ben, did you hear me? You brother-in-law has been killed."My daddy's voice came from inside the outhouse again, "I told you to get the hell away from this door!"By this time Marty had made it up the steps dragging her doll, Sally. Slowly we three turned around and made out way back down to the house, awed at my daddy's reaction to Uncle Marvin being killed in the coal mines.

Later on, after my daddy had completed "his business" and bathed and shaved, he and my mother drove off to Aunt Doney's house. When they returned that night, I ran out to meet them.
"Daddy, was Uncle Marvin really killed in the mines? Did you see him?"

"Yeah, son, a rock cut his head slap off. No, we didn't see him. The funeral man's working on him right now. He'll be laid out at home tomorrow evening and we'll see him then."

I didn't like this "we" business and said, "I don't have to go, do I? I really don't want to." I had already been dragged, protesting, to two funerals in my life, of people I had never heard of, because of my mother's belief that it was "good for me." I never did see any result from it other than bad dreams, and I sure didn't want to see a dead man without a head.

I asked my daddy again, "Can't I just stay with Mama Davis?" Mama Davis was living with us at the time. This was my mother's cue.

"Daniel Wayne, your Aunt Doney would be hurt if you didn't come, and I believe it's good for you to see these things."

The next day went by much too fast for me, and before I knew it, we were pulling up to Aunt Doney's house. Several cars were already lined up in the street in front of the house. We made our way up the steps to the front porch with me bringing up the rear.

My daddy didn't knock on the door; he just went ahead and opened it. I guess he figured it was all right, it being his sister's house. From inside, I could hear a chorus of voices, "It's Ben and Malva and Daniel Wayne's with them. Y'all come on in."

As I went in, I sort of nodded my head, but to no one in particular because it was just a blur of faces. I plopped down on the end of a sofa watching my mother hug Aunt Doney.

My aunt's living room was narrow, but it went back a good ways. From where I was, I could see a white casket sitting at the far end of the room. It was closed on one end, but open on the other. I could not see Uncle Marvin. An idea began to form in my mind. With this many people milling around, maybe I would not be noticed. Maybe I could just sit right there until it was time to go. If my mother or anybody asked me if I had seen Uncle Marvin, I would just say, "yes" and we could be on our way.

It was not to be! After about ten minutes of safety, my stomach started to churn when I saw Aunt Doney coming toward me. She was tall and lanky like my daddy.

"Come on, Daniel, you need to come and see your Uncle Marvin. He always thought the world of you, you know." I almost said, "No, Ma'am, I sure didn't know that," but thought better of it.

With Aunt Doney as my escort, I walked toward the casket. As we closed in on Uncle Marvin, I kept my eyes focuses on the closed end. I intended to keep my eyes looking in that direction while pretending to be looking at Uncle Marvin but after a couple of seconds she put her hands on my shoulders and pulled me up to the open end as if she knew what I was trying to pull.

I immediately closed my eyes and then barely opened them to a "squinch". Through the narrow mist, I could make out the upper part of a body--A BODY WITH A HEAD! I opened my eyes a little wider, and there was Uncle Marvin, head and all. I was too relieved to ponder how this miracle had come about. My aunt whispered, "Doesn't he look good, Daniel?" I said, "Yes, ma'am", almost adding, "specially since he's still got his head".

My aunt said, "You must be hungry child. Your cousin, Jerry Ray's in the kitchen. Go on in there and get yourself something to eat."

I said, "Yes, ma'am, thank you." I headed for the kitchen, feeling good that I had done my duty and it was over. As I walked away, I saw Molly Faye sitting in a chair crying. I didn't know what to say, so I just slowed down and went on by. When I entered the kitchen, I saw Jerry Ray at the table chewing on a chicken leg while hovering over a plate loaded down with baked beans, slaw and potato salad. When Jerry Ray saw me, he hollered, "Come on in, Dan, pull up a chair."

After I was seated, Jerry Ray became excited. "Hey, Dan, guess what? I got Dad's watch!"

He stuck his arm under my nose and, sure enough, on his wrist was a big man's watch.

Jerry Ray said, "This is a genuine ball-bearing watch, and it's mine now. And you know what else? Mama said I was going to be the man of the house now!" I wondered how he was going to handle that, being nine years old, but I didn't make any comment. Jerry Ray went back to eating his chicken leg.

I sure wasn't hungry, so I got up and walked out on the front porch. I was glad to see Ma sitting in a rocking chair on the porch. I sat down on the swing, and Ma began talking about Uncle Marvin.

"You know, son, he was a peculiar man. He was not like us."

I asked Ma why he was different.

"He was a refugee from Arkansas, son."

I asked Ma what a refugee was.

"Refugees was people who had to leave Arkansas because of a flood years ago. They came to Alabama, and some of 'em settled here in the camps. I don't know where Doney met up with Marvin. I guess in some beer joint. And I sure don't know why she thought she had to marry up with him. Doney was real pretty when she was younger and could've had any boy she wanted."

As Ma talked I became drowsy and laid down in the swing. Just before sleep overtook me, I heard a radio playing from a house somewhere down the street, ***"I saw the li-ight, I saw the li-ight. No more darkness, no more night."***

Uncle Marvin's funeral was the next day. His funeral was to be preached at Freewill Baptist church with burial in the church cemetery. My presence was, of course, required so I could receive all the benefits that could be gotten from the experience."

I'll admit it wasn't as bad as the night before. I sat in a pew with some cousins, and when everyone paraded around to have a last look at Uncle Marvin before they closed the casket, none of us were asked to join the march. There were a lot more people at the funeral than there were at Aunt Doney's house. I saw Ma seated in the pew cross the aisle from us. After a couple of songs, the preacher started talking about Uncle Marvin. He said Uncle Marvin was a good man who always provided for his family. He said, "I have no doubt that Brother Shook is in Heaven." I glanced over at Ma, but she had her head down like she was praying. The preacher said if there was anybody in the church who was not saved, it was time to come forward now. Nobody moved. I guess everybody was saved. Then the preacher dismissed everyone to walk over to the cemetery. As I was going out, I saw some men carrying the casket out a side door; my daddy was one of them. When I got to where they were going to bury Uncle Marvin, the casket was already sitting over a hole in the ground. Chairs were set up along one side. The chairs were for Aunt Doney, Jerry Ray, Molly Faye and an old woman somebody had said was Uncle Marvin's mother. I figured she must have been a refugee from Arkansas too. The preacher said some more good things about Uncle Marvin and said the Lord would be with his family during this bad time. After praying some more, the preacher went down the line of chairs shaking hands. When he got to Jerry Ray's chair, it was empty.

I had already seen Jerry Ray down by the road. He was showing his watch to three men holding shovels.

Chapter 4

In July of 1949 I turned 8 years old. It was a great summer for playing! Playing "cowboys" had now taken a back seat to playing "war". My friends and I had all seen, and been mesmerized by John Wayne in "The Sands of Iwo Jima". My usual comrades in arms that summer were Jimmy Spears, Thomas Dees, Charles Wright and Donald Mars. Donald was a year or so older than the rest of us and was always "the General". There was another reason for Donald's high rank other than age. His dad had been in the Army during the war and had brought back an assortment of wonderful things: helmets, duty belts, canteens, even a couple of bayonets. Donald would parcel out these items among us at his discretion. Then the Battle of Bayview would begin.

RAT-TAT-TAT-TAT!!! BAM, BLAM, BAM!!! KA-BOOM, KA-BOOM!!!

Battle sounds could be heard from early morning until late evening. One day we would fight the Japs, the next day the Germans. Bayview was safe from all enemies.

There was also an undercurrent of fear running through the camps that summer. The cause of this fear was summed up in one word: 'POLIO!' It seemed to be striking children everywhere although no one we knew had it. There was no shot to prevent it and no cure for it. We would over- hear our parents and other grown-ups discussing the cause of it: "Swimming in stagnant water, swimming in cold water and getting a chill, getting a hard lick to the head, too much sun, not enough sun", and on and on. Nobody really knew. In late August, the news spread like wildfire through the camps. Donald Mars had POLIO! The worst kind, everybody said. Donald was in the hospital three months. A few days later, after we heard he was home, all us boys went to see him. We were shocked at how Donald looked. He was sitting in a wheelchair. His face and dark black hair were the same, but his body seemed shriveled up. Next to Donald's wheelchair was a huge round thing with a mirror stuck on the front of it. Donald's mother explained, "This is where Donald will sleep at night. It's called an Iron Lung and will help him breathe." We were speechless at all this.

Then Donald, with his same voice as always, said, "Boys, I'll be able to play with you again in a few days."

After that, we went back several times and grew more and more used to Donald's condition. As he predicted, in about two weeks, he was ready to play again. After school, we would head for Donald's house. He was, of course, still "The General" and directed the battles from his wheelchair. Donald was to live another six years, dying in December of 1955. We heard his mother had said, "Christmas angels came and took Donald to Heaven."

Chapter 5

My daddy had two sisters and four brothers. One brother, Uncle Matthew, was ten years older than my daddy. In all the years he had worked at the #19 coal mine in Porter, Uncle Matthew had never missed a single day of work. This was even more amazing when you considered the fact that Uncle Matthew was a drunk. His breakfast at 5:00 a.m. every morning was a pint of whiskey. He would slip another pint into his lunchbox to get him through the day until he could make it to the package store after work. Uncle Matthew never married. The story had been told that he had been engaged to marry a young lady, years back. This mysterious young lady lived up in Walker County and Uncle Matthew drove there in his Model-T one day to see her. When he returned in a very short time, someone asked him why his trip had been so quick. Uncle Matthew didn't answer and went on to bed. When he was asked again the next morning why he had come back so soon, his only reply was, "I don't have nothing to say about it so don't ask me no more questions." The story was told that Uncle Matthew received two or three letters a week from the girl for the next six months. They were all burned unread.

This story came from family members because Uncle Matthew would never speak of it the remainder of his days. I guess today Uncle Matthew would be known as a "colorful character". To me he was just Uncle Matthew who was drunk all the time.

While his brothers and sisters were marrying and starting families, Uncle Matthew continued to live with his mother who was, of course, Ma. He would live with her the rest of his life.

Ma, being highly religious, hated Uncle Matthew's drinking and tried everything from prayer to trickery to stop it. She would find his "hiding places" around the house and empty his whiskey out in the sink. One time Ma emptied a bottle and peed in it and put it back where it had been hidden.

Uncle Matthew never said anything about it so Ma said he probably just drank it and didn't know the difference. A stunt Ma pulled that finally got Uncle Matthew's attention was when she emptied out one of his bottles and refilled it with tea. Ma set the bottle on the table and waited for Uncle Matthew to come home from work. When he opened the front door to come in, Ma grabbed up the bottle and ran into the room hollering and singing. Another one of Daddy's brothers, William, was there. He was in on it with Ma. Ma took a big swig in front of Uncle Matthew and hollered out, "I know now why you love this stuff sooo much! I feel wooonderful!" She then fell backwards on the floor, "out cold". Uncle William said it looked like Matthew went into shock right there. He screamed for Uncle William to "go get Doc Snow – git him down here, now!"

Uncle William told him, "I've been trying to stop her, Matthew! I think she's too far gone now for any doctor to help her!"

At that, Uncle Matthew actually started praying. "Oh God, oh God, if you'll let my mama live, I'll never touch another drop in all my born days!"

Ma then got up off the floor being her usual self while Uncle William laughed.

Ma said, "I heard your prayer to the Lord, Matthew, and Him and me will expect you to stand by it". As it dawned on Uncle Matthew what had happened, he pouted a little but he was too relieved to be mad. Uncle Matthew's promise to the Lord lasted about twenty-four hours.

Chapter 6

I'm not going to say the folks in Bayview were any more prejudiced than anywhere else in Alabama, or anywhere else in the country during this time, but prejudice was there. To Ma, the cause of the world's problems was women -- of any color. To Uncle Matthew, it was black people. "Damn niggers trying to act like white folks nowadays. Some of 'em thank they *are* white. If a family of 'em tries to move into Bayview, it'll be a sad day for that bunch!!" When Uncle Matthew would start winding down his sermon about blacks, Ma would usually chime in, "Now son, the colored are God's children just like we are. They're just different than us. God don't mean for us to mix with them, but they're still his children too. Just different, that's all."

"Well as long as they stay in their place and don't try to get biggety, they can be God's children. I don't give a damn!"
This way of thinking was by no means the sole property of Uncle Matthew. It was everywhere. Children would use the "N" word on a daily basis. "Last one to cross the line is a nigger!"
"Eenie, meenie, minee, moe- catch a nigger by his toe- If he hollers "let me go"-Make him pay fifty dollars every day!" Adults used black people to discipline their children. "If you don't straighten up and start behaving, we're going to give you to a nigger family, and they can raise you! We'll see how you like that!" Mothers would say "I worked like a black nigger to cook that supper, and I mean you're going to eat it!" The "N" word was used so much that it became meaningless. Everybody said it--Everybody but my daddy. At my very young age, I didn't "consciously" know my daddy didn't use the word. It was just somewhere in my brain along with the thousands of other things that run through a young boy's mind. Once, when I was six years old, my daddy took me to the Alabama Theatre in downtown Birmingham to see "Song of the South".

Afterwards we went to a "ten cent store" to get something my mother had wanted. Just to the right of the entrance stood two water fountains. There was a sign over each fountain, one said "white", the other "colored". My daddy stopped and looked at the signs for a second. Then he said, "Son, I want you to take a good look at them signs and remember 'em". When I asked him why, he said, "cause them signs will be coming down one day, 'cause it's wrong and people know it's wrong. Do you understand what I'm saying, son?"

I said, "yes, sir". I had no idea what he was talking about. Another incident happened a few months later that left me confused. My daddy took me to a barber shop in the nearby town of Ensley. On the street in front of the barber shop, we encountered an old black man. He and my dad recognized each other immediately. They shook hands and then hugged each other. "Radio, you old son-of-a-gun! What 'n the world you been up to?" Ben, you know I'm too ol' now to be up to anything!" They both laughed as if this was a great joke. Radio then turned his attention to me. "Lawd have mercy, Ben! Is that tadpole yore son?"

"Yeah, Radio, that's my boy! That's Daniel."

"Lawd, Daniel, me and your ole papa worked in 'em ol' flat mines years ago. He weren't much older than you an' still wet behin' the ears!" They both laughed again. They talked about the "old days" a few more minutes, shook hands again and Radio ambled off down the sidewalk.

When we entered the barber shop, several men were seated waiting their turn. After we sat down, an older man turned to look at my daddy. "Who's that nigger you was hugging around on out there, son?"

I saw a muscle in my daddy's jaw twitch. He stared straight at the man. That happened to be a good friend of mine. Why do you ask?"

The man acted as if he was going to say something else, but must have thought better of it. The shop stayed quiet while daddy and I got our haircuts. When we left, I didn't get the all-day sucker I usually got from the barber.

17

On the way home, my daddy was quieter than usual. Finally I spoke up.
"Daddy, why did you call that man Radio?"
"That's his name, son. That's the only name I ever knowed him by."
We rode the rest of the way in silence. In time I came to realize that my
daddy, in fact, did march to a different drum beat than most other folks.

The commissary had hired a young black man to unload trucks and stock the shelves. One Saturday, Charles Wright and me went into the store for a double cone. Eating our ice cream, we decided to mosey through the aisles to see what they had. Our moseying eventually led us to the back of the store where they kept the fruit and vegetables. The young black man was stacking produce on a table. When he saw us he said, "How y'all boys doing?"

I said, "Okay, I guess". Charles said nothing.

"What y'all boys' names?"

I said, "My name's Daniel." Charles said nothing.

"And this is my friend, Charles. What's your name?"

"My name's Carl, and I bet you boys could still eat an or'nge after finishin' off them cones."

"We don't have any money left", I told Carl. Carl said, "This here is a present from me to y'all." With this, Carl handed us each an orange. Charles accepted his orange but still said nothing.

I said, "Thank you."

Carl said, "Tha's alright boys. Y'all come back."

When we reached the sidewalk, Charles broke his silence. "Boy, I shore would hate to be in yore shoes." I asked Charles why. "Yore daddy goin' to wear your ass out with a belt he finds out you said "thank you" to a nigger.

I said, "Why would he whip me over that?"

"Boy, doncha know you don't say 'thank you' to a nigger? Why, it's agin the law!"

I said, "How's my daddy gonna find out? You goin' to tell him?"

Charles laughed.

"Hell, boy, yore daddy'll prob'ly find out the next time he goes in that damn store. That nigger'll prob'ly tell him hisself. Thanks he'd be bragging on you." Fear set in. A dark cloud descended. "Radio" and water fountains were one thing, but this was serious business. I had gone too far. My daddy had whipped me only a few times, and it had not been enjoyable to say the least. But this would be a bad one. It was even against the law!

Charles lived in a different direction than I did, so we went different ways after a little while. When Charles was about fifty yards away, I could hear his voice in the fading light,

"You really gonna get yore butt tore up!"

I headed on to my house. I had no choice. My conscience heavily burdened with the terrible deed I had done, I climbed the steps and sat down on the porch swing. I could hear my daddy playing his radio back in the kitchen. I knew it was him because the Grand Old Opry was on. ***"I'm walking the floor over you-- I caan't sleep a wink-that is true."***

Thoughts went flying through my mind. Charles said it was against the law. What if Mr. Bice, the white man who worked in the store, had heard me say "thank you" to Carl? He might go get Sheriff Clayburn. Now I was really scared. I decided right then and there to "fess up". Hadn't my daddy said one time that if I told the truth about something I had done wrong it wouldn't be as bad for me as it would if he found it out for hisself? Armed with that thought, I headed for the kitchen.

My daddy was seated in his usual Saturday night chair, smoking and drinking his coffee while listening to the Grand Ole Opry. The sound would sometimes fade away and then come back to normal, due to the great distance to Nashville.

I ambled up to the table and sat down, head hanging low.

My daddy said, "What's the matter, son? You look like you carrin' the weight of the world on your shoulders."

I said, "Daddy, I've done somethin' terrible, and I'm goin' to go on and tell it 'cause you said if I told you somethin' before you found out about it, it wouldn't be as bad for me." My daddy turned the radio off and lit up one of his Chesterfields. "Well, let's hear about it, son, but I want all of it now."

I said, "Well, there's a new person working at the store."

"Yeah, I know son. I seen him unloading a truck.""Well, I …. we, we … I mean."

"Come on, out with it, son. Did you git in a fight or somethin' today?"

"Well, no sir." Then I blurted it out. "He gave me and Charles an orange today, and I said 'thank you', but Charles didn't!"

My daddy looked puzzled. "What happened then? You and Charles git'na fight over them damn orn'ges?"

I was puzzled now. I figured I had blurted it out so fast he didn't catch it. I couldn't seem to get this over with. "Daddy, I told him 'thank you' for the orange." My daddy said,"Yeah, son, I heard that. Let's get on to whatever you done that might have you in trouble."

I blurted again, "Daddy I done told you! I said 'thank you' to a nigger!"
That kitchen got so quiet a feather falling would have made a loud bang. For
a minute I though my daddy was going to laugh. But he didn't.
His tight grin turned into a serious expression as I waited for him to jerk his
belt off.
Instead he said, "Son, I thank me an' you got some serious talkin' to do.
First off, the only trouble you might get in would be not telling somebody
'thank you' when they gave you somethin'."
"But Charles said it's against the law to say 'thank you' to a nigger!"
"Son, that Wright boy ain't got good sense, and I wish you wouldn't hang
aroun' with him. I worked with his daddy in the mines for years, and he
never had brain one."
Relief was flooding through me so fast I felt dizzy-headed. "But I want you
to listen to what I'm saying. They ain't no diff'rence between a black man
and a white man but skin color, and that don't mount to a hill o' beans.
Listen, son, you're going to grow up one day an' be out in this world. you're
goin' to meet good black people and some sorry ones. You goin' to meet
good white people and some sorry as hell. The differ'nce is black folks
ain't never had much of a chance. When you go out in this ol' world and
meet a man, find out what his idears are and what he thanks about thangs.
That's all that matters in the long run. Don't worry about what he looks like.
That don't mean nothin' in the long haul. Son, I know I don't have much
schoolin', but I've tried to explain all this to you the best I knowed how.
Has anything I've said got through to you?"
I said, "yes, sir".
As I got up from the table, my daddy said, "Another thang, son. Try not to
use that word anymore." I knew what word he meant and promised I
wouldn't. I went out on the back porch feeling fine. Charles Wright was an
idiot. I heard my daddy turn the radio back on. *I'm so lonesome I could
cryyy.*

22

The next afternoon I ran into Charles and a couple of other boys standing around in front of the commissary. It was Sunday, and the store was always closed on Sunday. Big-mouth Charles asked immediately, "Is yore butt too sore to set down today, or did you have the guts to tell your pappy whatcha done?" Embarrassed with the other boys there and under great peer pressure, I said, "Yeah, I told him. He let me go this time, but he said if I ever done it again, he was gonna wear me out with a belt." I was immediately ashamed of my lie but didn't have the courage to correct it. I steered clear of Charles from then on. I never knew why my daddy felt differently about some things than most other people I knew, even his own family. I wish I had asked him after I got older, but I never did. But I always had a strong feeling it had something to do with "Radio" and the flat mines.

Chapter 7

A wonderful thing came to Bayview that fall: TELEVISION. It was decreed by someone (I never knew who or what) that each family would have a TV set for a week. The way it worked with us was that when some of our kinfolk got the TV, we would go to their house every night to watch it. When we had it, they all came over to our house.The first of our family to get the TV was Uncle Henry, another one of my daddy's brothers. It was said that Uncle Henry had not spoken over fifty words in his life. His wife, Retha had once bragged that she and Uncle Henry had never had a cross word with each other in all the time they had been married.
Ma spoke up and said, "I guess not, seeing as how Henry don't talk!"

The first night we went over to Uncle Henry's house, I was excited, but it was not really my first time to see a television. I had seen one a few months earlier in the basement of Loveman's Department Store in Birmingham. A bunch of people were crowded around something, and my daddy wrangled our way up front to see what it was. And there it was, a TELEVISION! All I remember is a snowy picture and a young boy standing under a tree not doing anything. He was just standing there. The screen was small, and the picture wasn't clear, but I was thrilled beyond words.

When we got to Uncle Henry's, "Don Winslow of the Navy" was showing. He went around in a PT boat and killed a lot of Japanese sailors. Next was Wrestling, and this is what all the grown-ups were waiting for. That night a huge man named "Chest" Bernard wrestled two other men. It was no contest. Chest was unstoppable. He threw the other two men around like rag dolls. After Chest dispatched his foes, there were three or four more bouts. People would boo one wrestler and cheer for another. After the wrestling matches had ended, we got ready to go home. Out on the porch, my daddy said to Uncle Henry, "Boy that Chest Bernard is somethin' ain't he!" Uncle Henry spit tobacco juice over the porch railing and said, "Yep." That was the only comment I heard him make that night.Two weeks after Uncle Henry's family had their week with the TV, Ma and Uncle Matthew got it. We headed over to Ma's house every evening. Three weeks later it was our turn! The two men who brought the television in explained the operation to my mother. You could twist the "rabbit ears" around to get the best picture, and there was a large square glass that fit over the screen. The men said it was to help make the picture clearer like a magnifying glass, and it should be taken off and wiped clean every day. One of the men turned the TV on. It started making a buzzing noise, and the only thing on it was a picture of an Indian chief. One of the men said, "That's a test pattern. The shows will start later."

After the two men left, Marty and I sat on the floor and watched the Indian for two hours. I don't remember what channel it was, but it didn't matter because there was only one.

The shows finally got started. The first one was "Kukla, Fran and Ollie". Fran was a real woman and Kukla and Ollie were puppets. Kukla looked like a little boy with a big nose, and Ollie was an alligator. Kukla and Ollie were inside a puppet booth, and Fran stood outside the booth and talked to them.Fran would say, "How are you today, Kukla?" Then: "Have you been behaving yourself today, Ollie?"Ollie would say (in a deep voice), YA-HU, YA-HU, I have, Miss Fran." Sometimes Ollie would grab Kukla's big nose in his snout and pull him down out of sight. Marty squealed with laughter when this would happen.The next show was more to my liking, "Gunga the Elephant Boy". I had heard this show before on the radio and was thrilled to be able to see it on television. It was about a young boy in India who rode an elephant everywhere he went. He would run off man-eating tigers and go after bad men. He kept his village safe from all evil.After Gunga was through running around in the jungle on his elephant, "Don Winslow Of The Navy" came on. At the start of the show, a man's voice proclaimed, "**And Now,**

Doooon Wiiinsloww Of The Navy!" Don was still winning the war single-handed as he had at Uncle Henry's house. After Don, there was a show we hadn't seen at Uncle Henry's or Ma's house. It was a man sitting behind a big desk with two telephones on it and just talking. It must have been some sort of news show, but I didn't know it then. I just
knew it was boring, and I used the time to head for the outhouse. When I came out of the outhouse, I saw Carol Ashworth, a classmate of mine, walking down the alley toward her house. I yelled out proudly, "Carol, guess what! We've got the television this week!"
Carol threw her nose in the air and said, "So what! We had it last week, and you want to know what else? My daddy says he's going to buy us one soon, and we'll have a television *all* the time!" I headed down the hill depressed that the Ashworths were going to actually buy a television because I knew that would be a very slim chance at our house.

        When I entered the house, I forgot Carol and what she had said. I noticed some changes had happened. Now seated in the living room was my mother and daddy, Ma and Uncle Matthew, Uncle Henry and one of his daughters, Betty, who was sixteen. Another change was that every light in the house was off. That was the way it had been at Uncle Henry's and Ma's house. Everybody agreed that it made the picture clearer. They were there, of course, for the wrestling show, and it was just getting started. Chest Bernard wrestled again but just against one man this time. After they grappled around awhile, Chest got the other wrestler in some sort of wrestling hold, and the other man gave up. Betty started screaming, "That hold's against the wrestling rules. That's not right!"
I don't know where Betty got her wrestling knowledge from, but she kept hollering about it like she thought the referee was going to hear her and disqualify Chest.
 The next wrestlers were two huge men named Tarzan White and Farmer Brown. Farmer Brown was really big and wore a pair of overalls

and was bare-footed. Betty and people who were actually at the wrestling match all pulled for Tarzan and booed Farmer. Betty hooted and yelled and pointed out to the referee all the dirty tricks Farmer was trying to pull. The ref still paid her no attention. Tarzan finally "pinned" Farmer and everybody cheered, especially Betty, who jumped up in the air clapping her hands. About 10 PM the wrestling show ended, and somebody sang "The Star Spangled Banner". The picture went all snowy, and the buzzing noise stared. As everybody was getting up to go home, they were all talking about the wrestling matches and wasn't television something! Everyone but Uncle Henry, that is. I guess he wasn't very excited about it. The same routine was followed the whole time we had the television. A week later, the same two men came back and television went out of my life as quickly as it had come in.

Chapter 8

As 1949 came to an end, a tragedy unfolded that I would never forget. Phyllis Carnell, who was a year older and a grade ahead of me, seemed different than other girls her age. While other girls were playing "house" with their dolls, Phyllis would go from house to house talking to the grown-ups. Many times, she would come by our house and sit on the porch swing and talk with my mother just like a grown-up. I never knew what to make of it. I would hear my mother bragging on Phyllis to others, "that's the smartest kid I've ever seen. She talks like a grown person". I heard others say it too.
In early December, Phyllis became missing--She and her mother and her younger sister had went to the movies on a Friday evening.
Phyllis wanted to see "Angels with Dirty Faces" that was showing at the Ensley Theatre. Her mother and sister wanted to see a move at another theatre located in Wylam, about five miles away, so they dropped Phyllis off at the Ensley theater and went on.
When they came back later to pick her up, Phyllis was nowhere to be found. The theater manager told the police that he had seen a girl answering the description of Phyllis leave with a soldier before the movie ended. The next morning, Phyllis had still not been found, so the men in Bayview formed a search party. The crew my daddy was with was to search the woods between Bayview and Mulga, a nearby community. At 2:00 PM that afternoon, another crew found Phyllis. She was lying on a dirt road next to a small inlet on Bayview
Lake. She had been brutally assaulted and killed. The people in Bayview were stirred up. Nothing like this had ever happened there. Daughters were kept close to home, and accusations were thrown about on a daily basis. Kids even overheard adults talking about dark plots and conspiracies--Phyllis' mother and Sheriff Clayburn were lovers, or so it was said. Phyllis' killer

was never found, and my mother cried for a week. I heard her tell Marty that Phyllis was living with Jesus and all the Christmas Angels now.

Just as 1949 had ended in tragedy, 1950 also started with a tragedy. In early February, there was an explosion at Edgewater Mines where my daddy worked. My daddy was at work when we got the news. Women and kids were running up and down the sidewalks talking about it with panic in their voices."Dozens of men have been killed and Lord knows how many bad hurt!"
I had no idea where the news was coming from or if it was true. My mother started screaming, "Your daddy's dead, oh my Lord, help me Jesus!" She got me crying, and I went out in the front yard to wait for my daddy. I stood there with tears running down my face and praying as hard as I could until I finally saw his black '41 Chevrolet coming down the road. I had never been so happy in my life. After we all calmed down, my daddy confirmed there had been an explosion. "Yeah, she blew alright. I had just come out and was in the bathhouse when she went. Last I heard was that twelve men are dead. Damndest thang though, one of 'em kilt wasn't even in the mine. He was setting in his pickup close to the opening and a rock flew out, went through his winshiel' and cut his head slap off."

Two weeks after the explosion, a blizzard hit Bayview, at least by Alabama standards. It snowed all day and all night. When it stopped, there were five inches of snow on the ground, some said six. It stayed on the ground for five days, and Bayview looked different. Everyone said it looked like a winter wonderland. My daddy chopped wood into kindling for our wood burning stove we used for heat. The whole area was paralyzed. It was all just too wonderful because, of course, there was no school. Even the mines shut down because the men couldn't make it to work on the slippery, hilly roads. Not being used to snow, us kids caught on to it pretty quick, and snowmen were in every yard. And it didn't take us long to learn that a flattened cardboard box made a great sled for going down snow covered hills. Somebody knew how to make "snow cream" by mixing snow, milk, sugar and vanilla flavoring together and freezing it. We all thought it tasted just like home-made ice cream. Everybody but Ma was thrilled by the snow. Ma told me, "Son we had lots bigger snows that this when I was a young girl. Why, it would get so cold, big tree limbs would bust wide open. The men would go out and find squirrels and rabbits lying on the ground froze to death. They'd bring 'em home, and the women would make stew.The snow would be so high we could hardly open the front door". I believed every word. Nobody argued with Ma. I thought it would have been great to have lived back then. My happiness, of course, had to come to an end before the snow did. On the fourth night after the snow fell, my mother had a bad "spell" with her nerves. It was on a Saturday night. My daddy was at the kitchen table with his Chesterfields and coffee listening to the Grand Old Opry and Marty was under the table playing with Sally. I was lying on the living room couch reading "Hans Brinker and the Silver Skates'" a book Mama Davis had given me on my eighth birthday. I heard my mother say, "I'm going to lie down for a little while. I've got an awful headache". About ten minutes later, as my daddy would tell Ma the next day, "all hell broke loose". My mother ran screaming into the kitchen, "Benjamin, I'm smothering to death! I can't breathe! Help me, somebody! Lord Jesus! Somebody help me!" With that, she bolted out the back door with my daddy right behind her. Marty, who had just turned four in January, was confused and started crying. So was I. I had seen my mother have nervous spells before and go out the door, but this time it seemed worse. I told Marty everything would be all right. Half an hour later, our parents returned. My mother had quieted down, but she had a wild look in her eyes. They both sat in silence at the table while my daddy smoked and drank coffee. Suddenly my mother jumped up from the table and grabbed up my daddy's radio, jerking the plug out of the wall at the same time. She stood with it over her head for a second, and then threw it as hard as she could against the kitchen sink.

Tubes and pieces of wood flew everywhere. My daddy didn't say a word. He just sat there. She turned on him.

"I'm sick and tired of that goddamn shit you listen to all the time! You just do it to keep from talking to me, you sorry son-or-a-bitch!"

My daddy still said nothing, just smoked his cigarette. Marty started crying again. The shock of my life was coming. My mother turned her wild eyes on me.

"And I wanna tell you something, you little bastard – I hate your guts! You're the main cause of my nerves being like they are! Marty's the only child I love or ever will love! Why don'cha go live with Old Lady Knight, you love her so damn much! You ain't never cared nothing about Mama Davis the way you do that old woman!"

I was stunned. I felt like crying, but I didn't. My daddy finally spoke up. "Why don'cha leave the boy alone, Mal? You're saying thangs you're gonna be sorry for".She turned back on him. "The hell I am! It's the God's truth, and you know it!"My daddy told Marty and me to go to bed. He said, "Thangs will be better in the morning".

As I headed to bed, I heard my mother say, "The hell they will!"

Lying in bed, I could still hear them arguing at the kitchen table. A lot of it was muffled, but I did hear my mother say, "You know I told you when he was born that he was yours, and the next one would be mine!"

Then I did start to cry; but not loud enough for anyone to hear.

The next morning things were better as my daddy said they would be, for the time being anyway, but they would never be the same. That afternoon, my daddy and I walked to Ma's house. There were still patches of snow inpeople's yards and on the road, but the sun was out, and it was disappearing fast. Snowmen were just fallen clumps of snow. We would see lumps of coal that had been used for eyes and a nose lying on the ground where one had already melted away. The scenes together with what had happened the night before had me feeling as blue as I had ever felt. I couldn't explain it. It was just like the disappearing snowmen were somehow connected with my life.

At Ma's house, my daddy told her what had happened the night before. He tried to tell it from my mother's side of it.

"Mama, Mal's nerves are just real bad. She can't help the way she is. She don't mean the thangs she says."

Ma wasn't buying it. "Son, she's your wife, but she ain't got good sense. Nerves don't have nothing to do with it. Her whole family's the same way. We knowed 'em all years ago. None of 'em ever had brain one. And what she said to Daniel Wayne wasn't nothing but pure ol' meanness."

I could tell my daddy was uncomfortable while Ma went on, but he wasn't about to say anything to his mama.

Ma turned to me. "Daniel Wayne, you know I love you more than any of my gran'kids and much as I do my own kids. If Malva gets on to you again and starts acting crazy, you just come on and live with me!"

I said, "Thanks, Ma."

My daddy and I walked home in silence. I felt better now.

Chapter 9

In March I was still eight years old and in the third grade. I made pretty good grades, mostly A's with maybe a couple of B's. Carol Ashworth made all A's. There seemed to be a competition between us, not started by us, but by our teacher, Mrs. Barron. Maybe Carol thought there was a competition between her and me too, but it didn't mean a hill of beans to me. In May, Mrs. Barron announced to the class that Carol would not be going into the fourth grade in the fall, she would be going into the fifth grade. Carol was being "double promoted." That was fine with me; I didn't like Carol very much anyway.That afternoon, I was hitting a ball to another boy at recess when Mrs. Barron came out of the girls' side of the school outhouse. She came up to me, her hands on her hips. She was a fat woman with a big nose. She wasn't nearly as old as Ma or Mama Davis, but her hair was pulled back into a "bun" like theirs. She had a sneer on her face. "Well, Daniel, Carol moved ahead of you. I guess that means she <u>was</u> smarter than you all along."

I said, "I make all A's and B's"

"Yes, Daniel, you do, but it wasn't good enough. Carol's being double promoted and <u>you're</u> not. You could have been too, but I guess you just didn't care."

I didn't know what kind of response I was supposed to make to that, so I just kept quiet. She turned with her big nose sort of sticking up in the air like she had smelled something bad and waddled back toward the schoolhouse. It really didn't bother me. I just figured Carol getting double promoted had something to do with her daddy working at TCI and being a big shot.

In July I turned nine and another great thing came to Bayview, not as great as TV but close. And that was indoor plumbing! TCI owned the houses in Bayview, and everybody paid rent to the company. In July 1950, TCI announced that everybody had to buy the house they were living in or move out. Everybody we knew bought, including us. My mother and daddy went to an office somewhere and signed some papers, and we were now "buying" our house. Part of the deal if you bought was that TCI would build a full bathroom in your house--toilet, shower, sink and all. By the first week in August, the workmen had invaded the camps. Front yards were bulldozed for pipe to be laid leaving trenches and huge piles of dirt. For the grown-ups, this was annoying, but to us kids, it was great. The freshly dug ditches were used as "foxholes" and we would play "king of the mountain" on top of the huge piles of dirt. The only problem we had was having to bathe at least three times every night in a number three washtub just to get clean.

Hammering and sawing and the smell of new lumber was everywhere. I couldn't wait for our bathroom to be finished. Actually, I was a little scared using the outhouse, especially after it got dark. My friend, Jimmy Spears had told me that one time his grandfather, who lived out in the country, had been using his outhouse one night when a black widow spider bit him right on his balls. Jimmy said his granddaddy's balls swelled up so big he couldn't walk, and the ambulance had to back up to the outhouse to get to him. His granddaddy was in the hospital for two weeks sitting in a bathtub full of some kind of medicine until the swelling went down. I didn't know how much of Jimmy's story to believe, but I believed enough of it so that I always carried a flashlight with me to the outhouse. Every few seconds, I would jump up from the seat and shine the light around to see if any spiders were closing in. By the time school started, the new bathrooms were in and we all felt like "big shots" now.

My mother had a couple more nervous spells that summer, but nothing as serious as that Saturday night during the snow.

The worst thing that happened was that she started an argument with Mrs. Shoemaker who lived next door. Mrs. Shoemaker was working in her small garden in her backyard. My mother saw her and walked over and told Mrs. Shoemaker that she thought part of her garden was coming over into our yard.

Mrs. Shoemaker said, "Why no, Mrs. Knight, it's not at all on your property. Why don't you take some of these fresh tomatoes?" I guess she was a little scared of my mother because she and her husband had always had a ringside seat during my mother's "running fits".

My mother exploded. "You old bitch, call me a damn liar! I'll pull ever' one of your goddamn tomatoes out by the roots!" Mrs. Shoemaker headed for her back door. Luckily my daddy was home. He came out and got my mother by the arm and guided her back into the house. She looked at me in a funny way, but didn't say anything. I was thankful for that and for the fact that the Shoemakers didn't have any kids my age that I'd have to go to school with.

The relationship between my mother and me was strange, but I would still ask her permission to do things such as go over to a friend's house and things like that. It was a strained relationship, and she was like a stranger to me. I would sometimes pray at night that things would go back like they had been before the big snow, but deep down I knew they never would.

Ma always said, "Ben and Malva are too diff'rent from each other to have ever got married."--They were sure different to look at. My daddy was tall and lanky with brown hair and a receding hairline on each side of his forehead. My mother was short and plump with jet black hair.

Carol Ashworth told me one time, "You know, Daniel, your daddy looks just like Gary Cooper. I wish my daddy looked like that." Carol was real big on movie stars.

I said, "Who does my mother look like?"

She laughed and said, "Why, she just looks like Mrs. Knight, silly."

Chapter 10

I entered the fourth grade in September, and Mrs. Barron was no longer my teacher. Mrs. Fuller was my teacher now, and I liked her a lot better. Mrs. Barron was teaching fifth grade this year so she still had Carol and I was glad they were together.

In October, the fourth grade held a play in the auditorium. I don't really remember what the play was about, but we all wore old clothes and straw hats and rubbed black stuff on our faces and hands to make us look like negroes. There was a big pot that was set on the stage, and we all sat around it saying our parts. I do remember my one line was, "Lawd, have muh-sy, tha' pot sho is big. I'se wonda wha' they gone do wit tha' pot." I remember the parents in the audience laughing a lot.

Beside the outhouses (the school didn't get indoor bathrooms) at the school, there were also two bathhouses with showers in them, one for the boys and one for the girls. No one ever used them, but after the play was over, Mrs. Fuller told us to take our school clothes into the bathhouse and "wash that black stuff off and change before you go home." All the boys broke for the bathhouse. We pulled up short when we saw Miss Lolly, an old black woman, standing in front of the bathhouse with legs spread and her arms folded in front of her. I never knew Miss Lolly's job title. She seemed to be Mr. Earl's assistant because she was always helping him clean up around the school. When we stopped in front of her, Miss Lolly said, "Where y'all think you goin' with them black faces? Y'all done painted y'alls selves up to look like me, and that ain't no respec' at all! And y'all ain't about to use my bathhouse."

Mrs. Fuller had walked up in time to hear most of it and said, "You children just go on home and bathe there, and I'll talk to Miss Lolly." I don't know what she talked to her about, but the next day Miss Lolly was still in charge of the bathhouse.

Christmas that year was bleak. My daddy was out on strike from the mines. It seemed like he was out on strike a lot. My mother would carry on about it and act like it was somehow my daddy's fault.

On Christmas day, she was in a bad mood. When my daddy would try to talk to her, she would look away and not answer. I kept away. Marty got a new doll and a toy baby buggy, and I got a cap pistol with "The Durango Kid" written on the handles. Marty spent all day playing with her new doll and I stayed outside popping caps.

That night when everybody was getting ready to go to bed, my mother broke her silence. "We're all doomed, and I'm just gonna blow my damn brains out!" She screamed it so loud I'm sure the Shoemakers heard it next door. The only gun in the house, besides my cap pistol, was my daddy's single shot .22 rifle that he kept standing in the corner of the bedroom. After my mother's announcement, she headed that way with my daddy right behind her. She jerked up the rifle and started to swing it around when my daddy grabbed it and jerked it away from her. He looked sort of pale. "Don't you ever pull this stunt again, Malva, I mean it! If you do, you'll regret it!"

My daddy didn't raise his voice to my mother very often, and the shock of it seemed to calm her down. The rifle wasn't even loaded, but what my mother had done had really shaken my daddy this time. Later on, he took the bolt out of the rifle and locked it in his car trunk.

Chapter 11

In late January of 1951, the union called all the men back to work and things were fairly normal for a while. I was still making A's and B's, and I figured Carol Ashworth was probably getting ready for college.

One of the highlights for most of the boys in Bayview during this time was swapping comic books or "funny books" as Bayview kids called them. They could be bought for a dime and sometimes even a nickel, and just about everyone had a stack of them at home. Sometimes as many as three or four of us would meet at one of our houses and flip through each other's stacks to find some we hadn't read. Then we would start swapping. There would always be a large variety of choices: "Captain Marvel", "Nancy and Sluggo", "Fenimore Frog", "Henry", "Mutt and Jeff", and my favorite, "The Fox and the Crow".

There were even comic books written about the adventures of real people like Bob Hope and Roy Rogers and Gene Autry. I would never buy or swap for a Roy Rogers or Gene Autry comic book, and I didn't like their movies. To me, anybody who sang and liked girls was not a serious cowboy. My favorite cowboy was "The Durango Kid" because he didn't do either of those things. He just shot outlaws. It was hard to find a "Durango Kid" comic book. I had one put away, and I never took it to the swaps. I did have several ***"Red Ryder***" comic books because I considered him a serious cowboy too.

Carol Ashworth had always been big on comic books just like the boys were. If there was a "swap" going on, she was usually there. Her stack would have a lot of "Archie and Veronica" comic books in it, but she would have some good ones too.

Early in 1951 I took my comic books to Carol's house one Saturday to do a little swapping. Carol met me at the door and eyed the stack of books under my arm. I said, "Carol, get your funny books and let's swap, ok?"

She came out on the porch and studied me for a second.

She closed one eye and squinted at me out of the other.

"Daniel, I don't read funny books anymore. Mrs. Barron says they're childish, and honestly, I'm surprised that *you* still do." With this, she sort of sauntered back into the house and closed the door. I stood there flabbergasted for a couple of seconds, but I recovered enough to make it on down to Jimmy Spear's house where we did some heavy trading.

Daddy and I went fishing several times that summer, as we had most summers as far back as I could remember. We would usually drive as close to a river or creek as we could, and then walk through the trees down to the bank with our cane poles and worms. There was one place I always like to go because we would pass a small café where they also sold bait. I always got a kick out of the sign they had outside: "CAFÉ: HOT BISCUITS AND WORMS".

We never rented a boat when we went fishing. We would just fish from the bank. Sometimes men in a fishing boat with a motor would roar past us headed down river, and my daddy would say, "Look at that, son. That's big shots."

Ma went fishing with us sometimes. She would not tolerate any noise while she was fishing, not even talking. She would sit there with her cane pole and big sun bonnet and usually catch more fish than my daddy and I could catch together. Ma's favorite fishing spot was Brassfield Creek because of the perch you could catch there. Perch was her favorite to fry. The Palas bridge spanned the creek near to where we fished. As the sun got higher we would go under the bridge to fish to escape the heat.

In July of 1951, I turned ten and the Korean War was going strong. The Red Chinese were helping the North Koreans, and peace talks were getting nowhere. Three months earlier, in April, President Truman had fired General Douglas MacArthur, a hero of World War II. This had not set well with my daddy. "That son-of-a-bitch Truman don't have sense enough to pour piss out of a boot!"

I asked my daddy why President Truman had fired General MacArthur. He told me, "Son, this war is bein' run by China-- It ain't the North Koreans. They jus' do what China tells 'em to do. MacArthur wants to go on and invade China and end it now 'cause he knows we gonna have more trouble with them bastards later on. If we don't end it, you might wind up havin' to fight 'em before it's over. But the big shots ain't gonna let him invade China. They shut Patton up when he wanted to go head and invade Russia, an' this is the same thang. The money men in Washington get rich letting it go on an' on while pore boys die. If they'd turned MacArthur loose, we wouldn't have to still worry 'bout China, years on down the road. But then the money'd dry up, and they ain't gonna have that happen."

I didn't really understand how it all connected up, but I thought my daddy must be a pretty smart man.

Chapter 12

I guess the union didn't care much about the Korean War going on because the third week of September my daddy was on strike again. My mother was beside herself. I was in bed one night listening to them talk. My daddy was trying to keep his voice low, but my mother didn't care.

"It's all that son-of-a-bitch, John L. Lewis. He don't give a damn about the working man and his family, as long as he can line his own goddamn pockets. He don't give a damn if ever' miner's kid starves to death!"

My daddy tried to calm her. "Mal, don't wake the kids, they don't need to hear any of this."

"They need to hear it! Everybody needs to know they're going to starve to death!" I heard them going on about the strike until I finally drifted off to sleep. The next night as I lay in bed, it started up again. We were all going to starve to death because of some man named John L. Lewis wanting to be rich. I figured he must have something to do with the strike. My mother was pretty much covering the same ground she had the night before until my daddy said something that shut her up and shocked me from head to toe.

"Mal, when we was up at Charlie's and Clara's last month, me and Charlie talked about going up North and looking for work." Clara Aaron was my mother's sister and Charlie was her husband.

They had two boys: Roy, who was thirteen and Cecil, who was around Marty's age. They lived up in Walker County on a farm.

When I heard my daddy say this, I started to jump out of bed but lay still waiting for my mother to protest. She didn't. "What kind of work would y'all look for up North?"

"Well, Mal, most fact'ries are up North, an' I heard they're working 'round the clock because of the war."

"You know, Ben, that's just the very thing to do. But what could Charlie do? He ain't never done nothing but farm."

My daddy said, "Well, they told me they need men so bad they're taking on just about anybody. Course, I'm an electrician, so I won't have no trouble prob'ly."

My mother was getting excited. "You could send for me and the kids after you get settled in! Ben, why don't we ride up to Charlie an' Clara's tomorrow, and we can all talk about it some more!"

My daddy agreed that's what they would do, and Marty and I would stay with Mama Davis.

Mama Davis was old, but not as old as Ma. She didn't have a house like Ma did either. Mama Davis would live with one of her five kids for several months and then move on to another one. Now she was back living with us. I didn't get much sleep that night. I kept waking up and thinking about moving up North, wherever that was.

The next morning while my parents were getting ready to go to Uncle Charlie's and Aunt Clara's, my mother was in a good mood and talked about going up North.

"Daniel Wayne, we have to do what's best for you and Marty. We can't give y'all the things we'd like to with your daddy out on strike half the time." She seemed normal again. "As long as we stick together as a family, we can be happy anywhere."

I said, "I don't want to lose my friends and have to start in a new school where I don't know anybody."

My daddy spoke up, "Son, there's boys wherever we might move to that's your age and no diff'rent than the boys here. It's been my experience that ten year old boys are the same everywhere. Same thang with the schools."

I'll admit I was about halfway excited. I stood on the front porch and watched my parents pull out for Walker County in my daddy's '41 Chevy. Going back in the house, I asked Mama Davis what she thought about all this.

"Well, Daniel Wayne, your mama and daddy are trying to do what they think best for y'all. Why, you know yourself that your daddy's out on strike mor'n he's at work."

I said, "Why can't daddy get a job at TCI like Jimmy Spear's daddy?"

"Son, them jobs at the plant are just for big shots. Yore daddy couldn't get on there in a million years." I looked at Marty. She had discarded her new doll and was pushing Sally in the toy buggy. I asked Marty, "What do you think about us maybe moving up North, Marty?" Everybody said Marty sure talked well for a five year old. She said, "yes siree, we're moving up north." She might be smart, but I didn't think she understood what was going on. I watched her push the buggy into the living room. Mama Davis patted me on the back. "Now you kids go on out and play whilst I read my Bible." One thing she and Ma had in common was reading The Bible and talking about God. I hadn't heard Mama Davis ever say too much about women though. Another thing they had in common was both their husbands died before I was born, so I didn't have a grandfather. Jimmy Spears talked about his granddaddy all the time like the time he got bit on the balls by the black widow spider.

I sat out on the porch swing for a while thinking about where "up North" might be exactly. My daddy had a friend he worked with, Mr. Brock, who had come to Alabama from Virginia, and, sometimes he would bring his family to our house to visit. He and his wife had two daughters, one who was about a year older than I was, and the other was a year younger. They lived on the other side of the camps not far from Uncle Henry. We had been to their house several times also.

The girls had not been impressed with our big snow; they said it was nothing compared to the snows in Virginia. The older girl talked all the time about how great Virginia was and how much she hated Alabama. I wondered if my daddy was talking about going to Virginia, but then I figured that couldn't be it 'cause Mr. Brock had had to come to Alabama to find a job. As I thought about it some more I was pretty sure Virginia was "up North". I just didn't know where we would be going.

Late that evening, my mother and daddy came back from Uncle Charlie's and Aunt Clara's. Plans had been made. My aunt and uncle's preacher had been there too. He told everybody that he had heard that a plant that made boxcars for trains was hiring, and it was in Indianapolis, Indiana. I ran and got the Atlas. It was a big book of maps we'd had all my life. I found the map of the United States, and then I found Indiana. Indianapolis was shown too. It had a star by it. Indiana was "up North" all right.

This was on a Saturday. The plans were for my daddy and Uncle Charlie to leave the next Friday night bound for Indianapolis, Indiana. The preacher was going too. I couldn't understand why a preacher would want to go "up North", but my daddy was glad of it because the preacher had a brand new '51 Ford, and that's what they were going to make the trip in. My daddy and Uncle Charlie would help buy gas for the trip. There was still another surprise that night! They had stopped at McCrory's Department store in Ensley on the way home and bought daddy a new radio.

I lay in bed that night and tried to hear the talk at the kitchen table, but the Grand Ole Opry drowned out the words. ***"Blue moon of Kentucky, keep on shiining. Shine on the one that's gone and left me bluue."*** I finally drifted off to sleep.

Sunday afternoon, my daddy, Marty and I rode over the Ma's house to tell her the news. On the way over, my daddy said, "Y'all don't say anything to Mama. Just let me tell her in my own way." I agreed not to say anything. Marty was in the back seat with Sally. "I'll not say anything to Ma, no siree!"

Ma and Uncle Matthew were sitting in the living room with the front door open when we pulled up. My daddy opened the screen door and he and I went on in. Marty stayed in the front yard petting Ma's cat. We went into the kitchen where Ma had coffee on the stove and seated ourselves around the table. Ma was being awfully quiet. She poured coffee for daddy and Uncle Matthew and iced tea for me and her. As soon as Ma finally sat down, she looked at my daddy and said, "Well, son, so you're goin' north to seek your fortune air ye?"

There was a couple of seconds of silence. Then my daddy looked at me.

"Dan, was you down here at Mama's yesterday while we was up in Walker County?"

Before I could say anything, Ma spoke up. "Now son, I ain't seen Daniel yesterday, and you know it. You know the Lord reveals thangs to me, and he's done revealed to me that you're 'bout to do a foolish thang."

Daddy looked down at his coffee cup. "Well Mama, I cain't make a livin' in the mines no more, and there ain't no jobs here in Alabama. I got to do what's best for the kids."

Through the window over Ma's kitchen sink, I saw dark clouds out over Bayview Lake and a long streak of lighting. Daddy got up and went out on the front porch and hollered to Marty to get inside. She came in and jumped up into Ma's old rocker and started rocking Sally. My daddy sat back down at the table. By now, rivers of rainwater were running down Ma's kitchen windows, and the sky was filled with lighting streaks and rolling thunder. I thought for sure Ma would move us all into her storm pit like she had done other times, but she didn't seem to notice the storm.

"Ben, if you're wanting to do what's best for the children, you'll stay where you are. Matthew here's out on strike just like you are and we're gonna make it all right. I've lived in Alabama all my life, and I'm 75 years old. I've saw hard times, and I've saw better times, but I ain't never missed a meal yet. You goin' to take them kids off somewhere where nobody knows you or cares a buffalo nickel for any of yall. Them people up north ain't even like us. What if one of y'all gets bad sick like Daniel Wayne did when he almost died with the big red measles? Malva ain't got sense enough to take care of her own self, much less the rest of y'all."
Uncle Matthew spoke up. "Now, Mama, that's Ben's wife, and there ain't no need in talkin' 'bout her like that!"

Ma glared at Uncle Matthew. "If it's the truth I tell it, and God knows it's true. If you back-talk me agin, I'll wear you out with a switch even if you aire a grown man." Uncle Matthew dropped his head over his coffee cup as a deep rumbling sound of thunder rolled in the distance. I never did know how Ma could do things like that.

My daddy said, "Well, it looks like that storm passed on by us so I guess we'll head on back toward out house, Mama. I'll come back to see you before I go nex' Friday night."

When we reached the porch, Ma said, "I know you ain't coming to see me afore you go, but I'm going to be prayin' to the Lord to take care of you, son. The Lord's done revealed to me that they ain't no stopping you. Mal's done made up yore mind for you and nothin' I say will make any diff'rence."
My daddy didn't say anything.

Marty and me hugged Ma, and I said, "I'll be back before I move off, Ma."

Ma smiled. "I know you will, son."

Daddy picked Marty up before we left the porch so she wouldn't step off Ma's concrete walk on to the muddy yard. Ma's yard was always muddy after a hard rain because it was a dirt yard. Ma didn't allow a single blade of grass to grow. If some tried to come up she would be out in the yard with her sunbonnet on and her hoe, chopping it out of the ground. About once a week, she would go out and "sweep" the yard with a broom. She said she just liked a dirt yard better than grass.

On the way home, I asked daddy about the people up North being different than us. He said, "People are the same everwhere. People up north ain't no diff'rent than we are."

That week went by in a hurry. All day on Friday was spent with my mother packing things my daddy might need on his trip. I heard him say that they were going to drive "straight through" because he and Preacher could take turns driving and sleeping. He said Uncle Charlie never learned how to drive anything but a mule.

Around 6:00 PM Friday evening, Preacher and Uncle Charlie pulled up in Preacher's new Ford. Uncle Charlie bounced out grinning and punched me playfully in the stomach. Uncle Charlie was a little, wiry man with buckteeth. I had never seen Preacher before. When he got out of the car, I could see that he was tall like my daddy, but he had dark curly hair and a lot of it.

After my daddy had packed his things in the car, we all stood around in the yard, and the men looked at a map. Preacher said, "highway 31 to Nashville and then 41 on into Indiana and then we'll figure out the best way to Indianapolis."

Daddy looked at the map. "Yeah, that looks like our best bet." It all sounded exciting to me and far-away.Uncle Charlie said, "Well, I guess we best be gitting on the road." My daddy hugged everybody, even Mama Davis, and got in the back seat. My mother hollered out. "Take care of yourself, Benjamin!" Preacher started up his new Ford and the three men pulled out . I stood on the sidewalk and kept looking down the road even after they had went out of sight. I was wondering about what Ma had said and worrying about my mother having a "running fit" with my daddy gone. I was glad Mama Davis was there.

48

The Letter

A week after my daddy left, the first letter came. My mother read it and then she handed it to me. It was in my daddy's scrawled handwriting.

Mal and Kids,
We got to Indianapolis and I got hired on. Charlie and Preacher didn't.
They was going to check some other places around here. But when I went
back for my examination I found out you had to buy your own tools. I caint
do that of course. We heard about work in Tolledo, Ohio and are going.
We will be there by time you get this letter.
Love to all, Ben

I thought my mother would be upset, but she wasn't.
"I know your daddy is going to find a job somewhere. I'm just going to keep on trusting in the Lord."
I headed for the atlas. My daddy must have meant Toledo, Ohio because there it was right on Lake Erie, one of the "Great Lakes" the teacher had showed us on the big map at school. She said she had seen Lake Michigan, and it was so big you couldn't even see across it. I wondered if you could see across Lake Erie.

49

Chapter 13

Mrs. Fuller was my teacher now. A spelling bee consisting of the fifth and sixth grades was announced. Each grade would have spell-offs until each had five finalists. Two boys and three girls were finalists for the fifth grade class. I was one of them. For the sixth grade class, there were four boys and one girl. Carol Ashworth, of course, was the one girl. One week was given the finalist to study and practice before the main event to crown the Bayview Elementary School champion. Every night my mother would give me words to spell, not only out of the school speller, but out of the dictionary too. I had a dream one night that I would have to spell everything I said the rest of my life. Two days before the spelling bee another letter came.

Mal and kids, Have good news. Didn't find work in Toledo. Come on to Port Clinton,Ohio. Was hired on at a Army Ordnance Plant. It is called E.O.D. Found a place for us. Will send you some money for you and kids to come on the train as soon as possible. Charlie got hired at a gypsum plant in Sandusky,Ohio. It's not far from us. Preacher is going to get Clara and the kids and is going back to Alabama for good. He don't like this place he said. I think it's a nice place. I will write soon.

Love to all,

Ben

There was a picture postcard inside the envelope for me. It showed a white monument on what looked like an island in Lake Erie. On the other side, above my daddy's writing, it said this was Put-In-Bay where Commodore Oliver H. Perry defeated the British in the War of 1812. I couldn't believe I might actually live close to where something like that happened, but there it was. It even said it was near Sandusky, Ohio where my daddy said Uncle Charlie was living.

My daddy's letter to me said:

Dan you will really like it up here.

We can see Lake Erie from our place and a big river runs behind our place. Everbody here fishes all the time. See you soon. Love, Daddy

I was convinced. Ma's warnings were forgotten. I was excited and raring to go. My mother was the happiest I had ever seen her. That night we sat up past midnight, studying spelling words and talking about moving to Ohio. The big spelling bee was held on a Friday evening in the school auditorium.Folding chairs were set up for families and visitors, and my mother was there.The ten finalists were seated in straight chairs on the stage. Mr. Wilson, the principal, gave us the words to spell. The rules were that the speller would say the word, spell it, then say the word again. Several rounds went by with no one making a mistake. Jimmy Spears was the first to go down. The fatal word was "profession". Jimmy walked to the front of the stage. Mr. Wilson said, " the word is 'profession". Jimmy said in a loud voice, "profession.... p . r . . o .f . . .. f .. e ... s..i...o..n- Profession!"

"Sorry Jimmy. That is incorrect. " Please take a seat down on the first row. "

Jimmy kept standing there. The principal repeated, " Jimmy, please take your seat in the auditorium." Jimmy didn't budge. He just stood there staring at Mr. Wilson. Finally, Mrs. Russell came up on the stage and took Jimmy's arm and guided him down to his seat on the first row.Several more rounds went by, and there were more eliminations. They went quickly to their seats in the front row though, and didn't stand there and stare at Mr. Wilson like Jimmy had done. It finally came down to the finaltwo spellers, Carol

Ashworth and me. We each spelled three or four words correctly, and then It was my turn again. I walked up to the front of the stage. Mr. Wilson said, "the word is "physician". This was an easy one. I had spelled it a dozen times during practice. "Physician- P . . y . .s . i. . . cian." I knew as soon as I had finished spelling it that I had missed it.There were a couple of seconds of silence as though Mr. Wilson wasn't sure himself.Then he said, "I'm sorry, Daniel, that is incorrect. Please return to your seat. Carol Ashworth will be given the same word. If she spells it incorrectly, the contest will continue". Fifteen seconds later, Carol was the Bayview Elementary School spelling champion.

Chapter 14

Three weeks after the spelling bee, the next letter came. The envelope was long and heavier than usual.

Dear Mal and kids. I am sending two tickets for train. You and kids will leave Birmingham on Nov. 16th at six in the evening down there. This will give you time to take care of some things first. You will get here the next day. I will be at the train station. Marty does not need a ticket. Love to all.

Ben

Inside the envelope were two train tickets to Port Clinton, Ohio. There was also some money wrapped in brown paper. My mother was beside herself. "Finally we're getting out of this old place! Thank you, Jesus, thank you Lord! Maybe we can start living like human beings now!" That surprised me. I thought we had been living like human beings. Mama Davis only comment was, "I sure hope Benjamin got a big enough place to have room for me when I get to come." Nov. 16th was fifteen days away. On a Friday, my mother said there was lots to be done. The next day she sold Daddy's 41 Chevrolet to Mr. Bice for $50.00. When I protested, she said, " your daddy told me to do this before he left. You just let me handle it. When I need your advice, I'll ask for it." I was never to know what happened to the house or furniture or anything else we had.

The fifteen days went by in a hurry. I had one fight after school. Charles Wright cut in on me talking to Thomas Dees and Jimmy Spears about moving to Ohio and said, "Yore daddy must be nuts 'cause there ain't nothin' but nigger lovers live up North." I grabbed him in a headlock and wrestled him to the ground.

Getting astride of him, I got one punch in before Mr. Earl jerked me off of him, like I was light as a feather. He pulled Charles up off the ground and shook us both by the shoulders. "Now, no more fighting fellers! I ain't saying nothing to Mr. Wilson this time, but I don't wan'ta see no more of this!"

I said "Yes sir!" Charles jerked away and ran off hollering, "I'm gonna tell my Daddy about this! You"ll be sorry! You just wait! My daddy'll be here tomorrow!" I guess Charles' daddy didn't care because Charles stayed away from me the next day, and I didn't see any sign of his daddy.

In November, on a Wednesday, was my last day at school. I got my report card from Mrs. Russell to take to my next school in Port Clinton, Ohio. Mrs. Russell hugged me and said she would miss me. Mr. Wilson shook my hand and said he wished me and my family good luck. I walked out of Bayview School for the last time. When I left school, I walked all the way to Ma's house. The day was cool and cloudy, but Ma was sitting on her porch swing wearing a sunbonnet. I said, "Well, Ma, we're leaving on a train Friday for Port Clinton, Ohio."

She had received a letter from my daddy. "I know you aire, son. And I hate it more than anything in this world. But there ain't anything I can do about it. I just want you to take real good care of yourself and watch out for Marty. And I want you to know you've always got a home with me."

After we hugged, I saw tears in Ma's eyes for the first time in my life. She turned quickly and went into the house closing the door. It started drizzling rain as I started my walk home. If I had known what lay ahead of me, I would have turned around right then and gone back to live with Ma.

.

Chapter 15

At four o'clock on Friday afternoon , my mother's brother, Lloyd pulled up in front of our house. Uncle Lloyd was short and heavyset with dark hair just like my mother. He was a deacon in his church and very religious. He had a son my age named Bobby. I spent a week with Bobby one summer on their farm in Walker County, not far from Aunt Clara's house They were much better off than Uncle Charlie and Aunt Clara. Uncle Lloyd was a "big shot". The week I stayed with them, we went to church on Wednesday night, Sunday morning and Sunday night. I had never had so much "churching" in one week. The most church going I had been exposed to was going to Sunday School and preaching every once in a while with Ma at her church. I had never seen my mother or daddy inside a church.

The plan was that Uncle Lloyd would take us to the train station in Birmingham and then he would take Mama Davis back to his house to live for a while. Our luggage consisted of two large suitcases with cord tied around them, one small red suitcase that my mother was going to keep with her, and a cardboard box taped with electrician's tape. With Uncle Lloyd helping , we got it all loaded in the trunk of his car. My mother got in front with Uncle Lloyd, and Marty and I got in the back seat with Mama Davis and off we went to the train station in Birmingham.

To me, the trip to the station was the actual start of our journey since we didn't go into the city of Birmingham very often. When we went to the movies, or the "show" as we called it, it was usually to a theater close to

Bayview such as Ensley or Fairfield. It was a rare occasion to go "downtown", one of the few times being when my daddy took me to see "Song of the South" at the Alabama theater. A few times we had gone to Birmingham at Christmas to see the Christmas displays in the large windows of Loveman's or one of the other big department stores.

Uncle Lloyd took us through Ensley and up a hill they called "Bush Hill" with big houses on both sides of the road. My daddy had once told me that the people who lived in these houses were " really big shots" Our route took us by Birmingham Southern College. Once in the third grade, Mrs. Baron had brought us here to see a play about "Aladdin". Afterwards, Carol announced Birmingham Southern was where she would be going to college. College seemed so far off and strange to me that I never thought about it one way or the other.

We went by Legion Field, a large stadium that was called the "Football Capital Of The South". I wasn't sure what that meant, and I had always wanted to see it from the inside but never had. I had been in a stadium one time. It was where the fair was held every year, and my daddy and I had sat in the stadium and watched men shoot off fireworks. It was not nearly as big as Legion Field though.

Pretty soon we saw the large buildings of Birmingham, but Uncle Lloyd made a turn before we got all the way to them. After a couple of more turns, we pulled up to the train station. The building was big and people were streaming in and out. There were men in suits and hats and sailors and soldiers carrying bags on their shoulders. I wondered if they had been in Korea or if maybe they were on their way there.

A   black man came and loaded our green suitcases and cardboard box onto a cart with two wheels like I had seen Carl use at the commissary. He and my mother went in first. My mother kept the small red suitcase with her. I was more amazed when we got inside. Someone had carved statues all over the high ceiling. The station was full of people. Some were just sitting and some were trying to sleep . Others were just standing around. I saw a woman with her arms around a sailor's neck. The woman was hanging on for dear life and sobbing. The sailor wasn't crying; he was kind of red in the face and grinning. Uncle Lloyd found us some empty seats. My mother came over after checking on the train, still hanging onto her little red suitcase. "Well, the man said the train's on time. Our other bags are going in a baggage car, and I'm worried about it. We've got to change trains in Cincinnati, Ohio. How in the world will they know to put the bags on another train?"

Uncle Lloyd explained."Mal, those tags they gave you are for you to show when y'all get to Port Clinton. They've got "Port Clinton" on them, and the bags have the same tags on them. They know what they're doing alright. Don't worry about that. But my mother still had a worried look on her face.

We all sat pretty much in silence. Even Marty wasn't stirring much. All of a sudden a loudspeaker crackled--"**All passengers with tickets to Decatur, Pulaski, Nashville, Cincinnati, Akron and Cleveland will please board now through gate 3!**

Then the message was repeated. My mother jumped up looking bewildered. Uncle Lloyd took her by the arm and started guiding her toward gate 3 with the rest of us coming along behind. When we got outside, there it was. I had seen passenger trains before when one would pass by us while we waiting at a crossing, but this one looked cleaner and newer. The same black man who had taken our luggage in walked up.

"She's called the "Hummingbird" folks. Y"all know why? Cause she just hums along as purty as you please. Why, you can set a Dixie cup full of water on one of them arm rests by the seats, and you ain't gonna lose a drop all the way to where you going. She's that smooth." I don't know why, but my mother asked him if it had ever been in a train wreck. "Why, no ma'am, she surely ain't. Y'all be just as safe as can be on the Ol' Hummingbird." Mother thanked him for telling us, and we went to where a gray-headed man in a blue uniform had set a stool by some steps leading onto the train. My mother told him, "We're going to Port Clinton, Ohio."
The man said, "Yes, ma'am, you're getting on the right train."
"But we've got to transfer in Cincinnati, and our bags are on this train ". She must not have paid much attention to what Uncle Lloyd had said. The man assured her, "Ma'am, your things will be transferred to the train you transfer to. Don't worry about it at all. Y'all just get on board and enjoy the trip."

We went up the steps with my mother carrying Marty and turned right into a coach car. We sat down in the first row of seats. All the seats were big, and each seat had its own arm rests. It was the most comfortable seat I had ever sat in, in my life. There was even a lever you could pull to put the back in any position you wanted. I turned around and saw that there were several passengers already seated behind us.

It looked to me like most of them were reading a book or a magazine. I had the window seat, Marty was in the middle and my mother was on the outside. I looked out and saw Mama Davis and Uncle Lloyd right outside our window. It had gotten dark while we were inside waiting and lights had been turned on outside the station. Mother leaned over and waved at them. They both waved back, and Mama Davis said something, but we couldn't hear her. In a few minutes, the train gave a little lurch and stopped. Then it gave another little lurch, and we started moving slowly. I waved at Mama Davis and Uncle Lloyd as they disappeared from our window.

As the "Hummingbird" picked up speed, I looked out the window wanting to see the tall buildings in Birmingham, but I couldn't. I didn't understand it. Soon all I could see was what seemed to be the dark outlines of trees off in the distance and every once in awhile, a house setting way back with its lights burning. I knew then we were already past any hope of seeing the lights of Birmingham.

The same gray haired man who had been at the steps came to our seats. He said, "I'm the conductor ma'am . May I see your tickets please?" My mother handed them to him. "They said my daughter didn't need one." "No ma'am, the baby don't have to have one. Just you and the young gentlemen." I didn't think Marty was a baby, but I guess she was to a man that old.

After the conductor had left our coach, the lights were turned off, but there was a "reading light" above our heads that passengers could keep on if they wanted to read. Rain had started splattering against our window, and I gave up trying to see anything. I turned on the reading light and started reading a "Fox And The Crow"--a funny book that Mama Davis had bought me in the Birmingham train station.

Just then another man appeared. This one was a black man in a white coat."Ma'am, the dining car is still open if you and the children would care to

60

have supper." My mother said she didn't think so, but could he bring us something to us there? He said." Yes, ma'am, I can bring y'all a sandwich and something to drink. My mother asked, "What kind of sandwiches do y'all have. Have you got baloney?"

"No, ma'am, but we got ham."

"Okay, bring us three ham sandwiches and three soft drinks."

"Yes, ma'am." He was back in about ten minutes with three ham sandwiches and three Dixie cups filled with coke. "That'll be $3.00, ma'am."

My mother looked at him like he'd lost his mind. "Three dollars? Did you say three dollars?"

"Yes ma'am."

"For these little flimsy sandwiches?"

"Yes , ma'am, and the drinks." I was shrinking down into my seat, knowing a scene was coming.

To my surprise, my mother lowered her voice. "Mister, I know it's not your fault. You just work for the train."

"Yes ma'am." She handed him three one dollar bills.

"Thank you, ma'am. If y'all need anything else, just let me know."

"I don't think we can afford anything else."

He said, "Yes ma'am, I understand," and left. I started to ask my mother why we didn't eat in the dining car, but I knew the answer would be that it was for "big shots", so I ate my ham sandwich and read my funny book.

Chapter 16

It wasn't long before the "Hummingbird" started slowing down. The conductor came back to our car and said, "We're coming into the Decatur , Alabama station, folks. Anyone holding a ticket to Decatur will leave the train here. Decatur, Alabama , folks. For the ones going on, we'll be here about fifteen minutes."

After he made his announcement, He headed on to the next car. I peered out the window as we came to a stop. It was still raining, but I could make out a building with a sign on it saying DECATUR ALABAMA. It was a small station compared to the one in Birmingham. I didn't see any people at all. No one in our car got off, and nobody new came in, but we stayed there fifteen minutes.

When I had first looked around our coach, I had spotted a red-haired girl about my age sitting with a woman who I figured was her mother. When I looked around again to see who might be getting off, she was staring straight at me. I jerked my head back around so fast I almost broke my neck.

When we pulled out of Decatur, Marty was turned sideways in her seat with her knees pulled up and her arms around them. She was fast asleep. My mother was twisting around in different positions trying to get comfortable. The black man who had brought us the ham sandwiches appeared again carrying three big pillows. "Ma'am, I thought y'all might could use these."

"How much are they?"

"Don't worry about it, ma'am."

"Well, thank you so much."

"Yes, ma'am, y'all sleep good now." My mother said something about him being a real gentleman and then turned Marty around in her seat facing her and put a pillow under her head on the arm rest. She finally got into a position she liked and went back to sleep.

I was too excited to be sleepy. Thoughts of what Ohio was going to be like kept going through my head. What about the school? Were the kids going to be different like Ma said, or was everybody the same like my daddy had said? And what about all that fishing? The rain seemed to be hitting the window harder now. After all my daydreaming, I grew drowsy in spite of myself. I put the pillow and my head between my seat and the window and drifted off.

Somewhere in my dreams I heard the conductor say something about Pulaski, Tennessee and remember thinking that I was actually in another state for the first time in my life. I must have gone into a deep sleep because I didn't hear any other stops called out. The next thing I knew my mother was shaking me by the shoulder.

"Wake up, Daniel Wayne, we're coming into Cincinnati pretty soon." Still groggy, I satup rubbing my eyes. I heard my mother ask the conductor what time it was.

" It's 3:20AM Cincinnati time ma'am. You might need to reset your watch."

The conductor looked at me. "Thought you might want to know, son. We're crossing the Ohio River right now."

I gazed out the window. All I could see was steel girders zipping by. Further out it was too dark to see anything. I wasn't sure if I had ever heard of the Ohio River, but I had heard of the Mississippi River. Mrs. Russell had said it was the biggest river in the country. I wondered if the Ohio was anything like the Mississippi. We passed steel girders for a long time so it must have been mighty wide.

The "Hummingbird" was slowing down. I peered out the window. It had stopped raining and I could make out a couple of stars in the sky. Soon we started passing smoke stacks like those at the T.C.I. plant back home. All of a sudden I was startled when another passenger train roared right past us going in the opposite direction. It was so close I could have reached out and touched it. Then another one roared by on the other side of the train. Nothing like this had happened in Birmingham. It had startled my mother too. "My God, we're gonna be killed in a wreck before we make it to Cincinnati!"

The black man in the white coat was passing by our seats. "They all on they own tracks ma'am. Ain't nothing to worry about." My mother nodded at him, but I don't know if she really believed it. The "Hummingbird" slowed down some more, and my mother announced she and Marty were going to the restroom. When they returned, Marty's long blonde hair had been brushed, and my mother had put on lipstick and brushed her hair too. She opened the little red suitcase and handed me my toothbrush, toothpaste, a bar of soap and a wash cloth. I noticed there were also band aids and a bottle of aspirin in there. I knew my mother had headaches a lot, but I didn't know what the band aids were for; in case of a train wreck I guess. When I got back in my seat, we were barely moving. The conductor came in and announced that we were in Cincinnati and started listing off all the cities people could connect to from there. I heard Port Clinton and Sandusky. By the time he was through we were at a complete stop. Everybody was getting off this time. I saw the red headed girl go by us with her mother. We got off the train with my mother and me both holding Marty by her hands. I had never seen so many people in my life. My mother picked Marty up as we went through a turnstile and then a gate, and then we went inside. I forgot about the Birmingham station. I was awestruck. This had to be the biggest train station in the world. The ceiling was shaped like a dome and reached to the sky. Marty's eyes got as big as saucers. Right in the middle of the station, reaching almost to the ceiling was the biggest Christmas tree I had ever seen. When Marty tried to look at the top of the tree she almost toppled over. She had to lie down on the floor to see the Christmas Angel, all lit up, sitting high above the crowd of people.

My mother mumbled something about it being too early to have a tree up. I could tell her nerves were bothering her. "Lord have mercy, Daniel Wayne, I've got to find out where in the world we're supposed to go in this place!"

There was a counter stretching all the way down one side with ticket cages about ten feet apart. Each one had a line of people in front of it. My mother headed for the nearest one while I sat with Marty on a long wooden bench. A man walked by us with a turban on his head just like the characters wore on 'Gunga the Elephant Boy'. He was dark-skinned and had a beard, but he wasn't wearing a robe. He had on a suit and tie just like some of the other men.

Our mother finally came back and was out of breath. "Daniel Wayne, we've got to find Gate 22! The train's leaving in an hour and a half. And I don't know if we'll make it! You hold Marty's hand and carry the suitcase. Hurry up, let's go!" And away we went! I jumped up with the little red suitcase and grabbed Marty by the hand. My mother was already getting a lead on us. Marty couldn't move that fast, and I couldn't carry her and the suitcase too. I hollered out for my mother to slow down. She stopped and turned around.

"Daniel Wayne, there might not even be a Gate 22. We might be stuck in this place for eternity!" She turned back around and took off at a faster pace. She was soon out of sight in the crowd of people.

Across from where Marty and I had been sitting, there had been a big sign saying, Gate 15. Now we were passing a sign saying Gate 16. I had been practically dragging Marty along, but now I slowed down. I knew we would eventually get to Gate 22 and wouldn't be any hour and a half doing it either. We moseyed along talking about the big Christmas tree and laughing at people Marty thought looked funny. Marty said, "I'm so hungry, Daniel, I could eat a horse"

She had heard our daddy say that before. I told her I was too and we'd probably eat again when we got on the train. In about fifteen minutes we arrived at Gate 22. Our mother was sitting on a bench staring straight ahead. There weren't as many people here as there had been in the main part of the terminal. I didn't know what to expect when we got there. She acted like everything was fine. What took you two so long? I was beginning to think I was going to have to go on without y'all. With that, she laughed and pulled Marty up on her lap. "You know I wouldn't leave you behind, sweetheart." I said "Marty's hungry and I am too.".

She took the suitcase from me then and pulled two candy bars out of the inside lining. "Here, this'll hold y'all for awhile. We'll eat again when we get on this next train." I ate my candy bar and re-read my funny book. After awhile I became tired of waiting on the train. I got up and stretched and turned around. The red-headed girl and her mother were sitting on a bench right behind us. She was staring at us again. I quickly turned around and sat back down. How had they gotten there? I hadn't seen them since we left the "Hummingbird". Marty was curled up on the bench and sound asleep when the loudspeaker blared. **"All passengers holding tickets to Lima, Findlay, Freemont, Port Clinton and Sandusky please board now through gate 22!--ALL ABOARD PLEASE!"** We pushed through another turnstile and out through the gate with about a dozen other people. This train sure wasn't the "Hummingbird". It looked old and was painted a dark green color. On the side of each car was printed **NEW YORK CENTRAL.** The conductor looked a lot like our first one except he was a little older and fatter. My mother expressed her concern about her things. He assured her that her luggage was now on this train. As I went up the steps, I asked the conductor if this train had a name. He said, "No son, no name; it's just part of the New York Central Line."

When we entered our car, I saw the inside was worse than the outside. Green paint was peeling off the walls. Marty said, "this is an ugly old train." This time we sat on the right side of the aisle, and I sat by the window again. The seats were padded but were as ard as the wooden benches back in the station. There wasn't any overhead reading light.

I saw the red-headed girl and her mother sitting on the other side about two rows behind us. This time she was staring out the window. For some reason, I was secretly glad that she was still traveling with us. I wondered if she went to school in Port Clinton. After awhile, the train gave a couple of lurches and then starting moving. The old New York Central didn't hum like the "hummingbird". It creaked and groaned and made loud noises under our feet. As we picked up speed, it seemed to get louder. I thought my mother would say something about it, but she was just sitting there like she was in deep thought. Marty had something to say. "Daniel, why is this old train so loud? My ears hurt. I sure can't sleep on this old train." I said "it's just old, I guess, Marty."

After the conductor looked at our tickets he said, "It's 5:45 AM ma'am. The dining car is open." I was shocked when my mother asked him which way it was."It's just two cars up ma'am." The train was really shaking and rattling now. We made our way to the dining car holding on to the backs of the seats we passed. I could only use one hand because I was holding Marty's hand as tight as I could with the other. When we entered the dining car, there were already three men seated at different tables drinking coffee and reading newspapers. We sat down at the first table we came to. It was covered with a white tablecloth and already had spoons and forks and glasses on it.

A black man came to our table wearing a white coat just like the man on the 'Hummingbird'. The difference was his white jacket was dirty. He also wasn't calling anybody ma'am. He filled our glasses with water and asked, "what'll y'all have?"

My mother asked "Have you got corn flakes?"

"Yeah, we got 'em."

"Well, bring the kids some corn flakes and orange juice, and I'll have a doughnut and some coffee."

He sauntered off not saying anything. I looked out the window. It was breaking day now, and I could see we were going through hilly country, not like the rocky, red clay hills back in Alabama, but low, rolling, yellow-green hills.

After about fifteen minutes, the man came back. He put two small boxes of Kellogg's corn flakes on the table and two tiny glasses of orange juice. A pitcher of milk and a sugar bowl were already on the table. When he filled my mother's coffee cup and set a saucer with a doughnut on it in front of her, she asked him if he had to bake the doughnut himself since he had been gone so long. His jaw twitched a time or two, but he didn't say anything as he walked away. After we had finished eating, he brought the bill. I don't know how much it was but my mother paid it without any comment.

While we were in the dining car, the train had made a stop in Xenia, Ohio. Looking out the window, I saw it was another small station. Several old men in overalls were standing around on the platform looking at the train. They looked like the old men that sometimes stood around in front of my uncle's store in Walker County.

On the way back to our car, we passed the red-haired girl and her mother as they headed for the dining car. She looked at me and smiled. I sort of smiled back at her, but I could feel my face getting hot. By the time we got back to our seats we were creaking and groaning out of the Xenia station. A woman came into our car. She wasn't in any kind of uniform, and she had three or four pillows under each arm. She announced. "pillows folks! Pillows for rent, one dollar. Does anyone need a pillow?"

My mother looked up at her."The last train we were on, the pillows were free" The woman kind of sneered. "Well, lady, I guess this ain't the last train you was on, dear." Oh, Lord! She didn't know who she was dealing with. I sent up a quick prayer that my mother would just let it pass. My mother looked at her and said in a sweet low voice, "Well, I sure am sorry. I guess I'm mixed up." Her voice got louder, "but since you're here, how much would you charge me to stuff one of those pillows up your rear-end?- It's damn sure big enough !" The woman turned beet red and headed on down the aisle. I crunched down in my seat again praying the red-headed girl hadn't heard any of it. The New York Central rolled on. I wasn't seeing many hills now. The ground had flattened out and in some places it looked like I could see all the way to the horizon. I couldn't remember ever being able to see that far back home. I noticed my mother had pulled her knees up and turned sideways with her head back against the seat. Her mouth was part-way open, and I could hear her snoring quietly. Marty was already asleep curled up in her seat with Sally. I watched the country roll by for miles. I never knew when I fell asleep.

My mother was shaking me. " Daniel Wayne, Daniel Wayne". I raised my head up, groggy and confused. The train was stopped.

"Daniel, we're in Fremont. The conductor said we're not far from Port Clinton, and we'll be there in no time." She took Marty and headed for the restroom, leaving Sally sitting beside me. I stretched and rubbed my eyes, mad at myself for missing so much of Ohio. As my head started to clear and I thought about the red-headed girl, I stood up pretending to stretch. I casually turned my head to try to get a quick glimpse, but the seat was empty! They had gotten off somewhere while I was sleeping. A sadness swept over me; a feeling I could not understand. I felt like someone who had been an important part of my life was lost forever. My ten year old brain told me I was crazy. She was just a dumb girl who I didn't even know, but the strange feeling lingered.

Chapter 17

PORT CLINTON

It wasn't long until we were rolling again. The next stop would be Port Clinton---our new home! I could tell my mother was getting excited. She started rambling. "Daniel Wayne, this is Saturday, I probably won't enroll you into your new school until Tuesday so I can spend time in our new place seeing what needs to be done. There's no telling what kind of mess it's in with your daddy living there all this time by himself." I told her that was fine by me. I was a little nervous about it anyway. "By the way, Daniel Wayne, we haven't talked about it, but you know you'll be going to school with colored kids up here, don't you?" I told   her I hadn't thought about it. "Oh yes, colored and white go to the same schools." I said, "how do you know that's true?"

"Daniel Wayne, everybody knows the schools are mixed 'up-north' and we're 'up-north' now."

I gave her one of my Daddy's expressions. "It don't amount to a hill of beans to me."

"That's good. I know you"ll get along just fine." She turned to Marty. "You won't be going to school this year, baby, so you'll be there to help mother around our new place.Marty was not happy. "But I'm going to school too"

"No baby, you're only five years old. You won't start 'till next year."

Nobody we knew went to kindergarten in those days. Maybe big shot's kids did. I didn't know. Bayview didn't have a kindergarten. Maybe the schools up north did. I said, "They might have kindergarten in Port Clinton, and Marty can get started."

"My baby's not going anywhere this year. She's much too young. You just mind your own business, young man." Marty went into a pout, and I turned back to the window hoping I might get a glimpse of Lake Erie before we got to the station. I never did.

Soon after our big conversation, the old New York Central started slowing up. The conductor came through. "We're nearing the Port Clinton terminal, folks. Anyone holding a ticket to Port Clinton, this will be your station." He looked at me and winked. " For those going on to Sandusky, we'll be here about twenty minutes."

We were barely moving now. I craned my neck trying to catch sight of my daddy. The platform came into view. There were eight or nine people standing in a group. I spotted a red ball cap above the crowd. My daddy was wearing his heavy winter jacket. All three of us started waving out the window until he finally saw us and gave a little salute. Mother was the first off the train with me holding Marty's hand right behind her. The sky was dark and overcast. A bone-chilling wind swept down the platform and hit us head-on. Marty hunkered down holding Sally tightly in front of her. "It's too cold, Daddy! It's too cold!"After a few hugs, we went inside the station. My mother wanted to know why he hadn't written us about the cold weather. "All our coats are packed up and prob'ly somewhere in Georgia!"

"Well damn, Mal, it's been purty weather here, maybe a little chilly, 'til two, three days ago when it turned cold as hell. You wouldn't have had time to get a letter about it."

Mother glanced out the window and saw a man pulling a cart toward the front of the station. It had our two big green suitcases and cardboard box on it.

"Benjamin, there's four things. They did get 'em here! She looked like she was genuinely shocked. Then she asked, "How are we getting home from here?

"The feller I ride to work with is outside in his car. He brought me to get y'all."

"Well, that was nice of him,"

"Yeah, he's a purty good ol' boy. Now y'all stay in here 'til we get the thangs loaded, and then y'all can get in the car."

A couple of minutes later my daddy tapped on the window and motioned for us.

As we piled in I noticed the car looked a lot like my Daddy's old Chevrolet. Daddy got in front. "Mal , this is Mr. Lasner." Mr. Lasner turned around in his seat and shook my mother's hand.

" Pleased to meet all of you."

Mr. Lasner was wearing a navy blue watch cap and a leather 'bombardier' jacket like they wore sometimes in war movies. When he turned around , I noticed he had a mustache. Mother said later that he probably thought he was Clark Gable. He told my mother to call him Doug. Mr. Lasner said he lived in a trailer park close to where we lived and had two kids about

74

Marty's and my ages. Their names were Douglas Jr. and Alice, and his wife's name was Susan.

My mother said "I certainly appreciate you coming with Ben to pick us up."

"You'ens think nothing of it. Glad to help ol' Ben out". He talked a little like Daddy's friend from Virginia, only a little faster.--We drove straight through the town of Port Clinton. It looked about the size of Ensley. I saw a movie theatre and a J.C. Pennys-- I didn't see a McCrory's. It didn't take us long to get through town and out on the open highway.We went over a bridge that had a sign.

PORTAGE RIVER

My Daddy said "this is that river that runs behind our place"
Mr. Lasner looked over his shoulder at me. "Your dad said you couldn't wait to see Lake Erie."
"Yes, sir"
"Well, you're about to see it." We went around a long curve and there it was, coming almost up to the road! There was a wall about four feet high running beside the road. Mr. Lasner said it was there to stop the road from being flooded . I was amazed. It looked like an ocean! You sure couldn't see across it either. It was dark gray and the wind was whipping up whitecaps as far as you could see. Marty got on her knees in my lap staring out the window. My mother was impressed too. "I'll SWANEE, it is big. I didn't expect anything like this!"

All the women in Bayview would say "I Swanee" when they were told something or saw something that surprised them. I never knew what it meant. The road started leading away from the shoreline. In a little while you could just see a thin strip of the horizon.We passed the trailer park where Mr. Lasner lived. "We're in that third row about the sixth one down". The only trailers I had ever seen were parked behind the main runway at the ALABAMA STATE FAIR in Birmingham. I sure didn't know people lived in them. These looked a lot bigger though. A little ways after we passed the trailer park Mr. Lasner pulled off the road to the left in front of a long white building. I saw two small houses sitting next to each other in back and another one further on down by itself.

There was a big white sign with green letters in front of the long building.

WALTERS MOTOR COURT

George And Irene Walters, Prop.

My mother wanted to know which one we were living in--"It better be this big one up front." My Daddy sort of grinned. "Well, it is but we don't have the whole thing. "We're in this end down here." How big is it?" He handed her a key to the door on the end. There was a small porch in front of the door. "Ya'll go on in while me and Doug get the stuff in." My mother got the door unlocked and her and Marty and me went on in. We walked into a small room. There was an old red couch and chair over in one corner. There were rips and tears in both of them. A long, cord with a light bulb was hanging down just above the couch and chair. It had a long string coming from the socket but no shade. Close to the couch was something my daddy called a gas space heater. The only other thing in the room was a double bed at the other end. There was a door on the far wall. On the other side was an even smaller room. The only thing in it was a roll away bed standing upright in the closed position and a long pole running from wall to wall to hang clothes on. We came back into the front room. Just behind it was the kitchen. There was a tiny gas stove, a sink with a cabinet under it and a small refrigerator next to it. There were two wooden benches facing each other. The table was hooked to the wall. If you wanted to eat you had to unhook it and let it down between the benches. My Daddy was standing just inside the front door. Mr. Lasner had gone home. My mother wanted to know where the bathroom was. "Uh,…it's… it's just around the corner in the back. There's a shower an' everthang. "You mean we have to go outside to get to it?"

"Well , yeah, but it's just around the corner."

I thought this would do it. Surprised again. "Well, I guess it'll do alright." Maybe later on we can rent a bigger place." My daddy looked relieved . "Yeah, that's what I was thinking too." After the cardboard box was opened I put on my heavy mackinaw coat with the green and blue squares and my cap with earflaps that buttoned around my chin. I walked out on the porch and looked at the narrow strip of gray on the horizon that was Lake Erie. Bayview seemed a million miles away. I moseyed around the back and saw something I had missed earlier--a small blue trailer. There were curtains over the few windows it had but I couldn't hear anybody stirring around. Nothing was stirring around the three little houses either. I walked around to the other side of the trailer and walked right into an old bald headed man with glasses and a huge nose. He looked like he was wearing a fake "glasses and big nose" toy I had seen one time. You could put it on and look funny. But his were real.

He looked down at me and inquired,
"who do we have here?"

I said, "I just moved here from Alabama."

"Well, then , I guess you must be Mr. Daniel Knight."

"Yes, sir."

He said, "I'm Mr. Walters",

and stuck out his hand. While I was shaking his hand he told me

"You live on the other end and we live on this end."

What he didn't say was "his end" was the whole rest of the building with a bathroom in it. He hollered toward the house,

"Irene, come on out. Mr. Knight's family's here!" Irene came out the back door wearing a long red coat and red house shoes and her hair done up in curlers. "Oh, you must be Daniel. Let's go meet you Mother."

"Yes, ma'am."

We headed back toward our end with Mr. Walters' arm around my shoulder and Mrs. Walters twisting along behind, her elbows stabbing the air. Mr. Walters told me, "My boy's fighting in Korea. Did your dad tell you?"
"No, sir"
"Well, we sure miss him."
"Yes, sir" I led the Walters through the front door. Mrs. Walters immediately grabbed both my mother's hands in hers. "Oh, I'm so glad you' ens are here. I know you and the children are just worn out from the long trip."
My mother seemed to like Mrs. Walters. "Well, just a little I guess. It's good to meet y'all." I didn't remember anything in my Daddy's letters about anybody being nice.

"Oh, your husband is so sweet. We've looked out for him until you guys got here, you know?"

"I know y'all have and I so appreciate it", my mother said.

My daddy was standing there grinning like he was enjoying it all. I thought it was all a little embarrassing. I also didn't understand Mrs. Walters calling us 'guys' when my mother and Marty clearly weren't 'guys'. Then came the stunner--Marty came running out of the tiny kitchen. Mr. Walters caught her in mid-stride and lifted her up in his arms.

"And this pretty little doll's Marty, I betcha!"

With that he clamped his mouth around Marty's nose and starting sucking on it. I didn't know what to think. I looked at our parents, but they just stood there smiling like it was just fine. Marty jerked her head back and wiggled and pushed until Mr. Walters set her back down on the floor. She took off running into the other little room, slamming the door behind her. Everybody, including Mrs. Walters, still stood around grinning like this was normal behavior. Mrs. Walters said they needed to get back to their place so we could get some rest.

My mother wanted to know what time the grocery store back down the road closed. Mrs. Walters said she thought "around six on Saturdays". It was about 5PM now and had already been dark a while. My mother said "We're going to have to hurry down there cause Ben ain"t hardly got nothing here to eat. Mrs. Walters said something about that being like a man as they were going out. My mother and daddy went right out behind them, walking to the little grocery store. After they left Marty came back into the front room. "Daniel, that old man smelled terrible!"

"I said, I'll talk to daddy about it."

That night we had baloney sandwiches and Royal Crown Cola for supper. My mother said someone had told her that they didn't sell R.C. up north, but there it was in the very first store she had gone in.

Our parents sat at the little kitchen table eating and talking. Marty and me ate our supper sitting On the double bed. One of the items that had been packed in the big cardboard box was Daddy's radio. After supper he set it on the kitchen table and fiddled with the dials trying to pick up "The Grand Old Opry." He didn't have much luck. He thought, one time, that he could faintly hear it, but it faded away. You could see the disappointment in his face.

That night Marty and me lay in the roll-away bed with Sally between us. Marty was sound asleep. I lay with my hands behind my head starring at the ceiling while the bed springs creaked in the adjoining room. I guess we were living like human beings now.

Chapter 18

My Daddy arose every morning at 4:30 a.m. It didn't matter. Weekends, off days, holidays, they were all the same. Sunday morning I awoke around seven. I could hear my Daddy's radio playing from the little kitchen. " *There's a pawnshop on the corner in Pittsburgh, Pennsylvaniaaa.* "

I got up and dressed, putting on my heavy coat and cap. I went around the corner to the bathroom. I didn't see anyone else. When I came back in, my Daddy had fried some baloney and scrambled some eggs.

My mother and sister were both still sound asleep. I sat down to eat and talk with my Daddy. I asked him about the three little houses and the blue trailer. He told me the little houses were called cabins. He said, "We're the only ones here right now. Mr. Walters told me that others would be moving in come spring."

I told him I didn't like what Mr. Walters had done to Marty and she was real upset about it.

"Well son, he didn't really mean anything by it. And we can't say too much 'cause we got to live here."I asked him why we had to live here.

"Cause we ain't got the money to live nowhere else right now. But everthangs' gonna turn out alright. You just wait and see."

There was something different about my Daddy, but I couldn't tell what it was. I put my coat and cap back on and headed out to explore around some. There was a gravel path behind our building that led past the two little cabins that were sitting side by side and on past the little cabin sitting by itself. They were painted white just like the long building in front. Just past the cabins there was a big bale of hay off to the right with a bulls eye target pinned to one side. I wondered what that was for. About fifty yards further on I came to a footbridge of lumber. The bridge crossed over a small pond and ended at an embankment. At the top of the bank there was a set of railroad tracks. To my left the tracks went as far as I could see. I could also see the trailer park where Mr. Lasner and his family lived. The view to my right was blocked by two old boxcars. They were rusted out and looked like they hadn't moved in years.

Right in front of me was the Portage River. It was big. It was even wider than the Warrior River back home. The Portage was as gray as the sky and Lake Erie. The cold wind was scattering waves out in the middle of the river. I walked through some dead weeds down to the edge of the water. An old tree, with part of its trunk under water, was bent in a bow out over the river. One of its bare limbs was almost touching the surface. I knew this would be a good fishing spot in the spring because fish would be swimming around under the limbs trying to catch any bugs that fell off. Ma had taught me that when I was 5 years old. Out of the corner of my eye I saw something move in a big clump of weeds on the other side of the tree. I looked and saw the top of a man's head. He was wearing a dark blue navy watch cap. It was Mr. Lasner. He saw me at the same time.

"Daniel, come on over!"
"Yes, sir"
I pushed through the high weeds and found Mr. Lasner sitting on a big overturned five gallon can. He had a rod and reel in his hand and was casting out toward the middle of the river.

"Well, Dan, have you come up to do a little fishing?"

"No, sir."

I had never heard of anybody fishing at this time of year or in weather this cold.

Mr. Lasner told me, "I'm catching enough catfish for my freezer before this ol' river freezes over."

I said " do you mean this whole river turns to ice?"

"Yep, in a couple of months she'll just be a solid sheet of ice. Of course, you can still go out a ways and cut a hole in the ice and do some fishing if you want to." I was shocked. On cold mornings back home I had seen water, left in a bucket outside overnight that had turned to ice. But a whole river?! I figured Mr. Lasner was pulling my leg.

I asked Mr. Lasner if he had caught any catfish today. He pulled a stringer out of the water that had a dozen or more catfish on it. They were all about a foot long. He said, " these are channel cats"

I already knew that but didn't say anything.

I said, I guess I better head back for the house"

"Yeah, I'm about ready to call it a day myself. Tell your dad I'll see him in the morning."

I said," yes sir"

When I got back I told my daddy about the river freezing over. He said Mr. Lasner was probably just joshing me.

My mother announced that she had decided to enroll me in the Port Clinton School the next morning instead of waiting until Tuesday. "I don't want you getting behind." I told her it was fine with me. My Daddy was worked up over a news report he had heard on the radio. General Dwight Eisenhower was talking about running for President of the United States but wouldn't say if he was a republican or democrat. My Daddy said, "If he wants to be elected President of *this* country, he damn sure better run on the democrat ticket." I asked my Daddy why. "Well, son, the democrats are for the working man and the republicans ain't for nothing but the rich folks". I asked him why the republicans didn't like working men. "Cause that ain't where the money is. They go after the ones that just hang aroun' a damn golf course all the time. Big shots!" It didn't make much sense to me but I figured my Daddy knew what he was talking about.

"Yes siree , bud, if ol' Ike wants my vote he better run with the democrats!" I had heard my Daddy talk about his vote before but I had never known him to actually ever vote.

Chapter 19

The next morning at 7:15 my mother went over to the Walters' side to call a taxi. My Daddy said that's how we would have to get back and forth when we went into town. He had used one a few times and it was only 50 cents to anywhere in town, no matter how many people. Of course I would be riding a school bus to school as Mrs.Walters had said one came by every morning and evening. I had never ridden a school bus and didn't know what to think about it. When my mother returned from calling us a taxi she reported that the Walters had a television. In 10 minutes the taxi driver was blowing his horn outside. We had taken Marty to stay with Mrs. Walters which Marty didn't like at all.

My mother and me piled in the back and she told the driver, "Port Clinton Elementary School please". The driver said there was only one school and it went from first grade through the twelfth. As we pulled out the taxi driver asked if we had just moved here. My mother told him we had.

"Well you guys are going to like Port Clinton. The schools only about 4 miles, so the youngster won't have far to ride on the school bus." My mother said she was glad.

I saw Lake Erie up close again, then we crossed the same bridge we had crossed coming in. In no time we pulled up in front of a three story white brick building with narrow windows.

Kids were standing around in front of the main entrance. Some looked my age and others looked younger. Some looked like teenagers. We went right through the front door. I thought I could feel the other kids staring but I kept my eyes straight ahead. Inside the building my eyes widened. The walls were snow white with shiny metal handrails running down the middle. On one side of the hall there was a huge glass case filled with gold cups and ribbons. My mother asked a man in a suit and tie where the office was.

"Just around the corner to your left"

"Thank you"

As we started that way we were both startled. A loud speaker blared from somewhere. "Miss Carson please come to the counselor's office!"

In the office there were three women seated at desks behind the counter. One got up and came over.

"May I help you?"
"Yes, I need to enroll my son in this school."
The woman said, "Surely" as she handed my mother a white card.
"Just   have a seat over there and fill out this card."
While my mother was filling out the card a loud buzzer went off. I heard kids filling the hallways. When my mother had finished filling out the card, the woman said, "Please come with me".

As we were walking toward the back I saw her reading the card. We came up to an office door that was closed. She rapped on the door and then opened it. Another woman was sitting at a big desk.

"This is Mrs. Bauman, our assistant principal. And this is Daniel and his mother, Mrs. Knight".

Mrs. Bauman said, "Thank you, Shirley".

Shirley left us, after handing Mrs. Bauman the card. There were two big chairs facing the desk and Mrs. Bauman asked us to please sit down.

"Well now, so you just moved here from Alabama."

My mother said, "yes, we just got here Saturday and I wanted to go ahead and get Daniel Wayne enrolled."

She said, "Great, did you bring his last report card?"
My mother handed her my report card.
"All   A's and B's. That's wonderful."
Mrs. Bauman folded her hands on the desk and began talking about the school.

"Mrs. Knight, we consider ourselves a very progressive school- We will expect Daniel to participate in extra-curricular activities. We expect all our young men to participate in sports once they reach the 7th grade. Our teachers are tough but the children learn at an accelerated pace. I'm sure, with Daniel's grades, he will fit right into our program." I had no idea what she was talking about. The loudspeaker blared, "Will Mr. Graves please come to the gymnasium?"
My mother said, "Well that all sounds fine to me. Do you want him to start today?"
"No. We will make up his class schedule today and he can come by the office in the morning and pick it up and get started."

Mrs. Bauman shook my Mother's hand. Then she looked at me. "Have on your thinking cap tomorrow, Daniel."

"Yes, Ma'am"

One of the women in the front office called a taxi for us. As we stood out in front of the school waiting, my mother said, "I believe you'll like this school, Daniel Wayne." I wasn't so sure. "What's that extra-curriculum she was talking about?"

"Well I'm not sure, but I think it's doing things besides your regular school work, like playing baseball or drawing pictures or something."

The man in the coat and tie came out on the steps. "Mrs. Knight, Mrs. Bauman would like for you to come back to her office, please.

"What for?"

"I'm sure I don't know. Would you come back in, please?"
We went back in. Once we were back in her office, Mrs. Bauman said "I apologize, Mrs. Knight but I omitted asking a very important question."
"What is it?"
"Which side of the bridge do you live on?"
"What do you mean, which side?"
"Let me put it this way. Did you cross a bride coming here this morning?"
"Yes, we crossed a bridge."
"Oh, I'm so sorry. That means you live on the other side. It also means Daniel can't attend this school."
"What?"
"I'm so sorry, but that's the way the district is drawn. He'll have to go to Lacarne School. He *will* come back here when he reaches the 7th grade. Lacarne only goes through the 6th."
My mother was turning red in the face.
Wait a minute. How far is it to this Lacarne school?"
"Probably about 12 miles from where you live, in the other direction."
"Are you setting there telling me that you've got a 5th grade here, but he can't go to it, but he's got to come back here for the 7th grade and this young'un has got to ride a school bus 12 miles instead of 4? That's the stupidest damn thing I've ever heard!"

The typewriters on the other side of the door stopped clacking.

"Mrs. Knight, please. I agree it's confusing but it is the rule and we have to abide by it."

"Well I'll tell you this. Y'all are about the sorriest excuse for a school I've ever seen!" As we went through the outer office my mother hollered, "call us another taxi! That first one's probably gone!" Shirley said, "I'll be glad to Mrs. Knight". I was sure Shirley was not only glad to but anxious to. As for me, I was secretly glad to be getting away from there. I had not seen any colored kids. That evening my mother started calming down. She told me, "I didn't really like that school anyway, Daniel Wayne. Did you?"

"No Ma'am, not really"
"They all acted like a bunch of uppity ups"
"Yes, Ma'am."
When my Daddy got home from work, Mr. Lasner stepped inside to say hello. After my mother told them what had happened at the Port Clinton School, Mr. Lasner said, "that's my fault. I should have told you guys. Yes, Daniel has to go to Lacarne. That's where Doug Jr. goes. Catches the school bus right out front every morning."

The next morning my mother went next door and called us another taxi. In about 10 minutes it was outside honking. It was the same driver.

As we pulled out, my mother went through the story about the Port Clinton School. The driver said he didn't know about the rule or he would have told us. My mother asked him if he knew anything about the Lacarne School.

He said, "It's not that bad . "

We were heading in a direction we hadn't been before. The road led away from Lake Erie and you could no longer see it on the horizon. Soon we began passing farms; big two story white frame houses with red barns setting back from the two-lane highway. They didn't look like the farms I had seen back in Alabama. They look like farms in a picture book. Before long we passed a sign:

LACARNE

Pop. 1085

Just past the sign the driver turned right down a street lined with two story houses. After a couple of blocks the houses ended and the road went through a field and dead-ended at an old red brick building. The driver said, "Well, this is it, you guys. Lacarne School."

After my mother paid the fare, we headed toward the front door. Once again I was sure all the kids were staring at me. And they probably were, us getting out of a taxi and all. On the very top of the schoolhouse I could see a huge bell inside an enclosure with a dome top-- I could see over the door there was a slab of concrete with "1904" carved in it. We went up the broken concrete steps and through one side of the big, green double doors. Just inside a woman was standing in the hall, studying some papers in her hand. She looked up and smiled at my mother. "May I help you?"

"Yes, we're looking for the office. I need to enroll my son here. He's in the 5th grade. I'm Mrs. Knight and this is Daniel. "Well, we don't have an actual office at this time, Mrs. Knight, but I'll be happy to enroll this young man. I'm Mrs. Peterman, and I teach fifth and sixth grades. Let's step in here"

We followed Mrs. Peterman into a small room that had a big wooden desk and several metal folding chairs. I didn't hear any loud-speakers blaring. She reached in a drawer and pulled out a white card like the one we had filled out at Port Clinton. She handed the card to my mother and said, "Please fill this out. Do you have Daniel's last report card?" My mother produced the report card from her purse. Mrs. Peterman didn't look like the teachers at Bayview School. They all looked older and had snow white hair.

Mrs. Peterman had brown hair and looked like she was about my mother's age. She also wore glasses like my mother, but there the resemblance ended. Mrs. Peterman was tall and had a nose that looked like a hawk's beak. When she talked her head bobbed in and out like a chicken's. The school bell started clanging. Mrs. Peterman said, "Please excuse me. I'll be right back." I could hear stomping feet and chattering as the kids entered the hallway. In about five minutes everything got quiet and Mrs. Peterman came back in. My mother had filled out the card and handed it back to her.

"Oh, good."
"Do you want Daniel to just start tomorrow?"
"Oh no, I want him to stay today".
She didn't say anything about the school being progressive or anything like that. My mother asked Mrs. Peterman if she would call her a taxi. She was back in about a minute and said one was on the way. My mother thanked her and headed for the double doors. "I'll see you this evening, Daniel." Now it was just me and Mrs. Peterman. "Well, come on, Daniel and meet your classmates."

"Yes, ma'am."

This was the part I had dreaded. As we walked down the hall, Mrs. Peterman had her arm around my shoulder. "Daniel, do you like your bread buttered or plain?"

"What?"

"The cafeteria serves bread every day at lunch. I'll need to know each morning if you want your bread buttered or plain."

"I've never ate in a cafeteria."

"Well, you will here. How about that bread?"

"Uh, plain, I guess." At the end of the hall we turned left into a classroom filled with kids. Mrs. Peterman and me stopped at the front of the room, her arm still around my shoulder. "Class, we have a new student starting with us today." She looked down at me.

"Please tell us your name and where you're from."

I felt my face getting hot and knew it was turning red.

"My name is Daniel Knight and I'm from Bay .. uh, Birmingham, Alabama." Some snickering started in the back of the room. Mrs. Peterman jerked her head in that direction and it hushed immediately. She said, "Daniel, why don't you take that empty desk over there?"--The desk she pointed to was in the first row by the window, about half way back. I slid into the desk, glad to no longer be standing up in front of the class. Mrs. Peterman fumbled around in a cabinet and pulled out some books. She brought them over and set them on my desk.

"These are the books you'll need. Tomorrow you need to bring a 'big chief' lined notebook with you."

"Yes Ma'am."

'Big Chief' was the same notebook I had used back in Bayview and my mother had packed a brand new one in the big cardboard box. It had a drawing of an Indian Chief's head on the front. It looked a lot like the 'test pattern chief's head we had seen on television. Mrs. Peterman said "Alright class, I'm going next door to the see about the 6th graders.

Open your arithmetic books to chapter 6 and begin doing the problems on the first two pages." And then she was gone. Everybody opened their arithmetic book and got started.

A boy seated next to me gave me a blank sheet of 'Big Chief' paper and I started working the problems. Nobody whispered or looked around.

I could see there was one similarity between Mrs. Peterman and the teachers back home-- Foolishness would not be tolerated. Twenty-five minutes later, Mrs. Peterman was back. She started right in with us. "Julie, what did you get for problem one ? "

Julie gave her answer. Mrs. Peterman said it was correct. She asked several other kids to give their answers to the problems and then she got to me. It surprised me. I didn't think I would be called on the first day. "Daniel, what did you get for problem 9?" I gave her the answer I had come up with. "That's correct. How did you work that?" I told her. "Very good." I felt a little safer now. Mrs. Peterman then began teaching in earnest. I had never heard anybody talk that fast in my life. Her chalk streaked across the blackboard like lightening and her mouth moved like a machine gun. The surprising thing to me was, I was absorbing most of it. Mrs. Peterman alternated back and forth between us and the 6th grade until the bell on top of the school started clanging. Mrs. Peterman clapped her hands twice. "Lunch time. No pushing or shoving. Let's act like young ladies and gentlemen."

I followed the other kids out of the classroom and down a dimly lit stairway to the basement. Long folding tables and metal chairs were sitting all around a huge furnace with It's big arms going in every direction. I stood in line with the others at a long counter with a woman wearing an apron behind it. This was all new to me. We didn't have a cafeteria at Bayview School. Everybody brought lunch from home. I had took mine in a "Durango Kid" lunch box through the third grade. After that I thought I had outgrown it and started taking my lunch in a paper sack. I watched the kids inline ahead of me and did what they did. I picked up a tray and put a bowl on it and a paper napkin wrapped around a fork and spoon. When I got to the lady behind the counter, she handed me a saucer with three pieces of bread on it, plain. Then she took my bowl and scooped two big scoops of something out of a large can into it. She handed me back my bowl and steam was coming from it.

"You must be the new boy from Alabama?"

"Yes, ma'am."

"Welcome to Ohio."

"Thank you, ma'am. What is this stuff?"

"Goulash."

"What?"

"Goulash--It's good for ya. Put hair on your chest."

She threw her head back and laughed as if this was the funniest thing that had ever been said in the history of the world. The girl behind me in line giggled. I walked away with my bowl of Goulash. I seated myself at the other end of one of the long tables from where most of the other kids set. From time to time I could sense some staring, but I didn't care. For me, the worst part was over. I took a small bite of the Goulash, then a bigger one. Hey, this was pretty good stuff. Just as I finished eating my Goulash and unbuttered bread and polished off my milk, another boy sat down across from me---"Hi, my man's Doug."

"I'm Daniel."

"Yeah, I know. Your Dad rides to work with my Dad 'cause he ain't got a car." Doug looked like he was a little taller than me and had sandy colored hair. His nose turned up in front like a chipmunk's. In both nostrils you could see webs of snot. I was glad I had finished eating.

I said, "Well, we're buying one pretty soon."
Doug said, "let's go out back."

"Back of what?"

"Back of the school."

We went upstairs and put on our coats and caps and went through the back door. The first thing I saw was two long outhouses, just like at Bayview School. Somebody had painted "Boys" on one and "Girls" on the other. There was a merry-go-round' setting in the middle of the yard, sort of leaning to one side. It wasn't a merry-go-round like they had at the fair, with horses and all. It was just a circle of wood seats with metal bars to hold on to. It turned around a big iron pole in the middle. You could run holding one of the bars to get it going real fast and then jump on and ride. I had seen one in a park one time. Marty and me had rode on it. I would get it going fast while Marty held on, then I would jump on beside her. My mother had stopped it saying Marty might get hurt.

Several other kids were out in the schoolyard now. I asked Doug where the little kids were. "They go to lunch from 11:30 to twelve. We go twelve to twelve thirty." Doug looked at me and said, "You know what? You talk funny."

I said, "If you think I talk funny you oughta hear yourself.

"How do I talk funny?"

"You said, 'let's go out back'".

"What's funny about that?"

"It sounded funny to me." I was beginning to not like Doug.

The bell started ringing. I asked Doug "who's ringing the bell?" He said, "A sixth grade guy. We guys can do it when we get in sixth."

The afternoon was like the morning. Mrs. Peterman hadn't run out of steam. In fact, if anything, she got stronger. We had a spelling sit-down bee. When there were only four or five kids left standing, including me, I misspelled a word and sat down. I didn't want anybody thinking I was a smart-ass. Doug Jr. had went down on his first word. After the spelling bee we launched into our science books. Mrs. Peterman screeched a circle on the blackboard. The sun; 93 million miles. Gaseous storms on the surface. Hydrogen—blah, blah…Then she headed for the sixth grade class after telling us what pages to read. I thought about the school in port Clinton. I would bet that they didn't have a teacher as good as Mrs. Peterman.

At 3:00 the bell rang out. I got my coat and hat from the cloakroom and headed out the front door with the other kids.

Most of the kids walked on past the school bus that was parked in front. I figured they lived nearby and didn't ride a bus. AS I walked toward the bus, Doug fell in beside me. "Be careful what you say to the driver."

"I'm not going to say anything to him. Why?"

"He's an old German Nazi and he's mean. Hates kids."

About twenty of us got on the bus. Climbing up the steps I saw the mean German. He was wearing a cap. I had never seen one like it. It looked like it was made of leather and had a small bill that turned up in front. I said, "I get off at Walters' Motor Court." He kept looking straight ahead. "I noze w'ere youse gets off."

I went on back and found a seat. Doug plopped down next to me. "I told you he was mean."
I said, "I don't care as long as he lets me off at the right place."
After we had gone about a mile, kids started getting off. Some got off at the farms I had seen. Others got off where there was nothing but a row of mailboxes and a dirt road leading away from the highway. I figured they must still have a long way to go. The sky still looked like gray paint, but it had gotten colder since Saturday. It was almost 4:00 when we finally

stopped in front of Walters' Motor Court. There were about 5 kids still on the bus, including Doug, going on to the trailer park up the road. As I was getting off, the mean German said, "youse be out here in morning seven o'clock. I don't blow the horn. I von't wait." I nodded and hopped down the steps. As I went through our front door, I could hear my mother crying in the little bedroom. My Daddy was already home from work, sitting in the big torn chair in the front room, holding a handkerchief to his lip. I could see blood on the handkerchief. I asked my Daddy why his lip was bleeding and why was mother crying. He just shook his head. When she heard my voice, my mother tore out of the little bedroom, into the front room screaming, "that sorry son-of-a-bitch has brought us up here to this damn, God-- forsaken country. That's what the hell it's all about!"

I said, "What? I thought you wanted to move because of Daddy being on strike all the time."

"You little bastard, you're just like him. You keep your sassy mouth shut." Then she turned on my Daddy again. "You sorry thing, you set there with your mouth closed, upholding him in talking to me like that." My Daddy looked up at her. "Mal, the boy ain't done nothing. Why don't we all just settle down awhile?"

"Dear Jesus, they're both trying to kill me!" With that she tore out the front door. My Daddy slowly got up, still holding the handkerchief to his lip, and went after her. I found Marty sitting at the little table in the kitchen holding Sally. I sat down across from her and asked how long it had been going on.

"It's been going and going and going. Why does mother hate you so much, Daniel?"
I said, "I don't know, Marty."
Marty and me sat in silence until they returned. My mother went in the little bedroom and slammed the door. She didn't come back out that evening. Marty and I slept on the big bed and our Daddy slept on the couch that

night. When my Daddy woke me up at 6 am the next morning it was still dark outside. My Daddy said, "Big snow last night, son. Still snowing."

"It's snowing now?"

"Yeah, we got a big one going."

He turned on the outside light. In the light I could see it coming down. It wasn't just snowing like it had that time in Bayview. It was coming down in sheets. The yard was blanketed in snow as far as you could see from the porch light. I gathered up my school clothes, toothbrush, towel and soap, put on my coat and cap and headed around the corner to the bathroom. My shoes crunched in the snow. It was still coming down so fast I could barely see. When I came back my Daddy had already left for work. At 6:50 I was standing in the snow on the other side of the road waiting for the school bus. It was still dark and bitter cold. The wind felt like it was blowing right down the back of my coat. My face and hands were stinging. In about 10 minutes I saw the headlight of the bus. When I got on the mean German didn't say anything. He just stared straight ahead. Doug and the other trailer park kids were already on the bus. I plopped down in a seat by myself. After we had picked up a few more kids the boy who had given me the sheet of 'Big Chief' paper got on and sat down by me. He said, "hi, I'm Malcolm Finkling."

"Hi, I'm Daniel Knight."

"Yeah, I know. How do you like our school?"

"Just fine, I guess."

"Good. Do you belong to the Cub Scouts?"

"What?"

"Cub Scouts."

"No, I reckon not."

"It's a lot of fun. My mom's den-mother."

"What's that?"

"The troop meets at my house and she makes cookies and stuff. But we do a lot of other things too. We learn about crafts and we camp out all night in the summer with our dads." Malcolm talked about the Cub Scouts all the way to school. He never mentioned the snow. I guess he was used to it. When we were hanging up our coats and hats in the cloakroom at school I noticed the other kids taking big rubber boots off their feet. They were wearing them right over their shoes. Mrs. Peterman stared teaching right away, after we had lined up and stated if we wanted butter on our bread or not. At lunchtime we had goulash again. The woman behind the counter smiled at me but I just looked at her and headed for a table. This time Doug stayed on the other side of the room and Malcolm sat across from me, still talking about the Cub Scouts. I was starting to get interested.

Malcolm and me finished our goulash and headed outside. The snow was no longer falling but it was about a foot deep. By the time we made it to the merry-go-round my socks were soaking wet.

Malcolm had put on his rubber boots. We brushed snow off the merry-go-round and sat down, idly pushing it in circles with our feet and talking about the Cub Scouts.

Doug came outside with some other boys. They headed straight for the merry-go-round. After they had all found a seat, we continued moving in lazy circles and watching some girls standing down by the corner of the school. The girls would look at us and giggle and then duck around the corner. After they did this two or three times, Doug said, "stupid girls." I didn't know about that but they were sure different than the girls back home. I had never seen a Bayview girl act like that and if we had had a merry-go-round they would have been on there with us. Whatever it was, 'red rover' or "dodge-ball', the girls were right in there with the boys. They weren't shy either. Alabama girls would give you their opinion on something in a second, at least Bayview, Alabama girls would. Maybe they were the ones who were different. Maybe girls everywhere else were like these girls. Carol Ashworth even played 'Cowboy' with us when we were all younger (we drew the line at girls playing 'war'). After making another lazy circle on the merry-go-round, Doug looked at me and said "aren't you from Alabama?"

"Yep, I am."
"Ain't that in the south?"
"I guess it is"
"My mama said everybody from the South is ignorant."
I said, "maybe your mama's ignorant."

Doug leaped to his feet, his hands balled into fists, "Nobody can say that about my mama! Get up and fight!" I might have been ignorant, but fighting was one thing Bayview boys learned how to do by the time they could walk. I made one more full circle and then stood up facing Doug. He threw a long round-house right. I could have eaten another bowl of Goulash waiting for it to land. I had once read a booklet by Joe Louis called "Tips On Boxing". Joe said to always throw your shoulder into your punch because that would cause you to have more power behind it. I easily stepped back from Doug's hay-maker. I stepped back in, and putting my shoulder behind it. I landed a hard right punch right on Doug's snot filled nose. Doug Jr. didn't fall down. He sat down. Right in the snow. Holding his nose with both hands, Doug started hollering, "You broke my nose, damn it, you broke my nose!" Blood was dripping down between Doug's fingers and making little red dots on his pants and the white snow. I heard Malcolm say, "uh-oh".

I turned and saw Mrs. Peterman heading toward us. She really looked like a big bird now. She was taking giant strides, her head bobbing in and out, and holding her arms straight out from her sides. My stomach started churning. When Mrs. Peterman reached us, she grabbed Doug by the coat and pulled him up off the ground. He was still holding his nose with both hands.

"What in heaven's name is going on here!?" she demanded. "Someone better speak up and I mean now!" Doug nodded his head toward me. "He punched me in the nose!"

Mrs. Peterman turned to me, "Is that true, Daniel?"

"Yes, ma'am."

"This is only your second day in school and you've already struck someone?"

"Yes, ma'am."

"I'll tend to you later."

With that she grabbed Doug's arm and led him to the boy's restroom. Malcolm said, "Why didn't you tell her what he said? That he threw the first punch?"

"I don't know. It would be tattling, I guess."

"So what? It's the truth."

I guess they didn't live by the code here like the boys in Bayview.

Malcolm said, "Well anyhow, he's had that coming for a long time. He's a smart-ass." The other boys were standing around made agreeing noises. The girls were all huddled together down by the corner of the school staring at us. Mrs. Peterman and Doug came back out of the boy's restroom. Doug had a wad of toilet paper stuck in each nostril. The school bell rang. Mrs. Peterman and Doug stopped in front of me. She said, "I want you both to go to the empty room down the hall and wait for me there."

Doug and me went in and walked down the hall to the little room where I had enrolled. We sat down in two metal chairs facing the desk. Neither of us said anything. After what seemed a long time, Mrs. Peterman came in and sat down behind the desk. She looked at me and then at Doug. "I have just spoken with a student who witnessed this altercation." Looking at Doug she said, "Is it true, Douglas, that you made a remark to Daniel about people from the South being ignorant? And is it also true that YOU actually threw the first punch?" Thank God for Malcolm and the Cub Scouts. Doug dropped his head. "Yes'um, I guess I did." Mrs. Peterman glared at Doug. "I will not tolerate foolish talk of that sort from one of my students.

"Yes'um"

"And needless to say, I do not tolerate fighting."

"Yes'um"

"Douglas, you will write for me, five hundred times, I will not make foolish remarks about anyone again."

"Yes'um" Mrs. Peterman turned to me. Her glare softened a little. Daniel, you will write for me, one hundred times, 'fighting never solves anything'."

"Yes, Ma'am"

"These papers are to be turned into me Monday morning after the Thanksgiving Holiday. Douglas you may return to the classroom."

Doug got up and went out the door, the two wads of toilet paper still sticking in his nose. Mrs. Peterman smiled at me.

"Daniel, don't you have a pair of galoshes?"

"Goulash?"

Mrs. Peterman smiled again "No, not goulash-- galoshes. Galoshes are rubber boots that you wear over your shoes."

"No, Ma'am"

"Please tell your parents that you need a pair, and some gloves. The snow's going to get a lot deeper and the rubber boots will keep your shoes and socks from getting wet. We don't want you getting sick on us."

"Yes, ma'am."

I went back to the classroom a little relieved but I was worrying about my daddy. I was sure Mr. Lasner would get mad about me hitting Doug. He might not even let my daddy ride to work with him anymore. At the very least Mr. Lasner would say something to my daddy about it. That afternoon we all filed out to go to another classroom for a music lesson. Malcolm said they did it on Wednesday and Fridays. When we entered the music teacher's classroom, I was startled. Her name was Mrs. Randallson. She was much younger than Mrs. Peterman and beautiful. I started getting my first crush on a teacher. Mrs. Randallson said she had a new song for us. "It's a Hawaiian fishing song." She passed out sheets of paper with the words on it. With any other teacher I would have thought it was a silly song, but I figured that Mrs. Randallson could do no wrong. She banged away on the piano and sang along with us.

"We're going to the Huki-la, The huki-huki-huki-huki laa.--We throoow our nets out into the sea and all the little fishes come-a-swimming to me. Oh, we're going to the Huki-la."

I sneaked a quick look at Doug. He was singing right out about going to the huki-la. The toilet paper was no longer stuck in his nose.

The next day was Thanksgiving. School was out until Monday, but my daddy had to work. That morning I was lying in bed awake when I heard Mr. Lasner blow his horn. I figured I would catch it that evening when my Daddy came home.

When I finally got out of bed, Marty and my mother were in the kitchen. My mother seemed to be back to normal. "Well, It's about time, sleepy-head." she had me a plate of scrambled eggs and fried baloney with a glass of cold milk.

Unbelievably, it was snowing again. The first snow hadn't even melted and this one was falling right on top of it. To my surprise, my mother had already beat Mrs. Peterman to the punch. She had rode a taxi into Port Clinton the day before and bought me some rubber boots and a pair of gloves. The gloves had a little white tag inside each one: "Genuine Leather – Made In Formosa". I told my mother, "the rubber boots are called galoshes." She said she had never heard of such a word and anyway they were called overshoes. Whatever they were called, it was a struggle to get them on. I found out later that when you took them off, your shoes would always come right off with them. After finally getting the overshoes on and snapped up, I put on my ol' Mackinaw cap and my new gloves and headed to the river.

The Portage had not frozen over, but the wind off the water was so cold I couldn't stay long. After a couple of minutes, my face was numb and my hands were freezing even with my genuine leather gloves on. I headed home as the snow started coming down faster.

That evening when my Daddy got home, we had our Thanksgiving dinner. My mother had went all out, frying a chicken and making potatoes, gravy and cold slaw.

I asked my Daddy, "How was work today?"

He said," 'bout like always. Why?"

I said, "Just wondering, I guess."

At least Doug Jr. wasn't a snitch. That night I lay on me and Marty's bed reading comic books while she played on the floor with Sally. My mother and Daddy sat at the little kitchen table talking and listening to the radio. ***"The little white cloud that sat right down and criiied"*** --My daddy was now a big Johnny Ray fan.

The first week of December, I was lying in bed listening to my daddy complain. "Hell, Mal, I ain't making no money. That damn place just don't pay nothing. Shit, I was making a lot more money in the mines even with the damn strikes. And there damn sure ain't gonna be no overtime. I got in that double-time today, on Thanksgiving, but hell, that's it".

The next day my mother told Marty and me "we're not going to be able to do much for y'all this Christmas. It's taking every dime we can make and scrape to just get by and have something to eat." She was right. On Christmas Eve, Marty got a pair of white shoes and red mittens and I got a pair of pajamas. The top of the pajamas was some kind of pullover without buttons. On the front there was a picture of a cowboy on a horse. 'Gene Autry' was written inside the loop. When I said I had just as soon not gotten anything as something with Gene Autry on it, my mother said, "you have always been the most ungrateful boy that ever lived."

My Daddy told the story again about how all he ever got was one banana and one orange for Christmas when he was a boy and was thrilled beyond words. I really didn't care. It was Marty I felt sorry for. She still had a strong belief in Santa Claus. Laying in bed that night I told her that Santa probably couldn't find us because we had moved so far away, but we would write him and he would know for sure where we were the next Christmas.

In January the weather turned even colder. Not only did the Portage River freeze over, Lake Erie became a solid sheet of ice. I missed school the whole last week in January because the school bus couldn't make it. Each morning that week I would trudge across the highway at 6:45AM and stand in the dark and cold, waiting for the mean German. At 7:30 I would trudge back across the road, knowing he wasn't coming.

My Daddy proclaimed, "this is not a fit place for man to live." There was talk about moving back to Alabama. I was sure hoping we would, but no plans were really ever made. My mother had a few 'nervous spells' that winter but she didn't take off running. I figured the blowing snow and below zero temperatures had something to do with that.

In April the weather finally broke. Melting snow and heavy rains were causing flooding everywhere. Our yard looked like a small lake. A man on the radio said if the Portage River overflowed its banks, the people in the area where we lived might have to be evacuated. I heard Mr. Walters tell my Daddy, "they say that every year, and it's never happened yet." It didn't happen that year either.Talk of moving back to Alabama slacked off.

My Daddy was upset with General Eisenhower again because he had announced that he would accept the nomination to be President on the Republican ticket. "He damn shore ain't gonna git my vote."

I wanted to ask him what difference it would make to us who the president was, but didn't. The first week in May, two families moved in. They occupied the two little cabins that sat side by side. One of the families was a man and his wife and their daughter, Barbara, who was 12 years old. Their last name was Walters too. They were in some way related to Mr. Walters, but I never really understood how. Barbara called Mr. Walters, 'uncle George.' But he wasn't her real uncle. I heard Mr. Walters tell my Daddy that Barbara's father was his wife's great-nephew or something.

The other family was an old man and woman named Busby, whose grandson, Timmy, lived with them. Timmy and I were only 2 weeks apart in age, and became fast friends immediately. Timmy and his grandparents had moved to Ohio from Michigan. Timmy was very mysterious about his parents. He would only tell me that his mother and father were still in Michigan and he and his grandparents were "on the run." He seemed to like that expression. When I would ask about his parents or what it was like to live in Michigan Timmy would always say "Granddad said I'm not allowed to answer any questions because we're on the run."

Timmy was smaller than me and wiry and could run like the wind. Sometimes we would race through the motor court. I would stay even with Timmy for a while, then he would blast ahead. Timmy and I did not like Barbara. She had gotten off to a bad start with us right off. I had found out that Mr. Walters was a deer hunter. The bale of hay with a target pinned to it was what he used for target practice with his bow and arrow. One day Timmy and me were looking at the target, when Barbara moseyed up right out of the blue. She informed us that she was in the seventh grade and went to Port Clinton School. I told her that I was in the fifth and went to Lacarne. She sneered a little.

"Yeah, I know. That little country school."

Timmy said he had already finished fifth grade because his grandparents had taken him out of school earlier. Barbara sneered again."You were probably expelled."
Timmy turned red in the face. "Whadda you talking about, stupid! You go ask my Granddad."

Barbara ignored him. "What I came to tell you boys (she said it like she was an adult or something) is this is all my uncle's property and if I catch you messing around with anything I'll have to tell him."

I was getting mad. "Why donch'a go somewhere and mind your own business?"

Timmy was a little more blunt. "Go'ta hell, bitch!"

Barbara clasped both hands to her mouth and took off running toward her cabin. We both laughed, but I was secretly glad I hadn't said it. I was afraid she would tell her Daddy and "Uncle George."

My Daddy had bought a couple of cane poles and lines and hooks at a hardware store in Port Clinton. When I came home from school and on Saturdays, Timmy and me would dig up some worms from around Mr. Walters' pond and head to the river.

It was great fishing. You never knew what you were going to catch. Catfish, bream, rock bass, carp. We put most of what we caught in Mr. Walters' pond. The next day after the incident with Barbara we were sitting on the bank of the river with our lines in the water. As we were talking about how deep the river might be out in the middle, Barbara walked up behind us. We ignored her. Barbara stood around a few minutes and finally said, "I'm sorry about what I said yesterday, you guys. I just want to be friends if you want to be."

Timmy and me continued to talk about the depth of the river. Barbara sat down between us, right on the river bank.

"I'll tell you what. If you guys will be my friends you can look at my pussy anytime you want to."

I went into shock. I looked at Timmy. He had a silly grin on his face. We both were old enough to know she wasn't talking about a cat. Barbara tuned toward me. "Well, Daniel?"

Staring hard at my cork bobbing around I said, "I don't think so." My face was burning up. Barbara looked at Timmy. I waited for Timmy to tell her to get lost. Instead he said, "can I look at it now?"

"Sure"

They got up and went behind one of the old rusted out box cars. In about a minute they were back. Timmy still had a silly grin on his face. Barbara said, "Come on, Daniel, don't you want to look?"

Staring straight ahead, I just shook my head.

Barbara said, "You don't know what you're missing."

Timmy laughed, "He ain't missing nothing. That's the ugliest one I ever seen." Barbara broke and ran again. "You'll be sorry you said that!" I wondered how many Timmy had seen.

Chapter   20

The 5th of June was the last day of school. My final report card was all A's and one B. On the back Mrs. Peterman had written "Promoted to the 6th Grade" I was glad Mrs. Peterman would be my teacher again in the fall. I would see Mrs. Randallman again too. My crush hadn't faded at all. Malcolm and I promised each other we'd get together over the summer and I might even join the cub scouts.

That evening Timmy and me decided to go swimming in Mr. Walters' pond. We were splashing around and having a high ol' time when I got another shock. I saw Timmy's back and it was covered with scars from the bottom of his neck to his waist. I was too embarrassed to ask him about it so I just kept on acting like everything was normal, but I worried about it that night until I fell asleep.

Two days later, Timmy and his Grandparents were gone. They had left during the night. I heard Mrs. Walters tell my mother, "I just talked with Mrs. Busby yesterday evening and everything was fine. I don't understand it. This morning they're gone---lock, stock and barrel. Their rent was paid through June. I just don't understand it."

Timmy and his grandparents were "on the run" again. I never told anybody about the scars. I just hoped that Timmy and his grandparents could stay "on the run" until Timmy was a grown man.

On Saturday we were in for a big surprise. My Daddy rode a taxi into Port Clinton and came back driving a 1946 Hudson Hornet. It was the biggest car I had ever seen in my life. It was so high off the ground that Marty had to be picked up to be put in the seat. My mother was thrilled about it. That evening we all rode into Port Clinton to the picture show. The name of the theatre was the 'ERIE'. We saw Gregory Peck in "Captain Horatio Hornblower" and Richard Widmark in "Red Skies of Montana."

For the next few days talk was renewed about moving back to Alabama. A man named Werner Von Braun had been named to run a place called "The Redstone Arsenal" back in Huntsville, Alabama. It had been a place where rockets to be used in war were made. Now they were saying that with Von Braun there, they would begin working on rockets to go into space. Maybe even to the moon someday. My Daddy said, "hell, they going to need electricians there just like everwhere else."

We received an occasional letter from Aunt Clara in Sandusky. Even though it wasn't that far to Sandusky we couldn't visit each other because nobody had a car. Toward the end of June we received another letter from Aunt Clara. Uncle Charlie was bad sick. He was in a hospital in Sandusky where they were running tests. That Sunday, we loaded up and headed for Sandusky. After getting lost a couple of times, we finally found their trailer park. The trailer was easy to spot because their oldest boy, Roy, was sitting on the little steps, crying his eyes out.

When we pulled up, my mother said, "Oh, Ben, something bad has happened." My mother hugged Roy and said, "I'm so sorry." My Daddy patted him on the head as they went on in to the trailer. He was still crying, so I went in after them. While my mother was hugging Aunt Clara, she started squalling .

"They run them tests and said Charlie's got somethin' called Hodgkin's disease. His blood's all messed up. There ain't no cure or nothing they can do. The doctors said he might have two years to live if he's lucky!"

My mother started patting her on the back, telling her that the doctors didn't know everything and that God could cure people when doctors couldn't. Aunt Clara calmed down a little. "Lloyd's coming to get us all next week, when Charlie gets out, and take us back home. We'll be better off down there, where we know folks." My mother agreed. "Yes, y'all need to go back home." Then she added, "We knew something was bad wrong when we saw poor little Roy crying his eyes out on the steps."

Aunt Clara pulled back from my mother. "Hell, he ain't crying 'bout his Daddy. He's squalling 'cause I wouldn't let him go off somewhere with some other boys. He don't care nothing 'bout his Daddy."

A year later we heard that Uncle Charlie had been to see a "faith healer" and was completely healed. The doctors in Alabama had run all kinds of tests and they couldn't find anything.
Everybody said it was indeed a miracle. A year after that, Uncle Charlie was dead.

Roy joined the Navy two years later at seventeen and was never heard from again although I was sure I saw him one time, years later, getting on the Naval Base bus at the square in Long Beach, California. Before I could make it across the street, the bus pulled away.

Chapter 21

The first week in July, the weather was as hot as it had been cold in January. July 4th night, lying in the little bed with Marty, I could hear my mother and Daddy talking above the noise the little fan blowing on me and Marty was making. "Hell, Mal,we just ain't making it here, and this job's playing out."

My mother was getting worked up. "Jesus help us, what in God's name are we going to do?"

"Well, I was talking to some fellers at work. One of them's brother went to work at a steel plant in Chicago, Illinois. Making good money. Said he might go too." I guess the Red Stone Arsenal was forgotten. My mother said, "but what about all that talk on the radio about Truman having the government take over all the steel plants? Ain't they all out on strike now? We're just going to get ourselves into another mess."

"Nah, the big court in Washington put a stop to that shit. Most of the men have done gone back now. That's over."

"Well, how would you find out about it, Ben?"
"The bad part, I'd have to quit this job to go all the way to Chicago to find out."

"Ben, it's just a chance we're going to have to take. We gotta do what's best."

On July 15, 1952, my eleventh birthday, my daddy pulled out for Chicago in his 1946 Hudson Hornet. This time he was going by himself to look for work. Five days later he was back. He had been hired at a factory called "Press Steel Corporation". He had also rented us a trailer in a trailer park. "It's not really in what you'd call Chicago. It's a place a little bit south of there called Hegewisch, Illinois. It's not real big, but it's just across the line from Hammond, Indiana and that's a big town. Y'all gonna really like it there."On the 22nd day of July we packed our belonging in the Hudson and pulled out at 5:00 in the morning. We had said goodbye to the Walters the evening before. Mrs. Walters cried and said she would miss us. Mr. Walters reached for Marty, but she took off running. Mrs. Walters said she sure hoped we would come back to visit because we had become "just like family."

My Daddy said, "Don't worry none about that. You know we really think a lot of y'all. We'll come back to visit before too long. Of course, we would never see them again.

Chapter 22

As we pulled away from "Walters Motor Court", I looked toward Lake Erie, but it was too dark to see anything. I was sitting in the front seat with my Daddy. My mother and Marty were in the back seat. In twenty minutes they were both sound asleep. I asked my Daddy if Ma knew we were moving.

"Oh, yeah, son, your mother wrote and told her we were going. I got it off in the mail yesterday." That meant Ma hadn't got the letter yet. I wondered what she would think about it all.

We had received several letters from Ma and each one had a separate letter in the envelope for me, until the last one. I didn't understand it. I wondered about it until I found it crumpled up in the garbage can. At the bottom of this letter ma offered to send me the money to come back to Alabama if I wanted too--to stay with her.

It was still dark when we came into Toledo. I didn't know we had lived that close to a big city. It looked bigger than Birmingham. My Daddy had me helping him to spot a sign with "Highway 20 West" on it. We made a few turns and saw it:

20--WEST

We made the turn and we headed toward our new home.

My Daddy started talking about how much I was going to like it where we were moving. "I saw a lot of boys in the trailer park 'bout your age. They call the trailer park "Island Park Trailer Court". I guess cause there's a big lake surrounding a lot of it. Gotta be good fishing."

I asked my Daddy if we were going to be "big shots" now since he was working at a steel plant.

Ain't no workin' man gonna be a big shot anymore if ol' Ike goes in as president. And he had to go on and pick that damn Nixon as his vice-president on top of it." I asked who Nixon was.

"Big money man in Washington from out in California- Him and Ike'll stay on a damn golf course somewhere. Don't give a damn 'bout the working man. I'll say this for Ol' Nixon though. He damn sure hates the commies."

I asked my Daddy what a "commie" was.

"A communist, son, just like our boys are fighting right now. They're Godless people. They ever git a toe-hold in this country you can kiss it goodbye. They take everthang you got and give it to the gover'ment. You ain't left with nothing."

Just before we crossed the Indiana state line, we stopped at a roadside cafe in a little town called Columbia, Ohio. My Daddy had to have some coffee. It was full day light now. We sat at the counter, my Daddy drinking coffee and me sipping on a bottle of *Grapico* while my mother and Marty were still sleeping in the car.

An old man wearing suspenders over his shirt was sitting at a table and asked my Daddy "Where you'ens bound?"

"A place just outside Chicago", my Daddy said, "going to work in a steel plant. Done been hired and all." The old man said, "well, I guess you'll make fair money and I ain't never been to Chicago, but I hear it's a bad place to raise the kids."

My daddy said, "we'll do alright, I reckon."

As my daddy was paying the woman behind the counter, the old man said, "Well, you probably still have better'n two hundred miles or so. You'ens be careful."

My Daddy thanked the old man as we went out the door.

My mother and Marty were still sleeping when we crossed the Indiana line, but an hour later they both woke up hungry. We stopped at a little grocery store beside the highway where my mother bought a loaf of bread, some bologna, a jar of mayonnaise, and some cold RC Colas. The man who ran the store filled up our gas tank. There was a little place across the road from the store with concrete tables and benches. While we ate, my daddy commented that he hadn't seen another car pass the whole time we'd been there.

When we pulled out, all the Hudson's windows were rolled down because it was really getting hot. After a long time of seeing nothing but farms, we came into a fairly big town. The sign said, "South Bend." My Daddy had to connect with another highway here to take us to highway 6, which, my Daddy said, would then be a straight shot to Hammond, Indiana and Hegewisch, Illinois. A little ways out of South Bend we picked up Highway 6 and turned west again. My Daddy said, "it won't be long now, kids."

As we rode through downtown Hammond, I could see it was a large town, much bigger than Port Clinton. I saw there were two movie theatres; the "Parthenon" and the "Paramount." A little north of Hammond, we turned left on to a narrow winding road. The first thing we passed was a large garbage dump. Just past the dump was a sign:

ILLINOIS

STATE LINE

Around another curve was the trailer park. I had never seen so many trailers. It was a hundred times bigger than the trailer park Mr. Lasner and his family lived in. We started riding up and down different lanes while my daddy tried to find ours. "I just saw it that one time". We passed some huge trailers that were long and sleek looking with little white fences around the yards. I thought to myself that this might not be too bad after all. Then my daddy found ours. We pulled up to a tiny little trailer that was round on both ends. The top half was painted red and the bottom an ugly brown color. There were dark streaks all over one end that looked like somebody had tried to burn it down. A big round metal drum was on a wooden platform laying on its side and was up against the other end. I couldn't make myself believe it. It was pitiful to look at, sitting between the two big trailers on each side. I just knew my mother would say something now. She did.

"Well, Ben, It's not bad. Let's go on in."

Even Marty was horrified. "Daddy, why don't we have one of them big trailers?"

"Well, hon, this is the kind you get when you have to rent. Them big trailers are owned by the people living in 'em. They just rent the lot the trailer's setting on." I said, "you're working at a steel plant now. Why can't we buy one?"

My mother chimed in, "Daniel Wayne, you just let us worry about where we're living and just be glad you've got a roof over your head. When you get out on your own, which can't be too soon for me, then you can live like a big shot. "My Daddy said, "Ah Mal, he's just asking." My mother glared at me. "He ain't never goin' to be satisfied no matter how much we sacrifice for him."

I couldn't remember anything ever being "sacrificed" for me, but I kept quiet. I didn't want her to take off running and hollering through the trailer park our first day there. Inside the trailer it got worse. Our cabin in Ohio had been a castle compared to this. An old, wooden table with four rickety chairs was sitting right in the middle as you went in. A tiny stove was shoved up against a sink with a dripping faucet. On the other side there was a small refrigerator with most of the paint peeled off. Some kind of heater was setting next to the refrigerator. At the end of the little trailer closest to the door, there was a green couch with stuffing coming out of the cushions. At the other end a curtain was hanging. On the other side of the curtain there was a bed with a toilet setting next to it. A hand-written sign was hanging from a string tied around the toilet's tank:

Pleese dont use

NOT conected

It took about three seconds to see everything. I wondered out loud where Marty and me were supposed to sleep. Sounding as if he had discovered gold, my Daddy proudly announced, "That couch is a bed, Dan. You just take them cushions off and pull it right out. They call it a hide-away bed. Then he told us that the heater and stove ran off something called propane gas. "That big barrel in the back holds it. The trailer park people come around ever so often and keep it filled. It's figured in with the rent." The rent was forty dollars a month and that included electricity and everything my daddy said. My mother wanted to know, "what about bathing and using the bathroom?" It was taken care of. "That big brick building we passed coming in is the bath house. They got showers and toilets and everythang." I was slowly sinking. I said, "you know, ma said I could come live with her anytime I wanted to, and this place might not be big enough for all of us. Maybe I could just go live with ma." My Daddy's face got pale while my mother's was turning red. My Daddy spoke first. "Son, you can't go live with Mama. She's got her hands full with your Uncle Mathew. You gotta stay with your own family 'cause we need you here. It'd be again' the law anyway. They'd pick me up if we tried somethin' like that. Just git that notion out of your head. We're gonna git a big trailer before long, with a bathroom and everthang." I thought for sure that my mother would be agreeable to the idea, but she wasn't.

"You've always loved that old woman more than you do your own mother. I ain't never got the respect from you she's got all these years. You think the sun rises and sets on her. I sacrificed for you ever since you was born and she ain't never done nothin' for you!" I threw caution to the win. "I don't remember anything you've ever sacrificed for me. All you ever do is holler at me for no reason at all. I heard you tell Daddy that you loved Marty but didn't care nothin' 'bout me! I wanna go live with Ma!"

My mother bolted for the trailer door, my Daddy catching her just as she grabbed the handle.

"I can't breathe, Lord Jesus! Help me somebody!"

My Daddy glared at me over my mother's head as he maneuvered her back toward the curtain. I went out slamming the trailer door behind me. I stood around in the little yard awhile, then I started walking.

There were trailers as far as I could see in every direction. Walking down the row ours was on, I saw a couple that were small like ours, but they were in much better shape. I walked until there were no more trailers. After jumping over a bad smelling little creek and climbing up a bank, I saw Wolf Lake. It was bigger than I had expected. It was definitely wider than the Portage

River. I could see that I was down at one end of it. The other end appeared to curve around toward the far side of the trailer park. down on my end, there was an old wooden pier jutting out into the water. Next to it was an old ramshackle building. A sign was nailed to one of the porch posts.

ED'S FISH LODGE
Live Bait
Worms 25 cents a dozen

I didn't see anything stirring around the old house. I stood on the shoreline just looking at the water. It was a hot day but a warm wind was blowing causing a little bit of white foam to gently push against the shore. After an hour or so, I headed home, unsure of what to expect. As I neared our trailer, I could hear my daddy's radio playing. ***"Oh My Papa-To Me He Was So Wonderfuuul"***.

Inside it was like nothing had happened. My Daddy had gone somewhere and bought some stuff for sandwiches. My mother even asked me what I wanted on my sandwich. I sat on the couch with Marty, eating a baloney, tomato and lettuce sandwich and reading a funny book. Our parents sat at the old rickety table, listening to the radio and making big plans for the future. The next morning as my daddy was leaving for work, I went with him to the car. It was parked in a big parking lot right in middle of the trailer park. Everybody had to park there because there wasn't room in the small trailer lots to leave a car. My Daddy dug an old rod and reel out of the trunk that Mr. Lasner had given him that he had never used. I had used it a few times. At first it would "back-lash" on me and get tangled up. I finally learned how to control it by lightly pressing my thumb on the line rolled around the reel while I was casting. It was still fitted with an eight pound test line, sinkers and a bream hook.

My Daddy told me, "you be careful around that ol' lake now." I told him I would and took off toward Ed's fish camp. When I arrived at Ed's, I could see that the old building looked more like a house than a place of business, even with the sign. So instead of going on in, I knocked on the door. An old woman weighing about three hundred pounds opened the door.

"Come on in here, young feller."

"Yes, ma'am"

"I ain't never seen youse before."

"No, ma'am, we just moved here."

"Well, we're glad to have ya. What can I do for ya?"

"I want to buy a dozen worms."

There were old pictures on the wall behind her of men holding long strings of fish. I laid a quarter on the counter. In a little adjoining room I could see a man laying on a cot. His mouth was open and he was snoring to beat the band. The woman saw me looking. "That's my son, Ed. He ain't feeling real well this morning."

"Yes, ma'am."

She set a small paper carton on the counter. "Here's your worms, but I tell ya what; you just keep your quarter. Since this is your first time, it's on the house." I said,"yes, ma'am, thank you."

"You're quite welcome, youngster. You come back now and good luck to ya."

I thanked her again as I went out the door. I went about a hundred yards down the shore, away from Ed's. I found a small forked limb and stuck it in the soft mud. Reaching in the box, I came out with a lively worm that I threaded onto the hook. I cast my line out as far as I could and placed the rod in the fork of the limb. Since I didn't have a cork, I would be fishing, "tight line."-I set back to wait for the tell-tell sign of the tip of my rod making little jerks when I got a bite. An hour passed, and it was getting hot. Something was wrong. I reeled my line back in, sure that my worm had washed off the hook somehow. The worm was still intact but no longer lively. I took it off, put on a new one, and cast my line out to a different spot. I sat back again to wait. In about fifteen minutes a man walked up. It didn't startle me because I had seen him coming a good ways off.

He said, "Hi'ya, lad."
I said, "Hello".
He had a funny look on his face. "What the hell you doing, son?" I considered it to be a dumb question.

"Fishing", I said.
"Fishing for what?"
"Whatever bites, I guess."
The man laughed out loud. "Hell, they ain't ***nothing*** gonna bite. There ain't no damn fish in that lake. Hasn't been for twenty years or more." I asked, "Are you joshing with me?" He shook his head. "No son, I surely am not. Lake's been poisoned for years. Too much shit been dumped in it from the plants. Ya might catch an old newt or water lizard. They can live anywhere."--I asked the man what a newt was.

"Far as I'm concerned it ain't nothing but a shit-eating lizard. Ain't good for nothing , though I have heard of niggers eating 'em sometimes."-

I wanted to know, "why have they got a bait shop down there?"

The man laughed again. "Ol' Ed and his mama have had that place for forty years. When they built it, there was still fish in the lake. When it got ruined, neither one of 'em had sense enough to leave. Ol' Ed ain't nothing but a drunken sot now. Been that way since his woman left him 'bout fifteen years ago. Ain't never heard from her since. She had more brains than Ed and his mama put together."

I asked, "Where can you fish around here?"

A sad look came over him. "There ain't no place, son; there just ain't no place. You take care now." As he shuffled off toward Ed's Fish Camp I saw a brown paper sack sticking out of his back pocket.

I slowly reeled my line in. I had been fishing in a place worse than Bayview Lake, back home. Bayview Lake at least had fish in it, but you couldn't eat them because you would die if you did. Bayview Lake had been formed by backing up Village Creek years before. It was said that the hospitals in Birmingham dumped all their waste in Village creek and the coal mines did too. It all eventually worked its way into the lake. In the summer a green skim would form over the surface, and it would smell awful.

It didn't matter, because there were a lot of other places to fish not far from Bayview that were clean. The Warrior River, the Mulberry, the Sipsey, Flint Creek, even Birmingport. But here, there was no place to go fishing. I picked up my carton of worms and threw it out in the lake as far as I could. I didn't know if newts ate worms or not. If they did, they could have a good meal.

As I was moseying back through the trailer park with the rod and reel over my shoulder, a boy about my age came out of a trailer and fell in beside me.

"You been fishing?"

"Yeah."

"In Wolf Lake?"

"Yep"

"There ain't no fish in that lake."
"Yeah, I know that now."
"Anyway, my name's Frank Steenburger."
"My name's Daniel Knight."
"You mean like night time?"
"No, it's spelled with a K in front."
"What kind of a name is that?"
"What do you mean?"
" Well, like, we're German."
"We're American."
"Well, we're Americans too.
"I thought you said you were German?"
"I meant my forefathers came from Germany; what about yours?"
"Mine came from America."

"Everyone's forefathers came from another country.
"Not mine. They were all from America."

Frank changed the subject--"What grade are you gonna be in?"

"Sixth."

"Hey, me too! You'll be going to Henry Clay." Frank was about two inches taller than me and his hair was as blond as Marty's. I asked Frank, "where's the school at?"

"It's just about a mile and a half, down in Hegewisch. There's a school bus, but three or four of us guys just walk everyday until it gets cold weather"

"Do you like going there?" I asked.
"Yeah, it's ok, but it's tough."
"You mean the teachers are hard?"

Frank laughed, "Nah, I mean there's some tough kids. Lots of fights. Teachers are scared of some of 'em." I was amazed. I had never heard of anything like that.

"You mean teachers are scared of some of the kids?"

"Yeah, Polack kid, in the ninth grade knifed a teacher last year. Put him in the hospital for two weeks. Kid's in reform school now."

I couldn't believe it, but I knew Frank couldn't be making up a story like this.

I asked Frank, "What's a Polack?"

"Polish kids. Families came from Poland."

"Are there any colored kids in Henry Clay?" Frank laughed again, "You mean niggers? Hell no, ain't no niggers ever gonna get into Henry Clay. That's for sure."

My mind was still taking all of this in when Frank changed the subject again. "Do you collect stamps?"

"What?"
"Do you collect stamps?"

"Uh, I don't guess I do."

"I collect stamps from all over. I've got two stamp albums full and starting on my third. Let's go back to my trailer and I'll show 'em to you." We turned around and headed back toward Frank's trailer, my mind still on the teacher being knifed. Frank's trailer was three times bigger than ours. There was a little white fence around the yard. Frank's mother was washing dishes at the sink. She was tall and blonde like Frank. She had an apron on that had little red hearts on it. Frank's mother reminded me of the drawing of a mother in my second grade reader.

"Have you met a new friend, Frankie?"
"Yes , this is Daniel."
"Well hi, Daniel. How are you?"
"Fine," I answered as I followed Frank down the aisle toward the back. There were two bedrooms in the back with a bathroom between them. The first bedroom was Frank's-- all Frank's. I asked Frank if he had any brothers or sisters.

"No, I'm it." he said.

Airplanes were hanging from the ceiling by strings. Most of the planes had German iron crosses on the wings and a swastika on the tail. I told Frank that one of them looked like a Messerschmitt 109.

Frank seemed surprised. "Hey, you know about fighter planes. I'm impressed. That's exactly what it is." I said, "I know a little, I guess."

Taking up most of the wall behind Frank's bed was a huge red flag. There was a bit white circle in the centre. In the middle of the circle was a black swastika. Frank opened a drawer in his dresser and brought out two big books. "These are my stamp albums."

Now I was impressed. There were stamps from everywhere. As I flipped through the album, I could see different countries had their own section. There was a picture of each stamp underneath the actual stamp. Frank said the pictures let you know what stamps to look for. When you found one you placed it over its picture with a paper hinge. I had never seen stamps from another country. There were animals and birds. One huge stamp from

Belgium showed three men riding in a hot air balloon. Some pictured Kings and Queens. One, from the Philippines, had a picture of a man with a bandage wrapped around his head and down over one eye. Another from French Equatorial Africa had an angel with a sword in her hand flying over four army tanks.

Frank said he was a "philatelist." That's what a stamp collector was called. He said President Roosevelt had been a philatelist. To prove it he showed me a stamp from Nicaragua that pictured President Roosevelt studying his stamp collection. I wondered why Nicaragua would put out a stamp with President Roosevelt on it.

Frank pulled a magazine out of the dresser drawer. "I'm going to show you the most valuable stamp in the world."

"You've got it?" I asked.

Frank said, "I wish. Nah, it's just a picture."

The magazine had a picture of a stamp from British Guinea. It looked like the corners had been snipped off. There were strange words at the top and bottom and in the middle you could just barely see the outlines of a sailing ship. It didn't look nearly as impressive as the stamps Frank had but he said, "there's only two of these in the world and they're worth a hundred thousand dollars each. A private collector has one of them, but nobody knows where the other one is. I'm gonna find it someday." For some reason I believed he would. Two hours later I said, "Well, I guess I better head home, my mother'll think I drowned or something." As we went back into the kitchen area, Frank's mother said, "You come back anytime, Daniel."

I said, "Thank you."

When I reached the yard Frank hollered out "I'll probably see you tomorrow." I headed down the road toward our trailer with images flooding my head of swastikas, German fighter planes, stamps with wounded men on them, and a teacher face down on the street with a knife in his back. The rest of that summer, Frank and I became friends. I had talked my Daddy into buying me a stamp album at a little store in Hegewisch, along with two cellophane packets of stamps. My mother said it looked like a lot of foolishness to her. A lot of the stamps didn't have a picture in my album, but I was thrilled when I found one that did. I found ads in magazines where you could send off for a bunch of stamps for fifty cents. Along with these stamps, the ad said you would receive other stamps for your 'approval'. I sent off to three or four different places. In about two weeks I had stamps coming in from everywhere. Along with the fifty cents worth there were other stamps. There was a letter from each company saying if I 'approved' of these stamps to send twenty-five dollars or please return them. I threw the letters away. I ordered stamps through several other ads until I was caught up with. Coming home one evening, I found my mother holding letters from every stamp company.

"Daniel Wayne, what in God's name is this all about? These people are all demanding big money from you."

I explained to her about the 'approvals' and waited for the explosion. It didn't come. Instead she said, "just don't do it anymore."

That night my mother set down and wrote each company. She told them they were dealing with an eleven-year-old and if they didn't have any more sense than that, they needed to lose their stamps and if they wrote anymore letters she was going to sue them. I didn't receive any more letters. My stamp collection was off to a good start.

Chapter 23

The winter of 1952 was bitter cold and the snow never stopped. Our little trailer rocked in the wind at night. Ice formed on the insides of the windows. In the morning I would trudge through the snow to the spot where the trailer park kids waited for the school bus to take us to the Henry Clay School. Your feet didn't sink into the snow like in Ohio, because it was always frozen over. Some days we would walk to school, our backs turned to the cutting wind. At times the wind was so cold your lungs would burn if you took a deep breath. Henry Clay did have a lot of Polish kids. A lot of them had Z's and W's in their last names. Fighting was the main source of entertainment. Somebody was always going to, "meet you after school." I had several, losing most of them. Then, for some reason, a boy named Calvin Belski took a liking to me and we became buddies. This was great for me because Calvin had an older brother named Max who was the head of a 'gang' that roamed the neighborhood. Max and his gang were 15 and 16 year olds who took great pleasure in catching younger kids, taking their lunch money, and then de-pantsing them. "De-pantsing" consisted of having your britches pulled down around your ankles. The girls at Henry Clay took great delight in witnessing this event if they were fortunate enough to be close to the scene. One girl, named Norma, seemed to take a special interest in a victim enduring this embarrassment. When a target was chosen, Norma would shout, "depants him, depants him!" I never suffered this indignity because of my friendship with Calvin. A fat boy named George Towbridge was depantsed so many times it barely attracted attention anymore, except for Norma if she was in the vicinity.

In early December 1952 a great thing happened. We got a Motorola television. We didn't get it in a store; a man dressed in a suit came to our trailer. He showed my parents pictures of televisions in a brochure he had pulled from his briefcase. They settled on the Motorola. The man explained the payment plan and my Daddy signed some papers. My mother was to receive a "genuine" pearl necklace as a "premium" for buying the television. Two days later a delivery man brought the television to us. Wonder of wonders. We had 3 channels to choose from. Early in the morning the same Indian head test pattern would come on, but the programming started much earlier than it had in Alabama. My mother's favorite show was Art Linkletter's "House Party". Marty's was a children's program called, "Elmer the Elephant". A man talked to an elephant puppet and showed cartoons. Wrestling, live from Chicago on Wednesday nights, was me and my Daddy's favorite. Killer Kawalski, Hans Schmidt, Lou Thez, Argentine Rocca, became household words. They were the trailer park kid's idols. I was stunned one day when Frank informed me that Hans Schmidt had moved into our trailer park. I couldn't believe it. Frank showed me his trailer. It was a big, sleek, modern-looking one. We cased the trailer for 3 days. On the third evening the trailer door opened and a huge man with a shaved head walked out and picked up his newspaper--It was him! No doubt about it. Frank and I stood there, motionless, gawking. Hans looked at us and waved. "How you fellows doing?"

We both muttered something. Hans smiled and went back into his trailer. We were shaken. To me it was close to actually seeing the Durango Kid in person.

1952 ended on a bad note. Christmas Eve we had no tree, much less any gifts to go under it. My mother announced that her and my Daddy were going to a store and "get something for you kids".

My daddy was home every workday by 3:30 p.m. but not today. At four-thirty my mother started in. "Your Daddy's probably dead." I tried to ignore her. Marty started crying. At 5 pm darkness had settled over the trailer park. My mother was frantic. "What in Jesus' name will we do now?" At 6:30 pm I looked out the back window of our trailer. In a street light I could see snow starting to come down. Then I saw my Daddy's car coming, weaving from side to side. My mother looked out. "The son of a bitch is drunker than Cooter Brown." My Daddy's car went out of sight into the little parking area. A few minutes later he was trying to open the trailer door. My mother opened the door and jerked him inside. He stood there wobbling for a second and then just sat down in the middle of the floor. Then he threw up all over himself and the floor. My mother ran and got the mop. I thought she was going to mop the floor. Instead she started screaming, "you sorry bastard!" –While beating him across the head with the mop. He said, "Aw, Mal, I didn't mean nothing." I couldn't take it anymore. I jerked the mop out of her hand and threw it outside into the snow. My mother put Marty's coat on and reached into my daddy's coat for the car keys announcing, "this young'un ain't gonna do without a Christmas because of a no-good, sorry son of a bitch" Out her and Marty went. My Daddy struggled up with me helping him and headed for the back room. I heard him fall across the bed with a loud crash. It sounded like some of the bed slats had broken. I went outside and got the mop and tried to clean up the best I could. In an hour my mother and Marty were back. They had found a store open somewhere. Marty had a new doll under her arm. On Christmas morning I woke early. From me and Marty's sofa hide-away I could see my Daddy smoking a cigarette. His little radio was playing with the volume turned way down. I could hear Doris Day singing ***"Once I Had A Secret Loooove"***

Chapter 24

As 1953 began Russia and China, who were our friends in World War II, were no longer our friends. In March, Henry Clay School started something new. We still had fire-drills but now we also had air-raid drills. We were taught how to get behind our desks and shield our eyes from the blinding light should Russia decide to drop an atomic bomb on us as we had done to the Japanese. We thought it was stupid because we figured if we were close enough to be blinded we would be blown up anyway. But we carried on with the drills on a regular basis.

In July I turned 12. That same month my mother told Marty and me that she had found a job. She was going to work at Calumet Glass Company in Hammond, Indiana. We would be moving over the state line to Hammond so she would be closer to the factory. I would be changing schools again. The good news was, we would *not* be living in a trailer anymore. My daddy had rented a house. My elation was short lived. He had rented a house all right, but only part of it. We were going to live in the basement beneath the owners, the Robinsons. The Robinsons had a daughter, Gloria, who was 14, and a son, Eugene, who was 7.

I was devastated when I saw our basement "apartment". As you entered from the concrete stairs the kitchen was to the right. It consisted of an old wooden table with four chairs, a tiny gas stove, an old refrigerator that was

134

badly discolored, and a couple of cupboards hanging lop-sided on the wall. An enclosure made of unpainted lumber was built onto one of the kitchen walls. Inside the enclosure was a flush toilet. The toilet was about 4 feet from the kitchen table. Separating the kitchen from our "living room" and bedrooms was a large laundry room. Besides a big ringer type washing machine, there was a huge stainless steel sink. There was no door between the kitchen and the laundry room and only an old faded Curtain between the Laundry room and the living room. The living room sofa was also a hide-away bed and, of course, that's where Marty and me would be sleeping.

On our second day in our new "home" I was standing in the alley that ran behind the house when I spotted Gloria headed my way. She came striding up, hands on hips.

"I guess I might as well tell you the rules around here", she informed me. Gloria was about an inch taller than me and skinny as a pole. She smelled like sauerkraut.

"Your parents rent from us and that makes me your boss."
I told her I didn't see how that made her any kind of boss.
"Well, it does and what I say goes."
Removing her hands from her hips and folding her arms, she asked me, "Know what happened to the last family that rented from us?" I didn't answer so Gloria went on. "We threw them out. That's what. They didn't pay their rent on time and made too much noise."

I turned around and started walking away. Gloria yelled after me, "Your family just better watch their P's and Q's, that's what."
I figured she must have been kin to Barbara back in Ohio.

My mother would be riding the bus to the glass factory which was only about 7 miles away. My job for the rest of the summer would be to tend to Marty during the day while our parents were at work. That fall I would be going into the 7th grade at Washington Irving Jr. High. Marty would be going to Lincoln Elementary, about 2 blocks from our place.

Saturday night was the best night for television. My mother would make bologna and lettuce sandwiches and we'd sit around the T.V. and watch the "Jackie Gleason Show." My daddy would laugh when they did "The Honeymooners" skit. Afterward he would set at the kitchen table and try to pick up "The Grand Old Opry", but still failed. He would end up listening to a local station *"Where no one theeere will know your face - it's called, Hernando's Hide-Awaay - ole!"*

Two weeks after moving to Hammond, my mother located her a church. I was a little surprised at this as she had never been a church goer. It was on Hohman Street. It didn't look like a church. It looked like it had been a little store at one time. Attached over the door was a big sign,

CHURCH OF THE NAZARENE— G. Simmons-Pastor.

My mother attended every Wednesday and Sunday night. She said the preacher was really helping her with her "nerves". She nagged my daddy to go but he would beg off.

"Mal, I'm goin' with you one of these nights, but I'm just not up to it tonight."

Sometimes I would go with her but I didn't mind because I always sat with Preacher Simmon's daughter, Kathleen. Kathleen was my age and the most beautiful girl I had ever seen. Her hair was jet black and full of little ringlets that fell down over her shoulders. She always smelled like flowers and fresh chewing gum. She seemed to like me, too.

My mother and me would get to church early on Sunday and Kathleen and me would walk a little ways up and down Hohman Avenue and talk. She asked a lot of questions about Alabama and seemed really interested in everything I said. Sometimes we would get tickled during one of Preacher Simmon's sermons and would have to hide our faces behind our hymn books so we wouldn't be seen laughing.

The big night finally came when my daddy said he would go. Marty had on a new dress and smelled like white shoe polish. We all loaded up and headed for church. Preacher Simmons paced the floor back and forth preaching in a loud voice, waving his arms around. Sometimes he would pick his bible up and wave it around. He preached about how nobody knew when death was coming. Why, you could fall dead at anytime, even this very night on the way home from church. Then it was too late to be saved. You would not be going to heaven. You would be going to hell for eternity. At the end of the sermon, Preacher Simmons held "invitation." He was a tall man with wavy hair and when he held his arms in the air he looked even taller. "Won't you please come? If you don't know Jesus, this is the time. There may not be another chance. Won't you please come?" The little congregation was singing, *"Jesus is Caaalling, come hoooome."*

All of a sudden Preacher Simmons jumped down from his podium and started down the aisle. I thought he was leaving. He stopped at the pew where my mother and daddy and Marty were seated. Touching my father's shoulder, Preacher Simmons said, "Brother Knight, won't you please come up tonight and accept Jesus into your heart?"

My Daddy stood straight up. I was shocked. My Daddy was going to be saved! Preacher Simmons moved back to give him room to get out, saying "Praise the Lord." But instead of heading toward the altar, my Daddy turned the other way and went out the door. I looked at Kathleen. She had her hymn book in front of her face. Through the front window I could see my Daddy lighting a cigarette. The preacher leaned over to my mother and said, "Sister Knight, I believe the Lord touched his heart tonight." My mother nodded. I guess the Lord really hadn't though, because on the way home my daddy was madder then I had ever seen him!

"Who in hell does that son-of-a-bitch think he is! I ain't never been that embarrassed in my life. Picked me out as a sinner in front of all them people. What in hell does the S.O.B. know about me?"

My mother tried to calm him. "Ben, he's just worried about your soul." "What in hell does he know about my soul? The Son-of-a-bitch needs to worry about his own soul." That night, laying in bed, I could hear him still grumbling about it. I never knew of my daddy going inside a church again the rest of his life.

My mother's job didn't last long. Toward the end of August her "nerves" got real bad. She would wake up in the middle of the night screaming that she was smothering and dying. My daddy would talk to her until she calmed down.

One night Preacher Simmons and two other men came to our basement home. They were wearing suits and each man had a bible. They had come to pray for my mother. My daddy and Marty and me sat around the little kitchen table while Preacher Simmons and his friends prayed over mother in the living area across from the laundry room. The three men's voices grew louder and louder. I couldn't make out what the other two men were saying because Preacher Simmons was drowning them out. He kept hollering, "Lord, cast the devil from this woman!" This went on for a good half hour. Marty was scared. My daddy told her everything was all right. When the men left, my daddy shook each one's hand as they went out the door. The next night we had another visitor. Mr. Robinson from upstairs. He informed my Daddy that he didn't know "what in hell" had went on down here the night before but it had scared his wife and kids "half to death". He said he had never heard such carrying on. He said we had three days to get our stuff together and get out.

Chapter 25

I had been playing "horse" with Ray Gadhus, at an old basketball net that stood in one of the corners of the school yard when Coach Earl Thomas walked up. "I want you to come out for football this fall."

It was May, 1955. I was finishing up the 8th grade at Irving Jr. High. Irving went through the 9th grade so I would be there one more year before going on to high school.

After the Robinsons had kicked us out we had moved "up". We were now living in an attic that had been converted into an apartment or 'flat' as the old man who owned it called it. Mr. Mazurak looked very old. He always wore a gray sweater with wooden buttons and a little gray cap. He and his son, Johnny, who was as old as my daddy, lived below us. Mr. Mazurak couldn't speak English very well and was difficult to understand. His son, Johnny, didn't work and was always hanging around in the back yard where the stairs up to our flat were. You couldn't understand Johnny either because he was always drunk.When you went around to the back of the building to climb the stairs to our place, Johnny was usually there, swaying back and forth with his hands in his pockets. He would always say something that was not understandable. We learned to just nod in agreement and get on up the stairs. Sometimes Johnny's pants would be wet in front where he had peed on himself.--Coach Thomas repeated it. "I said I want you out for football this fall." I looked at Ray to see what his answer would be. Coach Thomas grabbed me by the shoulder and spun me around facing him. Coach Thomas was a small, compact man. I had seen him in nothing but running shorts and tennis shoes in the boy's locker room. Muscles bulged from his arms and legs.

"Ray's already on the team, I'm talking to you, Knight."
"Yes, sir!"
"Coach Thomas said, "come by the gym and pick up some gear. I want you and Gadhus to do a lot of running this summer. You'll get a letter on it, but report here to the gym on August 15th for a physical."

"Yes, sir."
Coach Thomas strode off.
Ray laughed, "I'm gonna knock your jock strap off, Dan."
We both laughed. Ray already had his "gear" but walked with me over to the gym. The equipment manager was a boy in our class named Ted Sparkman. Ted walked with a slight limp. He had told everyone back in the 7th grade that he had been born with one leg shorter than the other. Ted issued me a pair of football pants with pads already inserted in the knees and thighs, a pair of cleats, a practice jersey and a helmet. It didn't have a face guard like helmets would later have. Ted showed me how to unscrew the cleats from the bottom of the shoe to remove sod and grass that would build up. He said I would be issued shoulder pads and hip guards when practice started in August.

I was excited even though I had no knowledge of football at all. The past fall I had walked over to Irving Park and watched the 9th graders play a few times. Now I was on the team.

Ted and me stopped at the "Ice-Berg", a new ice cream parlor that had just recently been built. I was carrying my pants, jersey and helmet which I set down by a stool. The laces on my cleats were tied together and they were slung over my shoulder. As I sipped my milkshake I could see some girls from our class sitting at a table. Out of the corner of my eye I could see them looking at us and whispering. I felt proud and important. As if I was already a great football star. Somebody played the jukebox. *"**See You Later Alligator -- Afterwhile   Crocodile.**"*

I couldn't wait to tell my Daddy. I bounded up our back stairs without even a nod toward Johnny, standing there rocking back and forth, the front of his pants wet. My Daddy was home from work and just he and Marty were home. My mother had started back working at the Calumet Glass Company. She was on evening shift, 4 to 12. That way she could take Marty back and forth to school. Marty was in second grade and got out at 2:30 every day. I showed my Daddy my stuff and told him about Coach Thomas. He wasn't as impressed as I had wanted him to be.

"Well son, I guess that's alright. But you could be hurt or killed playing that game." I told him I had never heard of anybody getting killed playing football.

Then he floored me. He told me something I just couldn't believe. Unknown to me, he had received a letter from one of his older brothers, Oren, a few days earlier. Uncle Oren had offered him some of his land to build a house on if he would move back to Alabama. The coal mines were working good now and my Daddy could go back to his old job. I couldn't believe it! My Daddy had talked some about wanting to move back to Alabama but nothing serious. This was serious! I told him I didn't want to move back to Alabama now.

"Well, son, this ain't our home", my Daddy said.
I said, "Well, it's my home now. All my friends are here. I'm going to play football."
My Daddy lit a cigarette. "I don't think we'll be living here when school starts back this next time. You know, son, they play football in Alabama too." I was beside myself. "I don't care what they do in Alabama. I'm not going!" I saw my daddy's jaw start twitching. I had a room of my own now and headed for it. I slammed the door and fell across the bed. Late that night I woke up hearing my mother talking to my daddy in a low voice.

"Daniel Wayne's not running this family. We have to do what's best for Marty. We never should have come off up here to this place to start with." My daddy muttered something I couldn't understand. I was devastated.

Chapter 26

We now had a 1952 Chevrolet "Deluxe". The weekend after school was out we piled in the Chevrolet. My Daddy picked up highway 41 South and we headed toward Alabama to check out the land Uncle Oren was offering to give us. My worry had been put off some. The talk between our parents now was that it would be at least a year or longer before they could save enough money to start building a house back in Alabama.

About a hundred miles south of Hammond, Marty announced that she was hungry. Our Mother said, "I could eat something too." Our Daddy pulled into a restaurant parking lot.

I knew it was bad news as soon as we were in the cafe. White linen table cloths covered the tables. A nice- dressed lady met us at the entrance and let us to a table. Once we were seated she gave each of us a menu. Gleaming silverware lay on white cloth napkins. My Daddy looked stricken. The lady said a waitress would be with us shortly and she hoped we enjoyed our meal. We had blundered into a big shot place, for sure. My mother opened her menu. "My God, Ben, they want a dollar for a hamburger."

My Daddy didn't even open his menu. He stood up. "Come on, let's get out of here." We filed out. I held up the rear, my face burning as I could sense everybody staring at us. Once we were in the car my Daddy said, "hell, we just wanted a bite to eat. I didn't want to buy the damn place. Nobody can afford to eat in there, 'less they're big shots."

A few miles down the road we pulled up to a little grocery store. Across the highway there was one of those little road-side picnic areas just like the one we had eaten at traveling from Ohio. A concrete table with concrete benches running down both sides. We dined on home-made hot dogs and sodas.

We got lost in Nashville trying to find highway 31 to Birmingham. It was finally found and we were on our way. We pulled up in front of Ma's house early the next morning after riding all night. She had been watching for us because as soon as we stopped she opened the screen door and came out to meet us; wiping her hands on her apron. Ma hugged all of us, carrying on about how me and Marty had grown. We must have because Ma seemed even littler now.

"Daniel Wayne, I never would have known you. You've growed so much and got so good-looking." It was a little embarrassing. I told Ma I was going to be playing football in the fall. She said, "Well, I'll swanee."

Ma had a big breakfast already on the table. Mother said she didn't want anything to eat. She just wanted to lie down for a while. Ma looked disappointed. We had, recently, finally had a phone put in and I noticed Ma had one too. Our number was Westmoreland 2-1931. Ma's was State 5-2585. I guess phones were now available for all the "little shots."

The plan was for us to spend the day at Ma's and head up to Walker County to Uncle Oren's house the next morning and come back to Ma's. Ma went on all day about how happy she was that we would be moving back to Alabama. She kept saying, "I've lived in Alabama 80 years and I ain't never missed a meal. Y'all didn't have no business moving off up north in the first place."

I got Ma's phone book out and flipped through it to see if anybody I knew had a phone now. I saw Carol's daddy listed. I almost called her, but for some reason I didn't. I walked out on Ma's back porch and looked over at Bayview Lake. Everything looked smaller, I didn't know why. The next morning after breakfast we all got in the car and headed to Uncle Oren's. Ma wanted Marty to stay with her but she insisted on going too. Uncle Oren's house was about 25 miles from Bayview. He and his wife, Janey, were sitting on the front porch in a glider when we pulled up. Uncle Oren was a lot older than my Daddy and I hadn't been around him very much. They got up from the glider, when we got out of the car. Uncle Oren and my Daddy shook hands. Uncle Oren had one thumb hooked under the strap to his overalls. Janey spoke to my mother, "It's good to see y'all."--Uncle Oren patted me on the shoulder. Aunt Janey didn't acknowledge me or Marty. Somebody once told me that aunt Janey's people had come from France long ago. Inside, the house was so quiet you could hear the tick-tock of the big grandfather's clock that set in one corner of the living room. There was a smell of soap and furniture polish. My mother and Janey went into the kitchen. My Daddy and Uncle Oren went back outside and around toward the back of the house. Marty went out and started rocking back and forth in the glider. I sat down in a big, red leather chair. Next to the chair there was a wooden cut-out of a black man about three feet high. The man seemed to be dressed in one of the outfits that jockeys in horse races wore. One of his arms extended out with an ash tray in his hand. I didn't see anything to read and there was no television. I had been sitting in the chair for at least an hour listening to the tick-tock of the clock and the creaking of the glider when my daddy and

Uncle Oren came back in the house. My Daddy looked a little pale. "Mal, you ready to go?" My mother and Janey came out of the kitchen. Uncle Oren didn't say anything. Janey muttered something about us staying for dinner. Nobody replied to that. We all piled into the car and drove off. Janey and Uncle Oren had not come out of the house to see us off. My Daddy still looked a little shaken. "Hell, Mal, he wanted big money for them damn lots. I thought he was giving the damn things to me." My mother said, "I knew the way Janey was talking that it wasn't what it was cracked up to be. She told me that Oren could do whatever he wanted to, but she had to have a new room built on and a new bedroom suite out of the deal." My daddy repeated himself "Hell, I thought he was giving me them damn lots."

"Well, Ben, it wasn't Oren. Janey didn't want us having them lots. She'd already laid down the law before we got there."
Not much else was said on the way back to Ma's. I sure didn't say anything. It was all good news to me.

Chapter 27

"Turn your head and cough." The doctor had a finger dug into my groin and it hurt. "Now the other way and cough." He put a stethoscope to my chest and listened. Then he turned me around and put it to my back. Signing a form with my name on it, he said, "you're ok, next man."

Once our physicals were over, Coach Thomas marched us over to Irving Park, about 4 blocks away for our first practice. The first 3 days we wore gym shorts, t-shits, cleats and helmets. It was all running, jumping jacks, push-ups and leg lifts. But mostly running. Coach Thomas almost ran us to death. The temperature was in the nineties. The third day was the toughest. A couple of boys fell out. Their football career was over. One heavy-set boy named Kenny Linstrom vomited but hung on. There was no drinking water until we returned to the gym after practice. It was believed that drinking water while you were hot would kill you. The fourth day we came out in full pads. Coach Thomas had us blocking and tackling each other in "one on one" drills. He screamed and yelled and blew his whistle.

"Drive those legs, drive 'em, drive 'em! Don't let up! Come on, Knight! You must wanna be a cheerleader!" We all had the "cheerleader" remark thrown at us at one time or the other.

In the days that followed we started learning plays both on offense and defense. Coach Thomas moved us in and out at different positions. We began full speed scrimmaging. I had been at left guard. Coach Thomas moved me to center. There were only 17 boys left on the team. Most of us would be playing both ways. About the only one who wouldn't be was our quarterback, Mark Chappel. At the end of the second week of practice, Coach Thomas called out eleven names and positions. I was called in at center. When all eleven men were at their position, Coach Thomas said, "as it stands now, this is our starting offensive unit." I sort of threw my chest out and put my hands on my hips. Coach Thomas slapped me on the side of my helmet with an open palm. "Don't be so full of yourself, Knight. This can all change in a heartbeat."

"Yes, sir" -- My ears were ringing.

Our first game was against the 9th grade team at Woodrow Wilson High School in Gary, Indiana. All that week rumors flew. They had a player named Jaloveki.---Jaloveki was 6'3" or 6'5" and weighed 225 pounds or 250 pounds and was either 19 or 21 years old, according to whoever was doing the talking. On game day we loaded into an old school bus and pulled out toward Woodrow Wilson. Three 9th grade girls were our cheerleaders and they rode with us, wearing their cheerleader outfits and holding their purple and gold pom-poms. We were doing warm-up exercises at our end of the field when the Wilson team ran onto the field at the other end. Jaloveki was easy to spot. The rumors were true. He was at least a head taller than any other player on the field and looked too old to be a ninth-grader. We won the coin toss and would receive. I was on the receiving team. My assignment was to take out the kicker. I looked down field. The ref had teed the ball and naturally, Jaloveki was the kicker. The ref blew his whistle and Jaloveki's foot met the ball with a loud "whump"! We went sailing down field. I saw the ball flying over my head. Without a facemask I could see Jaloveki clearly now. He was coming right at me, grinning ear to ear. I left the ground attempting to bring him down with a cross-body block just like we had practiced. Something slammed into my helmet and I felt a searing pain in my side. I lay on the ground a couple of seconds trying to get my breath. My helmet was laying about 10 feet away. I could hear our cheerleaders. They sounded far away. ***Hit 'em again--Harder, harder!"***
I scrambled up and grabbed my helmet, running back downfield to the pile up. Jaloveki had dropped our return man on our own 10 year line. I thought

Coach Thomas would jerk me out of the game. He didn't. Three plays later we were still on our own 10 yard line. Jaloveki had made every tackle. We had to punt. Jaloveki broke through and blocked the kick, falling on the ball. They were on our 4 yard line. I moved to middle linebacker. Of course, Jaloveki was their quarterback. On the first play he kept the ball and started up the middle. Kenny Lindstrom was in the center of our defensive line at nose guard. He hit Jaloveki low around the ankles. I wrapped my arms around his knees. He dragged both of us into the end zone.

Toward the end of the second quarter, the Wilson Coach pulled Jaloveki out of the game, saving him for the next unfortunate team they played, I guess. The score was 20 - 0. Things got a little better but Jaloveki had us too beaten up to do much. Final score 27 - 12

Back on the bus, Coach Thomas told us, "Keep your heads up. I don't want to see any man hanging his head." He told us we had really not played all that badly and he had even seen some bright spots that boded well for the future.

The next week in practice we learned a new offensive formation. We would break from the huddle and line up in our old "straight - T" formation. But if the quarterback felt the opposing defense was set up right for it, he would call out "Shift". Our formation would then become what was called a "single wing". The quarterback moved over to his right and became the signal caller. One of the halfbacks, Rich Saebo (who became my best friend) moved over directly behind me and became a "tailback". The fullback stayed pretty much in his same position. The other halfback moved up closer to the line and became a "blocking back." Everybody, including Coach Thomas, was starting to recognize that Rich was the best athlete on the team. From his tailback position, Rich could do it all. Run, pass, or punt. Even quick kick on 3rd down if the coach signaled from the sideline to do it. Our second game was against a freshman team from Thornton, Illinois. They were bussed to

Irving Park, our home field, for the game. They didn't have a Jaloveki. We won 14 - 6. We played 6 games that season. Final tally was 4 wins, 2 losses.

Coach Thomas wanted me to go out for basketball when football season ended. I didn't want to but I couldn't tell him no. I wasn't very good but I got in enough to earn a letter.

Coach Thomas not only coached us, he talked to us about life. About character and morals. About growing up and becoming men who could be respected. Many mornings he would pick me up on my way to school. We talked a lot. He knew more about me in nine months than my parents ever would. I would never forget Coach Thomas.

Chapter 28

September brought bad news, especially for the girls. James Dean was killed in a car wreck. All that week every freshman girl walked around with a movie magazine that had James Dean's picture on the front. They stood around in little quiet groups. Some actually cried. The boys laughed. But most of us had seen "Rebel Without A Cause" and thought he was pretty cool. I got my first "crush" on a movie star watching that movie … Natalie Wood.

The first of December news from Alabama reached us. A black woman named Rosa Parks had refused to give up her seat to a white man on a bus in Montgomery. She had been arrested.

My Daddy went on about it for two days. "It just ain't right. That woman's got as much right to be on that bus as anybody else. He ain't much of a man to demand a woman give him her seat. No man at all would do that." I thought about Uncle Matthew and wondered what his thoughts would be on the matter. A lot different from my Daddy's, I was sure. There was good news. A Doctor named Jonas Salk had discovered a cure for Polio. We all received three vaccination shots over a period of time. Everybody was being inoculated so nobody would have to suffer from Polio ever again. I thought about Donald Mars and wished Dr. Salk could have discovered the vaccine in time to save him.

Chapter 29

"Come on guys, let's get them melons off them damn trucks! Time's money! Time's money!" It was July 1957. I had just turned 16. Rich Saebo and me had found summer jobs at Hanson's Curb Market on Indianapolis Avenue, a 4-lane main highway that ran through Hammond. The curb market was three blocks long. Mr. Hanson had hired five boys for the summer. Everyday, big trucks rolled in from Florida, loaded with watermelons. We would set up a relay team. One man on the truck pitched the watermelons down to the nearest man who tossed it back to the next man and on down the line to the last man who stacked it. From time to time we would switch positions. Mr. Hanson would holler about time being money through the whole process. We worked 6 days a week, 10 hours a day. The pay was 65 cents an hour. There was no lunch hour. We would eat a sandwich or something during a lull between trucks. We didn't receive a pay "check" and no taxes or anything was deducted. Each Saturday evening Mr. Hanson would hand you a small slip of blank paper to sign. He would then slowly count out 39 one dollar bills into your hand. We never understood why we were always paid one dollar bills. But we didn't really care. It was big money to us.

My family still lived in our "flat" upstairs over Mr. Mazurak. Drunk-Johnny was still there too. My mother was back working for the glass factory. She rode with a lady who lived down the street and also worked there. My mother helped pay for the gas. I was the only boy I knew who had a mother that worked. She said it was "helping her nerves". But she would still wake up in the middle of the night screaming that she was smothering and dying and calling for her mama. Sometimes I would get up and crack the door to their bedroom and talk to her and tell her everything was all right.

154

My Daddy no longer talked to her in a soothing way when she had a spell with her nerves. He just kept on snoring. My mother now had very little to do with me. It was all Marty. Marty would be going into the 5th grade at Irving. My mother made over her constantly. Marty this, Marty that. "My baby is so beautiful". She *was* a pretty girl. Her hair was long and still naturally blonde. Others commented on how pretty she was. I think some of it went to her head. She would stand in front of the dresser mirror staring at herself while trying to sing like Teresa Brewer. ***"Wouldn't anybody care to meet a sweet old fashioned girrl - doobady - dooby - dum"--*** Marty would even try to hold her mouth in a little 0- shape, like Teresa Brewer did. It was sickening. Sometimes I would have to leave the house.

My Daddy, now, had very little to do with either of us. Sometimes he would go for days without speaking to anybody, although my mother would get angry at times and demand he give Marty some attention. When he did talk, it was mostly about wanting to move back to Alabama and about his mama. At night he set on the couch in front of the television. He loved Arthur Godfrey and the "Westerns". I liked the westerns too. My favorite was "Cheyenne" with Clint Walker playing Cheyenne Bodie. My Daddy still got up every morning a 4 a.m. whether it was a work day or not. You could smell coffee being brewed in his percolator all through the flat. He would just sit at the kitchen table, drinking coffee, smoking, and listening to his radio***. "Day - O, Daaaay – O- Daylight come and I wanna go hooome."***

Our flat was located in an area called, "North Hammond". Washington Irving Jr. High was also in North Hammond. When you graduated 9th grade at Irving, you had your choice of two high schools to attend. Hammond Tyler High or Hammond Technical Vocational High School. Tradition had it that most of the kids from North Hammond went to school. Hammond Tyler was where the bit shot's kids from South Hammond and Munster went. The year before, Rich Saebo and me had chosen Hammond Tyler just to be different, I guess. We had been warned by several people including Coach Thomas. Coach Thomas had not come right out and said it but others had. If we wanted to play football, we'd better go to Tech. The stories were that Coach Ernie Kallas didn't cater to boys from North Hammond. It didn't matter how good you were. The boys from South Hammond and Munster did the playing. It was a very slim chance that we would even make the team. We went out. The rumors were true. One hundred boys went out. I practiced at left guard and Rich was put at defensive end. I thought I did fairly well but Rich was all over the place, tackling, making sacks and getting through to block punts. After two weeks of practice a list was posted in the locker room. If your name wasn't on the list you were cut from the team. There were 37 names on the list. Mine and Rich's names were there. We had made the team but we saw very little action. Not even enough to letter.

We were at practice with two games left in the season. A drenching, cold rain was falling steadily. Parkas with hoods had been distributed but we were two parkas short. We were doing calisthenics when Coach Kallas ordered me and Rich to turn our parkas over to two boys from Munster. Rich jerked his off, tossed it to one of the boys and walked off the field toward the locker room. One of the assistant coaches hollered at him, but he never turned around. He just kept walking. Coach Kallas said, "Let him go." I handed my parka to the other boy but hung on.

The next day at school I became deathly sick. I vomited my guts out in the boy's restroom. I was dizzy and every bone in my body ached. The boy's counselor drove me home. Nobody was there. I fell across my bed. I was burning with fever.

My mother and Marty got home first. My mother felt my forehead. She said "you've probably picked up a little something but I don't think it's anything serious."

When my Daddy got home he was a little more concerned. "This boy is really sick, Mal."

My mother had been going to a doctor in Whiting, Indiana named Dr. Rudser, who was giving her medication for her nerves. She called him, saying he was probably gone for the day. He was still in the office. He would wait for us. My Daddy helped me to the car and headed for the doctor's office. Dr. Rudser had me lay on the examination table with my shirt off. His nurse took my temperature. It was 103. Dr. Russell pushed around on my chest and back for a while and shined a light down my throat and in my ears. He announced that I had the "flu". He said it was going around and everyone was calling it the "Asiatic Flu" but technically it wasn't. It was actually a different strain but it was nothing to play around with and could have gotten very serious. His nurse gave me two shots in the butt. Dr. Russell gave my daddy a prescription for some pills I was to take.

I missed a full week of school. When I went back I still felt weak and ached some. I turned in my gear. My football days were over. But I felt a lot sadder for Rich than I did for myself because he was such a great athlete.

Chapter 30

I started my junior year in high school I had kept my grades up but Tyler was hard. I was now wearing my hair in what was called a "Detroit." Kind of a flat top on top but long enough on the sides to comb back I would put a dab of hair wax on the side and comb them back with a brush. Since I wasn't involved in a varsity sport any longer I was required to take a swimming class. Coach Kallas was the teacher. I could already swim fairly well and it was actually a fun class. But I hated that it was first period. It ruined my hair for most of the day. Also, included on schedule that year was Contemporary History, Advanced Algebra and Chemistry. The chemistry teacher swept into the room on the first day wearing a white lab coat. He announced, "Hi, I'm Mr. Simmons. I teach chemistry. And … oh yes, I have a private pilot's license. I love to fly." He looked like Mr. Boynton on "Our Miss Brooks."

All these courses were tough at Tyler. Tough for me anyway. The Munster kids seemed to already know this stuff. They actually stood around in the hallway between classes and discussed physics. You got the impression that high school was just a formality they had to go through before getting on through college when they could start discovering cures for all the diseases that plagued the world. Rich Saebo and I went everywhere together. We kept our jobs at Hanson's and worked part time after school. There were two walk in movie theatre in Hammond, about 10 blocks apart. The Parthenon and the Paramount. We were usually in one of them every Saturday evening. Nobody ever saw much of the movie. Everyone was too busy trying to find a girl to talk to. They came from everywhere. Hessville, Hobart, East Chicago, Whiting. Rich and me usually wound up with two, sitting in the balcony and making out like crazy. We would sometimes get their phone numbers and make dates for the next weekend.

My Daddy now had a 1956 Dodge. Rich and me both had our driver's license, but my chances of using my Daddy's car were non-existent. Sometimes he would come close to giving in but my mother would start raising hell. "What on earth would we do if he tears the car up? We can't buy another one. We'd be doomed!" That would be the end of it. Rich could usually get his father's Studebaker. When we double dated we always went to a drive-in theater. Most of the time it was the 'Calumet Drive In', just north of Hammond on the highway to Whiting. It cost a dollar for a carload to get in. No matter how many were in the car. One buck. They always showed 3 or 4 movies. We would park in the back row, pull the speaker in, roll up the windows and start making out. There was usually a lot of heavy petting but I was still a virgin.

I had another friend from my Irving days that I ran with occasionally. Red Perkins. I never knew Red's real first name. Maybe it was Red. It's the only name any of us ever knew.

Red and Rich didn't hit it off too well so seldom were we three together.Red's family had come to Hammond at about the same time we had. They had come from Kentucky.

In late December Red took my innocence away. It was on a Saturday night. Rich had to drive his father somewhere. I was setting in the living room watching television when Red appeared at the door. Red was already 17. He had quit school and had a full time job. He also had his own car. Red was cool. He had long blondish, red hair that was swept back in a 'D.A.' He always wore his shirt collar turned up and had cleats on the bottom of his shoes. Red called everybody, "daddy-O". He sat around for a few minutes with a little crooked grin on his face like he had a secret. Finally he said, "hey, daddy-O, wanna take a ride?" I said, "yeah" and grabbed my coat. My parents were sitting in the kitchen with Marty. Probably taking about moving back to Alabama. They no longer asked me where I was going or when I would be home. We went down the back stairs and around to where Red's car was parked. Red had a "51" ford. As we approached the car I could see two heads with long hair. One in the front seat ; one in the back. I asked, "who's that?"--Red grinned. "I brought you a present." The girls rolled down the windows. Red nodded toward the one in the front seat. "This is my girlfriend, Marcie and that one back there is her sister, Narcie. I looked at Narcie. She smiled. I was used to girls my own age. This was a full-grown woman. At least 19 or 20 years old. Like a fool, I yelled, "shotgun" and jumped in the front seat with Red and Marcie. They both looked at me like I was nuts. We rode around for a while with Narcie playing with my hair from the back seat. Red pulled over and parked. "I gotta take a leak. Come on, Dan." I got out. We went behind a tree and took a leak. Snow was on the ground. It was freezing. Red zipped up his Pants and turned and looked at me. "Listen, Daddy-O, are you going to fuck that woman or not?"

I stammered, "what? Well, yeah. Hell yes, I'm going to fuck her."
"Well, you sure as hell can't do it from the front seat so climb your ass in the back."
I got in the back seat. Narcie grabbed me. Her breath was hot and smelled like chocolate candy. I was starting to get into the swing of things. Red drove out to an old road that had been abandoned for years. The car radio was playing low. *"Peggy Sue, Peggy Sue, pretty, pretty, pretty, Peegggy Sue."*

In the front seat, Marcie mounted Red and began moaning. Narcie unzipped my pants and reached in. The next thing I knew, Narcie had thrown a leg over my lap and straddled me. I was no longer a virgin.

Chapter 31

The space race had begun between the USA and Russia. Our rockets were blowing up on their launching pads, but Russia successfully shot one up and put a satellite in orbit around earth. They called it, "Sputnik." There was more news from Alabama. An area in Birmingham called Fountain Heights was being bombed so often they were calling it, "Dynamite Hill." I thought about Radio. I wondered if anybody had bombed his house. Somehow, I doubted it.

At the start of 1958 we closed the gap in the space race with Russia when the army put a satellite in orbit. They called it, Explorer I. It would stay up until early 1970, when it would finally disintegrate.

My mother now rarely spoke to me at all unless it was to berate me for something. I couldn't do anything right, Marty could do no wrong. I was also required to pay twenty dollars a month out of my meager earnings at the curb market. This was for "room and board." My mother had been given a promotion at the glass factory. She was now "chief inspector" on her shift. Her job was to randomly check the mayonnaise jars that came down the conveyor belt to the "packing girls", who packed the jars in cardboard boxes to be shipped. If she found a blemish on a jar it was, by God, bad news. The machine that produced it was shut down until new molds had been put in place. My daddy had become a "loner" in his own family. He was like a ghost slipping around. He was arising even earlier in the mornings now. Most mornings he would leave for work an hour or more before he needed to. When he came home in the evening, he would watch a little television and head for bed. He was usually already asleep when I came home from the curb market. There were no more family meals at the table. Nobody cooked. It was every man for himself. My Mother had discovered "pot pies". This was a pre-cooked concoction that had a crust on the top with some sort of meat mixed with "only God knew what" on the inside. The refrigerator was always full of pot pies. Sometimes they were in the company of a gallon of Mogan David wine my daddy kept in there to sip on from time to time. Rich's father had become too old to drive. He had full time use of the Studebaker. After school, we would usually go to Jim's Drive-in to eat and flirt with the carhops before heading for the curb market. At least *I* flirted. Rich now had a steady girlfriend who worked there named Patricia Dembowski. If Patricia was on duty, we ate free. All the carhops had boy friends who ate free. Sometimes we wondered how Jim, whoever he was, stayed in business. That summer, Rich and me went full time again at Hanson's Curb Market. And, as usual, Mr. Hanson hired 5 other boys to help with the increased summer business and the watermelon trucks. One of the other boys was a black teenager named William Coates. Most of the black kids in Hammond went to Tech. There was only a handful at Tyler. William was one of them. William had an older brother named Ira who had received an athletic scholarship to Northwestern to play football. Rich and me had a couple of classes with William. William was one of the brainy guys. His big interest was astronomy. He liked to talk about light years and distances in space. It was interesting to hear William talk about outer space while we stacked watermelons. He also talked a lot about "time travel"--He believed that, one day, a time machine would be built that would enable a traveler to either go back in time or ahead to the future. William believed it would be more difficult to travel to the future, "because it hasn't happened yet." His theory was that everything that had happened in the past had left a form of energy behind that was much like a photo negative. All you had to do was find a way to develop the negative and you would be right in the middle of an event as it was happening. William would say, "we already have a very rudimentary time machine. It's called a camera. When you look at a 30 year old picture, you're actually going back in time. Once we learn to develop the negatives that have been left behind by energy; we're there." William acted like it was a foregone conclusion that it would be built someday.William wasn't all theories and equations. He also had a mischievous streak running through him. We had already found that out in Spanish class. Me, Rich and William sat three abreast at our desks in the back of the room. Mrs. Kerringer the teacher had assigned everyone Spanish first names. I was Antonio-Rich was Julio-and William was Pedro. She would begin class with, "Buenos Dias, Classe." The class was required to answer, "Buenos Dias, La Professora." Just this alone would send all three of us ducking down behind the students seated in front of us in muted laughter. Often during the class one of us would make a wise crack under our breath about La Professora's big butt. Down went our heads. Luckily we were never caught. Toward the end of July we were riding around in the Studebaker, after work one night talking about getting drunk. Neither of us had ever been. We all three decided it would be a cool thing to do. Most black people in Hammond lived in an area called "East Hammond". It's where William lived. He knew of a package store that was located on a street where winos hung out. They would do anything for a bottle. The plan was set. We would give a wino enough money to get us a bottle and one for himself. We found a wino right off, reeling down East Thomas Street. Rich called him over to the car. He stuck his head in the window. "What's happening my man?"Rich told him what we wanted and gave him a five dollar bill. The wino acted like he had done this a hundred times. We watched him reel through the front door of the package store. In a few minutes he was back out carrying two paper sacks. He stuck one of the paper sacks through the window to Rich and went lurching off down the street hugging his prize to his chest. An aunt had taken Rich's parents to Crown Point to see somebody. They wouldn't be back until the next evening. We got a pizza to go at Jim's Drive-in and headed for Rich's house.

The wine tasted horrible. But nobody would admit it. The pizza helped kill the taste. We were all three higher than a kite. Rich and William were sprawled on the couch, trying to sing.

"Preaching and a - crying, tell me that I'm lying, about a jooob that I never could find, get a job - shana na na na".

I was sprawled in a big easy chair. I was a little dizzy but I had a warm blow inside. Suddenly, Rich jumped up from the couch. "Let's do something!" William echoed, "Yeah, let's do something!" I was feeling good and at peace with the world. We batted around a few ideas. "Go cruising for chicks?" No, the hour was too late for that. Jim's Drive-in was out. Rich's girlfriend, Patricia might be able to tell he had been drinking wine. They were probably getting ready to close pretty soon anyway. We rode around for half an hour, finally ending up parked on the blacktop at Irving Jr. High. Rich and me got out to take a leak. William was stretched out in the back seat asleep. We stood around awhile and talked about the "old days" at Irving. I sort of kicked at a brick that was lying on the black top. Suddenly, in one motion, Rich jerked the brick up and threw it. Glass splintered. I gazed in amazement. "My God, Rich!" Rich started towards the Studebaker. "Let's get the hell out of here." We jumped in the front seat. William raised his head up. "What in hell was that?" We raced down Columbia Avenue on to Calumet and toward East Hammond.We let William out at his house and headed toward North Hammond. Rich slowed down on 150th street. He kept shaking his head saying, "I don't know why I did it. I just don't know." All I could come up with was "geez- oh - man."
We pulled up in front of my house and stopped. Rich shook his head again. "I must be nuts."

"Well, Rich," I said, "at least nobody saw it so I guess we're not in any trouble."
He mumbled, "yeah, I guess."
I got out and headed up the back stairs, tired, but sober.

Coach Thomas kept blowing his whistle. I couldn't understand why he wouldn't quit. The practice was over. As I slowly came out of a deep sleep, I realized it wasn't Coach Thomas blowing his whistle. It was the phone ringing. Ringing and ringing. Nobody else was at home. I staggered into the living room and picked up the receiver, saying a drowsy, "hello."

The voice on the other end was all business. "This is Lt. Hamaker down at the Hammond police station. I need to speak to Daniel Knight, please." I was instantly awake. "Uh, this is Daniel Knight."

"Mr. Knight, I need to see you down at the station in my office before 4:00 this evening. I'm sure you know what this is about."
"Uh, yes, sir,I think so."
If you're not here by four, I'll send a black and white around to pick you up."
"I'll be there."
The Lieutenant hung up.
The phone rang again immediately. It was Rich. Lieutenant Hamaker had already called him. Rich said he would pick me up in 30 minutes. I was Police station several black and white patrol cars were parked in front. We found an empty slot that said, "visitor." Over a doorway there was a sign: "PUBLIC ENTRANCE." A heavy set cop with sweat stains under the armpits of his uniform shirt set behind a desk. "What can I do for you fellows?"Rich told him who we were and who we were there to see. The cop half grinned and half sneered, as if saying "I've been expecting you and boy, are your asses in trouble." He nodded to the hallway behind him. "Third door on the right." The third door on the right was closed. "Lt. Hamaker"

was printed on the milky glass. Rich softly rapped on the door. A deep business like voice said, "come in." We went in. Lt. Hamaker was seated behind a metal desk. He was in shirt sleeves with his tie pulled down. He wore a gray fedora with the front turned down. Lt. Hamaker looked like a private eye from the movies. My knees almost buckled.

"You fellows have a seat."

We seated ourselves in two chairs facing him. The Lieutenant wasted no time. "You two are in serious trouble." We said nothing.

"Destruction of city property is a felony. You both could get time in a detention center for juveniles." My knees felt like water.

Rich spoke up. "I threw the brick. Daniel had nothing to do with it."

Lt. Hamaker ignored this. "If it was up to me, I'd throw the book at both of you, but Principal Lockhart refuses to press charges. You're going to have to pay for the window though. Two hundred bucks. A hundred from each of you. Mr. Lockhart is waiting for you at the school right now. "We started to get up. Lt. Hamaker held up his hand. "Stay seated. There's another matter." Rich and I looked at each other. "The witness said there was a third party with you." I need to know his name." We both said there was nobody with us.

The Lieutenant snarled, "Why in hell would you want to cover up for a damn spear-chucker?"

I didn't say anything. Rich asked him what a spear-chucker was. The Lieutenant's mind seemed to shift gears. He said if we didn't settle up with Principal Lockhart, we'd be right back there and next time it wouldn't go so easy for us. Then he told us to get our asses out of his office. We went. On our way to Irving, we wondered who had turned us in. They also would have to have known our names. It had to be somebody we knew. But nobody had been around - and it had been dark. Walking up the steps to face Mr. Lockhart proved to be much harder than walking into Lt. Hamaker's office. Thank God school was out.

Mr. Lockhart was waiting for us in the school office. We said we were sorry. He nodded his head. His eyes were watery as if he had been crying. The terms were 20 dollars a week from each of us for five weeks. After we agreed that we would be most happy to pay it and told him again how sorry we were, Mr. Lockhart turned and looked directly at me. "Daniel, if someone had asked me to list everyone who was capable of this, I would have put your name at the bottom of the list. Anybody but you , Daniel. Anybody but you."

I dropped my head. "I'm sorry."

Mr. Lockhart turned his back to us and looked out the office window. We quietly left.

In September we became seniors. A month earlier William and his family had moved to somewhere in Illinois. His father worked for a company that made boxcars and had been transferred. We would never see William again. Years later someone told me that he had gotten an academic scholarship to Northwestern and had eventually earned a doctorate at Stanford and was working for NASA. I wondered if he still dreamed of building a time machine.

Chapter 32

Patricia went to "Tech". In early October her Geography club held a "girl-ask-boy" sock hop. Rich, of course, would be going with Patricia. Patricia had a friend named Shirley Wyatt. Shirley had a boy friend in the Army. She needed a "date" so it was "arranged" that she would ask me. I went along. Shirley was a pretty girl with brown hair pulled back in a ponytail.

The gym was full and hopping. The usual wallflowers were seated in the bleachers - Mostly guys watching the girls dance with each other. Rich and I danced a couple of ballads with Patricia and Shirley.

Shirley had to pull "door duty" - taking tickets and stamping hands. "I'll be back, don't go away, now," she told me.

I said, "hey, that's fine, don't worry about me."

I sat down on the bleachers to watch the dancers. Some of the early wallflowers were out on the floor now. I recognized a couple of kids who had gone to Irving. Then I spied a tall girl dancing the bop with another girl. She was tall and lean with short brown hair. She wore a blue cap with a little bill in front like Mr. Mazurak's. She had on Levis and a sweatshirt - she was beautiful. I was staring at her when she seemed to suddenly turn and look directly at me. I couldn't be sure with the dim lighting.Then I lost her somewhere in the crowd. I was talking to a guy I knew at Irving when she appeared again. Standing no more than a foot away, alone. I had to say something. I racked my brain for a cool comment to make. Finally I blurted out, "how's it going?" I immediately felt foolish.

She looked at me and grinned, "Wanna dance with me?" I grabbed her hand and lead her out onto the floor. Ricky Nelson was singing, ***"There'll never be anyone else for me, but you."*** I didn't know it then but the song was an omen. We dance and talked. Her name was Rita Godski. She had been going steady with some guy but they had recently broken up. She gave me her phone number. She had not gone to Irving. She had attended George Rogers Clark in Whiting. She was now a senior at Tech. I explained that I was just an escort for Shirley, her boyfriend being in the service. She knew Shirley. "Nice girl, but watch yourself," she said. I didn't know what that meant.

The Platters came on singing, ***"Only You."*** The lights flickered. "Last dance",was announced. After a quick kiss we parted in the parking lot. Rita was with friends.

Shirley was already in the back seat of Rich's car. I climbed in. Shirley had her arms folded, looking straight ahead. Patricia, in the front seat, was as stiff as a board. Both were obviously angry about something. After a mile or so, Shirley spoke up. "How did you like dancing with the hood?"

I asked her, "what hood?"
"You know what hood. That Rita. She runs with a tough gang. You better just watch yourself." I had to laugh at that.

I called Rita the next night. She wanted me to come over. She lived on Brookfield Avenue, which was about 3 miles from me. Getting the car was out of the question so I headed out walking. When I arrived, Rita was alone. Her parents and younger sister were gone to visit relatives somewhere. We "made out" passionately on the couch. Rita put on a record. It was Elvis singing ***"Woncha Wear My Ring Around Your Neck".*** Rita kept looking at my class ring. She asked to try it on. It was several sizes too big. Rita wanted to talk.

"What's your religion, Daniel?"

I told her I wasn't much of anything.

"I'm Catholic."

I uttered something like "Well, that's great." I didn't know anything about Catholics.

"What's your nationality?"

"American. What's yours?"

"We're all Americans, silly. I'm Polish."

I stuck with 'American'. Still clutching my ring, Rita stretched out on the couch with her head in my lap. She tilted her head toward me. "Do you want to go steady?"

I said, "Yes I do."

Rita took a slender gold chain from around her neck, put it through the ring and hung it back around her neck. Then she turned over with her head facing down in my lap. She slowly unzipped my pants. I was totally gone. I would be forever in love.

Around 10:30 Rita's parent and her 9-year-old sister pulled up in the driveway. I was given the evil eye by both parents as they tramped into the living room. Rita introduced us. There were not friendly handshakes. Her father was tottering, back and forth on his heels as if he may have been hitting the bottle. Her mother didn't say, "hello, how are you?" or anything of the sort. She started in with the questions. The same ones Rita had asked. "Where are you from?"

"What religion are you?"

"What does your father do?"

I answered them all as best I could. But they were obviously the wrong answers. She gave me a look that said, "No way in hell is this going to work." I saw her eyeballing my class ring that hung from Rita's necklace.

Her mother turned on her. "What happened to that nice Polish boy you were dating?"

Rita's eyes rolled, "Mother, please."

Her father had not said a word. He lurched toward the stairs that let to their bedroom. He stumbled on the 3rd step, falling to his knees. Rita's mother turned on him. "Get on up to bed, you sot!" Mrs. Godski followed behind him.

Rita looked at me. "Let's go to my room."

I looked at her in amazement "Are you nuts?"

"No--They never come down again once they go up."

I followed Rita to her room which was downstairs in a corner of the house. She locked the door from the inside. We both undressed and climbed into her bed.

At 3 a.m. my eyes popped open. I groggily rounded up my clothes and shoes and got dressed. I tried to raise one of Rita's windows. It went up smoothly and silently. There was no screen. I crawled through and landed on some hedges. I heard Rita's sleepy voice, "I love you." I whispered back, "Yeah, I love you too." I headed home in an early morning drizzle.

When we were not in school, Rita and I were inseparable. The following June, Tyler High School and Hammond Tech held their graduation ceremonies on the same night.

While the rituals were underway, Rita and me were in a big field of wild onions that lay between the two schools.

Chapter 33

The lady at Rand McNally Incorporated asked me if I had ever operated a forklift.

"Well, no, ma'am"
"That's okay, we'll train you. You're going to be a fork lift operator."
I was thrilled.

I had turned 18 a month earlier. Rita and me wanted to get married. We were in love but each of us also wanted to get away from home. In fact, this may have been the overriding reason we wanted to marry. My mother's nerves had gotten much better. Working at them glass factory had become her life. My daddy was now drinking a lot of Mogan David Wine. He bought it by the gallon. Marty was the apple of his eye. He would down a couple of glasses of wine and tell her how beautiful she was and how Teresa Brewer wasn't even in the same league with her. I was more or less a nobody around the house. I was rarely even there, preferring to spend nights at Rich's house.

Rand McNally was a book binding factory that put together and hard bound all types of books, but their specialty was encyclopedias. One day after my interview, I was given a physical by a doctor in downtown Hammond. I was declared fit. I was to be on day shift which was 7:00 a.m. to 3:30 p.m. with 30 minutes for lunch. My pay was $2.00 an hour, which was considered fairly good money. I was there at 6:30 a.m. the next morning. I wanted to be early in starting my training as a fork lift operator. Johnny Frankovic was going to be my trainer. We passed several forklifts sitting idle as I followed Johnny into the warehouse from personnel. At each one, I thought we would stop. We finally did stop. Johnny declared:

"Well, there she is."

'She' was a hand operated forklift. I couldn't believe it. I had used one at the curb market. You shoved the forks into the slot in the pallet and then raised the pallet by pumping the handle up and down. You would then push the load to wherever it was going.

Johnny could sense my disappointment. "Don't worry, you'll graduate to a real fork lift before long." Johnny stayed with me for about 30 minutes. After that, I was on my own.

I was to be the warehouse man. A real forklift would bring a pallet stacked with books to my department and set it down. I had a huge roll of brown paper on a vertical roller. I had to wrap the pallet of books in brown paper, then scotch tape the ends of the brown paper together. I would then slap a "bill of lading" on the front, manually pump up the pallet and push it to the warehouse where I would set it down. Another guy, driving a real fork lift, would pick it up and take it to the shipping dock. This was 8 ½ hours a day, with 30 minutes for lunch. Most nights I would meet Rita and we would walk to Douglas Park and make love. I would fall in my bed later and be asleep by the time my head hit the pillow. I rarely saw my parents because of my work schedule. One thing worried me though. Marty and I had always been close. Now it seemed our two worlds were headed in opposite directions.

Christmas Eve 1959

Christmas Eve fell on Thursday. My mother had to work. The Mayonnaise jars had to keep rolling. That night my Daddy was hitting the Mogan David wine pretty good. He mumbled something as I went out the door. Walking to Rita's the cold wind stung my face. I walked backwards with my head down a good part of the way.

As I turned onto Rita's street I had a nervous feeling in my stomach. Something was wrong. I could feel it. As I approached her house I saw a police car parked at the curb in front. A cop was behind the wheel and Rita's daddy was seated on the passenger side. As I walked up the cop rolled his window down.

"Is your name Daniel Knight?"

I told him it was.

"Well, here's the thing, Daniel. These people don't want you coming around here anymore." I told him I was just there to pick up Rita. We were both 18. We were getting married. The cop knitted his brow. "Well, that's the other thing, Dan, Rita doesn't live here anymore. She … well she moved away and she ain't coming back!!" I stood there stunned. My insides were churning. I blubbered out something about "We're getting married."

The front door flew open and Rita's mother came bounding out, a big blanket wrapped around her. She threw something at me.

"Here, you can have that back."
I looked down and saw the streetlight glinting off my class ring lying in the snow.
I asked, "Where's Rita?"
She snorted, "Rita lives with her aunt in Wisconsin now and she's not coming back."

I felt numb. It just couldn't be. The cop lay his hand on my shoulder. "C'mon, son, I'll give you a lift back to your house."

I bent down and picked up my ring. Rita's daddy was still seated on the passenger side. The policeman opened the door and he got out in a zombie-like trance. I could smell whiskey on his breath. As we pulled away I heard Rita's mother scream at him, "get in the house, mush for brains!"--On the way home the policeman talked about it. "You know, my name's Wilson. We come from the same kind of background, me and you. We're true Americans, Protestants , such as that. These DP's come over here from Europe and think they own the damn place. Better to stay with your own kind, son." I just nodded. I had heard my Daddy and others use the term "DP's". It stood for "displaced persons." I had never thought of Rita as a DP. Hell, she had been born at St. Margaret's Hospital in Hammond. She was as much American as anybody else. All I knew was that my heart was broken. The policeman let me out in front of our place saying, "things will look better in the morning." I didn't think so but I said, "thank you." I walked to the back and slowly went up the stairs to our flat.

Chapter 34

I had continued working at Rand McNally's. I had even gotten a small raise. Now I was paying a hundred dollars a month for board. I kept waiting and praying for the phone call from Rita telling me it had all been an awful misunderstanding, that she was coming back and we were going to marry. The phone call never came.

On June 30th, 1960 two weeks before my 19th birthday I went to the post office on Calumet Avenue and joined the Navy. The draft was in effect at that time. The   law stated that any young man aged 18 to 26 must serve his country for a minimum of 2 years. A couple of guys I had worked with had already been drafted into the Army. Only the Army drafted. If you wanted into one of the other services you had to volunteer. I wanted to go in the Navy. There was nothing left for me in Hammond. It turned out to be the right thing to do because a draft letter from the Army arrived at the house for me 30 days after I had left.

I had to go to Great Lakes Naval Base in North Chicago for a preliminary physical. But my training (boot camp) would be in San Diego, California. The recruiter told me that San Diego was a little rougher than Great Laker but they turned out better sailors. I had no idea if that was true.

On July 5th I left on a train from the station in Chicago with 2 other boys headed to "Dago".Their names were Bernie Chandler and Mike Sopata. It took 5 trains and 3 days to get there but it had been fun.

We were all up and down the cars talking to girls. We told them we were Sailors on leave. Glad to be out of uniform for a while. Yes, we were going to sea when we returned to our ships. Going far away. Much danger. May never return. I picked up several scribbled addresses to write to which were taken from me in San Diego. The train tracks went over a large body of water which someone said was San Diego Bay. We were now at a crawl. The station came into sight and the train came to a complete stop. Bernie, Mike and me already had our overnight bags in hand. I had 3 changings of clothes and underwear, my toothbrush and paste and my shaving gear. As soon as we bounded off the train a guy in a white Navy uniform with a wide duty belt around his waist walked over to us. He read off 3 names from a piece of paper and asked if that was us. We told him it was. It was around 4 p.m. but the sun was blinding. He said, "let's go", indicating a gray van with "United States Naval Training Center" printed on the side. All three of us jumped into the back seat and away we went. We crossed several bridges. From the left window you could see the Pacific Ocean stretching away to the horizon. It looked so different than Lake Erie which had a green tint to it. This ocean was as blue as could be. The sun had now crossed over to the western sky causing the water to seem to sparkle. Soon, long two story buildings came into view. They were all white with red roofs. Everywhere you looked, men were marching with rifles over their shoulders. They all looked the same. White hats, blue shirts and dungarees and they all appeared to have some type of brown material wrapped around their legs from just below their knees to the tops of their shoes. We went through an arched gate. A sign on the gate proclaimed:

WELCOME ABOARD
YOU ARE NOW MEN OF THE
UNITED STATES NAVY

The van came to a stop by some bleachers that formed a pyramid. Men were sitting on the long wooden gray planks. Smoking and talking. Some were sleeping. They all had a sheet of some sort tied around their waists. As we slid out of the van the driver gave us each one. They were sheet covers to put a small mattress in. But they weren't called sheet covers. They were called "fart sacks." The driver told us to wait on the bleachers until someone came for us. I found an empty space and sat down. The California sun was blazing. It was hot as hell. I had no idea what to expect next. I had leaned my head back with my eyes closed when a gorilla-looking guy with hairy arms nudged me. "Ya wanna fight?" I opened my eyes and looked at him.

"What?"

He repeated it. "You wanna fight?"

I said, "Hell no. Are you crazy?" He said, "I'm smart enough that I want out of the Navy." I told him he wasn't even in the Navy yet. He looked away- "Yeah, but I been setting here all day and I don't like all this shit I see going on. Man, they're hollering and screaming at everybody. Cussing ever'body out. A man fainted this morning and some asshole kicked him in the head. I didn't sign up for that kinda shit. How about it? We can fake a fight and be out of this shit-hole pronto." I told him I thought I would stick around. "Suit yourself" he mumbled. He then turned and slapped the guy in the bleacher below him in the back of the head. "Ya wanna fight?"

I took the opportunity to move several bleachers away where I found another empty spot and sat down. I had laid my head back again and closed my eyes against the sun when I heard a loud commotion. Gorilla boy and the guy he had slapped in back of the head were rolling around on the ground. Somebody hollered out, "Fight!"

In about 5 seconds a gray jeep pulled up. Two sailors in dress blues, white helmets and carrying nightsticks hopped out. The two "fighters" were jerked up and shoved into the back of the jeep. Away they went. I never saw either one again. I figured they wouldn't have to worry anymore about taking any shit from the navy.

I had last took a shower the morning before
boarding the train. My shirt was sticking to my back from sweat. I could smell my own body odor as well as the man's next to me. As the evening drew on, a cool breeze began wafting across us. God, it felt good.

Another sailor in blues appeared. "If I call out your name, fall in behind me." He had a clip board and read from it. " Edward Hasenback, Thomas Bustamente, Ronald Haywood, John Milton, Bernard Smith, Daniel Knight"--I fell in line behind Bernard. The sailor kept calling out names. When about 80 of us had assembled behind him he stopped. He turned to face us. "Line up in 4 rows. I'm gonna march you guys to the chow hall. Look straight ahead. No talking or grab-assing. Try to stay in step. Forward, HO!" Off we went. "Hut, hut, hut, - your left, your left, your left." None of us had any idea what he was talking about. It seemed as if we had marched a mile before the sailor halted us in front of a large one- story building. "This is the chow hall. Get in line, single file and keep your mouths shut. When you come out, muster right here - I'll be back to get you."

The chow was some kind of meat concoction with sauce poured over toast. I found out later it was chipped beef and was widely known in the Navy as "shit on a shingle." It didn't taste all that bad which was good because I figured I would be eating a lot of it over the next 4 years. After eating, we all regrouped back outside as we had been told. But there was no sign of the sailor. In about 15 minutes a much older man walked up. He was dressed in brown khakis and was wearing a brown cap with a black, shiny, hard brim. He also had a clipboard. He frowned at us.

"You clowns come to attention, now! When I call out your name you will answer, 'here, sir'. Do I make myself clear?"--He had. He called out each name… no one failed to answer, "here, sir". I don't know what would have happened if one had.

After the roll call he introduced himself. "I'm Chief Williams. I've been in this man's Navy 32 years. That means I joined up in 1928 for those of you too dumb to figure it out. And I have to say that in all those years I have never seen a fucking sorrier looking crew than this one. You people look fucking pathetic. Of course none of you know what that means. It means sorry as hell. Don't pay any attention to that fucking sign at the gate. You are *NOT* 'men of the United States Navy'. Hell, you ain't even men. And most of you never will be. But the Navy expects me to do my best with you and that I will do."

He lined us up 4 abreast and marched us off. **"Your left, your left, your right foot, left!"** We still had no idea what we were doing. We marched over a long, green wooden bridge. We didn't know it at the time but we were going over to Nimitz Island where we would be quarantined for 3 weeks before being moved back to the main camp. Chief Williams halted us at a gray painted wooden building which would be our barracks. Chief Williams lined us up in formation in front of our barracks and gave us another speech. "You misfits will be company 389. I will be your company commander. I did not want this job. I wanted to go back to sea. But the Navy wanted me here so here I am. But I'm unhappy and that means 'tough goin' for you scroungers." He instructed us to file into the barracks and find ourselves a bed. "Then take a shower. You'll sleep in your skivvies tonight. And then you'll put back on the same smelly rags in the morning. After chow you'll be issued uniforms and get your first haircut, so you'll be getting rid of the fucking lice." We started filing in. Chief Williams startled me. "Knight, fall out over here. I want to talk to ya." I didn't know what in hell I had done wrong. I was nervous as I walked over to the chief. He was a big man. About 6'4". He looked down at me. Then he looked at the clipboard "you got a pretty decent score on your General Aptitude Test, Knight." I said, "Yes, Sir."--I had no idea what I had gotten on the test.

Then he asked me a strange question. "What would you do if some asshole took a swing at you?" I had no idea how to answer that. I stammered around and finally said, "I guess I would swing back, sir"

He looked at me and I could smell whiskey on his breath. I felt a little weak in the knees.

"Good answer, Knight. You're going to be my company Yeoman. Now get in there and find yourself a rack."

I took off vastly relieved that I was not in trouble. But I still had a problem. I had no idea what a company yeoman was. The chief followed us into the barracks to make a last speech.

"Lights out at 2100; that's 9:00 p.m. to you fucking boots - and you will all be in your racks at 2100. A duty officer will be around later and if you're not it's bad news. And another thing. If any of you girls are queer, get out of my fucking barracks right now. I'll be back in the morning and 'morning' comes earlier than you'll ever believe around here." With that he stomped out.

I found a bottom rack. Above me was James Sims, who went by "Jim". Jim was from Compton, California and we would become friends.

We were all worn out, so getting in our racks by 2100 was no problem. Most were already asleep by then. In the far distance I could hear someone blowing 'taps'. I was deep in sleep. My high school band was marching onto the field. The big drum was being beaten louder than ever. It was drowning out everything else. The closer the drummer came the louder it became. It was painful to listen to. Too damn loud. I wanted to scream for somebody to shut that guy up. Jim Sims was shaking me.

"Dan, better get up. Chief's here." I opened my eyes. The loud banging was still going on. I sat on the side of my bunk with my feet dangling over the side. I saw Chief Williams in the middle of the barracks.

He had a long iron bar in his hands and was slamming it back and forth inside a huge metal garbage can (known as a 'shit can'). Everybody was stirring now. I looked at my watch; it was 3:30 a.m.

The chief stopped beating the inside of the garbage can and started yelling. In five minutes we were standing at attention in front of the barracks in the darkness. Sunrise was still quite a ways off.

Chief Williams marched us off into the dark to a field. He said "this is where we'll do our physical exercises and learn to march for real." The Chief lined us up about four feet apart. He put us through about an hour of calisthenics. Jumping jacks, running-in-place, push-ups. When it was over we all thought, "hey, that wasn't too bad." We didn't know it would be getting a lot more intense as the days went by.

It was still dark when the Chief marched us to the chow hall for breakfast. While we were chowing down we couldn't help but notice the company two tables down from us. They looked straight ahead and were told when they could take each bite by the Chief sitting with them.

Chief Williams saw our interest. "That's company 4013", he said. "The fuck-up scrounge company. You screw up, you'll be joining them and time in that company doesn't count. If they get you straightened out you'll join a company just starting out. If they don't, the Navy will kick your sorry ass out. So you girls take a good look at them". When breakfast was finished we lined up in a huge building for our second physical. Again we were stripped naked. Our blood pressure was taken standing up, sitting down, lying down and after running in place for 60 seconds. We were probed and pushed and kneaded. More urine samples and blood samples and X-rays. We all had to face the wall and bend over spreading the cheeks of our butts apart. A doctor came around and at each man, stopped and shined a light up the man's rear. I had no idea what he was looking for. The physical seemed to go on for hours.

Our vision was checked once again, including a test to see if any of us were color-blind. One man was but he didn't fail and stayed with the company. He told us they had informed him that he could stay in the Navy but would be restricted to special duties-- whatever that meant. Then we were run through the dental building. More x-rays. I needed fillings in 2 teeth but some men were going to have to come back for further work. Some teeth were so bad they just pulled them all and fitted them with dentures. We didn't make it to noon show until 2 p.m. (1400 hours).

After chow we were taken to a large wooden building. We lined up at a counter and each man gave his hat, shirt, shoes and pants size. We were each issued 4 blue shirts, 4 pairs of dungarees, 4 white hats and a pair of work shoes called 'boondockers' and 4 pair of 'skivvies' - boxer underwear. - and 4 white t-shirts. We were also issued toothpaste, soap, and shaving cream that was in a large tube like toothpaste. It was called "Barbersol". We were also issued a razor.

We went from there, carrying our newly issued gear, to an outdoor area where we all stood at wooden work benches. We were issued cardboard boxes and told to strip down completely. Every civilian item we had we placed in the box: clothes, underwear, jewelry, watches, shoes, socks - everything. We sealed the boxes with tape and wrote our home addresses on them. Then we were issued stencils and markers. We had to stencil our number on everything that had been issued to us. Then the boondockers and "leggings" which wrapped around the legs from the ankle halfway up the calf and were made of leather. Once you had wrapped them around your leg, the leggings had to be laced up on one side. The Chief then herded us back to the barracks where we stowed our gear into our lockers. There was now a big blue flag with gold trim in the barracks. It had "Company 394" printed in white. We were each issued an old Springfield military rifle (.30-06 caliber). Weight 9.2 lbs. No ammo was issued. Each man's rack had slings hanging from the left side. This is where your rifle (or piece) stayed when you weren't marching with it. The next stop was the barbershop. It didn't take long. The barber completely shaved your head in about 3 minutes and another man took your place. There were 7 barbers so we were out in no time. We were issued a seabag and the rest of our gear. Dress blue uniforms, undress blue uniforms, whites, black shoes that would be spit-shined until the Chief could count his teeth in their reflection and our boondockers and work dungarees. There was even a blue "Donald Duck hat" with a ribbon on the side. This would be worn when overseas.

I was wondering when the Chief was going to mention my being company yeoman again. It came late that evening. I was summoned to his office down the passageway from the berthing area. The Chief went over my duties. Basically I would be his assistant doing his paper work for him. I would also make up the watch list, assigning men to two- hour barracks watch during the night. The Chief looked at me. "You are never to put yourself on watch." He handed me a heavy webbed duty belt. There was a scabbard hanging from it with a bayonet in it. Chief said this was my "badge of office." He also told me my rifle would stay in its sling all through boot camp. When we marched I would be carrying a clipboard with "the plan of the day" on it. This was put out early each morning to inform the company what it's agenda was for the day. It would be my job to see the company got to wherever it was supposed to be. Classroom study - fire fighting- survival class –gas chamber--ordinance-- marching drills. I thought, "this yeoman business is not going to be too bad."

Boot camp was a very busy 9 weeks and 5 days. From reveille before sunrise until taps at 9:00 p.m. (2100). Marching, calisthenics, fire fighting, class room studies, swimming and survival courses, knot tying, training films and more fire fighting. We were taken to the rifle range and given M-1 rifles. We fired standing; we fired sitting; we fired from a prone position.We were yelled and screamed at but we were slowly becoming sailors. We learned that Chief Williams was a lot more bark than bite. And we learned that in the Navy, cleanliness really was next to Godliness. The Navy, more than any other branch of service was huge on tradition. Everything stood for something. The 13 buttons on the flap of our dress blue trousers stood for the 13 original colonies and on and on. The days wore on. We became proficient in fire fighting. We learned about 5 inch mounts and 40 millimeter anti-aircraft guns. We learned what the different colors on the noses of artillery shells meant. We learned to recognize a ship by its configuration. And cleanliness, cleanliness, cleanliness was beat into our heads. We joked among ourselves that if we were attacked by an enemy, we would throw bars of soap at them. And we learned how to tie knots - every knot known to man: Sheep-shank, half-hitch, full - hitch, clove- hitch, bowline, slip- knot and several others. We even learned the rudiments of Morse code. And we drilled on marching until we could turn "right oblique" as one man. I had a difficult time with "about face" but finally had it down pat. We came to march like a well-oiled machine. We didn't even have to think about the moves. They became an automatic reflex. Even though we all knew, being in the Navy, we would never march again once we were out of boot camp.We each went before a Navy Counselor to discuss what we wanted to do in the Navy. I said I wanted to be an engineman. I got it. Graduation day finally arrived. We had lost 2 men to company 4013. And one man received a medical discharge under honorable conditions for bed-wetting. We were decked out in our dress blues, and wearing white leggings. Ten companies were graduating that day. I had two diagonal red stripes on my sleeve which denoted a "fireman apprentice", which meant I would be in the engineering department aboard my ship. We had received our orders two days earlier. Some were headed to ships. Some were headed to Guam or Wake Island for shore duty. I was assigned to a ship named the "USS Clay Country" (LST 824)-- "LST" stood for 'Landing Ship Tank.'

for "Landing Ship Tank" (Chief Williams told me it stood for 'Long Slow Target')---

The USS Clay County was part of Amphibious Forces - Pacific. It was presently tied up to a pier at Long Beach Naval Base. We were all at "parade rest, looking sharp in our dress blues, some 900 men. Rumors were flying that President Eisenhower was in the reviewing stand to see us graduate. Finally the order was given. "Attenshun—Forward, March!" A Navy band broke into "Anchors Away"-- As we marched by the reviewing stand the order was given "eyes right". Each man carrying a rifle snapped his head to the right toward the reviewing stand. Men without a rifle, such as me, would look to the right and sharply salute, holding it until the order "two" when you dropped your salute and everyone faced forward again.

While I was holding my salute, my eyes scanned the glass enclosed box on top of the reviewing stands. I could make out gold braid and men in civilian suits. But I couldn't see their faces well. I never knew if the President was up there or not.

Chapter   35

The Clay County (LST 824)

Night had fallen when I arrived in Long Beach. I stood on the pier looking up at the "Clay County". My seabag was hoisted onto my right shoulder and a big white envelope with my orders in it was under my left arm. A cold, light rain was falling. The topside running lights were shimmering in the gathering fog.

Chief Williams had told us that there had been complaints from the fleet about new men coming out of boot camp who didn't know how to properly come aboard a ship. So it was drilled into our head. When you reached the top of the gangplank you turned and faced aft saluting the ensign flying from the fantail. Then you turned to the quarterdeck watch and saluted smartly while giving your name and serial number and saying "reporting for duty - request permission to come aboard." I went over this in my head several times and started up the plank. At the top I did it all correctly and smartly. I don't know what I expected. Congratulations I guess. Instead, I received no response from the quarterdeck watch. He was sorta slumped over a wooden podium that looked a little like a preacher's pulpit. He was wearing a peacoat with the collar up. His white hat was pulled down low. A white duty belt with a flap holster and a .45 automatic was around his waist. I cleared my throat a few times- Nothing. I said, "Hey!" He pushed his hat back.

"Yeah?"

I went through it all again. He looked puzzled. I was pretty sure he had been asleep. Finally he muttered, "lemme see what you got there, Sailor"-- I handed him my orders. He took the orders out of the envelope and looked at them. "Well, you came to the right place, buddy." Another sailor appeared. He was younger, about my age. He was also wearing his peacoat and a white duty belt. He was unarmed. He was known as "the messenger." An officer walked up. I saluted. He just nodded. He also looked at my orders. "Well, we got us another snipe." I had no idea what that meant.

The officer had one stripe around his sleeve. An ensign . He handed the messenger my orders.

"Take him down and turn him over to Suds in engineering."

The messenger led me aft and through an open hatch. We went down a metal ladder and stepped into the mess deck. Three or four men were sitting around drinking coffee. One of them was Suds. The messenger led me over to him, handed him my orders and took off. Suds was a lean, wiry guy with sandy curly hair. He looked about 30 years old. A lot younger than Chief Williams but still old to me. Suds looked up at me,"have a seat." I set my sea bag down and seated myself across from him. I glanced at his sleeve. Suds was a first- class shipfitter. He asked me if I was hungry. I said, "a little, I guess." Suds took me to the galley. The mess cooks were cleaning up. Evening chow was long past. Suds handed me a metal tray and told one of the mess cooks, "give him some of that shit on a shingle."

We went back down to the mess decks. There was a huge coffee urn on a metal table. There was also a fresh milk dispenser. I got a cup of milk and Suds and me sat back down. He said,"Well, Dan, this being Friday night not much will be going on until Monday morning."

Suds informed me that he was lead petty officer in engineering. Chief Burns (an electrician's mate) was Chief Engineer and Mr. Lingan; Lt. J.G. was

engineering officer. I would be meeting everyone Monday. He said there wouldn't be much for me to do the next two days."Just learn the ship"
He wasn't going to put me on the watch list as I had no training in any of the engineering spaces. Plus, Mr. Lingan and Chief Burns would have to decide exactly where I was going. Engine room, boiler room, pipe shop, electrician's shop, or what I would be "striking" (training) for. I asked him about the snipe remark. He laughed. "That's what the rest of the crew call engineers because we rarely come up for fresh air at sea. But pay no attention to them bastards. They're just dumb deck apes. Too fucking stupid to be engineers."
Suds said there wasn't many men aboard. There were three duty sections. Sections 1 and 2 had weekend liberty, leaving just section 3 aboard. "But they'll all be spilling back aboard Sunday night and early Monday morning."

I didn't know whether to or not but finally decided to mention the slackness of the quarterdeck watch. Suds grinned.

"Well, we're amphibious forces but we're also called the "gator navy." Some call us the dungaree navy. We're a little more informal than the big boys. The cruisers, carriers, destroyers. Of course the quarterdeck watch should have been more alert than that. Anyway, come on back and I'll assign you a rack."

We went through a hatch on the starboard side, headed forward. After passing sick bay we went through another hatch and stepped into the engineering berthing space. It consisted of three compartments. Each compartment had 12 canvas racks to a tier. They hung from the overhead by chains. The first two compartments were for petty officers. And one was for firemen and fireman apprentices which is where Suds assigned me to a middle rack. There would be a man above me and a man below me.

A middle rack seemed about right to me. Suds told me he would give me a liberty card and I could go ashore if I wanted to look around Long Beach a little but I said I would just hang around. –Saturday I went down to the main engine room. Two huge General Motors V012 diesel engines powered the ship. The two big engines took up a lot of space in the engine room. It was quiet down there. I didn't know how much that could change until I heard them lit off a few days later. No one was on watch in the engine room as nothing was running. And no one was on watch in the auxillary engine room just aft of the main engine room. In this space were three smaller diesel engines that ran generators supplying electrical power to the ship. Suds had given me this information before I went exploring. Suds said the auxillarys weren't running because we were hooked up to electrical power on the pier. There was a security watch who went down into all the engineering spaces once an hour to check everything and sign a log book stating everything was secure. I found out that in the Navy you had to log in just about everything you did. There was a long time running joke that pretty soon we would have to log in when we took a crap. The Navy wanted everything logged in so your ass could be hanged if something went wrong. If you said something was secure, it damn well better be secure.

My next stop was the boiler room. The boiler was running and there was a man on watch . His name was Gary Bailey, from somewhere called Cheney, Kansas. He told me the boiler produced steam for the galley and heating. "It's a 300 pound fire-side boiler." --There were two huge evaporators used to convert sea water into fresh water. Gary showed me a diagram or blueprint of the ship that showed the steam lines. I noticed that each side of the Clay County consisted of salt water ballast tanks, voids, freshwater tanks and diesel oil tanks. Between the port and starboard bulkheads was the tank deck that led up to the big bow doors at the forward end. Gary informed me he was a "short timer."

"Twenty three days left on this fucking tub and I'm gone. I been on her 3 years and 11 months and still a fucking fireman. My older brother is a fist-fucking lifer. Been in 12 years. He's a chief turd-chaser on the 'IWO JIMA'. I wasn't sure what a turd-chaser was. Gary explained it was a shipfitter. Shipfitters were the ship's plumbers and everybody called them 'turd-chasers'.

I mentioned that Suds was a shipfitter.
"Yeah, Old Suds' is alright. He's a fist-fucker, but he's alright."
It seemed that Gary used the term "fist-fucker" to describe just about everything. He told me the boss of the boiler room was Patrick Bertella, a 2nd class boiler technician who had been in the Navy 8 years. "That son of a bitch is half Jew and half fucking Italian. Can you believe that? And to top it off, he's from the fucking Bronx in New York City. The fist fucker sounds like it too. But hey, he's alright. Knows his job. We sit around and shoot the breeze a lot. It's just me and him down here. Say, Pat's gonna be needing a striker with me leaving. Why don't you do it"

I said, "who me?... nah, I wanna work in the engine room."

Gary grinned. "You don't wanna work with that bunch, believe me. They got a 2nd class engineman in charge down there. A fist-fucking Philipino named Macaleo. They call him Mac. The bastard'll work your ass off while he struts around blowing off about when he was a professional boxer. He'll make you look at his fucking scrapbook. Just tell Chief Burns you wanna strike in the boiler room."

Just to be polite I said, "Well, I'll think about it."

That seemed to satisfy Gary. But I still wanted to work in the engine room. I wanted to help run the big diesels. Gary started taking readings

.

on the various boiler gauges and logging them in. As he pointed out different things I tried to look interested but wasn't. Little did I know, standing there with Gary, that in 2 years I would be in charge of that same boiler room.

Sunday morning I sorta just took it easy. I found a paper back book lying on a bulkhead ledge. It was by an author named Richard Prather titled "Strip for Murder." It was about a tough LA Private eye, Shell Scott, and his exploits. I became engrossed in it and spent most of the morning lying in my rack reading it.

As the evening wore on into night, the liberty parties began coming aboard. Mostly younger, single men with whiskey on their breath. Some of the older married men lived in Navy housing or an apartment with their wives--They wouldn't be coming back aboard until 0600. But if you weren't aboard at 0745, you were AWOL - that was it. You would stand Captain's Mast for sure. If it had happened before you stood a chance of a general court martial and you could wind up in the brig for 30 days. It seemed the only excuse accepted was your death. Several of the guys introduced themselves to me. Each man told me where he was from.

"Richardson, Salt Lake City."

"Petrie, Ogden, Utah"

"Moreno, El Paso."

There seemed to be a lot of guys from Texas. I asked if anybody was from Indiana or Alabama. No, there wasn't. It was starting to look like the whole engineering department was from the west.

Then Bill Beylor walked up and stuck out his hand. Bill was just an apprentice fireman like me and had only been aboard two months. Tall and lean, Bill was from Hershey, Pennsylvania. His white hat was on the back of

192

his head and his neckerchief knot was pulled back against his throat. There was nothing "regulation" about Bill. The sleeves of his dress blues were rolled back, revealing stitched dragons. So this was a custom-made uniform. We had been warned about having custom uniforms made by Chief Williams. Very non-regulation. Glancing around I noticed several sleeves rolled back revealing Chinese dragons. I guess Chief Williams had never been on the Clay County.

Bill was hanging by the chain holding my rack. He was a little loaded. Under his pushed back white hat, I could see his hair was curly and jet black. He didn't seem to want to leave. Over the ship's PA system came "Taps, taps - lights out. The smoking lamp is out in all berthing spaces." The lights went out.

Bill sat down on the unoccupied rack below me and lit a cigarette. He offered me one and I took it. A Phillip Morris. We talked into the night. Bill had a girlfriend back in Hershey named Virginia. They had went steady from 8th grade through high school. Bill and Virginia were getting married as soon as he was out of the Navy. But Bill had received a "dear John" letter from Virginia 2 weeks earlier. She was in love with someone else. In fact they had already married. Bill was a little broken hearted but philosophical about it all. "Hell, she's probably doing me a favor. I'll only be 22 when I get out and that's too damn young to get married." I agreed with him. Bill went on. "I don't even know if I ever really loved her. She was like a habit. And comfortable. A sure date on Saturday night and for the junior and senior proms. I never had to worry about asking a girl for a date because I had 'all purpose' Virginia. But I'll tell you this, we started fucking when we were freshmen in high school and she was a terrible piece of ass. Wouldn't even push back half the fucking time. A'course I didn't know it until I got a real piece of ass from Carolyn Stubek one night behind the gym. JESUS! She went crazy. But hey, Danny! -- There's pussy all over the place out here in California. And the women love the shit out of sailors. Hell, don't ask why, just accept it. But you gotta get out of these shit-hole Navy towns. Too many fucking swab-jockeys. Hitchhike out to Orange County or up around Bell Flower. The women think you're a fucking admiral. Fall all over your ass."

I liked Bill. I knew he liked me. We both knew we were destined to be close friends and running mates.

Somebody was shaking me.

"Hey, Danny, wake up buddy."

I opened one eye."Whatcha want?"

" I'm Oswald, the security watch. Suds wants you to take the 4 to 8 shift with me and train you to stand the watch." I sat up on the side of my rack, holding my head. "What?" --Oswald repeated it. I slid to the deck and put on my dungarees and boondockers. Oswald handed me a wide, webbed duty belt. "Here, put this on." I put it on and we started out. First stop was the mess deck. Deck force was milling around filling their coffee cups from the giant urn. We got us some coffee. Oswald told me to call him "Oz"

I said, "hey, Oz, deck force is up early."

Oz said, "fuck 'em". He didn't add anything so I didn't say anymore about it either. We went down a 30 foot ladder into the port shaft ally and then over to the starboard shaft alley. The shafts came all the way from the engine room and out aft of the shaft alleys to where the big screws were that propelled the ship. We checked the bearings and oil seals that circled the shafts. Everything was logged in. We hit the reefer down below the mess deck, checking temperatures. Then we went down into the boiler room and both engine rooms. After that we dropped down into the forward fire room where the emergency generator was located. The round took about 45 minutes so we had 15 minutes before we made it again. We went up on the fantail and smoked. The air was cool. Cool enough for a jacket.

Looking east you could see a faint streak of light. Looking west, out over the Pacific it was still pitch black. Oz had been aboard 6 months. He wanted to strike for electrician's mate but was still stuck in the engine room. He was a full fireman. Three red stripes. A rank above me. Oz said he was probably going to be a 'lifer'. Twenty years or more. "Anything's better than working on a damn dairy farm in fucking Borgman, Minnesota, sliding around in cow shit all day."

At 0630 Oz and I were relieved for chow. At 0700 we made our last round. "All hands not on watch muster topside" came blaring over the shops' PA system. I went up with Oz. All the different ship's departments were separated into their own groups: Deck force, communications, supply, engineering and ordinance. A Chief Petty officer who I figured was Chief Burns and a Lt. J.G. who had to be Mr. Lingan, stood facing the engineers. The chief called the roll. To my surprise my name was on there. I called out "aye, Sir"when my name was called as the others had done. Chief Burns introduced me as the new man--There were nods in my direction. The chief told us everything was going to be pretty much routine the next few days and then there was a good chance we would steam down to a gunnery range about a hundred miles off Baja. We would be gone about 5 days. Some groans were heard. They came from a few of the older men who were married. Chief Burns grinned. It was his chance to use an old Navy saying. "We didn't issue you a wife with your fucking seabag - so stow it! " Everyone laughed, including the married men. I had already heard it several times in boot camp. The P.A. system came to life. **ALL HANDS TURN TO—COMMENCE SHIPS WORK"**

Chief Burns and Lt. Lingan called me aside after muster. I would be working in the main engine room for Mac. Suds joined us. He was appointed to give me the "orientation tour". I was issued bedding then we went to sick bay where I met Chief Nichols, a chief pharmacist's mate and the ship's "doctor". In fact everyone called him "doc". He was in his 40's and had been in the Navy 27 years. This meant he had joined in 1933. Doc had seen it all: Doc gave me his little talk, "don't come running to me with every little thing. But when you get the fucking clap, then you come to me. I'll handle it." He didn't say "if"-- he said "when" you get the clap.

I figured getting the clap must be an on-going occurrence on the Clay County. Doc went on, "When you get up one morning and take a piss and scream and grab both sides of the urinal, you've got the clap. You go running up to see Lt. Lingan or Chief Burns, they're gonna send you over to the dispensary on base and them bastards will fill you so full of penicillin, your ass will turn green. Plus it goes in your jacket where it stays permanently. So you come see me and I'll take care of it." I told doc I sure would. On the way to the laundry room I asked Suds what doc was talking about when he said my "jacket." Suds told me,"your jacket is your service record. By the time you get out it'll be a foot thick. Everything you do; good, bad, indifferent, doesn't matter - it goes in your record. Save a man's life or fart on a windy day. It goes in. And it will follow you everywhere you go the rest of your life. You can bet your sweet ass that when you stand before God on judgement day, he'll be flipping through your fucking jacket." --In the laundry room I met Larry Bowie. Suds had already showed me the huge white bag in every compartment where you stuffed your dirty laundry, and this is where it came. Larry was operating a big steam press, pressing a pair of khaki pants. It was hot as hell in the laundry room. Larry was wearing a white T-shirt, dungaree pants and shower shoes. Sweat was pouring from him. Larry had an assistant he called "Igor" - I didn't figure that was his real name. Igor was the one who brought the dirty laundry bags down to the laundry and sorted them. And pretty much anything else he was told to do. Larry also doubled as ship's barber but Suds told me later to not even think about it. "He'll ruin your hair for life. You'll never get it looking right again." -Walking down the tank deck, Suds talked a little about Larry and the laundry room. "He's got it made really. Never stands watch and has liberty every night and weekends. He don't belong in any duty section. Even at sea. Works pretty much when he wants to and the rest of his time is free to do whatever he wants.""Pretty good duty," I said. Suds laughed, "It is if you don't mind handling another man's skivvies with shit streaks and cum stains where he's been beating his meat all night." I was a little startled. "I hadn't thought about that. That sure as hell wouldn't be for me."—Suds laughed again. "I didn't think so. And on the subject of jacking-off, It's ok, just don't get caught. Hell, every man on this tub beats his meat, including the fucking Captain. But when you do, find yourself a private spot. Don't jack-off in the shower and for God's sake, don't jack-off in your rack with a sock on your dick."

I said, "What?"

Suds shook his head. "Some of these guys put a sock over their dick and beat off in it and then throw it in the laundry bag. They had a guy over in deck force they called Sully. One night Sully put a sock on his dick to whack off. Trouble was Sully fell asleep before he finished. When they turned on the lights the next morning there was ol' Sully snoring away, with his limp pecker hanging out with a sock on it. Hell, the damn bosun's mate sent a man around the whole ship to tell everybody, not on watch, to come see it. When Sully finally opened his eyes there were 15 or 20 men, including two officers, staring at him and grinning. When Sully finally realized what they were grinning and staring at he started crying like a fucking baby. His life on the Clay County was over. Captain got him transferred a few days later because he knew Sully's life would be hell, even though ever mother's son standing there grinning and pointing at Sully had done the very same thing. But Sully got caught. See what I mean?"

I nodded, "Yeah, I see what you mean."

I didn't know what else to add to all that. We went to the engineering log room where all engineering records and logs were kept. We hit the electrician's mates' shop. Men had holes in their dungarees. "From battery acid splashing on them" Suds said. We hit the shipfitter's room where Suds, himself, was in charge. Somebody was welding. I closed my eyes from the bright sparks being thrown off.

The last stop on my orientation tour was the Captain's cabin to see the man himself. On the way Suds filled me in, "Captain Dodd is a full commander which is a notch too high to command an LST, so he'll likely be transferring soon, but we hope not. He's a mustang-came up through the ranks. Started out as a fireman apprentice just like you. He's a hell of a seaman and knows the ropes. Saw action in the Korean War. Just don't laugh while you're in there."-I said, "Why in hell would I laugh?" Suds looked at me. "Cause he talks like Elmer Fudd. Some of the other officers even call him Captain Fudd. --A' course they don't do it to his face." We went through officer's country. Somewhere a radio was playing Marty Robbins, ***"out in the west Texas town of El Paso, I fell in love with a Mexican girl."***

Suds rapped on the door of the captain's cabin. A strong voice said, "come in."--Suds went in first and I followed. There stood Captain Dodd. Suds and I both went to attention and saluted. Captain Dodd returned the salute, "Come in, men. Be at ease, have a seat." He motioned to a leather sofa. Suds and I sat down. The Captain was wearing Navy Blue pants with white shirt and a navy-blue tie. There were gold oak leafs on his collar. His shoes were spit-shincd. He asked me where I was from and went into what I figured was his usual talk to a new hand. "We're vewy glad to have you aboard, Dan. Just keep your nose clean and be a sailor, that's all I ask. Do your duty at all times and keep away fwom men with low morals. Remember, Dan, wherever you are, you're representing the United States Navy and the Navy is what you, yourself, make it."-I was too awed to laugh, even if he did talk a little like Elmer Fudd. The imposing figure he struck more than made up for that. His face was lined and his eyes spoke of many years at sea. He looked a little like Alan Ladd. I could see he was a true mustang.

He told me he had read my jacket and he had noticed my GCT scores were high. "This means you can go as high in the Navy as you want to, Dan." He seemed to be genuinely interested in me as a person. Captain Dodd stood and we stood. Suds said, "By your leave Captain." We both saluted and Captain Dodd returned the salute saying, "Good luck, Dan."

Chapter 36

The engine room was hot. The blowers were mostly throwing off hot air. Mac turned out to be ok. He had us all wiping down the engines. Mac ran up the ladder to get his scrapbook from his locker to show me. The photos were impressive. Mac in his robe and trunks climbing through the ropes. A referee holding Mac's hand in the air in victory. Mac being presented a trophy stating him to be the Philippine National Champion - Welterweight division. And a lot of pictures of Mac in action in the ring. I noticed a few of the guys rolled their eyes when I looked up from the album. I guess they had seen the pictures a few times. I also noticed that none rolled their eyes while standing where Mac could see them. Mac showed me around. We walked over to the starboard side of the engine room and he showed me how to operate the ballast tank pump and explained how it operated. We went down into both shaft alleys to check the oil level in the bearings that kept the shafts turning smoothly. Mac said this would be one of my duties as new man.

The day went by in a hurry. At 1600 the ship's PA system blared.

"Knock Off Ship's Work--Liberty commences for sections one and two!"

I was in section #1 and so was Bill Beylor. Bill met me at the top of the ladder. "Get into your blues, Knight, we're hitting the beach."

By 1700 we had showered and shaved and got into our dress- blue uniforms. We asked permission to go ashore, saluted the Ensign on the fantail and headed down the plank.

Blue buses carried Navy personnel back and forth to town. One was just pulling up when we walked through the gate and we piled on. I was starting my first liberty call.

We got off the bus at the square in downtown Long Beach. Bill seemed to know where we were going. The sidewalk went down a hill. I could see bright lights and hear organ music playing. The top of a Ferris wheel came into view behind a building. We walked onto the fairway of "The Pike"-- Long Beach's amusement park. Bill took us to a beer joint he heard about where they would serve beer to underage sailors. We each had a hamburger with fries and a beer. It came to a buck and a half each. We knew we couldn't afford to stay in there long. Outside Bill said, "hell, they must think they're a high class joint."

As we ambled down the fairway, music was blasting from the Ferris wheel area. *"Like a rubber ball, I come bouncing back to yooooou, bouncy - bouncy."* Bill grinned. "That's the dumbest fucking song I ever heard."-I agreed with Bill. Sailors were everywhere. It was like an ocean of dress blues moving in both directions. Sometimes you would see a sailor with a girl on his arm but it was rare.

Bill had a scowl on his face. You gotta get out of these Navy towns if you want to meet any women. Too many hard-tails around."

I grinned to myself. Bill was the old, wise one, with his whole 2 months in the Navy.

There was a strong scent in the air, a mixture of cotton candy, salt air, and stale beer. Bill asked me how much money I had. I said, "about five bucks."

202

He said "me too. Let's go back to that joint we were at earlier and get a coupla more beers."

A steady, light rain was beginning to fall. We ducked in the door by the red, neon, "Schlitz" sign. The bar had taken on a different look than it had earlier. The lights were dimmer and different colored lights played on the ceiling. ***"Let it Be Me"*** by the Everly Brothers was coming from the juke box. Several sailors were seated at the bar and others were in booths. Two older women were dancing together in an embrace by the juke box. The shorter one had her head on the other one's shoulder.

Bill and I set at the bar with our backs to it, surveying the scene, sipping our long neck Budweisers. We spotted a lone woman seated in a booth by herself. She smiled at us. Bill sort of whispered, "If she comes up here, don't talk to her."

"Why?"

"Just don't. I'll tell you later."

And then she was there. Standing between us. Close up she looked older than she had in the booth. She put her hands on both our knees.

"How about one of you cutie-pies buying me a beer?"

I said, "ok". Bill looked over at me and shook his head. I didn't know what in hell was going on but it was too late to stop the beer order. The bartender set a bottle on the bar in front of her and I paid. She moved closer to me and began massaging the inner part of my upper thigh. Then her hand moved up. "I'm Anna," she breathed. I gulped a swig of beer.

"Oh, yeah?"

Anna became serious looking. But she didn't move her hand. "Hey, I'm just a girl trying to make a living. I'm honest and I wanna save up enough money to get back to Texas. I don't charge much and I really will show you guys a good time. The best you've ever had."

Bill came up from his stool. Reaching over and grabbing my jumper he jerked me from mine. "Let's go, Dan, we gotta get back."

Anna grabbed my arm. "Aren't you even gonna ask what I charge?"
Bill said, "Sorry, baby, not tonight.
"Halfway to the door I looked back to see Anna move next to a lone sailor. When we hit the sidewalk Bill laughed. When I looked at him he said, "She was a cop. LAPD vice. Suds pointed her out to me a couple of weeks ago in another joint. The bitch wanted us to ask how much she charged. If you had, she would have slapped the cuffs on you." I guess I looked a little confused. Bill said, "don't worry about it. You did ok, but there's a lot of things you have to learn and you will. But it takes time." When we arrived at the square to wait for the little, blue Navy bus to take us back to our ship, the rain was falling harder and a cool wind was blowing. I asked Bill to tell me something else I needed to know. He kicked at a pebble. "Well, one big thing you'll learn is that the civilians in these Navy towns hate sailors. They love our money we spend but despise us. The women are afraid we're going to fuck their daughters and the men think we're out to fuck their wives. They think sailors are the scum of the earth. They're too ignorant to know we were screened before the Navy let us join and we're the cleanest and smartest of all the services. Oh, hell no - they think we're all wild, drunk and running around with our dicks hanging out. Hell with 'em!" I pulled the collar of my peacoat up against the wind and began to ponder all this.

Chapter 37

The ship's PA system blared throughout the berthing area.

"Now, Reveilie, Reveilie" All hands heave out and trice up. The smoking lamp is lit in all authorized spaces – Now Reveilie!"

We were all stumbling around trying to get our dungarees on. Somebody threw open the overhead deck scuttle to let in fresh air. It was still dark outside. I looked at my watch. 0430. The speaker over our heads came to life again.

"Now make all preparations for getting underway!—Set Special Sea Detail—Working Party Lay To The Pier For Casting Off All Lines!"

I could hear the big diesel engines being lit off down below. I scrambled down the ladder to the engine room. The bridge was already ringing the engine room. I tried to act cool but I was excited. A man named Hatcher walked over to me. Hatcher was close to having his 20 years in and had seen action in the South Pacific and the Korean conflict. He grinned at me."First time out, Dan?"

"Yeah, it is."

"Well, don't expect to be cutting through the water like the destroyers and cruisers you see in the recruiting films. This old flat bottomed tub just bounces along."

The wheelhouse was ringing the engine room furiously now. Mac was answering by moving the handle on the engine telegraph to the same speed being demanded by the bridge. We jerked back and then forward and then back again. Then we started moving slowly ahead. I was holding on to an air duct over my head. The overhead lights blinked off and back on. Mac sidled over to me and said, "since it's your first time out, go on up topside and get a look." I scurried up the ladder, went through the berthing area and climbed the ladder to the main deck. The pier was still in sight aft of us, but we were picking up a little speed. A deck hand named Turnbull walked over. The ship did a little bounce. He asked me, "Well, whadaya think?" I said "a little rough." Turnbull threw back his head and laughed. "Hell, you ain't seen nothing yet. We're still in the channel. Wait till we hit the open sea. You'll see some bouncing then." We both lit up cigarettes and started talking. Turnbull's first name was Anthony but everyone called him "Tony". He was from a small town in New Jersey. He had had it rough growing up. His father ran off when he was 10 years old. He was never seen again. Tony had to quit school at 16 and go to work to support him and his mama. Two years later his mama got a divorce from his father claiming desertion and married some guy from Pennsylvania. Tony joined the Navy. That had been 3 years ago.

Tony told me, "Listen, Danny, it's not that bad in the Navy. Three square meals a day, free room and board, even if it's on an old tub like this one. Hell, free medical and dental."

While Tony was telling me all this, we hit open water. We were not only bouncing, we were wallowing.

About 200 yards to port were two huge fishing trawlers. On the trawler closest to us, I could see men standing around the big nets hanging on the stern. I said, "Wonder what they're fishing for."

Tony laughed. "Those bastards are fishing for information."

I said, "Information? What kind of information? "

Tony said, They're not real fishing boats. They're Russian spy ships."

My mouth hung open. Tony went on,"they're monitoring the radio transmission of every ship in the area." I couldn't grasp this new revelation. "Hell, why don't we blow them out of the water?"

Tony shook his head. "We can't. We're beyond the 3 mile limit. This is international waters we're in now."--This sounded crazy to me. Since we *were* still in sight of land.

Tony said, " Most countries have a 12 to 20 mile limit. But not us. Hell no, 3 miles! That's why the Commies are here. Fucking Russkies."

One of the men on the nearest vessel actually waved at us. Tony grabbed his crotch and shook it at him. The Russian showed Tony his middle finger. Tony kept shaking his crotch at the Russian. The old Hawk bounced on until the trawlers were out of sight.

At 1300 we arrived on station. This cruise was for gunnery practice. General Quarters was sounded.

 "ALL HANDS MAN YOUR BATTLE STATIONS--THIS IS A DRILL-

THIS IS A DRILL!"

A gong was sounding furiously. My battle station, at the time, was with the #2 damage control team. We mustered in the mess hall wearing our life vests and steel gray Navy helmets. The Hawk had slowed; we were barely moving. All was quiet. Then it came. **BLAM! BLAM! BLAM!**

I jumped a little. A man called Pierce handed me some ear plugs.

"Hell, we forgot to tell you how loud those 40 millimeter guns are. That was #3 gun tub, right over our heads."

I could hear the other gun tubs firing. Then #3 started up again. I could hear brass shell casings hitting the deck. I asked Pierce what they were shooting at. He grinned. "They're firing at a "sleeve" being towed a thousand feet behind a plane, but they ain't gonna hit it. Our gunners couldn't hit the broad ass side of a barn if they were standing inside the S.O.B."

At 1500 the firing stopped. The ship's PA System blared again. **"Secure from General Quarters - Set the regular underway watch."**

I had the 1600 to 2000 security watch. I took the duty belt from the man I was relieving, strapped it on and started making my rounds. Around 1930 I moseyed up topside. It was very dark as the Hawk moved thru the night. Looking up, the stars looked bigger to me than they ever had before. Looking down from the stern at the water, large green streaks of phosphorus looked like big fish swimming beside the ship. I went back down to the engineering spaces. At 1945 I was relieved. I was fumbling through my locker when the speakers came alive:

"Now, Movie Call! Movie Call! Tonight's movie will be shown in the mess deck. The name of tonight's movie is "Shane" starring Alan Ladd, Van Heflin, and Jean Arthur."

Most of us had seen "Shane" as boys but you couldn't see "Shane" too many times. I headed for the mess deck. The electrician mates were hanging up a sheet. The projector was about 30 feet away. I looked at the film case. "Shane" consisted of 3 large reels. Bill and I found a mess table close to the screen. We all had our coffee mugs and cigarettes in front of us.

"Shane" was as great as ever. We all cheered when Shane (Alan Ladd) outdrew the evil gunslinger, Wilson (Jack Palance) and killed him. We all clapped when Shane rode off at the end with little Joey (Brandon De Wilde) yelling, **"Come back, Shane".**

I headed for the head where I showered and shaved and then fell into my rack. I would be going back on security watch at 0400. I immediately fell into a deep, dreamless sleep.

The sound of running feet grew louder. I could hear men shouting. Suddenly something hit one of the chains my rack was suspended from. I fought my way out of my deep sleep. I set up just in time to see the executive officer rush by my rack. He was wearing a white duty belt and holster and had a Navy issued .45 automatic in his right hand. Several men followed him. One of them was Suds who had a huge pipewrench in his hand. In my muddled half-asleep mind I thought there must be a busted pipe somewhere on the ship. But I didn't understand the .45 automatic. I struggled into my dungaree pants and shower shoes and followed behind them. They tore down the ladder to the tank deck and mustered outside the ship's laundry. I asked Suds, "what in hell's going on?"

He told me, "Chow's in the laundry and he's got the hatch dogged down. He went nuts about an hour ago, running all over the ship with a meat cleaver threatening to kill everbody. He hit your chain with that damn cleaver - He's totally lost it, even foaming at the mouth."

Chow was one of the ship's cooks. I had not spoken with him much. I never knew his real name. Everyone just called him Chow. He was a big guy of Chinese descent.

Finally the executive officer posted an armed guard at the laundry room's hatch. The Hawk turned and headed back to port where the Naval Station Police would be waiting to take Chow away. Our cruise had been cut short. I crawled back in my rack to ponder all this. Soon I was back into my deep abyss of sleep.

Chapter 38

In January 1961, John F. Kennedy was sworn in as president. I had been promoted to fireman and Pat had talked me into transferring to the boiler room to work for him. The operation of the boiler and fresh water evaporators didn't take long to learn. But striking for boiler tender on the Hawk (the nickname of the ol' Clay County) meant I had to learn the entire fresh water, salt water, and diesel oil systems. Which meant I spent a lot of time crawling on my back through the bilges of the engineering spaces, mentally mapping out diesel, salt water and fresh water lines. There were 133 valves in the boiler room alone.
Pat was on his second hitch with about 2 years to go. He would have 10 years in but was getting out. Pat wanted to be a real estate tycoon.

"Santa Anna, Anaheim - all that out there is going to boom. People are going to be coming into this state by the millions over the next 20 years - I wanna be part of it all. I'm gonna be somebody, Danny. Maybe even run for political office! Whada'ya think of that - huh, Danny? Wouldn't that be something?" Over and over he talked about it. I was starting to believe he really would make it big someday. Pat also talked a lot about his wife, Jackie. According to Pat, she was the 8th wonder of the world.

"How could I have been so lucky, Dan? She's so beautiful, so much class. And the best part is, she worships me. She loves the ground I walk on. She stands behind me in everything I want to do. I want to give her the finer things in life, and I sure as hell can't do it on Navy pay. It's the real estate world for me, baby."

In April, Pat invited me to his house for dinner. I hesitated but he insisted, "Jackie's looking forward to meeting you." Pat and Jackie had rented a house in Signal Hill. Pat and I rode the bus to Signal Hill. We got off at Cherry Street and had to walk a couple of blocks to the house.

When Pat opened the front door I caught the warm aroma of something baking in the kitchen. Jackie came out to greet us. She looked like a housewife you would see on television--Short blond hair swept up at the ends and wearing a red dress, white apron, and high heels. She was very good-looking. Pat introduced us and I stuck out my hand, but she ignored that and hugged me instead. There was just a trace of great smelling perfume. She looked a little like a young Barbara Stanwyck, only prettier. Jackie had invited her sister, June and her husband, Frank, over to meet me. We ate steak, baked potato and a salad. Jackie brought out a lemon cake that was the best I had ever tasted. I knew one thing about her - she could damn sure cook. Jackie ushered us into the living room after dinner and served us some kind of coffee called El Supremo or a least it sounded like that. It wasn't bad. Jackie said, "We're having a kaffeelatsch", which I think meant we were going to drink coffee and have a conversation. I didn't see much resemblance between Jackie and her sister. June had dark brown hair, and a deep tan. At least she did on her face and arms. Frank was actually wearing a white shirt and tie, which I thought was strange for our little gathering. June was wearing a pink blouse and light brown slacks. She appeared to have very good legs. June was nice, with a smile that seemed to be genuine. Frank, on the other hand, seemed to have a permanent smirk on his face that said, "all this is beneath me." He seemed to want to give the impression that he was tolerating our little Kaffeelatsch because he was such a swell guy.

Frank was gaunt and hollow-cheeked with a badly receding hairline. He looked over at me, sitting on the couch with Pat and Jackie. "What did you do before the Navy?"

I told him, "I was a supervisor with Rand McNally." It was a lie, of course, but I wasn't about to tell him I had ran around with a hand-operated forklift, shuffling books from one place to another.

I asked Frank what he did for a living. The little smile/smirk appeared. "Let's just say I'm in the information business. "I wanted to ask him if he was a telephone operator but instead I said, "What kind of information?" "Let's just say government stuff."
I was beginning to get a little irritated with Frank.
Pat felt the tension and began talking about the coming Orange County real estate boom. Jackie was rapt with admiring eyes for her husband. Frank's smirk came back. Julia looked like she would have loved to have been anywhere else on the planet.

It was late. I had to get back to the ship. I thanked Jackie for a great meal. She blew me an air kiss. Even though I still had a couple more days of liberty left, I was broke and there was nowhere to go anyway.

Pat took me back to the bus stop in Jackie's car. We set and talked till the bus came. Pat told me, "Frank's a real jerk-off. He's got some little government job. Thanks he's J. Edgar Hoover." We both laughed. Pat added, "What the S.O.B. doesn't know is that his wife is balling their insurance man at least 3 times a week. She told Jackie all about it. She's in love with this guy, going to leave Frank."

I grinned thinking I wouldn't mind having a little of June myself. Pat picked up on my thoughts. "Hey, buddy, I know what's going through your mind." We both laughed again.

The bus pulled up and I told Pat I would see him Monday. The bus was packed with sailors but I managed to find a seat. It was cold on the bus. I buttoned my pea coat and folded my arms. It was quiet. No one was talking. I soon fell asleep as the old bus rattled through the darkness.

Chapter 39

December 31, 1961

Colorado Boulevard was alive with people. The sun was going down and it was getting colder. Bill and I buttoned our peacoats and turned the collars up. Small campfires were burning on both sides of the street.Tents were set up. Sleeping bags and lawn chairs were scattered about in the grass and on the sidewalks. Throngs of people were moving in both directions on the Pasadena street. All vehicle traffic had been blocked. Everyone was trying to maneuver into a good spot to watch the Rose Bowl Parade that would be coming down that very street the next morning. It had been Bill's idea for us to come up to Pasadena for the big parade.

"Hey, it'll be great for meeting women. We'll stay in uniform, they'll love us."

So far I hadn't seen many eligible women. It was mostly families, moms and pops with the kids and a lot of older people. And ,of course, sailors. You could see white hats moving through the crowds. Bill and I ambled 5 blocks south on to another street and found a small, dimly lit cafe still open.
"HAPPY NEW YEAR" had been sprayed on the window using fake snow from a can. There was no waitress. There was only an old man behind the counter. He wore a dirty white shirt and a grease-stained apron. The old man grinned a toothless grin. "What'll it be lads?"

We both ordered a cheeseburger and a beer. He didn't ask for any I.D. We sipped our beer from long-neck bottles while the old man cooked the burgers. The only other customer in the little cafe was a woman with long, straight, snow-white hair that hung down to her waist. She was seated at a table near the jukebox guzzling a glass of draft beer. The Drifters were singing ***"OH DARLING—SAVE THE LAST DANCE FOR ME!"***

From the light of the jukebox she looked pasty pale. The big smear of bright red lipstick made her look a little like a clown. Her and Bill were eyeballing each other. Bill nudged my leg with his, "check out the babe at the table."

I laughed, "you mean Witch Hazel ? Come on, Bill, she's a hundred years old, man."

Bill glanced back at the table. "She's not all that bad and you know what they say, 'any old port in a storm, right?"
I said, "That's a little too stormy for me."
Bill picked up his beer, "I'm gonna talk to her."
I grinned, "have at it, buddy."
She was at the jukebox when Bill walked up beside her. Connie Francis was crooning, ***"Wheeere the boys are, someone waits for me."***

From the light of the jukebox I could see her smiling up at Bill. They talked a few seconds, then started checking out the songs that were listed. Bill put in some quarters and she punched in her selections. With Bill's arm around her, he guided her back to her table. I ordered another long-neck and listened to the old man who was telling me how he had won WWI single-handed. The old man's memory had us deep in France where he captured 25 German soldiers all by himself, when Bill returned to the bar with his woman in tow.

He introduced her. Her name was Imogene. Up close she looked a little better. Her eyes had a humorous sparkle. Bill patted me on the back, "get your peacoat on, Daniel, we're going to Imogene's house."

I objected, "I'll just stay here till you get back."

"We ain't coming back", Bill said. "We're spending the night at Imogene's."

Imogene spoke up in a deep raspy voice, "Come on, Danny, sweetie, I won't bite you." Bill turned his beer up and finished it.

"Imogene's gonna fix the couch up for you."

It sounded good. I was dog-tired and sleepy and a light rain was beginning to fall. Imogene was walking a little unsteadily but Bill had his arm around her waist with me trailing behind. Imogene's car was parked about a block away. A green 1958 Pontiac Fire Chief. Bill insisted on driving. Imogene didn't object and surrendered her keys. I climbed in the back seat and crouched in the corner, pulling my white hat down over my eyes. Imogene was pretty tipsy but she managed to get out the directions to her house.

We finally pulled up in front of a small frame house with a wide porch. When we started up the walk a big black cat jumped from the porch and tore around back. I thought it was fitting that Imogene would have a black cat. But she was a great hostess. We three sat at the table in her small but neat kitchen. There was a big plastic owl over her stove with a clock in its belly.Imogene made ham sandwiches that were delicious. Her and Bill drank Coors beers. I was sick of beer and drank a cup of coffee. In her raspy voice Imogene told us how she had come to California ten years earlier with her husband and two daughters from Ohio. "Oh my God", she rasped. "He was a mean son-of-a-bitch. I finally ran the bastard off and got a divorce." The daughters were grown now and living back in Ohio, but Imogene had stayed in California because Ohio winters were too cold for her and her arthritis. She worked at a bookstore in L. A. called, "Vineyard's Book Mart" and loved her job. I was telling Imogene how much I liked books when Bill butted in about all the far away places he had been in the Navy. All lies, of course. My eyes were closing. Imogene jumped up, "let's get you settled in, Danny boy."

I followed her to the living room. "I'll be right back", she said. Bill came sauntering into the room. Imogene returned with a clean sheet, pillow and a red blanket. She spread the sheet on the couch, punched up the pillow, and put the folded blanket at the foot. "Now, if you need anything, Danny - just whistle, ok?"

I said, "Ok."

Her and Bill headed off down a short hallway. I took off my jumper and dress shoes. My feet hurt. I was rubbing them when I saw a bookcase at the far end of the room. I moseyed over. They were all hard backs. There were books by authors I knew such as O. Henry and Jack London and other I had never heard of like Maria Edgeworth and Mary Roberts Rinehart. --Heading back toward my couch I turned on Imogene's Zenith TV while wondering why she would have a book by Jack London. A rerun of Jack Paar's "Tonight" show was on. Jack was trading quips with his announcer, Hugh Downs. I laughed. I had always thought Jack was funny. I watched it until a big-nosed young woman came out and started singing something about a bee. I clicked it off and stretched out on the couch, pulling the red blanket over me. The pillow case smelled fresh and clean. I was tired and sleepy and felt snug. It didn't take long for me to fall asleep.

The 40 millimeters were firing. **Blam! Blam! Blam!** But I was confused because nobody had called for general quarters. Somebody was yelling. I slowly opened my eyes remembering where I was. On Imogene's couch. Someone was pounding on the door and yelling.

Imogene and Bill came stumbling into the living room. Imogene was clutching a sheet around her. Bill was fumbling with the 13 buttons on the flap of his dress-blue pants.

I said, "what the hell?!"

Imogene pulled her sheet tighter. "It's my damn husband, Wallace."

Bill stared at her in disbelief. "Your husband?!"
"We're divorced but the bastard won't leave me alone."
The door pounding continued. Imogene looked at Bill and said, "I'll get rid of him" and headed for the door. Bill jerked up a brass doorstop shaped like an owl. I said, "Hell, Bill, don't hit him with that damn thing. We'll be in jail."

"Yeah, but what if he's got a gun or something?"

There was no time for further discussion of the matter. Wallace was coming through the open door. I was relieved that he appeared to be unarmed. Bill eased the owl doorstop back down onto the floor. Wallace stopped and stood there looking from me to Bill and back at me. I wanted to say, "I didn't do anything," but kept my mouth shut. Wallace was a slight built man with thinning red hair. He looked to be at least as old as Imogene, probably older. He was wearing a red jacket that had frayed sleeves and green work khakis that stopped about three inches above his ankles that made me think of Little Abner in the comics. We all four stood in stunned silence. I sure as hell didn't know what to say. Wallace broke the spell by walking over and sitting on the couch where I had been sleeping. He dropped his head and held it in his hands. His shoulders started shaking. I thought he was laughing but then I heard the sobs. Imogene walked over to him and began rubbing his shoulders. Bill and me grabbed our things and took off out the door and down the steps. Bill was walking a little bow-legged and holding his crotch. I asked him if he was ok? "Damn, she was giving me a blow job when that bastard started beating on the door. Bitch bit my dick - hurts like hell."

We found a gas station that was open all night. Bill got the key from the attendant and walked bow-legged to the men's room to check out his injury. While he was gone, I drank a Grapico out of the soda box. Bill came out declaring no major damage. "Still hurts like hell." I told him he should have Doc take a look when we got back to the ship.

Bill said, "no way am I letting Doc fool around with my pecker. Plus it's embarrassing. Doc would blab it all over the ship."

I said, "I'm sure as hell not going to say anything about it."
"Hell, I know that, we're buddies."
    We had walked about 2 blocks when we both bursted out laughing. We headed back toward Colorado Boulevard. When we got back to where the action was, there wasn't much going on. The crowd had grown quiet. Most were in their tents or sleeping bags dreaming about the big parade. The lucky ones who had tickets would be watching UCLA and Minnesota play in the Rose Bowl the next day. I looked at my watch. 0230. It was already the next day. Bill was still walking a little bow-legged and my feet were hurting. We both were cold and needed sleep. We weaved our way around the campers and their dying little camp fires and finally came across a bowling alley that was open. There was a heavy set woman with glasses behind the counter where you rented your bowling shoes. She was totally

engrossed in a paperback book and paid us no mind. We located a round leather bench with no backing. We sat back to back for support, folded our arms and conked out.

Sunlight streaming through the bowling alley's window woke us.

While we were in the men's room throwing water on our faces, two middle-aged, well-dressed men walked in. They had definitely used Old Spice after they had shaved that morning. They both wore dark blue suits, white shirts and red ties. Each man had a round medallion with blue ribbons hanging from it. Printed on the medallions in gold were the words, "Rose Bowl Official."

One of the men looked at us and said, "Hey, Paul, the Navy's here."
Paul was drying his hands with a paper towel. "I can see that, Keith- how you guys doing?"
Bill and I nodded.
Paul walked over and shook our hands. "You guys here for the parade? Well of course you are. Stupid question. Tell you what, that's a big crowd out there and you're not going to be able to see much. Keith and I are both officials and we can get you guys ring-side seats. How about that?"

Bill said, "Sure." Paul looked at me.
I said, "sounds good to me."
Keith cut in, "and we can get you into the stadium later to see the game. And you boys are invited to a big party at my house after the game. Lots of girls."

I said, "hold on, why are you giving us such special treatment?"
Paul actually looked hurt. "Hey, we're grateful to our servicemen. You sacrifice a lot for us and we like to do what we can for you fellows."--I was a little ashamed for questioning their hospitality. Paul and Keith went out the door with Bill and me following.

Bill whispered, "maybe we died and went to heaven."

I said, "maybe, but I doubt it."

Outside Paul grabbed my elbow and guided me right through the crowd. We got some angry looks but nobody said anything. I looked around for Bill and Keith. Paul said,"don't worry, they'll catch up to us later."--Paul took me right to the wooden bleachers that were set up and reserved for important people. I spotted the actor who played "Wally" on the "Ozzie and Harriet" TV show sitting about 4 rows up. Paul and me climbed to the 6th row and set down. Roy Rogers and his wife, Dale, were just riding by on Trigger and Buttermilk. Trigger reared up on his hind legs and Roy waved his cowboy hat at the crowd. This was neat. I couldn't believe my good luck. The actor, Guy Madison, came by on a horse. A float came by with "Wizard of Oz" characters made of flowers. There was a real girl dressed to look like Dorothy at the front of the float, waving to everyone. Paul explained that every float had to be made entirely of flowers or natural plants like leaves or bark. The US flag came by made of red, white and blue flowers. Then came a huge snow-white swan. Standing inside the swan and waving was a beautiful blond-haired girl wearing a blue gown, long gloves and a crown. There were several other girls standing around the swan and waving. The blonde girl was cradling a bouquet of flowers with her left arm and waving with her right hand. When she turned our way, her smile was dazzling.

Paul said, "Whadaya think of that? Lot of woman, right?" I agreed that she most certainly was a lot of woman. Paul took this opportunity to put his hand on my thigh. I roughly shoved his hand away. "What in the hell do you thinkyou're doing?" Paul grinned, "I was just checking to see if you had a hard-on after seeing that gal."

I said, "You're fucking nuts, pal."

I stood up. Paul started apologizing, "I didn't mean anything by it, I'm sorry."

As I reached the bottom steps I heard him yell, "What about the party?" I figured he must be insane. I pushed through the crowd looking for Bill. I saw a white hat coming my way - it was Bill. "Let's get the hell out of here, Dan - These bastards are queerer than a three dollar bill!"

I said, "I know, where's the other one?"
Bill nodded behind him, "on his ass where I put him."
I looked in that direction. A crowd of people were looking at something that was apparently on the ground. It had to be Keith.
I said, "you're right-- let's get the hell out of here!"

We headed west. A motorcycle cop was coming down the sidewalk towards us. His lights were flashing as he weaved in and out of people. He went right past me and Bill without even looking at us. We walked faster, cutting down an alley, headed south. Three blocks down we turned back east. When we reached Arroyo street we found an old red-brick hotel with a blue neon sign that told us this was the "Court Plaza Hotel."

The skinny, dark-haired woman behind the counter couldn't speak much English but we finally understood it was ten bucks for the day. Two beds and a bathroom down the hall. The lobby smelled like mildew but we took the room. We trudged up the old wooden stairs to the third floor which was the top floor. The mattresses felt like they had been stuffed with rocks but the room smelled ok. It even smelled clean. Bill was snoring as soon as his head hit the pillow. I lay awake a while looking at the green-wood ceiling and rehashing, in my mind, the events of last night and today till sleep overtook me.

When I awoke, Bill was sitting up on the side of his bed flipping through the Los Angeles phone book. I grinned, "You got relatives in LA?"

Bill tossed the book back on the nightstand. "Hell no, I would never claim any relative who would live in this shit-hole."

We took turns going to the bathroom down the hall to wash up a little. We looked fairly decent but there wasn't much we could do about us both needing shaves.

We hobbled down the old stairway to the lobby and walked over to the desk to turn in the key.The dark haired woman came out of an adjoining room in the back. She was dabbing at her eyes with a handkerchief as though she had been crying.

Bill and I looked at each other but neither of us said anything. We handed her the key and left. We started walking, looking for a bus stop so we could get on back to Long Beach and our ship. There was still plenty of daylight left. A few blocks north the sickening sweet smell of dying plants hit us. Flower petals were 2 and 3 feet deep on the sidewalk as well as the road. Rotting flowers were strewn as far as you could see.
We kicked at them as we made our way down the deserted street.

Chapter 40

February 6th 1962

The Hawk had steamed into San Diego Bay the day before and tied up at pier 20 inside the San Diego Naval Base. I had not been in San Diego since boot camp and now San Diego would be the Hawk's home port. The scuttlebutt had it that the Navy was phasing out Long Beach.

We had steam, fresh water, electricity and salt water for flushing coming in from the dock so the boiler and auxiliary engines were shut down.

Pat and I were down in the boiler room where I was working on a centrifugal pump while Pat talked about becoming a millionaire and maybe even the governor of California someday. Pat and Jackie had been skiing at Big Bear over the weekend, and Pat was beside himself over San Bernadino County. When he paced back and forth orating, he made me think of Burt Lancaster in the movie "Elmer Gantry". He even looked like Burt Lancaster. Sometimes the guys would kid him by calling him "Burt".

"The California real estate boom actually started 15 years ago", Pat said, "and the surface hasn't even been scratched. New people are piling into California everyday and servicemen are staying here going to work in the aircraft industry. Hell, nobody's going back to Wallerbutt, Kansas and raising goats anymore. I had to laugh about "Wallerbutt". My wrench slipped and I busted a knuckle. I yelped, "Jesus Christ!" Pat kept talking. "Jacqueline and I are both studying for our real estate license." Sometimes he would call his wife "Jacqueline" instead of Jackie. He had also mentioned, several times in the past, about his wife having the same first name as the president's wife. I never understood the connection.

Pat went on, "the money's out there, and I'm gonna make it big, me and Jackie." I dabbed a rag at the spot of blood on my knuckle and said, "You know, Pat, I believe you will make it big, - You and Jackie."

Then he surprised me by saying, "hey, Dan, you can make it big too, you can be in on it. Hell, you're smart and Jackie thinks you've got a great personality. You'd make a terrific real estate salesman."

I grinned, "thanks, Pat, but Bill and I have been talking some about going to Australia when we get out. You know, the new frontier and all that." Pat stared at me for at least 5 seconds. Then he said, "Australia?! -What in the fuck is in Australia but fucking kangaroos?!"

I said, "Well, actually that's what some of it is about. According to this book on Australia that Bill has been reading, the Kangaroos are becoming overpopulated. Eating the crops, drinking the stock's water. There's a bounty on 'em. The Australian government will pay a hundred dollar bounty for every hide you bring in. Bill thinks we could make a lot of money down there. And there's tons of precious stones like rubies if you're willing to dig them out of the ground. Bill says it really is the new frontier. " Pat stared at me as if I had two heads and four eyes. Just then, the ship's speakers boomed.

"All hands not on watch muster topside - All hands not on watch muster topside, on the double!"

Pat and I looked at each other and said in unison, "What the fuck?" Up the ladder we went. We fell in with the rest of the ship's crew. We weren't mustered by division. One hundred and ninety men and officers were lined

up together, less the ones on watch. I had already seen Captain Dodd on the bridge looking down at us. He came down the ladder and all 190 men and officers snapped to attention. He said, "at ease,men" and clasped his hands behind his back. He scanned us with his eyes without saying anything as though he was gathering his thoughts. Then he began. "Men, we have received orders from AMPHIBPAC. There is a crisis in Laos as we speak. The North Vietnamese are in Laos building staging areas from which to attack South Vietnam. If the Godless communists are allowed to take South Vietnam, other democracies will also fall. Laos, Thailand, maybe even the Philippines. President Kennedy has vowed this will not happen on his watch. Our orders are this - We will depart San Diego on the morning of February 20th. Two weeks from today. We will proceed to Pearl Harbor Naval Base where we will take aboard a contingent of 100 Army personnel. We will then proceed to our destination, which is unknown at this time, where these soldiers will disembark. I am stressing to you that these soldiers will not be in combat roles. They will be acting as military advisors only. And this is very important--During the next two weeks *do not* talk about our mission to a barmaid or anyone else. As far as your wives and families you are to tell them you will be on an extended tour. And that, gentlemen, will be the gospel truth. I have no idea when we'll be back stateside. As always, I expect each man to carry out his duties in order for this mission to be successful. And I know you will. You are a fine, top notch crew. That's all I have at this time."
The old Chief Bosun's mate called out, "**ATTEN-HUT!**"

Captain Dodd went back up to the bridge. The old bosun' told us to "fall out." We mingled around discussing these new developments. The ship's yeoman asked, "where in hell is Waos?" Someone explained to him that was the way the captain pronounced "Laos." The yeoman looked confused. Bill was talking to Suds when I walked over.

"You mean we already have soldiers fighting in this Vietnam place?" Suds said, "Nah, they're just there as advisors and such to the South Vietnamese Army." A radioman from operations named Carr butted in, "that's bullshit, Suds, and you know it." Suds frowned. "It probably is bullshit, Carr." Suds added, "why don't you trot up to the Captain's cabin and tell him that? Tell him it's all bullshit and you ain't going." Carr looked sheepish. "No, I don't think I'll do that."

"Then shut up."

Carr headed back down below. I had noticed that Pat had not hung around for the chatter. He had left as soon as we broke ranks. I found Pat in after-steering punching the hell out of a Kapok Lifejacket.

I said, "Settle down, buddy, it's not the end of the world."

Pat exploded, "It's the end of *my* fucking world!"

I patted him on the shoulder. He jerked away as though I was in on some conspiracy to keep him from his dream. "Mother-fuckers know I don't have long to go till I'm out. But could they wait a few months for this bullshit to get started? Fucking hell no! "

I said, "Pat, you're not making any sense." I don't believe he even heard me. He kept raving, "Fucking Dodd loves this shit, strutting back and forth like General MacArthur."

Then Pat seemed to settle down. His face brightened as if he had just thought of a great idea. He had. He said, "no problem, I'll go through the chain of command and see the exec. He'll understand my situation and transfer me to shore duty. No sweat. He's a good guy. We talk a lot and he's got his shit together. He'll understand."

Pat headed up to officer's country to see Mr. Lingon to get permission to see the exec. I went back down to the boiler room and resumed repairing my centrifugal pump. Half an hour later, Pat came down the ladder. I looked up and said,"well,what did you find out?"

He just shook his head and said,"that son-of-a-bitch."

Chapter 41

Bill said, "Damn, I've never seen this many swabbies." Broadway Street in San Diego was teeming with beer joints and sailors. We had joined a locker club called "Ebb Tide" earlier that day and bought some civvies. Of course, nobody was fooled into thinking we weren't sailors. The spit-shined shoes, the haircuts, even the way we carried ourselves were all dead give-aways. But it still felt good to be out of uniform sometimes.

Unlike Long Beach we couldn't find a bar that would serve anyone under 21. We decided to try an old trick. We found a bowling alley that served beer. The place was packed. You could hear bowling balls roaring and pins crashing. We stood around until two sailors got up from a table and left. Two empty beer bottles were still on the table. Bill and me quickly slid into the vacated chairs. We pretended to be drinking from the bottles until Bill caught the eye of a roving waitress.

"Could we get two more over here?" Bill said, holding up two fingers. She brought them over thinking someone had already checked our ID's since we were already drinking. We were in. On our third beer I spotted a girl with reddish blonde hair, sitting at a table with an elderly woman. They were drinking cokes. I caught her glancing at me and she smiled. Bill said, "why don't you go talk to her?" I said, "fat chance with that old woman with her." Then, as though she had heard us, she got up and walked down to the bowling lanes. When she went by me she smiled.
Bill said, "there you go, stud."
I said, "I'm gone."
She smiled as I came up to her and said, "I knew you would come down here."
I said, "really? And how did you know that?"
She dropped her eyes, "I just did." She was even more beautiful close up and smelled like Ivory soap. Her reddish-blonde hair was cut fairly short and sort

of curled inward. Her name was Cindy Hollister from Colorado Springs, Colorado which was "dullsville" according to Cindy, so she had come to California to live with her grandmother.

We both glanced at the grandmother. The old woman was standing up and rummaging through her purse. Cindy said, "I've got to go but can I give you my phone number?"
I said, "sure," when I really wanted to drop to my knees thanking God.
She wrote her number in a small notebook and tore out the page. When she handed it to me she squeezed my hand. "Do call me, please." I said, "you got it" and immediately felt stupid. What a dumb thing to say, "you got it" - pitiful.

I saw the grandmother looking at us and scowling. When Cindy reached her, the old woman paid for the cokes and followed Cindy out the door.

Bill said, "man, she's alright. Did you get her phone number?" I showed it to him.

"Way to go, hoss."

We had another beer and decided to head back for the Hawk. We started toward the Ebb Tide Locker Club to change back into our uniforms. We were strolling along the sidewalk, looking in store windows. About every fifth building was a "photo studio" where a sailor could get his picture taken with a pretty girl in his lap for 10 bucks. He could mail it to his old buddys back home and impress the hell out of them. They were all packed with sailors waiting their turn.

 I saw it developing before Bill did. Two civilians headed our way. One was tall and lanky like Bill. The other one was about my height, but twice as wide. They appeared to be quite a bit older than Bill and me. Probably in their late 20's. They were coming right at us. Then Bill spotted them.

Trouble on the hoof. They were not going to yield and I knew Bill wouldn't. The tall guy's left shoulder slammed into Bill's left shoulder. The civilian turned around and said, "Think you own the sidewalk swab-jockey?" I knew Bill wouldn't back down---"Fuck you, dirt-ball."

They went at it. Dodging, ducking, dancing and swinging. They looked like two guys shadow boxing. No one had landed a blow. The wide guy walked over to me. He had a huge head that was shaved and no neck. His breath smelled like Redman chewing tobacco. The corners of his mouth were brown stained. He had so many freckles he looked like he had the measles. I was sure he outweighed me by a hundred pounds or more. He put his big hand on my chest and shoved me.

"What you gonna do sailor boy?"
I said, "I'm not going to do anything."
"I didn't figure you would, candy ass." Freckles then turned to watch his buddy and Bill going at it. Whish, whish, dance, feint, whish, whish. Still, no one had connected. .
 Freckles said, "finish him off, Gene, and let's get outta here."
That's when I hit him. I caught the area on the side of his nose and just under his eye. But it was a solid punch. Freck didn't go all the way down - just to his knees, right between the two gladiators which broke up their fight. Freck's buddy picked him up under his arms and held him from behind telling him, "Keep your head back Ed, you're bleeding from the nose." Gene looked at Bill, "hey, partner, we don't want any more trouble. Hell, I'll apologize for both of us. What ship you guys on?"

Ed still had his head back holding a handkerchief on his nose that was getting redder and redder. I hit him again. This time it was a solid left blow to his right temple. He didn't go down again but he fell away from Roy's arms and stumbled out into the street before going down on one knee. He stayed there with his head down. A San Diego police car cruised up with his lights flashing. The cop got out.

"What's going on here?" Bill started explaining. The cop cut him off and pulled us out of ear shot of Gene and Freck. "Hey,guys--I'm ex-Navy. I'll handle this - You guys take off before the Shore Patrol shows up."

We thanked him and took off. About five blocks down we ducked into a coffee shop. While we were sipping our coffee and recapping the events of the night, the waitress came back to give us a refill. She glanced down and said,"did you hurt your hand?"

I said, "a little, I guess." My hand was swelling and becoming a little discolored and starting to hurt like the dickens. By the time we got back to the locker room, my hand was throbbing. With Bills help, I got out of my civvies and back into uniform. I wasn't up to waiting for a bus so Bill hailed a cab to take us back to the base. The cab brought us back down Broadway, past the spot where Ed went down. Gene, Ed and the policeman were gone. Bill said, "you sure cleaned his clock."

I winced a little from the pain in my hand. "Listen, if I had gone toe to toe with that freckled-faced ape, he would have killed me."

Bill grinned, remembering it. "Maybe so and maybe not."
"But," I said, "you and Sugar Ray *did* put on a brilliant display of fancy footwork." We both laughed.

I was lying on my back in my rack when Mr. Lingan came through on his rounds. There was no hiding the hand. It was lying on my chest. "Good God, Dan! What in hell happened to your hand?"

I had already decided to tell the truth about all of it, so I told him about the run-in with the civilians, leaving nothing out.
Mr. Lingan told Bill, "go get Doc."

Bill took off and came back with Doc in tow. Doc gently picked up my hand and slowly turned it over and back. I let out a small yelp. He turned to Mr. Lingan. "Doesn't look good; not much I can do with this. With that discoloration it looks like a probable fracture but there's no way of telling without an x-ray." Doc took my temperature. "100.2-- Low grade fever," Doc said, "I'm gonna send him over to the dispensary on base in the morning. Mr. Lingan nodded his head in agreement. I sort of dozed off. I came awake with a start and found my hand in a bucket of ice water. Doc said, "just take it easy. I'm gonna wrap it in a pressure bandage."

I had only taken off my jumper, with Bill's help, and my dress shoes. I was still wearing my dress trousers. Doc said, "just stay like that and try to get some sleep." He handed me a paper cup of water and three APC pills - known in the Navy as "All Purpose Capsules." It was a running joke that they would cure anything, from the clap to pneumonia. I choked them down. Somebody switched off the lights. The only light was from the red-glowing battle lanterns.

It was a fitful night for me. Falling asleep and waking up. Around 0300 sheer exhaustion put me out for keeps. Someone was shaking me. It was Doc. My hand was throbbing in pain. They had let me sleep till 0800. Doc had my medical work-up in a folder. Doc and two of the guys helped me get my jumper and shoes on. Doc set my white hat on top of my head saying, "don't worry about shaving or anything, just get on over there. Bill's taking you. He's waiting for you on the pier with the jeep."

I went down the gang plank and hopped in the jeep. Bill pulled away, headed for the base dispensary about two miles away.

We drove up to the double doors of the dispensary and Bill parked. We talked a bit then I said, "Well, I guess I better get on in there."

"Yeah," Bill said, "call me as soon as they're through with you and I'll come get you." I said, "You got it, partner."

The place was packed. I got in line leading to a Navy corpsman seated behind a gray metal desk. When I finally reached him I handed over my medical file Doc had given me.

"OK," he muttered, "go over to the port bulkhead and wait until your name is called. Next!"

I fell in line with about 50 others. A couple of Navy Waves were also in the line. There were at least that many on the opposite bulkhead. The sailor in front of me kept looking back at me. I ignored his eyes because I knew he wanted to strike up a conversation and I didn't feel like talking. He finally cranked up anyway. What ship you off of, buddy?"

I told him.
Gator Navy, eh?"
I said, "yep."
"I'm off the Iwo Jima, myself. LPH - Whirlybirds."
I said, "yeah, I know."
He looked down at my hand. "Whoa! - what happened - get inna fight?"
I sure didn't want to discuss it with him. I said, "nah, nothing that dramatic. Wrench slipped down in the boiler room." He was talking about the same thing happening to a buddy of his when a fat corpsman walked out and yelled, "Knight, Daniel - 542-09-01"

I said, "that's me"
The Iwo Jima sailor said, "hey, I was here before you."
I said,"look, I just go when and where they tell me."
He nodded, "yeah, I know. Well, good luck."

The fat corpsman led me through a door with a sign above it declaring that this was Radiology. He had me lie down on a cot and placed my hand on a raised flat surface. Then he rolled a machine over. It looked like the x-ray machines the dentists had used in boot camp. But this one was set vertically right over my hand. The corpsman went out of sight but I could hear him clicking pictures. Then he came back and jerked my hand over. I said, "what the fuck you doing, dumbass?" It had hurt like hell. He became haughty. "Hey, I don't have to listen to that! You can't talk to me in that manner!" I said, "go get me a doctor, fat boy - right now!" His demeanor changed. "Look,we don't need that. I apologize for causing your pain." I lay my head back down and said, "Just take it easy with the hand." "I will - I promise." And he did.

He left with the x-ray plates under his arm. Fifteen minutes later, the doctor came in. He gingerly probed my hand. "The x-rays show you have a fracture of the fifth metacarpal bone. We're going to put a short arm cast on and scoot you over to Balboa."

I asked how long all that was going to take because I needed to get back to my ship. He laughed, "You're not going back to your ship today, son--You're going to Balboa for further evaluation and I imagine you'll be there a few days."

I said, "but what about my ship? They don't know anything about this." The doctor smiled, "Well, you don't worry any about that. Your ship will be duly notified." The fat corpsman rolled me into another room that smelled like wet plaster where they put the short-arm cast on and then he rolled me out a side door sitting in a wheelchair. I felt embarrassed and ridiculous at the same time. There was a gray ambulance sitting there with "U.S. Navy" printed on the door. I hopped up into the passenger seat. The driver was a third class pharmacist mate named Dave. We went out the main gate with the red light turning on top of the ambulance. We lit up and yakked all the way. It was great fun going around other vehicles and straight through red lights and stop signs, especially with the patient sitting up in the front seat, laughing and smoking with the driver. Dave took me right up to the emergency room doors. As I went through the door, the mediciny- clean smell all hospitals seem to have hit me. I handed my file and the large envelope with the x-ray picture in it to a sailor seated at another gray metal desk. He glanced at the file and said, "Have a seat until they call your name."

There were several rows of hardwood benches that looked like church pews. They were about half full of sailors and marines. I took a seat in the second row at the very end. My hand started throbbing again and I was growing sleepy. I leaned my head back against the corner of the hard-wood bench andclosed my eyes. Somebody was calling my name, "Knight, Daniel - 542-09-01!" I came up out of the deep and stumbled back up to the desk.

The sailor said, "down the hall, fifth door on your left, Dr. Gunter." I said,

"Thanks." but he was already calling out another name. "Stewart, Robert R.

617-07-06!"

Dr. Gunter clipped one of the x-rays to the front of a lighted area and crossed his arms saying "hmmmm - definitely a break of the fifth metacarpal. I'm calling up to the orthopedic ward and get you a bed. We have to get that hand elevated as soon as possible."

I asked him when I would be able to return to my ship. He shook his head,

"Not sure--You'll be with us a few days." Another sailor with a wheelchair pulled up. I protested. He said, "regulations, buddy", so I set down and away we went. We climbed on an elevator and went up to the fifth floor. He pushed me down the hall and through a door into the orthopedic ward.There were sailors and marines in hospital beds lining both sides. The nurse told my pusher, "fifth bed on the right."

I got out of uniform with his help and crawled in the bed. Everything smelled clean. Real sheets and spreads. I had just gotten settled in when I saw the nurse coming with an aluminum pole on wheels with an aluminum arm sticking out. She said, "I gotta get you elevated right away."
I grinned as a thought went through my head. She caught it.

"What's so funny?"
I said, "Oh nothing"
Then she smiled. She knew what I was thinking. She said "don't be thinking ugly thoughts now."
I said, "What I'm thinking is far from ugly."
I didn't want to push it too far because, after all, she was an officer in the United States Navy. But she just smiled that beautiful smile.

Chapter 42

I was lying there with my arm in a sling and elevated when a corpsman brought me a tray. He raised me up a little and set the tray on a little table he had placed across my lap. There was some kind of meat, mashed potatoes with dark gravy, candied yams and coleslaw with a plastic glass of iced tea. In a little container on the side there was banana pudding. It wasn't bad, not bad at all.

The next morning I was classified as "ambulatory" which meant I could stay in bed until 0800 with my arm elevated and then I could amble around wherever I wanted to go just as long as I was back in my bed and elevated by 2100. Each morning at 0930 I had to see Dr. Gunter to be re-evaluated. They seemed to put a lot of stock in "evaluating" around here.

I had not slept well the first night. The man across from me had cried out in pain all night. I looked over at him now and saw that he was finally asleep. I looked at his feet. They were wrapped in bloody bandages – His toes had metal rods sticking out. I asked a passing corpsman what was wrong with him. He said, we don't know. His toes started curling under and wouldn't straighten back up. The orthopedic surgeon put those damn steel rods in his toes trying to straighten them out."

I said "damn"

The corpsman said, "Yeah."

I climbed out of bed, putting the robe they had furnished over my hospital gown. I headed for the head. I looked a little like a hobo in the mirror. I got in the shower and turned it on very hot. The stall steamed up. I toweled myself dry and put my gown and robe back on. I came out and there were Bill and Suds. They had brought me a set of dress blues, a set of undress blues and a dungaree shirt and bell bottomed trousers. They had also brought me three sets of clean skivvies, my shaving kit and 20 bucks. They looked like angels to me. We had coffee out on the screened in sun deck. There wasn't much news back on the Hawk, other than getting ready for the big voyage. Today was February 16 - Four days to go.

Suds asked me, "You'll be back by then … right?"
I said, "hell, yes."
But I was worried.
After Suds and Bill left, I headed back to the head where I shaved, changed underwear, and struggled into my undress blues, leaving the cuff buttons unbuttoned on my left sleeve so I could pull it over the cast. I was stuffing the dress blues I had been wearing into a large paper bag when something fell out of the jumper pocket. A slip of paper. It was Cindy's phone number. I went out into the passageway and located a pay phone. I dropped in my dime and dialed the number. She answered on the second ring.

She said, "Oh, Daniel, I'm so glad you called. I didn't think you were going to call me."

I told her about my adventures since I had met her in the bowling alley.
She said, "Oh, you poor thing. So you're at Balboa. I know right where that is. Are you allowed visitors?"
I said, "Sure, can you come up here?"

She said, "I'll get Granny's car and be there around seven."

I told her I would meet her in the lobby.
She said, "I miss you."
I said, "I miss you too."
I couldn't believe it. I hung up a happy man.

    I heard my name being paged, telling me to return to my ward. A different nurse was on duty. This one was older and had a nose like Jimmy Durante's. I said, "did you page Daniel Knight? That's me." --She threw her big nose back, "yes, I certainly did. You need to go to Doctor Gunter's office for evaluation." I took off.

Dr. Gunter took my fingers that were protruding from the cast and gently bent them back and forth. "Well, it seems to be healing nicely," he said. I said, "yes sir." He thought for a moment and said, "We'll change that cast tomorrow and get another x-ray." I asked him when I might go back to my ship. He said, "We'll see - I'll see you tomorrow morning."

I said, "aye-aye, sir" and left.

I went down the stairs to the lobby. This is where I would meet Cindy tonight. I went outside through a side door. Concrete steps led down to a geedunk area. There were wrought iron tables and chairs outside the Geedunk. I went in and got a hamburger and a coke and came back outside to eat it. Every table but one had two or three people seated around it. There was an elderly lady seated alone at one of the tables, dabbing at her eyes. She reminded me a little of ma. She had on a ladies hat with a feather sticking up from it like the one ma sometimes wore to church.

I asked, "is it ok if I sit here with you?"

She looked up holding her hand over her eyes to block out the sunlight and get a better look. She said, "Why, of course, young man. Please sit here." She began dabbing her eyes again with the handkerchief. I asked her if there was anything wrong or anything I could help her with. She said, "Oh no, thank you for asking. I received quite a shock here yesterday morning, but

everything's ok now." I asked her what had happened. She told me that her husband had been in a private room on the third floor. She had been with him all night, sleeping in a reclining chair next to him. At 0600 yesterday morning she came down here to the geedunk for fresh air and coffee. She had been gone an hour. When she returned to her husband's room no one was there, including her husband. The bed was made up. New sheets and blankets and pillow. All his flowers were gone. At first she thought she was in the wrong room but she wasn't. She grabbed a corpsman. "Where is my husband?" The corpsman told her,"Oh, he passed away about an hour ago. His body is down in the morgue." She dabbed at her eyes. "I ran down the hall bawling and ran right into my husband's doctor. He asked what was wrong. I thought he had lost his mind asking me such a question. She told the doctor 'My God, my husband has died." The doctor, she said, was astounded. The doctor told her that her husband was very much alive. He told her he had moved him to a better private room on the fourth floor and thought she had been told. "I fainted dead away right there in the hall. They put me in a bed and stuck an IV needle in my arm." She told me that when she started to feel better they put her in a wheelchair and rolled her to her husband's room. He was propped up eating Jell-O. She said, "My emotions are still on a roller-coaster and that's why I'm still tearing up a little."
I said, "you have every right to tear up. That's awful, what they did." I asked her what happened to the corpsman who had told her that. She smiled a little, "he's in deep doo-doo."

She had told me her husband was a retired rear admiral, so I knew the corpsman's head would roll and probably the doctor's too.

I showered and shaved and changed uniforms. At 6 p.m. I was seated in the hospital lobby thumbing through an old issue of "Stars And Stripes". At 6:45 p.m. Cindy came through the revolving doors like an angel coming through a cloud. God, she looked good. I stood up. She spotted me and headed my way. Every sailor in the lobby was staring at her wide-eyed. A wolf-whistle came from somewhere. I was proud that I was the one she was walking toward. I said "hi, stranger". She slapped at my arm.

"Hey, I'm no stranger."

I said, "Let's go for a walk".

She grinned, "I'm with you."

Cindy took my arm and we went out a side door. The sun was setting, giving a golden aura to everything, especially Cindy's hair. We went to the geedunk and found it still open. We each had a burger and a Grapico soda. We split a plate of French fries and talked. She wanted to take acting lessons and get a real screen test. She showed me her card where she had already joined the Screen Actors Guild. Cindy had actually been in a movie called "Flower Drum Song".

"It was a bit part," she said. She didn't have any lines. She was just a young woman walking down a street in San Francisco. She smiled remembering it all. "It lasted about five seconds, but you can plainly see me. And best of all, it didn't get cut and they paid me a hundred bucks."

I was duly impressed and said so. But, inside, I was getting a sinking feeling. If she really started acting in films that would be the end of me in her life. But I didn't say anything.

I hit the highlights of my life so far. Nothing much exciting there. But she was fascinated by it all—Moving from Alabama to Ohio and then Indiana. She said, "Alabama sounds strange and far away." I said, "Well it is far away and it's been known to be a little strange too." She laughed and squeezed my hand.

Some guy was sweeping the floor. We left. Outside it was completely dark but there were a billion stars twinkling. There was a chill in the air. I put my arm around her shoulders. As we strolled along, I kissed her cheek. We were somewhere in back of the hospital. We passed a huge brick smoke stack. Toward the bottom you could see flames leaping between cracks in the bricks. Cindy said, "What in the world is that for?"

I told her, "that's where they incinerate the body parts they hack off."
She glared at me, "are you serious?"
I grinned, "no, I just made it up."
She hit me in the chest, saying, "Oh, you!"
We both laughed but for all I knew that might have been what it was used for. We were getting further from the hospital into a field of grass that was dimly lit. Cindy tugged on my arm. "Let's sit a while." She pulled me to the ground with my arm still around her. We kissed, long and deep. I felt her tongue dart into my mouth. Jesus! This girl tasted good! I began kissing every spot on her face. We fumbled with each other's clothes. She was doing her best to get the thirteen buttons on the front of my uniform trousers unbuttoned. I helped her with it. I felt like a space traveler. I was floating through galaxies and planets were blowing up all around me. When it was over we lay holding each other with our bodies pressed together. We were both damp with perspiration. I held her close until our breathing calmed down.

As we walked back toward the hospital I said, " I really want to see your dreams come true but if you become an actress in movies, I'm afraid

I'll lose you." Cindy stopped and pulled me close and kissed me long and hard. "You'll never lose me," she said— " never."

When we got to her car, I told her my ship was getting underway on the 20th and I didn't know when we would be back. She looked away for a few seconds. When she looked back, there were tears in her eyes. "Well, I can tell you this, I'll be right here waiting for you and I'll write you every day. Just come back to me." --I said, "you can rest easy on that." After we kissed again, I said, "I love you."

She held me tighter. "I love you too, so very much."
As she pulled away the night was getting colder. I watched her until her grandmother's car went out of sight.

Chapter 43

At 0800 I was seated in Dr. Gunter's office. He was turning my hand this way and that. He told me, "it's still healing beautifully but you've got a ways to go!"

I said, "Well, Sir, I need to be getting on back to my ship."
Dr. Gunter shook his head and smiled. " I have never seen a sailor want to get back to duty as much as you do. Most of the men like it here. No duty, just lie around and rest; the life of Riley, really."
I said, "Yes, Sir, but my ship is getting underway soon and I need to be getting back."
Dr. Gunter said, "We'll take another look tomorrow morning, but right now I want you to go to the cast room and get this one cut off and a new one put on and then I want you to stay in your bed with it elevated for the rest of the day. I see you running all over this place."
I said, "aye-aye, sir."

This time I walked to the cast room. The smell of plaster of Paris or whatever it was, was strong. It wasn't an unpleasant smell. It sorta reminded me of the smell of the wallpaper paste the men had used at our house in Bayview one time. The corpsman used a small, circular saw to cut through the cast, and pull it away from my arm. My arm and hand were both whiter than the rest of me. The corpsman started slapping new plaster on and in no time I had a new cast. While this was being done, I had been watching several corpsmen hovering over a sailor who appeared to be asleep. They were wrapping gauze around his waist and both legs. I asked my corpsman what that was all about. He said, " they're putting him in what they call a 'full-body cast.'"

I asked him why—"Did he break both legs?"

The corpsman looked over at him. "Nah, he ain't hurt at all. The dumb fucker tried to kill himself by jumping off the stairwell up on the eighth floor. He won't be going anywhere now."

I said, "I guess he won't"

The corpsman shook his head."A lot of 'em go straight from here to the loony bin."

The wheelchair rules had changed again. This time I was wheeled back to my ward. I climbed in bed and put my forearm through the sling hanging from the metal pole. Lunch was roast beef, mashed potatoes with gravy, slaw, stewed carrots and a couple of rolls. There was also a slice of apple pie in a side saucer. The chow was the only thing good about this place.

Around 2130 I went to the restroom. I came out and walked past the nurse's station, headed for the hall pay phone. I didn't make it. The nurse stood up. " Back in bed, big boy!" Her finger was pointing toward my bed.

I said, "Oh, I'm just going to make a quick phone call."

She didn't say anything. She just kept pointing toward my bed. I turned around and headed that way. It was plain I would not be calling Cindy that night.

Dr. Gunter grunted, "Ok son, I'm discharging you this morning. You're going back to your ship. But it's strictly limited duty for six weeks."
I said, "Yes, sir."
He shook his head as if he was still amazed that I would want to leave this glorious place and go back to duty. "Your ship has been notified and they're sending someone for you. Get your gear and wait in the lobby downstairs. And take care of that hand!"
"I will, sir,and thank you."
He shook his head again.I headed for the pay phone.
Cindy answered.
I said, "It's me."
She whispered in a voice so low I could barely hear her, "Oh, Daniel, I can't talk now."
I could hear who I figured was the grandmother yelling in the background. Cindy whispered, "Call me back tonight. I love you."
I said, "I'll try, but ...." I was talking to a dead phone.

I was a little worried but I told myself it was just a spat with her grandmother. Everything would be ok.I felt better. The nurse gave me a laundry bag to put my things in. As I was loading it up I saw a corpsman coming with a wheelchair. I couldn't believe it. He saw the look on my face. "Regulations, buddy."

 I didn't argue. I just said, "of course" and sat down with my laundry bag on my lap. As I was rolled past the nurse's station, she called after me, "Stay out of fights!" Now, how in the hell did she know about that? I was seated in a leather chair close to the front entrance when I saw Suds pulling around in the ship's jeep. Suds told me that in about an hour they were moving the Hawk from its berth next to the pier. They were moving two other LST's in and we would be the third ship out from the dock. This was because we were pulling out the next morning on a short shake down run to check out all

248

machinery. When we came back in tomorrow evening, we would tie up at Broadway Pier. This was the pier most ships tied up to prior to an extended cruise. It was February 17th.

Cindy appeared in a dream and then was gone. The rest of the night was dreamless. The loud speaker over my head was blaring. I buried my head under my pillow. **Chow line open- …. Make all preparations… getting underway!"**

I was able to maneuver pretty good with my cast by now. I grabbed my toilet kit and ambled to the head where I shaved and showered. I climbed into a fresh pair of dungarees and headed up to the chow line. Scrambled eggs that were undercooked, sausage links that were still fighting for their life and burnt toast. It was plain that I was no longer in Balboa Naval Hospital and I was glad. I was home.

I climbed down the ladder to the boiler room. Pat was reseating a valve. He said, "glad you're back, buddy."
He started whistling.
I said, "you sound like you're in a good mood." Pat grinned.
"I am. I'll tell you, Dan, that Jackie has a level head. Just one more reason I love her so much. She made me see reason. After all, I am in the Navy and it's my duty. Like she said, it won't be that long. We'll be gone probably less than a year and then I'll be getting out and we have a long time to be together.

I said, "that's good, Pat."

The "shakedown" run lasted longer than we thought it would. All machinery worked fine except #1 auxiliary engine. The lights kept blinking off and on. We stayed out until the problem was located and repaired.We didn't pull into Broadway Pier until 2330. Then we were up half the night hooking up for shore services and running hoses for fresh water. I helped the best I could with one hand. In my rack I feel into a deep sleep with no dreams about anyone. The next morning, right after muster, I hit the pier looking for a pay phone. I found four under a shed. I dropped a dime in one and dialed Cindy's number. The grandmother answered. I said as nicely as possible, "this is Daniel, could I speak with Cindy, please?" She answered. "Cindy ain't here. I sent her packing. She's on her way back to Colorado."

I stammered something. She went on.

"That gal ain't nothing but trouble and I'm too damn old for it. If you've got any sense you'll be glad to be well rid of her. Sent 'er back to her mama and her no-good husband. Put her on a Greyhound yesterday. She oughta be getting there about now!"

I stammered out, "What ?.... husband?"--I got a dial tone. The old woman was gone. I put the receiver back in its cradle and stared at it a couple of seconds. The wind off the water picked up a little and was blowing a piece of paper across the pier. There appeared to be handwriting on the paper. I absently wondered why a letter would be blowing around on a dock. I watched it until it went over the side into the bay. There were pieces of gravel around the pay phones. One was big enough to kick. I kicked it all the way back to the Hawk.

Back at the ship there was a flurry of activity. Working parties were moving up and down the gangplank bringing on stores. Vegetables, meat, coffee, ice cream. The captain was topside looking down on it all. He saw me. I gave him a salute. He saluted me back and turned and left.

Chapter 44

We had been steaming for 8 days. On the morning of the 9th day someone shouted down the boiler room shaft that Diamond Head was coming up on starboard. Pat and I hustled top side. There it was. Flying fish were flying out of the water and around the ship as if welcoming us to Hawaii. Doc spoiled the magic by saying, "Well, they're really not 'flying fish'. They're just great jumpers." I still preferred to think of them as 'flying'. The water was bluish green and looked great. I didn't see any rainbow-colored oil streaks floating by as you did off the coast of California. We started down the long channel that led to Pearl Harbor Naval Base. Both sides of the channel were flush with green. Palm trees, vines and undergrowth. We passed two other naval vessels going the other way, headed out to the sea. I wondered where they were going. The bay opened up as we entered the Naval Base. To port a flag pole was jutting high out of the water with the United States flag waving at the top. As we started past, everybody topside saluted and held it until we had passed. The USS Arizona was down there with 1800 men still aboard her. She had been sunk when the Japanese had attacked Pearl Harbor in 1941. Passing close by her gave you a feeling of pride mixed with sadness. Somebody said they were going to start building a permanent monument over the site someday. We tied up to our assigned dock. On the other side of the concrete dock a British destroyer was tied up. Somebody said, "that's a sleek looking son-of-a-bitch." It looked to be brand new, her big guns glistening in the sunlight. A Quartermaster named Bell said, "makes us sorta look old and used-up." Someone else spoke up, "stow that shit, the old Hawk can outdo that pile of junk anyday. The British couldn't fight their way out of a used condom anyway."

The dock offered full services. In a couple of hours we were able to shut down all machinery. No liberty was granted for anyone . After nine days at sea maintenance checks had to be made. I was glad I would be sleeping in my rack tonight without hearing the auxiliary engines whining below me. As night came it seemed to get hotter and more humid. The little berthing fans were giving it their all but not having much luck. Several of us went back up topside for some fresh air. We couldn't believe it. They had placed powerful spotlights along the dock and had them shining up against the British destroyer. Bill said "what the fuck?" Suds said, "crazy bastards". A guy named Bobbie Whitman spoke up, "those bastards must think it's a fucking Christmas tree!"

Suds shook his head, "what a target that would make if somebody made a bomb run on us tonight."

The next evening, Bill and Suds and me hit the gangplank with our liberty cards. Outside the main gate taxis lined the street. We jumped in one. The driver charged us fifty cents each to take us to Honolulu. As beautiful as Diamond Head was as we had approached Oahu the day before, Hotel Street in Honolulu was that ugly. The smell of fish, stale beer, vomit, and rotten fruit hung in the air. Servicemen were everywhere. Soldiers, sailors, marines and airmen out of Hickam crowded the street. Added to that were servicemen from just about every country in the world.

We ducked into a darkened beer joint called **"ZUMA'S".** We groped around in the dark until we finally made it to the bar. We ordered three beers. We were shocked. Fifty cents each! Suds said, "What the hell is this, the fucking 'Shangri-La'?" I knew we wouldn't be in this dump long at those prices. Suds had been here before. He told us that in 1957 the beer here had been a quarter just as it was in California. Of course Hawaii had not been a state at that time. Even now it had only been a state 7 or 8 months. An older

252

civilian seated on the stool beside Suds said, "you boys can drink out on the beach at fancy places for the same price - fifty cents a beer." Suds asked him why he wasn't out there.

"Cause I like the atmosphere here better."

We had two more beers each and left.

Walking back up Hotel Street there was a commotion up an alley. A crowd was gathering. We took off up that way to see what was going on. It was a fight. A sailor and a marine, both in uniform, were going at it tooth and nail. Each man's face was bloody and so was the front of their uniforms. Neither man was giving an inch. We watched the blows being passed a while when Suds said, "let's get the hell out of here before the HASP shows up."

I said "What the hell is the HASP?"

Suds said, "It's the Hawaiian Armed Services Police. Made up of mean-ass sailors and marines. It's their permanent duty. Even the local police don't fuck with 'em. They get their hooks into you, it's big trouble."

Bill said, "Hell, we're not doing anything."--
Suds said, "You don't have to be doing anything."

Back on Hotel Street we grabbed a bus just pulling up. We rode it back to the main gate. Hawaii, so far, had been a disappointment. It rained every day. An hour after it stopped it was as if it had never rained at all. The hot sun quickly dried everything up.

A couple of nights after our Hotel Street excursion, we three musketeers took off again. This time we went out to Waikiki Beach. We ended up in a hotel bar called the "Outrigger Reef On The Beach". As the old man had said, beer was fifty cents a bottle, same as on Hotel Street. The bar was going all out to look authentic with a Hawaiian out-rigger canoe propped against one wall and a fake fishing net spread out on the wall above it. A stuffed Marlin was mounted on the wall behind the bar. We all agreed that it too was probably a fake. Our table had a candle burning in a short red vase that had a net wrapped around it. The bartender set a bowl of what looked like small pieces of some kind of meat on our table. We each ate a couple. Suds asked the barman what it was. "It's octopus", he said. "It's good for you." It was a little stringy but tasty. There weren't many sailors in the bar but there were a dozen or more women. Three and four to a table. Several smiled in our direction. Bill commented on it. I said "Yeah, but I don't see any under 50 years old or 200 pounds."

"Yeah, I noticed that", Bill said.

Suds filled us in on the scoop. "They're retired school teachers for the most part. They come over here to get their ashes hauled by a serviceman and then they go back stateside acting prim and proper again. This summer, when school lets out, younger teachers will be headed this way looking for the same thing. Bill smiled, "Well, at least we've got that to look forward to."

Suds shook his head. "We'll be long gone before then."

This led to a discussion of when we were going to pick up these military advisors to take them wherever we were going to take them. Suds was the senior lead petty officer in our division and he had heard nothing. "Shit, even Mr. Lingan doesn't know what's going on. Hell, I doubt the old man knows."

Back on the Hawk, Pat had been ashore too. He was proudly showing a set of salt and pepper shakers he had bought for Jackie. It seemed she collected them.

"She's got 'em from all over the world", Pat said.

These were shaped like hula girls and had leis around their necks.

That night Bill and I sat in the mess hall and made plans for Australia. He said we were going to have to stop blowing our paychecks on beer and chasing women. I agreed. When we got back stateside we would open up a joint savings account at the bank on base. They could automatically pull out a percentage of our pay each month. Bill loved to talk about the plan and I loved to hear it.

"I'll get out a couple of months before you. I'll get a cheap pad up in Long Beach. When you get out, we'll head for San Francisco. Catch a tramp steamer for Sydney. If we agree to work in their boiler room we might even get free passage!"

I said, "sounds good to me."

Two soldiers of fortunes headed for adventure. We talked on into the night. When I finally climbed into my rack I lay awake and thought about things. Cindy? Would I ever hear from her again? I figured I wouldn't. I thought about my family. It would soon be two years since I last saw them. I usually received a couple of letters a month. Usually they were from Marty. Sometimes my daddy would stick a note inside telling me to take care of myself. And sometimes my mother would write a short letter usually talking about Mama Davis illnesses. Often, she would bring up the subject of my cousin who, she would remind me, was also in the Navy in California and she couldn't understand why I had made no effort to find him. I always got a chuckle out of that one. I was thinking about some of my old buddies back in Hammond and wondering what they were doing when sleep finally overtook me.

Chapter 45

Mr. Lingan mustered engineering in after-steering to give us the dope. We would not be picking up the military advisers here in Hawaii. They had been flown to the Philippine Islands for further training. We would be departing Pearl Harbor in two days and steaming to Subic Bay, Philippines. We would load these advisers on there and proceed to Laos.

Suds, Bill and I had liberty that evening. We figured we would hit Waikiki one more time. We had heard Tempest Storm would be appearing at a club on Kapiolani Boulevard called "Forbidden City". Tempest was a world famous strip tease artist. We had all seen her pictures in various magazines. Now we wanted to see her in person. We caught a taxi to the club where we each had to pay a three dollar cover charge to get in. Inside, a bottle of beer was a dollar. But we considered it was worth it to see Tempest.

A young woman opened the show. She appeared to be Oriental and very beautiful. She sang several "show-songs" really belting out, **"There's No Business Like Show Business"** and **"The Man That Got Away"**. After she finished to a lot of applause and whistling there was an intermission. Then the house lights dimmed and a spotlight began reflecting different colors on the curtain. The band started playing "Stormy Weather" as the curtain slowly opened … and there was Tempest. Her hair was long and red although the colored lights made it sometimes appear to change shades. She began slowly gyrating to the music, wearing a sequined slinky black dress. She danced and whirled - She would turn her back to the audience and reach behind her and pull the zipper half way down and smile and zip it back up. Finally the tight dress fell off. There was another black garment under it. She danced around in that a while doing the zipper thing. Finally that fell off and she was in what I guess they call a G-string. Then the bra finally came off. Her nipples were covered with little cones with tassels hanging from them. She bent over forward with her hands on her thighs and began slinging her breasts in a circle, causing the tassels to whirl like little propellers. The crowd went wild. A lot of applause and wolf whistles. We three looked at each other. I don't know what we had expected. I guess we thought she would strip down bare-ass naked. It was obvious by now that this was not going to happen. After the whirling tassels act, Tempest went behind a screen and came out wearing short-shorts, a tuxedo coat, a top hat and carrying a cane. She strutted a while and the tuxedo coat came off. Beneath was a black blouse that had straps. She would pull a strap off her shoulder, smile, and pull it back up. Bill said, "let's get the hell out of here."

Suds said, "I'm already gone in my mind!"

We got up and left. Ambling down Kapiolioni we talked about how good-looking Tempest was and what a great body, but the show itself wasn't much to write home about. Three blocks down, there was a movie theatre called "The Aloha". The next showing of the movie was starting in ten minutes. We each got ourselves a bag of popcorn and found seats about half-way down. We watched, "The Man Who Shot Liberty Valance" with John Wayne, Jimmy Stewart and Lee Marvin. It was a great Western.

257

Chapter 46

Officer of the deck's log entry

May 10th 1962

00-04 Anchored in Subic Bay Harbor in 80 feet of water - coral and sand bottom with 50 fathoms of chain to the bow anchor. Ships present include various units of the Pacific Fleet. Conditions of readiness V

Lt. R. Bowen

We dropped anchor in Subic Bay on April 6th. We had now been here over a month. But no advisers had come aboard and no word had come down from on high. Rumors were flying but most of us paid it no mind. It was just Navy scuttlebutt. One yeoman had told everyone that we were going back to Pearl. We all laughed at that. There were no dock services available to us so all machinery was running but the diesels. Pat and I had the evaporators running around the clock, pumping salt water in, desalinizing it and pumping it on to the fresh water tanks making sure they stayed topped off. Subic Bay was much better liberty than Honolulu. For one thing, the people were a lot friendlier and the women were better looking. We had found us a place called the "Tennessee Bar and Grill" to hang out at in Olongapo City. Long neck bottles of beer were a quarter and there was country music on the juke box. One night disaster struck. The bar was packed. Cigarette smoke was hanging like a cloud. There was loud talk and laughter. Marty Robbins was coming from the juke box, *"Blacker than night were the eyes of Felina, Wicked and evil while casting a spell."*

Down at the end of the long bar, facing us, sat a man and woman in intimate conversation while smooching it up. The woman was in her twenties and good-looking. Bill said, "looks like he's gonna get lucky tonight."

I said, "looks like, alright" and turned to look at them again. I was just in time to see the woman smash a beer bottle on the side of the man's head. She gave it everything she had. The loud thud was sickening. He went down hard, out of sight. Then he emerged from behind the bar on his hands and knees. He made it to the juke box and fell flat. He rolled over on his back and was still. Blood was trickling from his head. His eyes were wide open. Bill had just gotten out, "What the fuck?" when the woman moved to the stool beside me. "What ship you guys on?" I turned to Bill and said, "let's go", but Bill was already up.The laughter and merriment had not died down at all. It was as if nobody had seen it but us. Someone must have finally noticed because three blocks up the street we heard a siren headed that way. We went into a USO canteen and drank coffee while we debated whether or not the man was dead. We decided he was.

Officer Of The Deck's Log Entry

July 12, 1962

04-08 Anchored as before 0430 c/c to 035 0600 c/c to 215 – 0730--
Mustered crew at quarters.

Absentees: None

Lt. J.G. Higgins

Still lying at anchor the long hot days and nights seemed to be getting longer and hotter. Most of the crew slept in the gun tubs wearing just their skivvies. Pat and I took turns sleeping in the boiler room under one of the blower ducts. It blew warm air but at least it was air. Salt-pill dispensers were placed throughout the ship to replace the salt our bodies sweated out. Morale was low. Arguments that many times led to fist fights were a daily occurrence. Our mail was several weeks old by the time it got to us. Several of the men received "Dear John" letters from wives or girlfriends who had found someone else. The days wore on with no word. The captain appointed Mr. Lingan "morale officer". We all got a chuckle out of that. But he went at it in earnest. He even created a recreation committee that I was drafted into. In an old bos'un locker that hadn't been opened in years, we found baseballs, softballs, baseball gloves, footballs, basketballs, and nets. We got the nets up and they proved to be very popular with the crew. You could hear basketballs being dribbled on the steel deck late into the night. We also found several pairs of boxing gloves. Mr. Lingan wanted to set up some "smokers" immediately. "Let'em burn off some of that pent up anger," he said.

A makeshift ring was set up. An old chief radioman by the name of Masters said he would do the refereeing. Everybody on the recreationcommittee was expected to participate. Each fight would be for 3 rounds and each round would be three minutes long. It turned out to be even more popular than basketball. Tempers flared up a couple of times but mostly it was just good sport.

My turn with the gloves came on the third night of the smoker. The second fight of the night. They put me in with a guy named Tommy Wingo, a gunner's mate. I had heard that Tommy had boxed some before the service. We were about the same height and weight. I pretty much held my own till half-way through the second round when I saw a bright, white star flash in front of my left eye and the deck flew up to meet me. Tommy was the first one over to see if I was OK.

I said, "Did you get the license number of that truck that hit me?"

Tommy laughed and said, "he's okay."

We headed to the mess hall for coffee.

Chapter 47

The Word Comes Down

The captain had an announcement to make. All hands not on watch were mustered topside. The captain paced back and forth a little before speaking. "Men, we will not be picking up advisers. The Washington County will handle that job. We have been assigned a much more important task. Tomorrow morning at 0530 we will get underway for Pearl Harbor. There, some of you will be trained in radiation detection and more. Special equipment will be brought aboard the Hawk. After this is completed, we will steam to what is termed "The Johnston-Christmas Island Danger Area" to join Operation Dominic, where we will participate in nuclear testing. I cannot express enough how important these tests are to the security of our country. As always, I expect each man to do his job to the best of his ability." We went to attention and saluted. The captain returned the salute and went back to his cabin.

Nineteen days later we steamed back into Pearl Harbor. We tied up again across from the British destroyer with the floodlights hitting it from the dock. It appeared to never have moved since the first time we saw it.

All liberty was cancelled the first evening for machinery maintenance and for deck force to use 4-inch hoses to spray down the main deck to get rid of standing salt water. The radio operators in operations were busy doing whatever it was they did. Quartermasters were running around with charts folded under their arms. The guys up in the crypto room seemed unusually busy with their secret doings. The crypto room was off limits to everyone but the captain and the men who worked there. They were a close-knit, closed-mouth bunch. They looked at you as if they were saying, "We know things you don't and you never will." They only buddied with each other.

I had stumbled into crypto a couple of times. Nothing was said because a guy I had went to boot camp with worked in there. But you could tell the others didn't like me being in there at all. I got some mean stares. It was always bathed in a reddish/green light. There were big round monitors that had hands sweeping in circles. I knew these were sonar and radar equipment but I really had no idea how to read them. And a teletype was constantly clicking away as messages poured in from wherever-- I had no idea. Most of it was in code. I could not have told anyone what in hell was going on in there if they had put a gun to my head. My boot camp buddy was Spence Dubois from Louisiana. Spence was quiet and tight-lipped in boot camp, so I guess he was cut out to work crypto.The next night, Suds, Bill and I hit the beach.

We stopped at a little bar out on Waikiki that advertised "Live Entertainment". We went in. The live entertainment was a long-haired girl sitting on a stool, picking a guitar and singing folk songs. She wasn't very good but she was giving it her all.We found us a table over in a corner and ordered draft beer.We discussed the upcoming deployment to the Johnston/Christmas Island Danger Zone for these nuclear tests. Suds had known a couple of guys who were on Bikini back in 1958 for tests. One was now dead and one was dying.

"It's not a good thing guys. Not good at all. We will more or less be guinea pigs. I just don't want to be one of the poor guys that has to go topside to take radiation readings after they drop one of those bastards. I want my ass to be deep, deep below decks."

I went to the bar and got us three more drafts.While waiting for them to be pulled, I chatted with the folk singer. Her name was LuAnn and she was from Columbus, Ohio. She played these gigs (as she called them) while attending the University of Hawaii. When I asked her why she didn't stay in Columbus and go to Ohio State she stared at me as if I had gone daft. I grabbed our beers and headed back to the table. When I arrived the conversation had changed. Bill and Suds were in a discussion about poetry. Bill was talking about a man named Shelley, a name I vaguely remembered from high school literature class. Suds said Shelley had a fascination with death. "Just read his 'Queen Mab' and you'll see what I mean." --Bill said he had and it was one of his favorites. Bill said "death has a beauty of its own and, in fact, may be the most beautiful part of life."

I was a little surprised when Suds said, "I've heard you write a little poetry" and Bill said, "I dabble at it. It's not very good but I enjoy it."

They were thinking out of my league so I just sat there sipping my beer. Bill sensed this and said, "Do you have a favorite poet, Dan?" I said, "Well, I sorta' like that Poe guy, I guess, and the poem where he looks for El Dorado. I guess that's about it." Suds sorta' smiled as if I had said I preferred comic books to John Steinbeck. Bill picked up on that and quickly said, "Poe has always been under-appreciated. He was actually an extremely profound writer." I didn't know where Bill was getting words like "profound" from, but I was glad to see it wipe the smirk off Suds' face.

There wasn't much action going on in the little bar and we didn't care. We were all three worn out and ready to go hit our racks early. Lu Ann was demolishing "Red River Valley" as we went out the door.

September 2, 1962

At muster the next morning it was announced that three men had been chosen to attend radiology school for five days. These men were:

First Class Electrician's Mate, Howard Sayers

Second Class Boiler Technician, Patrick Bertella

Third Class Engineman, William Beylor

This would be the team who would be taking radiation readings topside after a nuclear detonation. I was inwardly glad that I had not been picked for this duty but didn't much like the fact that the others had been. Sayers was an African-American from Kansas and would be senior man on the team. He was a quiet guy who knew his job as an electrician's mate well. Mr. Lingan later confided to his engineering department that no one from any other departments had been assigned because the powers that be expressly wanted engineers. These classes would begin on Tuesday, September 4th and continue through Saturday September 8th. The Hawk would steam out of Pearl Harbor on Monday morning, September 10.

The next evening, out mail finally caught up with us. We all gathered in the mess hall as names were called out. "Burns, Jenkins,Conroy"---- Letters were passed from one man back to another until it reached the person it was meant for. I had three letters. One from Ma, one from Marty, and one that was thick, but with no return name in the corner, just an address I didn't recognize. I noticed that Pat had grabbed a letter that he seemed thrilled to get. He took off down the boiler room ladder with it. I went up on the fantail, lit a cigarette and looked at my mystery letter again. hen it hit me whose hand-writing it was. Rita's! A little thrill surged through me as I tore it open.

The stationary smelled like lavender. I began reading. She still loved me. She would always love me. She had been so stupid. Her mother just wants what would make her daughter happy and that would be me. We could marry and all I would have to do would be to take instructions on raising any children as Catholics. We would be so happy. The letter went on. I stopped and tried to picture Rita in my mind. I looked out at the gathering dusk and tried to see her face. I couldn't. I stood there a minute and then I let the wind carry the sheets from my hand and over the side. I tossed the envelope over with them.

The last I saw of the letter was a couple of sheets washed up against a barnacle covered pylon. I had not even read the last sheet.

Reveille was sounded at 0530. Sleepy men were climbing into their shower shoes, grabbing their shaving kids and stumbling toward the head. I noticed that Pat was already up and gone. Many times he had gotten up before reveille. He was probably already in the mess hall drinking coffee. A couple of the guys were carrying on some horseplay, slapping each other in the ass with wet towels. I found an open sink where I shaved before hitting the shower.

Bill and I hit the chow line together. Scrambled eggs, toast and bacon. The eggs were awful. They tasted like someone had put mint in them. Bill said, "Where's Pat?"

"I don't know - I thought he would be in here."
"Probably down in the boiler room."
I said, "probably."

At 0730 we mustered topside. After he had called the roll for the engineering department, Suds turned to Mr. Lingan, saluted, and said, "all present and accounted for but one, sir."

The one missing was Pat. We stood around after we had been dismissed. Mr. Lingan came over and asked me about Pat. I said, "I don't know, sir, he was here yesterday for mail call. That was the last time I saw him." There were agreeing murmurs from the other men. It seems that was the last time anyone had seen him. Mr. Lingan said, "Well, he's officially AWOL as of 0730 this morning. I'll cover for him the best I can, but he better have his ass back aboard in the next couple of hours. In the meantime, we'll have a team search the ship."

I went down into the boiler room. A fireman apprentice by the name of Hooks was taking readings on the boiler. I told him I would handle it and sent him over to the engine room to work. I set in my metal chair and thought about it all. It didn't make sense. Pat seemed happy at mail call, grinning when they handed him a letter from who, I figured, must have been Jackie. Jackie …. I started thinking about Jackie. Boy, she was a looker… and what a personality. She was what they called a "cool customer." And she truly loved Pat, but yet …yet. What the hell was in that letter anyway?

My thoughts were interrupted when the messenger of the watch came down the ladder to inform me that Mr. Lingan wanted to see me in his stateroom. Up I went.

I tapped on Mr. Lingan's door and stepped inside. A storekeeper by the name of Ambruzzi was there. Ambruzzi was from Brooklyn like Pat. Nodding toward him, Mr. Lingan said, "he tells me Pat received some bad news in the mail. His wife is divorcing him. Ambruzzi here found him sitting in a store room late last night in pretty bad shape. Did you know anything about that Dan?"

I said, "no, sir, I thought they were making big plans for the future. I thought everything was fine."

Mr. Lingan nodded and told Ambruzzi that would be all. After he left, Mr. Lingan said, "Well, he's definitely jumped ship. It's no longer in my hands. The HASP has been notified. It's official now. He's AWOL."

I said, "how did he get off the ship?"
He shook his head. "We don't know. We're looking into that next. All of his personal things are still in his locker."
I nodded. Mr. Lingan looked at a sheet of paper on his desk. "By the way, Dan, you're now on the radiology team."
Somehow, I knew that was coming.
I said, "Yes, sir."

There were over 80 men in the radiology class. Larger ships had as many as a dozen men on their radiology teams. The Hawk was small so she rated just three. The class was taught by a chief warrant officer who claimed to have a degree in physics. We were each issued a numbered Mueller-Geiger counter that we had to sign for. Each man would be responsible for the care and maintenance of his counter until the end of the tests when they would be turned in.

We were instructed in calibrating the instruments to take radiation readings. These readings would be read as roentgens. We also learned about ionizing radiation and its "half-life". We learned about alpha and beta particles and gamma rays. We were trained in "wash down" procedures. By the end of the five days of classes not one man knew what in hell he was doing.

Chapter 48

There seemed to be an unnatural stillness about the base as the Hawk steamed slowly up the channel headed for the open sea. It was still dark with a faint light to the east. No other vessels were moving in either direction. I was alone on the fantail with my thoughts. Pat had not been found. I wondered if he had caught one of those small planes and hopped to another island in the chain. Some of the islands in the Hawaiian chain were pretty remote. One was even said to be a leper colony. Then I wondered if Pat was even alive. If he was how would he live? I had heard the stories in the Philippines of Japanese soldiers who had recently been discovered by hikers and picnickers, hiding out in remote areas, believing the war was still going. Some refused to believe that Japan had surrendered. All of them were sent safely back to Japan. Pat was smart and resourceful, I knew that. But what he had done was not too smart. Had Jackie found someone else? The idea went through my head that maybe I would go see her. I was immediately ashamed of the thoughts that conjured up. I threw my Chesterfield over the side and headed below decks.

Chapter 49

Officer Of The Deck Log Entry

September 12, 1962

20-24 steaming as before. 2012 C/C to 195.

2013 C/S to10.3 kts. 2115 C/C to 125. C/S to 7.5 kts. 2143 observed shooting star bearing 140, angle 30, traveling northeast to southwest. 2147 set material condition Zebra. 2201 commenced maneuvering to maintain station.   2215 set course 015. observed nuclear air-burst range 100 Mi. bearing 090. 2234 set condition Yoke.

R.A. Emmets *ENS. USN*

The farther we steamed southwest the more reality seemed to become suspended. Even the sea looked different. Darker. No phosphorus streaks brightened the wake behind the Hawk. Stars were becoming rare. It was impossible to tell where the sky ended and the sea started. There was no horizon. A black dome seemed to have been placed over the sea where the Hawk was steaming. Even breathing was difficult. On our third night of steaming, it seemed that every man not on watch was topside. The old salts who had been at sea for years had bewildered looks on their faces. Old Doc, who had sailed on all seven seas shook his head. "These latitudes are not meant for men. This is Satan's playground. Satan and his demons."

Just as Doc finished his sentence the southern sky flashed a bright white light. Brighter than any sun. Then it turned a greenish hue and then it was gone. Somebody said, "What in God's Name?" Doc said, "That was a nuclear air burst. And we haven't even reached our destination yet, where we're going to see the bastards up close for real." A light rain started to fall. We all headed below decks.

Chapter 50

We anchored 1000 yards out from the breakwall that had been built around Johnston Island which was really not an island, but an atoll. And a small atoll, at that. Standing on the main deck you could see the sea on the other side. There was a short runway running the length of the atoll. Men and equipment were moving about. We watched a 4 - engine cargo plane coming in on final. You could hear him cut back on the engines while he was still skimming the water's surface. The nose- wheel touched down just where the runway met the water. The pilot knew it was a short runway and he was good. We could hear his brakes squeal as he brought the plane to a stop 30 yards before the pavement ran out.

Somebody said, "Jesus Christ!"

Mr. Lingan called the engineers together. We were all issued a dosimeter--a small, black round object that would hang from a cord around our necks. We were told these would be "read" from time to time to detect how many roentgens we were being exposed to. They never were. The "uniform of the day" would be t-shirts and dungaree pants because of the heat. Then he hit us with, "no ship's personnel from the Philippines or Canada will be allowed to go ashore on Johnston Island for the duration of the time we are here."

None of us liked that at all. There was grumbling through the ranks. Mr. Lingan held up his hand to quiet us. "This is not from the Captain.

These orders are from on high. The Captain has already made a formal complaint to the Navy Department."
We doubted that. But maybe he had.

Chapter 51

Bill, Howard Sayers and I were seated on the deck just inside the port hatch. We were all three wearing asbestos fire-fighting suits. Sweat was pouring from our bodies inside the suits. The only part not made of asbestos was the plexiglass in front of our eyes to see through. Howard muttered something about us looking like creatures from a B-grade science fiction movie. My body was itching. My face was itching. There was no way to scratch. Howard said he was having trouble breathing. We each were holding our Mueller-Geiger counters. Johnston Island was radioing messages that were being piped throughout the ship. One phrase was repeated over and over.

"APRIL WEATHER - APRIL WEATHER - APRIL WEATHER".

We had no idea what it meant.

We knew a B-52 had left Hickam headed our way with a payload. It would be a surface drop of a multi-megaton nuclear bomb. It would be detonated at a certain altitude for the "rainbow effect".

These drops were designated "air-bursts". We had no idea where the Hawk's position would be in relation to this drop. The damage control teams were seated in the mess hall below us. The rest of the crew were at their General Quarters stations. This drop was designated **"Shot Lighting"**. We had no idea what the fuck that meant either. The countdown was blared throughout the ship.

"D - MINUS TEN MINUTES" We three looked at each other. Howard shrugged - that was all he knew to do.

"D -MINUS TWENTY SECONDS …
…19…18…17…16…15….14…13…
12…11…10…9…8…7…6…5…4…3…2…1"

The overhead lights blinked off and on. I could hear the engines changing speeds trying to maintain some sort of station. The engines shut down. There was silence. The speakers blared. ***"Brace for base surge."*** We had been warned about the "base surge". We were told that when a bomb detonated a mighty wave would emanate in a circle from surface zero, and would strike the ship with "significant force". The base surge countdown began.

"Ten seconds to base surge - 9…8…7…6…5…4…3…2…1…"

It was like a giant's hand had slapped the side of the Hawk. I was thrown against the bulkhead behind me. Bill's head slammed into the bulkhead behind him. Howard hung on to a rung to keep from being thrown down the ladder to the next deck. The Hawk took a 20 degree list to starboard and then bobbed back up on an even keel. On the deck under us we could hear the damage control parties.

"What the fuck!"

"Mary, Mother of God."

The ship's speakers crackled, **"damage control teams to port and starboard shaft alleys for damage inspection. Report to CIC.--- Radiology team lay topside."**

That was us. We got the hatch undogged and stepped outside. The heat was worse than inside. Daylight was just breaking. The sky on the southern horizon was unnaturally white with a greenish hue. It was like being on another planet, looking at an alien sky. We headed out in different directions. I went midships on the starboard side, working my way forward. I slowly ran the counter's probe wand over the railing. The meter fluctuated between 30 and 40 roentgens. I ran it over a hose rack and it hit 50 roentgens as the clicks per minute increased. These were pretty much the average readings I received over my area. I dutifully logged in locations and the readings. The radiology team met back at the port hatch thirty minutes later. Howard's reading had been about the same as mine. So were Bill's, with the exception of the forward gun mount where his needle had pegged. We noticed the greenish hue in the sky had become larger. Then the rain came. We headed below decks, stripped down and hit the showers. Doc stationed himself outside the shower stalls with his own Geiger counter. I had my shower running with only cold water. It felt good. I let it hit me full in the face for a long time, trying to get rid of the stink of the damned asbestos suit, before I started soaping down. Howard came out first. He stood with his arms out and legs spread while Doc ran the wand over him. There was no clicking from the Geiger counter. I came out next and assumed the position. Doc pronounced me "clean". Bill came out. There was some clicking under his right armpit. He went back into the shower. When he came back out, the clicking had stopped. Bill was clean.

Mr. Lingan came in and talked with us while we were getting dressed. He looked at our logs and whistled when he saw the high readings Bill had picked up in the forward gun mount. He said, "I need to get these up to the captain right away" and took off with the log sheets.

That night Bill and I sauntered into the mess hall at a little before 2000 hours to get a good seat for the movie. I asked the electrician's mate setting up the projector the name of the movie. He said, "It's called, 'Flower Drum Song', it's a good movie." He started to add something else but I cut him off.

"That's ok", I said--I headed back to my rack. I climbed in and read a western by Max Brand until I fell asleep.

Chapter 52

At least 20 of us were fishing off the fantail. We were anchored just inside the breakwall. We didn't have poles or rods - just lines with hooks. We used washers for sinkers and biscuit crumbs for bait. You would just barely get your bait into the water when you would hook another one. It was beginning to get a little boring. Just to test, I dropped my hook with no bait. Sure enough, one grabbed the bare hook and I hauled him in. The fish probably weighed around four pounds each. They were black with white stripes. Doc said they were "some kind of salt water bass". But he didn't know for sure. I noticed the cooks were hauling some of the larger ones down below. I looked at Doc, "Hell, they're not going to cook those damn fish, are they? We don't even know what they are!" Doc said, "Hey, they've got scales. You know the rule of thumb. If they've got scales, they're edible - if they don't, stay away." That evening they served fish for chow. I just had a salad and a piece of pie.

The next test was two days later. This time the weapon would be carried aloft by a **Thor** missile and detonated in the ionosphere above us. All hands were required to observe this one. It was designated "Blue Bird." We were each issued a pair of dark goggles with one-inch thick lens. At 0100 hours we were all seated topside with our knees pulled up. Even with the goggles you had to bury your head into your arms because the initial flash would blind you.

The control room on the island was coming through the ship's speakers.

"The blue bird has left the island – stand by"--We didn't need to be told that. We were close enough to see the Thor missile lift from its pad and hear the roar and see the flame. It quickly disappeared into the blackness of the night. We waited. Then the countdown.

"D - minus 30 seconds."

We buried our heads and closed our eyes.

"10 - 9-8-7-6-5-4-3-2-1"

With the goggles on, my face buried in my arms, and my eyes shut, I still saw a flash of light.We waited. The speakers came alive. **"All Hands May Now Observe Detonation."** We removed our goggles and looked up. The sky was on fire. A deep, dark, boiling red, covering the entire sky. There seemed to be lightning bolts flashing through it. There were audible gasps all around me. I heard an unknown voice somewhere behind me "Now we know what hell looks like". Somebody else said, "the hell we do, this fucking shit would scare the piss out of Satan." Then a band of light appeared, arcing form horizon to horizon. The ship's speaker told us we were looking at the Van Allen Radiation Belt. We were told that the lights that looked like tracers headed for it was actually ionizing radiation from the detonation being pulled into the belt. Some of the guys had already left. The rest of us went below. Everybody was quiet getting ready to get back into their racks. The usual horseplay and laughter was muted. Somebody propped open an overhead scuttle to let in some air. It was raining again.

Bill and I caught the LCVP and went ashore on Johnston Island for the first time. We headed for the little bamboo hut that had been set up as a bar. We walked by a storage building that had a naked female mannequin standing on the flat roof. Someone had pasted hair over her crotch. A sign hung from a string around her neck that said, ***"Someday."*** The little bamboo bar was full. Servicemen, scientists, engineers and workers were all packed in together. Two sailors were vacating a table by the window and we grabbed it. Drinks were free and served in huge dixie cups. Bill went up to the bar and got us each a rum and coke. Nobody gave a damn how old anyone was. It was an atmosphere of "We're all in this boiling hell together."--There was a hand painted sign over the bar that said, '**EAT, DRINK, AND BE MERRY FOR TOMORROW WE DIE!'**

 Bill and I were getting pretty well lit when Suds and Howard came in and joined us.

They each had a Black Jack and Coke. The talk turned to Pat and where in the hell was he? We pondered that for a while then Suds asked Bill and I if we were still going to Australia. Bill was feeling the rum. He put his arm around me and said, "hell, yes - me and my best buddy in the whole world are going to Australia!" I agreed that we were still going. We started talking about the tests. Suds asked Bill about the "hot spot" he had found n the forward gun tub. Bill got serious. "Suds, that son-of-a-bitch was hotter than a Tijuana whore's cunt. The needle pegged out. The C.P.M's were off the scale. I got my ass out of there in a hurry."

Howard said, "deck force washed that gun tub down with hoses for two hours before they finally got a clean reading!"—

Suds said, "Jesus!

"Six days later there was another surface drop. We were advised that the Hawk would be stationed closer to surface zero for this one. The day before the test, we saw the USS Carroll County pass us pulling a barge. The open barge was carrying animals in wire cages. Mostly goats and pigs from what I could tell. The cages were so small the animals couldn't move. Gruman, from operations, said, "What the fuck is that all about?" Doc, who seemed to know more about all this than anyone else, said, "those are test animals… They'll take them in real close to surface zero and tie the barge to an anchored buoy. Four or five days after the air-burst, when the radiation level has fell, they'll go in and get what's left and ship the carcasses off to laboratories to be studied."

Gruman said, "study-study what! Have they lost their fucking minds?" There were no answers. We all just shook our heads.

0530 HOURS: SHOT REDWING

We both felt and heard this one. The overhead lights went out long enough for the battle lanterns to automatically switch on, throwing their eerie red light. We could hear the wind howling. The base surge hit us from aft this time. There was a loud whining sound. We found out later that the starboard screw had actually come out of the water about four feet. The radiology team waited. The damage control teams were sent to the shaft alleys but there was still no word for us. We three just looked at each other. My face was sweating so much, I could barely see. My eyes burned. Still we waited. Howard complained again that he was having trouble breathing. Then the word came down. **"Radiology team lay to main deck."**

Out we went. We three stood there in our asbestos fire fighting suits and stared open - mouthed. A huge mushroom cloud extended from the sea to the heavens. The cloud was white. The sky behind it was tinted red. Howard said, "too bad they confiscated our cameras before we left for this hell-hole."

When Howard said that it made me remember that we had all also signed paperwork that we would not speak of any of this to anyone for a period of twenty years under penalty of death. That would be 1982. That sounded far away . We three headed out in different directions. This time it was Howard who found the "hot-spot" at the forward wench.

All three of us had to hit the showers twice this go around before Doc would pronounce us "clean."

Suds met us in the mess hall for morning chow. After we were seated he told us, "Ed Mitchell had a nervous breakdown earlier this morning." Bill said, "who the hell is Ed Mitchell?"

Suds said, "he's a storekeeper."

Howard wiped his mouth with a napkin and said, "why would a storekeeper have a breakdown?"

" Suds said, "I don't know.

I asked, "Where is he?"

Suds said, "Doc gave him something to make him groggy. They put his ass in the liberty boat and took him ashore. We won't be seeing him again."

We looked at each other and bursted out laughing. I never knew why.

Palmyra Island

October 6, 1962

We had steamed southeast to Palmyra Island and anchored just outside the lagoon. We were here for what the Navy called R and R (Rest and Relaxation). Hot dogs, hamburgers - we were even allowed beer brought from Johnston Island. Some of the guys were in the lagoon splashing around. A baseball game was underway. Bill, Suds, Howard, several guys from deck force and operations and me had a game of tag football going. The longer our game went the more competitive it became. Pretty soon the "tagging" was replaced by full contact tackling. Bill and Suds and their crew were on the opposite team from me and Howard and our guys. When it finally ended, there were bloody noses and torn t-shirts. I don't even remember which side won but it was great fun. Everybody seemed to be in a good mood as we piled aboard the LCVPs and the sun was setting. Bill set down in a corner of the boat. "Man, I must really be out of shape. Damn, I'm tired and ache in every bone."

I said, "hell, we all do."

Suds said, "what about an old an old guy like me? I'm 32 years old. How do you guys think I feel? You young whippersnappers shouldn't be tired. Hell, I'm the one who's tired." We all grinned.

October 10, 1962

Bill didn't feel like eating chow that night. I said, "they've got ice cream. Do you want me to bring you a bowl?" He thought a second. "Nah, I don't think so."

After chow I went back to the berthing area to get Bill for the movie but he was sound asleep. I went back to the mess hall and watched a goofy movie called "Duel of the Titans". They were speaking English but it was definitely dubbed in because the actor's lips weren't in sync with the words. Halfway through just about everyone walked out, including me. Reveille came at 0600. I tied a towel around my waist, grabbed my shaving kit and stumbled to the head. An engineman named Mosley was shaving at the sink next to mine. I never cared much for Mosley. He resembled a chipmunk to me. Buck-teeth and all. He said, "Where's your buddy, Beylor?"

I said, "Probably looking for you to whip your ass."

Mosley was patting cheap after-shave on his jaws. "No man, I'm serious. He was supposed to stand the mid-watch on the auxiliary engines. I went to wake him up but he wasn't in his rack. Hell, I couldn't find him anywhere. Mac had to take the watch."

I went back to my rack and climbed into my dungarees and boondockers. Headed down the passageway I passed sick bay. The hatch was cracked about a foot. I could see someone was in the small hospital bed Doc had in there. Doc was flipping through some kind of medical book. I stuck my head in and said, "who you got there, Doc?"--He shook his head. "It's Bill, Danny. He's a very sick young man." Somehow I already knew who it was. I stepped inside. "What's wrong with him, Doc?" Doc said, "don't get too close. I don't know what's wrong with him. He woke me up around 0100 saying he was in pain everywhere. I got him in here and he started throwing up. I gave him something to put him out. I didn't know what else to do. He's resting pretty good right now."

I said, "could this be from that football game yesterday?

Doc gave a sad smile and shook his head, "this ain't been caused by no football game." I said what we were both thinking. "It's radiation sickness, ain't it, Doc?"

Doc held up his hand. "I can't say that. This is way beyond my expertise. I'm suspicious, of course, because of that "hot spot" he ran into. But there's no way of knowing. Nobody knows what that shit's capable of doing. And I mean nobody. The top brains of the world don't know. That's why us dispensable fools are here. So they can learn more. Maybe someday they'll know more. Maybe someday they'll stop this madness, although I doubt it. But the bottom line is, I just don't know what's wrong with your good friend." I said, "What's going to happen next?"

Doc said, "Corpsmen from Johnston are coming out to get him. He'll be flown back to Pearl. From there, I don't know." Mr. Lingan stepped through the hatch. He looked at me.

"Danny, would you do me a favor? And I know Bill would want you to be the one to do it. Would you get some bolt cutters and cut the lock on his locker and put all his things in his seabag?"

I said, "yes, sir."

I went down to the tank deck and down the ladder to the forward emergency auxiliary engine room and through a hatch to the area where each man's empty seabag was hanging with his name stenciled on the strap. I found Bill's and headed back up. I carefully packed all of Bill's gear. There were three books in his locker. One was titled **"Animals Of Australia."**

That jolted me a little. When I opened it a folded piece of paper fell out. I unfolded it. It appeared to be a poem or notes of some kind. I folded it back and put it in my shirt pocket and placed the book in Bill's sea bag. I left the sea bag just outside the sick bay hatch and went topside. Suds was up by the boat davit. He had already heard about Bill. News traveled fast on a Navy ship. We saw a large motorboat headed our way. The back half of the boat had a full canvas covering with red crosses painted on the sides. As it pulled along side, the step-ladder was lowered down to it. Three corpsmen came up carrying a stretcher. Suds and I stayed topside. Ten minutes later they came back up. Two of them were carrying Bill on the stretcher and one had his sea bag. They got Bill down to the boat and under the canvas and shoved off toward the island. Suds and I smoked and talked a while. Doc came up and joined us. We three just stood there smoking without many words being passed. We saw a C-130 Electra lift off the runway and turn north.

Suds said, "there goes Bill."

Doc shielded his eyes from the sun. "Yep, there he goes."

I wanted to be by myself awhile and said,"Well, I've got some valves to reseat."

Suds flipped his cigarette over the side. "And I've got a welding job to do."

Doc said, "I think I'll hang around up here a while longer and think about philosophy."

Suds and I grinned, but there wasn't much humor in the grins. We both headed below decks.

Down in the boiler room, I pulled up my old metal chair and propped my feet on a fresh water line. A fireman was running the evaporators and doing a good job. The needle was in the green, meaning good, fresh water was going into the tanks at a good rate. I closed my eyes and then I remembered the piece of paper in my pocket. I took it out and unfolded it. It was definitely in Bill's handwriting:

Steaming On A Sea of Red

By William Beyler

Steaming, Steaming, Upon A Sea Of Red.

Steaming, Steaming, Upon A Sea Of Red.

Dare We Pray Tonight For Sleep Or Rest?

Or Would A Moment's Lack Of Vigilance Bring

Us That Eternal Sleep That Knows No Sound?

Being Young And Foolish, We Do Not Know.

Once Again The Giant Sleigh With It's Huge Wings

Has Lifted Up From The North Pole … Bringing What?

Bearing Gifts For Us From A Long Ago

Pine-scented Christmas?

Being Young And Foolish, We Do Not Know.

We Laugh, We joke – But The Fear Remains

Deep In Our Bowels!

Fear Of … What?

Being Young And Foolish, We Do Not Know.

A Great Flash Of Light On The Horizon!

The Deep Bellow Of Rolling Thunder!

But It Is Not Thunder .. Nor Is The Intense

Heat Caused By Lighting Bolts From The Sky!

Being Young And Foolish, We Do Not Know.

Wise Men Now Appear Before Us As

They Once Did The Manger.

The Sage Tells Us That Our Deeds Will

Bring Peace On Earth Forever.

Peace … For Who?

Being Young And Foolish, We Do Not Know.

O' Captain, From Your Quarters O'er Us

Where Many Wonderful Secrets Are Kept,

Will You Protect Us?

And If You Shall … From What?

Being Young And Foolish, We Do Not Know.

The Great Wave Moves Mightily Upon Us!

Then Silence! Is God Still In His Heaven, Sir?

Do Christmas Angels Tread These Depths?

Is It Snowing Somewhere?

Are Children Laughing Out Loud?

Being Young And Foolish, We Do Not Know.

From Beneath Our Feet, The Muffled

Sound Of Bells! Could It Be St. Nick?

No, It Is Only The Wheel House, Ringing The

Engine Room It's Frantic Need For More Speed!

More Speed To Go … Where? Or Away

From …What?

Being Young And Foolish, We Do Not Know.

On Dawn's First Light, A Voice Booms Down

The Passage Ways!

"Awaken, My Sons! Santa Came During The

Long Night"-- But, Father, You Know

We Have Not Slept For It Is Forbidden By

Your Own Law And Tempered By Our

Expectations Of Good Things To Come….

But May We Lie Down This Day, If

Only For An Hour, That We May Dream Of

Toy Soldiers And Dancing Girls Of The Night?

"No, My Sons, For If The Yule Eagle Should

Fly Tonight And Find His Sons Aslumber,

His Wrath Would Be Great. He Would

Find Shame Among You, As I Would.

Steaming, Steaming, Upon A Sea Of Red.

Might It Be Red From The Blood Of Those

Who Have Sailed These Waters Before Us?

Being Young And Foolish, We Do Not Know.

I read it a second time. I figured Bill was referring to the nuclear tests but I didn't understand what he meant by some of it. But I knew it meant something to him. I decided to make myself a copy and when I heard from him I would mail him the original. And there was always the possibility he could get better and come back to the Hawk. And we would still make it to Australia. But even as I was telling myself this, I knew it would never be.

Chapter 53

October 17, 1962

We were steaming 100 nautical miles southwest of Johnston Atoll when the ship's speakers came alive. **"All hands not on watch muster topside."** We wondered what it would be this time. We were all grouped as one unit when the captain began speaking to us.

"Men, we may be going to war with the Soviet Union." There was some shuffling of feet. The captain continued, "Yesterday, a U.S. reconnaissance aircraft mission spotted twelve SS-4 nuclear missiles in Cuba. Our president is meeting with Foreign Minister Gromyko as I speak to you, demanding they be removed immediately. As most of you know, there are Russian subs in this area. They're here to monitor these tests and that's fine. Let the bastards witness America's power. But if this crisis should lead us into a war we must be ready for any type of action these vessels may initiate. I know my crew well and I know I can depend on each and every one of you to do his duty to the best of his ability." We returned the captain's salute. We all drifted back to our work places without much talk. It was like each man was deep into his own thoughts.

October 18, 1962   0400 Hours

Shot Chamalan

2.5 Megaton – Air-Burst

This one was the biggest one of the series and would have the most yield so far. Unlike the other surface drops, all hands were required to be topside for this one. We all had our goggles and battle helmets on. With my head buried in my arms, I had my left eye at a squint. At the initial flash of light I saw the bones in my leg, like an x-ray. I closed my eyes tight. I didn't want to see that again. Behind me I heard Mr. Lingan say, "damn, I saw my own bones!"

        Then the heat and wind hit us with force. Once again it was difficult to breathe. When we finally raised our heads we were again in awe. This mushroom cloud was *much* larger than the first one. It was mostly boiling red but that damned green hue was there. This air-burst was supposed to have been 130 nautical miles to the south but we all agreed it sure as hell looked closer than that.The crew hustled below decks before the radioactive base surge hit us. We all held on to something. When it hit, the forward part of the ship went almost vertical before we slammed back down. Many of the men were thrown violently to the deck. Cursing could be heard coming from below.

Howard and I climbed into our fire fighting suits and took up our post just inside the hatch. The damage control teams went to the shaft alleys and then Howard and I went out. --The cloud was still there but had turned white with red streaks**.** And it seemed to be reflecting light from the sun rising in the east. This go around, Howard and I both found hot spots. We dutifully logged them in. I had no idea who would eventually read these logs or if they would even be read. Howard and I finished and went back inside before the rain started to fall. The executive officer informed the crew that a naval blockade of Cuba had begun and military alert was set at **DEFCON 3.**

The Hawk went to **"set condition yoke"** which was a state of readiness just two levels below a full general quarters.

October 24, 1962 - Anchored inside break wall.

The executive officer informed us that Russian ships had reached the quarantine line 800 miles from Cuba and stopped. They were maintaining their position awaiting orders from Moscow. Military alert was reset to **DEFCON 2**. --The Hawk went up a notch to **Condition Zebra**. At 1600 hours we went to General Quarters. A Russian sub had surfaced 40 nautical miles from Johnston Island and was heading in a general direction toward the atoll. At 1630 the word came down that the sub was changing directions away from the island. I had to run up topside and see what was going on. A group of men were by the starboard boat davit wearing their gray helmets and life jackets. Mr. Lingan and Suds were among them. Mr. Lingan looked at me and nodded south. "That damn Red sub is hauling ass away at around 30 knots."

I couldn't see anything. Then we saw why the sub was hauling ass. On the horizon, the USS John S. McCain was cutting through the water in that same direction. The McCain was a Destroyer Leader, armed with the big guns and depth-charges. We all cheered.

Suds laughed, "Sounds like a scene from a WW2 movie." Then he turned to me. "How would you like to be on that baby, Dan? The *real* Navy."

I said, "Nah, I'll just stick to the Ol' Hawk."
Mr. Lingan slapped me on the back as he headed for the conn.
"Me too, Danny - me too."

We remained at general quarters until 2300 hours when we finally went back to Condition Zebra. Some headed for their watch station while others hit their rack knowing they would soon be going on watch.

Friday, October 26, 1962

President Kennedy receives a communication from Soviet Premier Khrushchev stating that the Soviets would remove their missiles if President Kennedy would guarantee Cuba would not be invaded and all U.S. Missiles are removed from Turkey. President Kennedy refuses to make any guarantees.

October 27, 1962

Khrushchev announces that all Russian missiles in Cuba will be dismantled.

USS Clay County

Officer of the deck log book entry Tuesday 10-30-1962

0408: Steaming Independently At various speeds maintaining position on station 7 cap B.

0440: Crew observes Shot Beta Air-Burst – 8.3 megaton yield. The ship is approx. 137 nautical miles from detonation. Material condition yoke set.

LTJG V. Byron USN

Officer of the deck log book entry Sunday 11-04-1962

22-24 Anchored in Johnston Harbor in 30 fathoms.

2320: Crew observes high altitude detonation over Johnston Island designated Kingfish.

SOPA is CTG 8.3 in USS Princeton. Condition of Readiness V

LJG. S. Salter USN

On November 16th the Hawk was the last ship to depart Johnston Island. We never knew why we were required to stay another 3 days after everyone else had left. We steamed out of Johnston Harbor at 0500, headed back to Pearl. We were all tired to the bone. We were also hungry for something real to eat. We had run out of groceries a week earlier and we were subsisting on powdered eggs, spam, powdered potatoes and powdered milk. The refrigerated reefer ship that was on it's way to Johnston Island to re-supply us never showed up. We had no idea what the situation was on the larger ships. They sure as hell didn't offer us anything.

At 0200 on November 19th we tied up to a pier in Pearl. We hooked up to shore steam, electricity and fresh water. After that the engineering crew was so tired we weren't up to getting undressed and climbing into our racks. We just threw our pillows on deck and flaked out in our dungarees.

Early the next morning, the supply trucks were on the pier. The whole crew went down to help bring it aboard – officers, chiefs, non-coms, E-2's, E-3's, everybody. It seemed we were all after the same thing – ice cream!

Everyone was tearing into the 5-gallon cardboard tubs of ice cream and eating it with their bare hands. I was right in there with the rest of them. Later that day I went to the base bank and exchanged a ten dollar bill for ten dollars in change. I found a pay phone and called Hershey, Pennsylvania information. The operator had one Beyler – a Norman Beyler. I said, "are you sure?" - She was sure. And this one didn't actually live right in Hershey. But he was in the county. She rang it for me after I put in ten quarters for the first three minutes. A man answered on the third ring.

I said, "Bill?" Although I knew it wasn't his voice.
He said, "you must have the wrong number, this is the Beyler residence."
"Do you know Bill Beyler?" I asked.
"No, I don't. My name's Norman, I don't know a Bill, sorry."
I asked, "Do you know *any* Beylers?"
"No, I don't know any other Beylers, I'm sorry."
I said, "thank you" and hung up.I walked back to the Hawk and ran into Mr. Lingan on the quarterdeck. I asked him if there had been any word on Pat. He said, "nothing, nothing at all. If he had been picked up we would have been notified so I guess he's still running loose out there somewhere." I walked aft to the starboard boat davit, lit a cigarette and leaned on the railing. I wondered how two men could totally disappear like that? I knew Pat was totally self-reliant and would probably stay uncaught. I finished the Chesterfield before I headed down to my boiler room.

Friday, December 8,1962
Officer of the Deck Log entry.

16-24 steaming as before. 1612 c/s to 9.3 knots

1624 sighted Point Loma Bearing 075 Distance 25M cls to 2.1 knots. 1630 set special mooring detail – maneuvering at various courses at various speeds conforming to enter San Diego Harbor channel. Buoy #5 a beam to port – 1640 entered inland water –draft fwd 6'3", aft 12'9" - 1720 commenced maneuvering to approach berth – 1740 moored starboard side to Navy Pier – Ships present include various units of the US Pacific Fleet and various foreign and domestic merchant vessels. Condition of readiness V.

J.E. Elwell

LJG USN

The diesel engines went silent. We were home. I went topside to have a look. There was a cold mist falling and a fog was rolling in. It was a welcome change from the unbearable heat of the past ten months.

There was a small group of people on the pier and a small Navy band trying their damnedest to play "Anchors Aweigh"--The group was made up of mostly women and children; families of some of the Hawk's crew. After the gangplank was lowered, the ship's speakers announced that anyone with family members on the pier had permission to escort them aboard and down to the mess hall for coffee and cake. The speakers also informed us that all profanity would be banned during this reunion.

I watched the dependents being escorted aboard. The children were wide-eyed and so were some of the women. The small Navy band left in a gray van. Then I noticed there was one person still on the pier. Her head was covered with a red scarf; she was wearing a red leather coat. She saw me and gave a little wave. Hell, it was Jackie! I bounded down the gangplank to her. She grabbed me and hugged me. I couldn't tell if she was crying or if it was the falling mist. She held my right hand in both of hers.

"Daniel, please tell me how to find Pat". I said, "I have no idea where he is, Jackie. I thought you were divorcing him." Now she was crying. "No, no … it's …. it's all so stupid. I thought I wanted one. I thought I had met someone but I was just lonely – so very lonely. Please understand, Daniel, you have to understand."

"I said, "It's not my place to understand, Jackie."
She dabbed at her eyes with a handkerchief, "but you have to so you can explain everything to him if you hear from him."
I lied and said, "well, sure I understand."
She wrote her phone number on a slip of paper and I put it in my shirt pocket. She grabbed my hand again.
"And if you talk to him, please tell him what I've said and that I love him so very much. And if we haven't found him by the time you get out, we can look for him together."

I guess she had forgotten there would be desertion charges against Pat if and when he surfaced. But I said, "sure, don't worry, we'll find him."

I asked her if she wanted to come aboard for coffee and cake. But she just smiled sadly, hugged me again, and walked away dabbing at her eyes. I watched her until she vanished into the fog. I would never see her again.

The Hawk was steaming straight toward the sandy beach on San
Clemente Island along with nine other LST's. We had been at it three days,
carrying out amphibious exercises along with marines from Camp
Pendleton.We had over one hundred US Marines aboard along with twelve of
their armored tanks tied down on the tank deck. The Hawk would hit the
beach with just enough force to stabilize itself on the sand. Then the big bow
doors would open and the tank crews would drive their armored vehicles up
the ramp and off onto the beach. This would be our sixth and final time to
beach for this operation. I was in the boiler room setting in my metal chair,
reading. I had picked up a book someone had left in the mess hall. It was
called "Tropic of Cancer" and was written by some guy named Henry Miller.
It didn't make a lot of sense. Miller lived with another man in France and
they spent time picking crabs off each other. Miller falls into a woman's
vagina and it's so big he meets a motorcycle cop in there. The blurb on the
back cover informed me that the book had been banned in the USA until
1961. It also stated that such notables as George Orwell had praised it. I
shook my head. I had always liked to read but had grown even more addicted
to it since joining the navy. Maybe it was because of the lonely hours of
being on watch in the boiler room. I had went through "The Bridge of San
Luis Rey", "To Kill a Mockingbird", "Atlas Shrugged", "From Here to
Eternity","Cannery Row" and my favorite, "Studs Lonigan" and many others.
But this book was trash. I thought about George Orwell praising it. I was
learning just how little the "experts" really knew about anything. I was also
learning that most people would do or say anything if they thought it would
make them look intelligent to others. But I had enjoyed Orwell's 1984 and
wondered if things might actually be like that when 1984 rolled around
someday. I threw "Tropic Of Cancer" in the shit-can. Over in the engine
room I could hear the diesels cutting speed as we approached the beach. I
grabbed a fresh water line and braced myself. I had been through this 15 or
20 times the past three years and I knew we would hit the beach fairly hard.
We did. But it wasn't too bad. I climbed the ladder and

stood on the small poop deck above the tank deck to watch the marines drive their tanks off. They knew what they were doing and it was all going like clock work. I went back down into the boiler room. An hour later, I heard the diesels crank up and go into reverse to pull us back off the beach. We didn't seem to be moving. I heard the RPM's move up a notch. Then wide open. It felt like the stern was moving in a starboard direction. The RPM's cut down and then the Hawk shook as the whole starboard side seemed to make contact with something.

I went topside where I couldn't believe the scene. Most of the starboard side was actually upon the beach. We were stuck like a beached whale.

The other LST's were pulling away. The crew on the closest one were hooting and hollering at us and waving bye. It was embarrassing as hell. I went back down below. Four hours later three tug boats out of San Diego showed up. Using cables and winches they finally pulled us off and back into the water. They pulled us out a ways before cutting loose. The Hawk headed for San Diego. An hour later we were steaming at a 10 degree list to starboard. I didn't have a role in beaching and working with marines and their equipment but this would come under the heading of my area. I would be expected to solve this one. I soon found the culprit. Ballast tank V404 on the starboard side had filled with salt water. I hot-footed it down to the engine room, opened the valve to that tank and lit off the ballast pump. It took a suction. Thirty minutes later I checked my bubble indicator. We were on an even keel. An hour later we were back listing ten degrees to starboard. Back down in the engine room the ballast pump took a suction. The tank had filled up again. Mr. Lingan came down the ladder. He said, "what do we have, Dan?"--I said, "we've got a problem, sir."

The Hawk entered dry dock being pulled by two large cables. Once in, the water gates were closed and the shipyard started pumping the water out of the dock. The Hawk settled on to six huge concrete stanchions, high and dry.

The gangplank was extended horizontally over the side of the dock. The captain, Mr. Lingan, Chief Burns, Suds and me along with several shipyard workers clambered down the long ladder to the bottom of the dock. Looking up at the ship's hull above us made the Hawk look much bigger than it had looked in the water. We saw the damage immediately. Under the starboard void there was a 12 foot long gash, about 12 inches wide at it's widest point. The entire hull was also encrusted with barnacles a foot thick. These would have to be sand-blasted off. The captain made the decision that as long as we were in dry dock anyway, we would go through a complete overhaul. We would be here a while.

Shore services would consist of electricity and water, but no steam. The fire tubes on the boiler would be swabbed out using long wooden poles and rags to get the soot out that had built up. The back doors of the boiler would be removed and the asbestos insulation replaced. I would be assigned three firemen to assist me. I had been through this once before with Pat. It was a hot, dirty job but one that was necessary.

The noise of sand-blasting underneath us and deck hands chipping paint on the main deck over us was pretty much around the clock. Once again, sleep was a rare commodity. The one bright spot to being in dry dock was getting to eat at the base mess hall. We had heard they had great chow and it was true. There was also a variety. There were always at least three different meats to choose from, several deserts, iced tea, rolls. And the meat wasn't still fighting for its life as was sometimes the case on the Hawk, with blood oozing up through it. We would all stroll back to the Hawk, chewing on toothpicks and loudly bragging about the base cooks. Our cooks would glower at us but didn't say anything. I don't know where the Hawk's cooks were eating but we never saw them, even once, in the base mess hall. We figured they were afraid they might learn something.

Friday, November 22, 1963

1140 Hours, Pacific Time

Several of us from the Hawk were in the chow line, laughing and joking. The line wasn't moving yet, so I cut out to go to the head. Inside, a marine was washing his hands. When he saw me, he said, "have you heard anything about the president being shot?" It sounded like the opening line to a joke to me.

I grinned, "No, what's the punchline?-Did Jackie shoot him?"
The marine said, "No man, I'm serious. It's all over the place that he's been shot in Texas."
I saw he was serious. I said,"is he ok?"
He shook his head, "I don't know. I've just heard he's been shot."
Back in line, Suds and the others had just heard it too. Suds said, "It's probably a load of crap, somebody trying to start some shit."

The mess hall was alive with talk about it but no one knew anything for sure. When we got back to the Hawk, the black and white TV in the mess hall was on. Most of the Hawk's crew were in there. The president had been shot in Dallas, Texas. President Kennedy was dead. A silent pall fell over the mess hall.

August 5th 1964

The ship's yeoman gave me the papers I would need to take with me. I was heading over to what they called "Receiving" on base, only I was "leaving". This was where you went to be processed out when your time was up. A fireman apprentice named Scurlock asked me if he could carry my seabag down to the pier – I said, "sure". This was an old Navy tradition and was considered an honor to carry an older man's seabag to the pier for him when he was being discharged. I had carried a couple myself. I had already shook hands with the captain and many of the Hawk's crew including Suds who was still aboard her. Mr. Lingan had been gone since the past February. There were a lot of new faces on the Hawk. I shook hands with Scurlock on the pier and wished him good luck. With my seabag heaved over my right shoulder and my paperwork in my left hand, I turned and walked away. I was dressed in my dress whites and the ends of my black neckerchief were blowing over my left shoulder from the breeze coming from the bay. Just before I reached a warehouse where I would turn left putting the Clay County out of sight, I stopped. I set my seabag down, turned around and saluted the Hawk. I could swear someone on the bow saluted back but I would never know for sure.—

The receiving station was organized confusion. Men being discharged, men being transferred, men waiting for a ship they had been assigned to, to come back into port. They assigned me to a berthing area with the other men being discharged. I found myself a rack and threw my seabag on it. The next morning, after chow, we went through a battery of physical exams that lasted half a day. That evening I was sitting at an outdoor wooden bench drinking coffee and idly going through my billfold when I found Jackie's phone number. I had forgotten about it. I found a pay phone and dialed it. The line had been disconnected.

.

That night at 2300 I was awakened to go on watch. I had been told it was coming. All NCO's had to stand a watch. It was the Navy's way of saying goodbye. I put on dress blues, a white helmet, a white duty belt with a holster that had a Navy .45 automatic in it and a full clip. It was a cool night when I walked outside. Several others were already waiting.

A small, gray Navy bus picked us up. Each man was dropped off at the place he would stand watch. When the driver called my name, we had stopped at a deserted baseball field that belonged to the Navy. There was actually a small guard house at the entrance. I stood in there and bravely guarded some old wooden bleachers, and a backstop. I smiled – the Navy had had the final word after all. At 0345 I saw the little gray bus coming to get me.

303

The Greyhound Bus crossed the Mississippi River at St. Louis into Illinois. We pulled into the depot in Edwardsville where the driver announced we would have a one hour layover for supper. I was still in uniform when I climbed off the bus and stretched a little. It was a small bus station but it was neat and clean compared to the station in Los Angeles where I had first transferred buses. It was huge but filthy.

I headed for the little cafe inside, along with several of the other passengers. I found a booth next to a window. Dusk was falling. The jukebox over in the corner was playing a .45 record. ***"Baby, I need your loving, got to have all your loving."***

There were two young ladies in the adjoining booth who had not been passengers. I could see the one facing me fairly well. A real looker. She had long curly red hair cascading down her shoulders along with very cute freckles. I could only see the back of her friends' head. I caught the one facing me looking at me a couple of times. She wasn't being coy about it either. Each time, she would lean over and whisper to her pal. Suddenly, the one whose back was to me turned around. Also a looker. In fact they favored.

"Are you in the Navy?"
I grinned, "well, technically I am until I get home to Hammond, Indiana. I've been honorably discharged after serving four years."
She gave me a big smile. "Were you on a boat?"
I said, "Ship."
"Where all did you go?" They seemed to be fascinated. I guess a sailor was a rare sight in Edwardsville.

I said, "look, why don't you and your buddy come over here and join me? We can talk better."

Here they came, sliding into my booth facing me. They were even prettier close up. Both had long red hair and freckles and were obviously sisters.

Introductions were made. I was in the company of Arlene and Darlene Newell. We all three ordered cheeseburgers, french fries, and chocolate milkshakes.They peppered me with questions. Was I married? Did I have a girlfriend? No and no.--Arlene was my age -– Darlene was two years younger. They both worked at Glenn's Shoe Store right here in Edwardsville and often ate here at the bus station after work. No, they didn't have steady boyfriends at this time. Darlene informed me that the young men in Edwardsville were "sooooo booooring." Glenn's Shoes had a store in Springfield and they both had put in for a transfer there.

They talked about what a big city Springfield was, being the capital and all. We were having a great time when the station's speaker told us it was time for the passengers to return to the bus. I started to get up. Arlene looked shocked. "You're not leaving now, are you?" I reckoned as I had to since my bus was leaving. Arlene was adamant, "Oh no, I know Bobbie, he runs this place. I'll talk to him and you can leave in the morning."-I said, "Well, talk fast before the bus pulls out." She was back in a flash. "It's all set. Bobbie will change your ticket. You can leave at 10:30 in the morning." I said, "Well, alright then."-- Arlene had a '62 Monza. We rode around town with Arlene driving and me up in front in the middle of her and Darlene. Darlene pointed out some landmarks and houses that were well over a hundred years old. She said Edwardsville was one of the oldest cities in Illinois dating back to the turn of the 19th century. Many of the homes did look very old but they were also immaculate. The girls rented the left side of a brick duplex. Darlene said an old couple lived on the other side but were always gone to visit their daughter somewhere in Kentucky. The apartment was small, clean and efficient looking. Arlene brought out three bottle of Pabst from the

fridge and uncapped them. Then she filled a bowl with pretzels. "We're having a party," she smiled. Darlene cranked up the .45 record player. Elvis started singing *"It's just breaking my heart 'cause she's not you."*

Elvis was their favorite, Darlene said. "But we're also starting to like the Beatles."--I said, "the what?"—

"The Beatles – you know? - the four guys from England?"

I said I didn't know. I laughed, "the only beetles I've heard of are bugs that destroy crops."--They both thought that was funny. Arlene said, "play the Beatles." Darlene put another .45 on the spindle. ***"Oh yeah, I'll tell you something – when I say that something, I want to hold your hand!"***--I wasn't sure what to say. But not wanting to spoil anything, I lied and said, "Hey, that's pretty good. Do you have anymore by Elvis?" They sure did. We were on our third round of Pabsts. I guess I looked a little tired. Darlene massaged the back of my neck. "You look like you're about ready for bed."

 I said, "Yeah, I'm pretty tired, I guess." --But my brain was churning. What was the situation here? Was I going back to the bus station? Was I going to sleep on the couch? Nothing had even been hinted at as far as what the deal was . It was starting to be a little awkward, at least for me when I made the decision to just bring it up and be done with it. I asked, "are you ready to take me back to the station?"--They both looked stunned. Darlene spoke up, "Why would we do that?"

I said, "Well, I wasn't sure exactly what you two wanted to do." Arlene had a big grin. "You're staying here tonight and you're sleeping with both of us. That's okay with you isn't it?"--I stammered out, ..what?..well, sure..well, yes… that would be good …that would be great." To myself, I said, "Thank you, God."--The girls hit the bathroom first. I had brought my shaving kit so I was able to brush my teeth and shave. I fell in the bed between them. The lights were out except for a low-watt lamp in a far corner. They both rolled over into my arms. Darlene whispered into my ear, "we like to do kinky things." I thanked God again.

The next morning, after one hell of a great night, Darlene cooked up scrambled eggs, sausage, toast and opened a jar of peach preserves they had canned themselves. It was the best eating since the last time ma had cooked for me. We were all three fairly quiet on the way back to the station.

I believe we were all disappointed that I had to leave. It even crossed my mind that maybe I should stay. But I knew, in the back of my mind, that an arrangement like that couldn't go on forever. They stayed with me until the bus pulled out. I had their phone number and swore I would call and I would no doubt be back.The Newell girls were still waving when the Greyhound turned a corner.

Chapter 54

Rolling through the Illinois farmland, I wondered again about the wisdom of going back to Hammond. My father had written me several times the past six months wanting me to come home and so had Marty. My mother had even written me a couple of times that she wanted me to come home! But still, it just didn't feel right for some reason. I really would have liked to have gone to Australia with Bill. But I didn't want to try it alone. Maybe someday Bill and I would meet up again and head for "down under", as he called it. But down deep, I knew it would never happen. I didn't even know if he was alive. Somehow,I doubted it. I thought back on all I had seen and experienced the past four years. I thought about Pat and wondered where in hell he was. And where did Jackie go? Howard had been transferred to the Carrol County. What was he doing now? And ol' Suds- still aboard the Hawk. Suds was a good man.

Then the sweetest memory of all invaded my mind. Cindy. I had really fallen for her hard. I had seen her only twice and still missed her to this day. The taste of her. The scent of her hair was with me now. It would come like that. Just out of nowhere. I would hold it as long as I could before it faded away. But I knew it would be back. There would never be another one like Cindy.

After a two-hour layover in Chicago where I had to transfer buses for a thirty minute trip, we rolled into the Hammond depot at 8:00 pm. I spotted Marty standing by the glass door that led to the waiting room. When I left she was a child and now she was a beautiful young woman. As we hugged, I couldn't get over how she had grown up. I guess four years is a long time for some things. She even had her own car. A 1960 Chevy Bel-Air. I retrieved my seabag from the luggage area and threw it in the trunk. Marty was full of information. Daddy was drinking a little. He had gotten sick and finally went to a doctor. He was diagnosed with silicosis of the lungs. He had stayed in the mines too long after all. But he was still working. He and mother both were now working at the glass factory. Daddy was there now, working evening shift. Mother worked day shifts. Daddy would be home around 11:30 pm. "Daddy sure wants to see you," Marty said. "He's so glad you've come home." Then, like an afterthought, she added, "Oh, and mother too, of course." And then she hit me with the big news. She was getting married in December. I was stunned. "But …you're too young to be getting married!" I stammered. Marty laughed, "I'm almost nineteen, Dan"--His name was Jeff Landrum. He was two years older than Marty. Jeff had spent two years active in the army, stationed at Ft. Knox, Kentucky and now , according to Marty, had a great job as a keypunch operator at Inland Steel in Gary. He had helped her buy her Chevy. All I could think of to say was, "I guess I'm going to have a brother-in-law."

Marty said, "Oh, I've told him all about you. You're really going to like him, Dan, you really are."
I said, "I'm sure I will."
We pulled up in front of the house they were living in now, on Hoffman Street. It looked small but at least it was a house and not somebody's basement or attic. I grabbed my seabag and followed Marty in. My mother was waiting at the door. She hugged me and said, "I'm glad you're home,

Daniel Wayne. I would like to set up and talk but I've got a splitting headache. I gotta lay back down."

I said, "sure, I understand." I could tell Marty was a little embarrassed. "She really has had a headache ever since she got home from work."

I said, "hey, she needs to lay back down. It's OK." Marty made us bologna and tomato sandwiches and uncapped two bottles of Royal Crown Cola she had brought out of the fridge. I smiled to myself. Some things might change in four years, but some things didn't. We talked about our daddy's illness. The doctor had said that silicosis was a progressive disease that inflamed and scarred the lungs and eventually the patient may get to the point where he had to carry a portable oxygen tank around with him, but hopefully that wouldn't be for a long time with the proper care. I asked Marty if he should still be working. She shook her head, "no, he shouldn't, especially at that damn glass factory." She suddenly changed the subject to Rita. I've ran into her several times in Goldblatts and we've had lunch together a bunch of times. She always talks about you and when you're coming home. She still loves you very much." I made little circles with my finger on the checkered table cloth. "To tell you the truth, Marty, I don't remember much about her." Marty's eyes widened. Then she softly laid her hand on mine. "Daniel, I know you've been through a lot but after you've rested a few days and gotten used to being home, you'll be your old self again. I had no idea what she was talking about but didn't say anything, I changed the subject this time by asking about our daddy's drinking.

"It's not a lot but it's enough to worry me. The doctor says it probably cuts through the mucus in his chest and makes him feel better." Marty seemed to remember something she had forgotten. "Oh, did you know Uncle Matthew died?"

I said, "no, I didn't When did that happen?"

"About three months ago. He passed out in the front yard and laid there all night in the rain. Ma found him the next morning. She thought he was still in bed. He died of pneumonia in the hospital three days later."

I laughed, "it would have took a lot of whiskey to have made that old cob pass out. What about Ma? Is she living by herself?"
"As far as I know," Marty said. "Daddy didn't go to the funeral; mother wouldn't let him. She always hated Uncle Matthew, anyway!"—
 Our father came through the door. I stood up. He looked almost shocked as if he had forgotten I was coming home. We embraced and shook hands. He was still four inches taller than me.

Marty poured us a cup of coffee and we three talked until 5 A.M.-- Daddy was still dreaming of living back in Alabama someday. "But there just ain't no jobs there 'right now." I said, "well, maybe after you retire from working."--He poured some coffee in his saucer and sipped it from the saucer as I had seen him do many times. "I've got this damn silicosis of the lungs now."

I said, "Yeah, Marty told me. Maybe you should go ahead and think about retiring now. I bet you would feel better in Alabama. The cold weather here can't be good for you. "

Daddy nodded his head, "yeah, I been thinking about that too." My Mother was up now and had heard us talking. "We ain't moving back to Alabama or anyplace else. The boy Marty is marrying was raised here and has a good job. Marty and him won't be moving to Alabama, so we're not. I'm not leaving my baby."

Marty looked embarrassed.

Daddy said, "I reckon not."

I didn't say anything.

Mother poured herself a cup of coffee. She still hadn't looked in my direction. Then she did. "Daniel Wayne, I'm glad you came back, but you're going to need to help us on groceries and utilities and such." I said, "Well, I had planned to for ever how long I'm here."

Marty was upset with our mother's comment. "Is that all you can think of to say to him, mother? Hell, he just got home and the first thing you say to him is to ask for money!" Mother looked a little sheepish. "Well, Marty, I just meant ...."__ I cut in. "Hey, it's OK. I understand and sure, I'm going to help out." I went to my seabag and unlocked it. I pulled out a large white envelope with an eagle on it. In it were all my discharge documents. There was also a book of Travelers Checks in there. Over 850 dollars worth, for unused leave time I had sold back to the Navy. I tore one out for a hundred bucks and handed it to my mother. It definitely made her happy. "Daniel Wayne, you know you don't have to run out and find a job tomorrow. That's not what I meant. Of course you need to rest a few days." I said, "Well, actually I want to get started soon looking for a job. I've got to buy me a car of some kind and then I'll start applying." My mother shook her head, "no, no … you rest a few days first." I heard the words but I knew it was the hundred dollar Traveler's Check that had bought me a small grace period with my Mother. Our Father went to bed and our mother left for work. I was dead tired. Marty took me down a short hall and showed me my room. It had been her room but now she was mostly staying over at Jeff's. The room was small but looked fine to me. It had been a long time since I had slept in a bed that didn't rock me to sleep other than at the Newell girls' house. I had noticed earlier, in the single bathroom, that there was another door inside on the opposite wall that was latched from the inside. I asked Marty about it. "Oh, the Martins share the bathroom with us. When one of them is in there they latch the door to our side so we'll know. And we latch the other door when we're in there." I could barely get it out, "are you telling me other people live in the back of this house?"

Marty said, "Yes, the Martins. They own the house." Then she hit me again. "And the Easterwoods live over us." I just stared at her. I didn't have any words. I said, "what about my things? My clothes, my big radio, my barbells, all that?"

Marty looked down at the floor. "Mother got rid of everything because she really didn't think you would ever come back." I set down on the side of the bed and stared out the window at a tree that's leaves were blowing a little in the wind. I kicked off my shoes and stretched out. Marty was saying something, but I couldn't make it out. I fell into a deep sleep.

On my third day home I walked over to Columbus and Hohman Avenue to Ed's Used Cars with my book of traveler's checks under my arm. It had been located in the same spot as far back as I could remember. I had gone to Irving with Ed's son, Ed Dembrowski Jr. As I walked onto the lot I saw Ed Junior. So he was working for the old man now. Ed spotted me at once.

"Hey, Dan, what in hell? Where've you been man?" Ed was pumping my hand. He was wearing a green checkered sports coat, a white shirt, green pants, a green tie and smoking a cigar. He was taller but other than that he hadn't changed all that much from the ninth grade.

I said, "How're you doing, Ed?"
Ed patted me on the back still holding my hand. I finally got myself loose. I said, "well, I've been in the Navy the past four years."
Ed said, "how about that? Hey do you remember Lamar Mazak?" I said, "I sure do."
"Hell, he joined the Marines. He came back dead. Killed over there in Asia or China or somewhere like that."

"Probably Vietnam or Laos," I said. "Yeah, yeah, something like that. Hell, I wanted to join up myself but I know you remember I've always had bad knees."--I lied, "I sure do remember."

Then I said, "look Ed, I need to buy a used car, something dependable. "He grinned ear to ear. "Well, we got 'em old friend and you know *you'll* get a hell of a deal."

Ed told me his dad was sick a lot so he was more or less running the show now. Ed went inside the little office and came back with a handful of keys. I cranked and looked under the hood of several cars before I spotted a 1959 Ford Galaxy. It was black with a red interior. A 2-door hardtop with an automatic transmission. I drove it down Hohman Avenue to downtown Hammond, cut around the civic center and opened it up a little. I loved it.

Back on the lot I tried not to look too enthusiastic. I asked Ed, "how much you asking for this pile of junk?" Ed smiled, "I knew you would like that Ford. It's yours for 500 bucks. That's exactly what I've got in it." I was a little taken back. I had expected it to be twice that amount. I said, "What's wrong with it?" Ed looked genuinely hurt. "Nothing as far as I know." He kicked at the ground. "I told you since it was you, it would be a great deal." I knew then that he was being truthful. I felt a little bad. I said, "hey, Ed-- I was just joshing you, buddy. I'll take it."

Fifteen minutes later, I drove off the lot in my Ford Galaxy, short 500 bucks in traveler's checks.

I drove south on Hohman Avenue to downtown Hammond, wanting to check out the old stomping grounds. I turned east, down Isbel Street. The building that held Millikan's Record Shop was still there but it was no longer Millikan's Record Shop. It was a used furniture store. A sign said, "Easy

Credit". I made the block and came back out on Hohman at the Parthenon Theatre. It was still going. "Dr. Strangelove" was showing. The five and dime across the street was not. The store where we would crowd in to a booth to have our pictures taken now had newspapers covering the windows. I guess the picture show business was still good because, farther on down, the Paramount Theater was open. It was a double feature, "Apache Rifles" and "Atomic Brain".

I cut over to Calumet and drove to the Hammond Tyler football field. The football team was going through its August drills. I walked up to the fence and watched a few minutes. Coach Kallas looked over at me and I gave him a little salute. He waved back--I don't know if he recognized me or not.

I drove north on Calumet to Jim's Drive In. It was too hot to sit in the car and flirt with the car hop so I parked and went in and found a booth. I looked around and saw some familiar faces but I couldn't exactly place them. Then a face came through the door that I knew, George Brumm from high school. He recognized me immediately and came over. I stood up and we shook hands. George said, "Long time no see. Mind if I join you?"

I grinned, "I insist."

After I told my story, George brought me up to date on him. He had been drafted into the army but had been lucky enough to get into the Army Corps of Engineers. George had spent two years helping build a road in the Panama Canal Zone. I told him I was a little embarrassed because about all I had done was chase women in the Philippines. George chuckled over that.

I said, "Do you remember Rich Saebo?"
George said, "Sure, you and he were buddies."
I asked him if he knew anything about Rich. "I know he married that cute blonde and they had a couple of kids. Somebody told me they were living somewhere in California." It was hard to believe that Rich had been living in

California during the same period I had been in and out of there and neither of us knew it. George asked me if I had located a job yet.

I said, "No, but I'm getting ready to start looking. Probably hit the steel mills." He shook his head.The waitress came. We both ordered the luncheon special. After she left, I said, "why did you shake your head?" George salted his food. "Look, Dan, the steel mills are ok but if you haven't already been there 20 years you're always subject to getting laid off according to how the economy's going. Hell, a new home today can run you as much as nineteen or twenty thousand bucks. You buy a house or a new car on credit, which you will eventually, and get laid off, then what?

I asked him what he was driving at. "We need somebody where I work. You were a boiler technician in the Navy. They'll grab you up in a second. There's 190 million people in this country now and very few know anything about boilers or heating or air conditioning – things like that."

I asked, "Where do you work?"

"Carson, Pirie, Scott – downtown Chicago, the big department store. I'm in the engineering department. That building is ten stories high. The store has the first seven floors. The next two are rented out as office space to doctors and lawyers and such. The top floor has a tower with a 300,000 BTU chilled-water air conditioner with ducts running to all the floors. We do all the maintenance and run all the machinery. There's nothing to it and the money is the same as at the mills with benefits just as good.

I was interested. "Yeah, I've seen that building from the outside. It's a beautiful building. Did you say you guys need somebody?" George tore out a small piece of paper from a notebook. "We had a guy retire and we need to replace him. Can you go up there tomorrow?"

"Sure," I said, "I'll go up there and talk to them."

George slid the piece of paper over to me. "Ask for Stash. I'll call him this evening and tell him you'll be there. He gets there around 6:00 A.M. So if you get there about nine, that would be about right."

I said, "you got it."

George told me he went in at two in the afternoon and if I was still there he would see me tomorrow. We shook hands and left. I noticed George was driving a new, 1964 Ford Fairlane.

     I pulled out in my old Galaxy and headed up Calumet toward Hoffman Street. I switched on the radio. A group called 'The Four Seasons' were belting it out, ***"Dawn, go away from me – I'm no good for you."***

At 8:00 A.M. The next morning I found a place to park right off Lake Shore Drive. It was a big parking lot with a lot of cars. Best of all it was free. It meant having to walk nine blocks but that was ok. George had told me to go past all the main entrance doors until I came to a small green door. That would be the entrance to maintenance. I glanced in the showroom windows as I went past. This was a high-class store. I found the green door and went in. A long metal stairway took me deep under the store. I spotted a 1200-pound super-heated steam boiler. Engineering was a large area with a lot of men scurrying around wearing work clothes and tool belts. I saw right off it was a much larger operation than the Hawk's engineering department. On the wall there was a time clock and a rack full of time cards. A man wearing Khaki pants and shirt walked over to meet me, putting out his hand.

"You must be Danny boy, I'm Stash. Come on back to the office." Stash seated me at his desk and handed me an application and a pen. "Here, fill this out and we'll talk, ok?"

I said, "yes, sir."

Stash grinned, "hey, you're not in the military anymore. 'Stash' will do just fine."

I said, "ok, Stash." I liked him right off. Filling out the application wasn't complicated. My main experience was the four years in the Navy. Stash was back before I had finished. "That's enough filling out." He threw the application in a desk drawer. "How about some coffee?"-I said, "sure."

We talked about the Navy. Stash had been in during the War. Gunner's Mate. After we chatted awhile about the glories of the Navy, he reached into the desk and slapped two W-4's in front of me. "Fill these out – you're hired. Can you be back here at 2:00 A.M. In the morning? Your shift will be 2:00 A.M. To 10 A.M." I thought that was odd hours, but I said, "sounds good to me."

Stash and I rode an employee elevator up to the tower where the 300,000 BTU, chilled water air conditioning unit was located. "This is where you'll be working. Just keep an eye on it and at random times hit three or four floors at random and get temp readings. That's pretty much it. In the winter we still run air through a couple of ducts to areas like the lamp department. They keep all them damn lamps on around the clock. Always hotter than a two dollar whore in there. Any questions?"

I wondered why he was putting me on the air conditioner unit instead of the boiler but I said, "no questions"- Coming back down on the elevator, we talked about pay. I would be starting at $3.50 an hour. Damned good pay and a hell of a lot more than I ever made in the Navy.

After I left, I took highway 41 until I picked up Jeffries Ave. and headed south. At 7th Street I took a right. About three blocks down there was a restaurant called the Skillet, where Rita and I had eaten several times. It was great food and I was hungry. I was also disappointed. The Skillet was gone. In its place was a parking lot with busted beer bottles scattered about on the blacktop. I drove back over and picked up 41 south crossing back into Indiana at Whiting where I picked up Indianapolis Boulevard South. I wanted to see if Hanson's Fruit Market was still in business. It now seemed a long time ago that I had worked there. I pulled over on to the gravel parkway in front of Hanson's. The old sign was still there but the small buildings were shuttered and boarded up. From the looks of the place it had been shut down for quite a while. I looked across the street at Wicker Park. There was something exciting going on over there. The large swimming pool was surrounded with people in street clothes. Both men and women. My first thought was that someone had drowned. I strolled over. I couldn't believe my eyes. It was an amazing sight. They were all holding fishing poles and had lines in the water of the pool. I watched for a minute, totally confounded. I noticed a middle-aged fat guy wearing red shorts and a Hawaiian shirt sitting in a lawn chair. There was a small scale with a hook on a table next to him. I said, "what in hell are those people doing?"

He looked up at me shading his eyes with his hand. "They're fishing – what does it look like?"

I was a little stunned, "there's fish in the swimming pool?"

"Sure, I stock it ever morning."

"And they pay you to fish in the pool?"

He lit a Lucky Strike. "Well, they keep the fish, take' em home and eat 'em. But they bring their catch over here first and I weigh 'em. They pay according to the weight."

I said, "This is all a joke, right?" He looked a little peeved. "No, it's not a joke at all."

Then he grinned, "Barnum said there's a sucker born every minute."

I shook my head.

"He had that right."

I drove back down Calumet Avenue and stopped at Maid-Rite Hamburgers. It was starting to look a little seedy but at least it was still there. Inside, I spotted Lou Burnham. He saw me at the same time and waved me over. I slid into the booth across from him. As we shook hands, Lou said, "Good grief, where in hell have you been hiding?"--After I told him my story, Lou said he had received a Bachelor of Arts degree in education from Purdue University Extension here in Hammond. He was teaching English at Wilson Elementary. Lou had married Bernice Bergstedt and they had twin girls, two years old. Lou chuckled, "the best part is, it's keeping me out of the draft."

"Amen to that," I said.

He added, "Seriously though, we're getting out of Hammond. I've accepted a job in the Dayton, Ohio School District. I start teaching there next month; the girls are already there. I'm just here tying up some loose ends. I said, "Hammond has changed over the last four or five years, that's for sure."

Lou laughed, "you don't know the half of it, brother. Most of the kids you knew in school are gone. Some went off to college and never came back. Others took jobs out of state."

"What's the problem?" I asked

"Hell, you name it. Crime on the rise, unhealthy polluted air, dirt, soot, drugs. Fucking US Steel laying off people because of all the foreign steel coming in. People going fucking nuts."

I grinned, thinking about the people fishing in a swimming pool.

Lou went on, "The Fabulous Fifties are history. We saw Hammond in its best days, but it's over now. Hell, they're closing down the Paramount Theatre after the first of the year. The Parthenon will no doubt follow. Goldblatts Department Store is going downhill fast – it'll soon be gone. It's been shoplifted into bankruptcy." --I had to grin at that one. I had known a few girls who had contributed to that.

Lou continued with the bad news, "Hammond will be a ghost town in a few years. At best, it will be a ghost of it's former self."
Just for the fun of it, I said, "what about Vivian's Record Shop in Gary?" This had been our primary place to buy records in the 50's. Vivian also had a radio show we all listened to.
Lou wiped his mouth with a napkin and smiled. "Hell, yes, Vivian's will still be there a hundred years after the world ends."
Lou and I finished our burgers and shook hands, wishing each other luck. I took Sheffield road and crossed back over into Illinois passing Wolf Lake on the right. The trailer park we had lived in when we first moved here from Ohio was still there. I didn't see our old trailer-They were all big and fancy-looking now. Unbelievably, Ed's Bait Shop was still there. But the old house was vacant. The porch had collapsed and all the windows were broken out. The wooden pier still stood. I walked out to the end and sat down. I lit a Chesterfield and let my thoughts drift back. I was becoming lost in my memories when I remembered I had to be at work at 2:00 A.M. When I arrived home, my daddy was watching "McHale's Navy" on TV. I watched it with him and then went to bed.

I clocked in at 1:45 A.M. There was pretty much only a skeleton crew in engineering. A man walked over and asked if I was Knight. I said I was. He said, "Stash left this for you." He handed me a tool belt loaded with tools. Then he was gone. I strapped it on and stood around a minute but no one else approached me. I caught the maintenance elevator and rode up to the tower. No one was in there. I walked around the air conditioner, and sat down at a metal desk with a telephone, a notepad, and a lead pencil and that was it. I opened the top drawer. There was a portable temperature gauge setting atop two Playboy magazines. It was the type of gauge you whirled in a circular motion before reading the temperature.

I flipped through the magazines awhile admiring Miss March 1964 and reading, "The Girls of Russia". After awhile I put the mags back and picked up the temperature gauge. I found the lamp department on the third floor. Stash was right. Every light was burning and it was hot as hell. The gauge registered 83 degrees Fahrenheit. I hit a couple of more areas and headed back up. One of the elevator buttons said "Roof". I punched it. Stepping out on the roof, I felt a breeze. You could see the lights of Chicago to the north extending as far as you could see. The Palmer House Hotel, next door, had several lights burning. I saw a couple of guys I had seen down in maintenance earlier. They were over by a huge vent, smoking and laughing. One had a pair of binoculars. I walked over and introduced myself. They were Russ and Bernie. They were quite a bit older than me. Probably in their late thirties. I said, "What are you guys looking at?" Bernie pointed to the Palmer House. "Look in that window straight ahead of you. The one all lit up." I looked. I could see a woman walking around in the room who appeared to be naked but I couldn't make out many details. Bernie handed me the binoculars. They brought her close in. Now I could almost read the title of the magazine on the dresser.

The woman was a beauty. Jet black hair (everywhere), and tall with perfect-looking breasts. I thought she had to be a model. She was sorta pacing the floor and smoking as though she was worried about something. I greatly enjoyed looking at beautiful women and I was far from a saint but for some reason, I couldn't define, this didn't seem right. I gave Bernie his binoculars back and said,"boy, that's something, alright."

He said, "Fuck, that's nothing. We've watched orgies going full blast over there. Just about anything you can imagine, we've seen it over there. "

Russ grabbed the binoculars and took over the watch. I headed back to my tower.

At 10:00 A.M. I rode the elevator down to engineering. I stuck my head in Stash's office. He was watching some show on a small TV. I said, "Hey, Stash." He looked over his shoulder, "Oh, hi, Danny. How'd it go?"
I said, "It went good."
"Great." Stash turned back to his TV show.
I clocked out and left.

When I arrived home, Jeff was there. Marty introduced us. He seemed ok – maybe just a little too sweet. I noticed he was already calling mother, "mom" - which was causing "mom" to beam.

I chatted with Jeff awhile and headed for bed. My mother followed me in, shutting the door. "Danny, could you help us out a little?"
I said, "I don't get paid for two weeks."
"Well, don't you have any more of the traveler's checks?"
I had 150 dollars left. I tore out the 50 and handed it to her. She took it and closed the door behind her.

In October the weather turned cold. All of my old clothes were gone, including my black leather jacket. I dug my peacoat out of my seabag. I had gained a little weight but it still fit me fine and was snug and warm. On November third I entered a voting booth set up at Irving Park to vote in my first presidential election. Barry Goldwater, a senator from Arizona, was running against the incumbent, Lyndon Johnson. I liked some of the things that Goldwater said but Johnson's people ran ads claiming he would have us in a major war. I had my doubts about that but pulled the lever for Johnson solely because of my admiration for John Kennedy and the fact that Johnson had been his vice president. Nobody knew then that Johnson already had us in a war that would last over ten years.

In December the weather worsened. It had been snowing almost daily since the last week in November. Now the temperature hovered in the low teens in the day and colder at night. I had forgotten about the winters here. I didn't know if it was because my body had become accustomed to the hot weather the past four years---I just knew I was freezing most of the time and no one else paid it much attention. The wedding was scheduled for December eighteenth, at 7:00 P.M., a week before Christmas. The ceremony would be held at Aunt Gert's house. Aunt Gert was Jeff's aunt who had supposedly raised him since he was a baby. She lived about two miles away over by Columbia Park. That day, after work, I went to Goldblatt's and bought a white shirt, pants, and tie. I also bought a red pullover sweater. I was decked out in all of this garb when I pulled up in front of Aunt Gert's house.

Gert was a nice lady. She took my peacoat and folded it carefully on the bed.

The bride and groom were already there and so were my parents. Marty looked more beautiful than ever. There were faces seated around the room that weren't familiar to me. But on a couch with my parents was one who was. I almost wiped my eyes to make sure. It was Rita! She was staring straight at me. I had no idea what I was supposed to do. I edged into the kitchen where I saw Marty talking to a girlfriend of hers. Marty saw me coming. She said, "I'm sorry, Danny – I didn't know about this. It seems that mother invited her."

I said, "Listen, don't worry about it, this is your night."
Marty hugged me and said, " thanks."

Not knowing what else to do, I walked over to the couch. Rita slid over and I sat down next to her. I said, "how've you been doing, little lady?"
A little icily she said, "fine, how about you?"
I tried to be funny, "Well, nobody's shot me yet."

She obviously didn't think it was funny. She glared at me. " We need to talk."
I said, "We do?"
She glared even more, "you don't think we should?"
"Sure," I said, "sure we should."
"We'll talk after the ceremony." I said, "OK."
The ceremony went beautifully. One of Jeff's buddies was best man and our
daddy gave Marty away. Mother and Gert had tears in their eyes.

By each plate on the long dining room table there was a little paper sack
filled with rice. This is what we would throw at Marty and Jeff as they
headed out after the reception. .

The reception was underway when Rita whispered to me, "let's sit in my car
awhile."

I got a dixie cup full of black coffee and followed her out. We climbed into
her car and she started it up and turned the heater on.

I said, "thank you so much for the heat."
The windows were iced over. Rita sighed, "let's just cut to the chase. Do you
still love me?"
I said, "I care about you."
She said, "that's not the same."
Even with the heater I was cold and shaking. I sipped the hot coffee. " I
don't know, Rita, it's been a long time."

"Time means nothing if you love someone"

I said, "Maybe it's according to what all happens during a time period that
determines how long or short it is."

She played with her gear shift. "I've been seeing Jerry Haskell."

325

I said, "who?"

"Jerry Haskell, surely to God you remember Jerry Haskell?"

I had never heard the name in my life, but I said, "Sure, I remember him. A nice guy." She looked doubtful. "Yes – yes, he is."

We were quiet for a moment. Rita broke the silence, "look, we're not getting anywhere with this conversation. You're obviously confused and have a right to be. I probably shouldn't have come here tonight, but I did want to see you. Listen – think all this over. Think about what we meant to each other at one time. Will you do that for me?" I said I would. "And then call me and let's talk some more, ok?"

I said, "ok"

I opened my door, got out and walked around to her side. She lowered the window and I kissed her on the forehead. She said, "you won't call will you?" I said, "no."

Her tires spun out as she jerked away from the curb, splattering the legs of my new pants with dirty snow. Back inside, Marty grabbed my arm and whispered, "How did it go?"

I said, "I think it went well."

She grinned, "no, it didn't."

1965

In March the blizzard came. When I went out at 1:00 A.M., the snow was up to the top of my tires. I went back inside and got a broom to sweep the snow off my windshield. I finally got the door open and slid in behind the steering wheel. I patted the gas pedal a few times and then held it to the floor. The engine turned over a few times and cranked. I was relieved. But getting out of the snow bank was another story. Putting the automatic transmission into drive or first did nothing. I couldn't budge. I put it in reverse – it came back a little. I started alternating between drive and reverse using the "rock the boat" system. I was making a little headway when I heard a loud "**POP**" I had blown my reverse gear. I got out with my sack lunch, cursed, and started walking. It was a little over two miles to the South Shore Train Station. The heavy snow had stopped falling but the wind cut like ice. I pulled the collar of my peacoat up and walked with my head down. When I finally made it to the station my feet were numb. I went up to the man behind the cage, who looked like he had been sleeping, and bought a ticket to the Loop Station in downtown Chicago.

My feet were just starting to thaw out which made them hurt like hell, when I heard a far off clanging. When I walked outside the moon was out but it had gotten even colder. Far down the track I could see the headlight of the train coming from Gary. Snow was being thrown up in front of the engine.

I head a small "chirp" and looked up. A little sparrow had landed on a telephone line. I was wondering why it had not flown south with the others when it suddenly teetered and fell to the ground. I walked over and gently covered it with snow. I said, "I know how you feel, little buddy."

It was a nine block walk from the downtown station to Carson, Pirie, Scott. When I clocked in, I felt a little feverish. The shift went by sort of in a dream.

I didn't leave the tower. At 9:45 A.M. I rode the elevator down to engineering. A guy named Weaver was watching TV. I didn't see Stash. Weaver was watching the news, eating a doughnut and drinking coffee. The news people were talking about and showing film of black people in Selma, Alabama trying to hold a civil rights march and being tear-gassed .Weaver finished his doughnut and licked his fingers.

In his Yankee clip, he announced, "damn niggers, they oughta shoot ever one of 'em." He turned and looked at me. "Hell, Danny –you're from the south originally. I know damn well you feel that way too, right?"

I thought about Radio and William and Howard and Miss Lolly. Several others were in the room now.

I said, "the truth is, if I was down there, I'd probably be marching with 'em." A silence fell over the area. I clocked out and left.

When I arrived at the Hammond Station I didn't believe I could make the walk home. I used the pay phone and called the house. Marty was there and answered. When she picked me up at the station she said, "Good God, you are really sick." I guess I looked awful. After 3 aspirins and a fitful night I didn't feel any better. Marty had spent the night and insisted on taking me straight to Dr. Rudser's office . I protested, but not much. I said, "Is that old codger still around?"

Marty laughed, "he's not that old, really."

Dr. Rudser remembered me from when I was a kid. At least he said he did. The nurse took my blood pressure and temperature which was 103 point something. After looking in my ears, down my throat and some stethoscope listening, Dr. Rudser said I had a viral infection. I told him about my long walk in the cold. He said, "that wouldn't have caused it," which surprised me.

He said "you've probably had a cold and it's turned into the flu. And you look completely run down. How old are you now?"
I told him I was 23.
"That's awful young to be as tired looking as you are, son. You're going to need some bed rest." Marty had come into the examination room and heard most of it. Dr. Rudser wrote out two prescriptions and handed them to Marty when she reached for them.

Marty took me home and made sure I climbed in bed before she left to get the prescriptions filled. When she came back she made chicken noodle soup and poured me a glass of tomato juice. But I couldn't get much of it down. Marty called Jeff and told him to pack some things and come here. She told him I was still very sick and they were going to stay here for a couple of days. By the third day I was feeling better. I was mostly just weak. Maybe I was going to live after all. That evening I found myself alone in the house. I phoned the Greyhound Bus Station. They had a bus leaving for Birmingham at 7:00 P.M the next evening. The estimated time of arrival in Birmingham was 10:40 A.M. the next morning. Next I called Ma. I asked her if I could come live with her awhile. Ma said, "you know better than to even ask such a foolish question." I told her what time the bus would get into Birmingham. Ma said, "one of your cousins will be there to get you, probably Jim. You just come on home, son."

Next I called Stash. He hated it but understood. He said he would give me a good recommendation wherever I went.

That night Marty and Jeff came over. My mother and Father were seated on the couch and Jeff was sitting in the recliner chair with Marty on his lap when I made the announcement of my next day departure. My daddy didn't look surprised at all. He asked quietly, "did you call Mama?"

I said I had. Marty said, "Well, I do feel like you'll be happier there, Danny, I really do."

There was a short silence before my mother said what I had heard so many times--"You go on down there to that old woman. You've always loved her better than you ever did me!"

Marty cut her off. "Not now, Mother, please, not now. Let it go."

The next evening I packed my few civilian clothes and shaving gear into my seabag. My mother was gone somewhere but I didn't ask. My daddy was taking me to the bus station. Marty called me and we talked awhile.

We arrived at the station at 6:00 P.M. I bought my ticket and we set on a wooden bench and waited. We didn't talk much, just waited. An announcement came over the loudspeaker, *"All passengers for St. John, Terre Haute, Evansville, Henderson, Nashville, Birmingham and Montgomery, your bus is now loading in lane three."*

We both stood up and hugged. Daddy said, "Tell Mama I'll see her before long."

There wasn't many people on the bus and I found a good window seat on the starboard side. The driver climbed on, wrote something in his log, closed the door and the big engine in the rear came to life. Night had fallen and the street lights were burning on Hohman Avenue, reflecting off the piles of dirty snow. The bus was moving slowly through the traffic. As we passed Goldblatt's, I saw Rita going through the revolving doors. I knew I was getting a last look at the town I had called home. Now I wondered if it really ever was.

The bus turned south on Indianapolis Boulevard and picked up a little speed, headed to pick up highway 41 South. Our first stop was St. John,

Indiana. A family of black people got on. Two set across from me and two behind me. As the bus headed back down 41, the family began talking in quiet tones about Doctor King and the events in Selma. I heard an elderly lady's soft voice behind me. "We really are going to be free at last, just like Doctor King said."

I wasn't black but, for some reason, her words comforted me, as though they were meant for me as well. In some small way, maybe I also was free at last.

The Greyhound felt safe and warm – a feeling I had not had in a very long time. I switched off my overhead light and bundled my peacoat between my seat and the window to lay my head on. I watched the lit windows in houses go by.

Just before I fell asleep I heard the big engine pick up more speed as the Golden Eagle rolled south through the night.

THE END

CPSIA information can be obtained at www.ICGtesting.com
Printed in the USA
BVOW07s1002280414

351917BV00008B/373/P